BECOME LEGEND

THE BLOOD REGENT

3

MARISSA ALLEN

Become Legend: The Blood Regent 3

Copyright © 2023 by Marissa Allen

All rights reserved.

This is a work of fiction. Names, characters, places, and events are used fictitiously and any resemblance to actual events, locales, or persons is entirely coincidental.

This book or any portion thereof may not be reproduced or used in any manner whatsoever without the express written permission of the publisher except for the use of brief quotations in a book review.

Edited by Cait Marie

DEDICATION

To my husband.
Thank you for always entertaining my ever-changing requests for the covers of these books.

CONTENT WARNING

Become Legend follows Vi and the resistance as Kabria falls into a civil war. This includes references to combat, torture, trauma, and PTSD, as well as the repercussions of war. It also includes a healthy dose of how a healthy support system can help someone who is struggling.

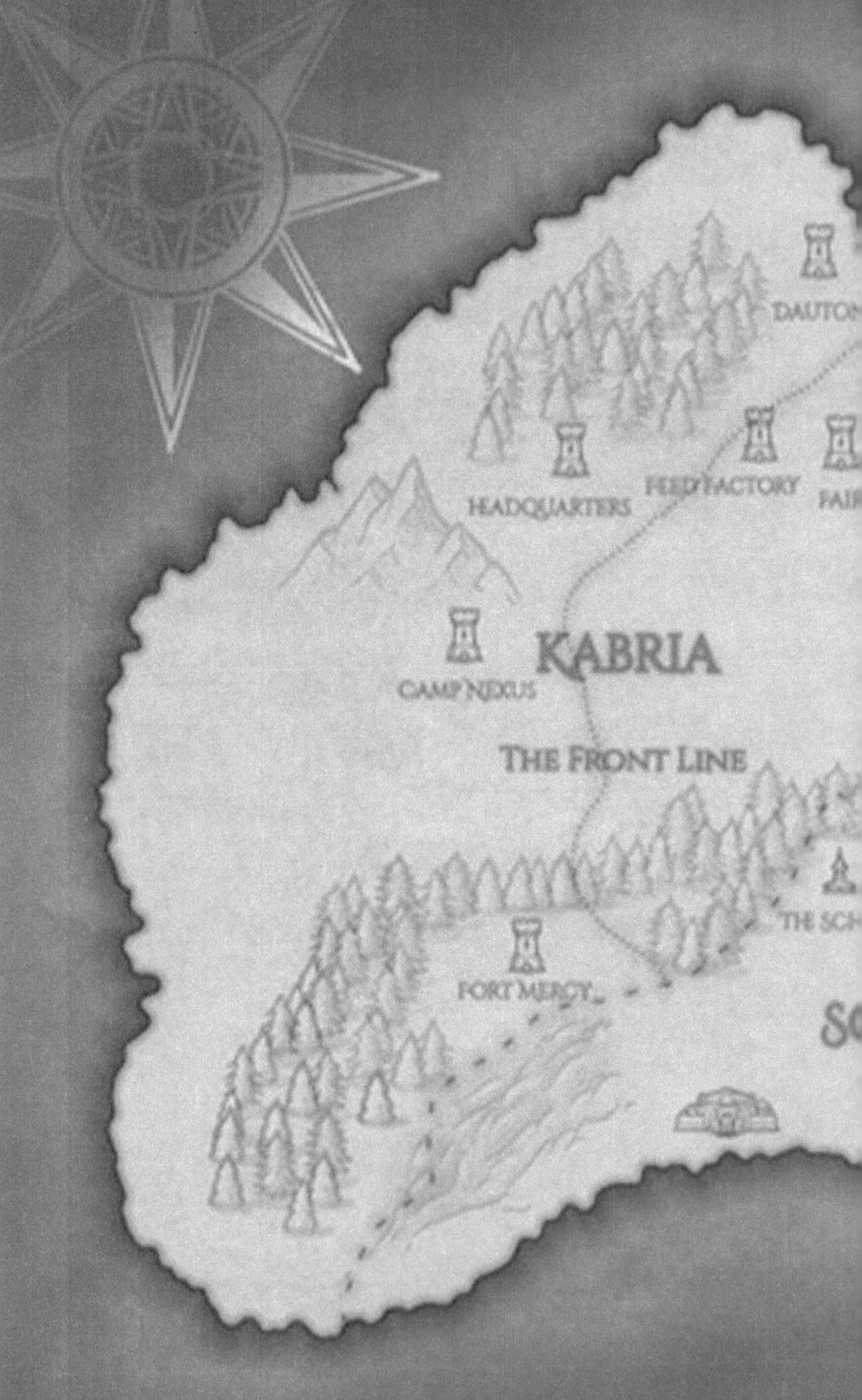

DAUTON
HEADQUARTERS
FEED FACTORY
FAIR
KABRIA
CAMP NEXUS
THE FRONT LINE
THE SCH
SO
FORT MERCY

LONGDALE
NERIA
ND

THE RISE

1

ESMERELDA

My glass exploded as it crashed against the wall, and my scream echoed around the room. An almost-priceless liquid splashed across the lavish wallpaper. Rage boiled within me as I watched the video of my stepdaughter, the bane of my existence, running through my father's palace.

That stupid oaf Jasper, my enforcer, hadn't been able to bring her to me or even finally manage to put her down. Now, she chased after him like a hunter after her prey. It should be the other way around. He had reported that she was fully healed from the DNA-targeted biological weapon we gassed her with—somehow.

Apparently, I had underestimated her friends.

Friends. The word left a bad taste in my mouth. I had shown that you could get exactly what you wanted without them. They did nothing but hold you back, and I would prove to her the truth of that statement soon enough. Her compassion was her weakness.

"Captain." My tone was clipped, barely able to control my anger.

The man jumped to attention and gave me a salute. "Yes, Your Majesty."

"Launch the attack."

He nodded and ran off to do my bidding.

I had recently found out the location of a rebel cell here in Kabria. That girl and her friends were causing me enough trouble in Neria. They had been disrupting the constant flow of test subjects I had manipulated my father into sending to me.

The Nerian rebels and lower classes had been a threat to him, and he was happy to get them out of the way. Which worked out perfectly for me as the survival rate was still under one percent no matter what changes we made to the serum.

So, I would bring Genevieve Astor and her friends home. The people were flocking to her, and it was dangerous. I needed to take her out of the equation. I would punish the rebels and the people of Kabria, and I would make her understand their blood was on her hands and all of it was her fault. If I could break her, that would be the largest victory.

She would find out that if someone resisted me, tested me, or even merely inconvenienced me, they would be crushed under the might of my power.

"Nolan," I muttered under my breath. Of course, Genevieve's father had managed to rescue her. Although, I couldn't help but enjoy the fact that it took him six years to do so. Letting him live was one of my biggest mistakes. I had been soft back then. Deciding to give my husband the chance to walk away. To take the throne without bloodshed. Never again. I knew better now. Kill them as soon as they become a problem. Because now, I had this annoying resistance to deal with.

If only I didn't need to keep Genevieve alive. At least, for now. All that data tucked away in her cells was priceless. I needed to get my hands on it. Once I had what I needed, I could finally be rid of her.

I dropped down into my chair as I watched the camera footage of the rebel attack against my father. With the losses he had taken over the last few weeks, I had no doubt he would fall. Jasper hadn't even managed to turn the tides in his favor.

Good riddance. As I had come into my own as a queen here, I realized how pathetic he had been. How he had denied me my birth right because of the disease that destroyed my body but didn't seem to realize my younger brother, Edward, was an idiot who would destroy everything our family had built. How he would get the keys to the kingdom just because he was a male and healthy, like that predisposed him as a good ruler. My father couldn't see how everything I had lived through only prepared me to be strong, ruthless, and cunning.

You'll never find a husband, Esmerelda.

I wish this sickness would just kill you already, Esmerelda.

Why couldn't you have just been normal, Esmerelda?

I slammed my arm down to stop the thoughts. Who was going to have the last laugh now? The joke was on them because their heads would be on pikes soon enough, and I still sat on a throne.

I had been the one smart enough to have Nolan's wife killed. I had her poisoned so I could take her place and prove that I was a true ruler. I managed to take control of our oldest enemies without a single shot fired. I managed to get Nolan to fake his own death and leave me the throne. I was the one to remove Genevieve from her line of succession.

Me.

I would prove those of the true Nerian bloodline were still a mighty force to be feared. I wasn't given my power. I took it.

Eventually, once things were settled here, I would set my sights on retaking Neria. I'd salt the Earth just to keep the so-called resistance from having it. I would punish them for thinking they could topple the Ravensbones. My father might have been worthless, but it doesn't change our lineage. I would break them. I would take back everything that was rightfully mine. I just needed to deal with the Astors first.

I turned my attention to the view of the jets taking off toward the Kabrian base. A smile slid across my face. The reflection of my perfectly white teeth showed behind my blood-red lips. They were striking against my pale skin and surrounded by my raven hair. I never could look away from my reflection. I was stunningly beautiful; despite everything I had lived through.

I didn't even try to temper the laughter as the bombs dropped. Nolan, Genevieve, and all their allies would rue the day they crossed me. I was going to burn it all. Starting with what they called the feed factory.

Get ready Astors because I'm coming for you.

12 hours later...

My vision blurred through the unshed tears as I stared up at the tree that had been a refuge for me for so long. When I had first been rescued, almost three years ago now, this tree was where I went to hide and heal as I tried to figure out my new life. Now, I was breaking beneath it. Returning to my task, I slammed my shovel into the ground, ripping the dirt free and tossing it over my shoulder.

As I dug, I wished for the pain from sore muscles, but it never came. My body might have been close to indestructible now, but my mind wasn't as lucky. Just a few weeks ago, I had a run-in with a deadly toxin, created to tear the body apart cell by cell. My friends and the resistance in Neria managed to create a serum to save me from its effects.

Their cure ended up supercharging my already enhanced healing. Now, I couldn't even break a sweat, my lungs didn't burn for oxygen, my muscles didn't cry for rest. I couldn't wallow and hide in exercise like I used to. I just had to sit here and feel all these soul-crushing feelings. My mind unable to pull itself away from the vision of my friends dying that was stuck on a never-ending loop.

Today should have been celebrated for victory, and instead, I was digging graves for my friends. We had just liberated Neria. The resistance, with our help, had taken the palace and was going to create a new government—one run by the people, for the people.

Just hours ago, my friends had been alive. How had it only been hours? Here with my guilt, it felt like it had been an eternity. Why did I deserve to be here, and they didn't? Why was I the one who made it out alive? It wasn't how things should have happened. I was supposed to keep my friends safe. Atty, one of my best friends, was dead. Marco was dead.

I hadn't known Marco long, but he had changed my life. He had used his wealth from creating the technology for the biologic implants that fueled Neria's expansion, to try and save his people. His king had perverted his work and he wouldn't give up without a fight. He had been the founder of the resistance in Neria. We understood each other because the fight was personal for us both.

It was my fault. I should have been able to save them. If I had been fast enough to get to Atty... If I had managed to stop Jasper sooner... If I hadn't been so distracted, I could have stopped the canister that released the mist that killed Marco. It was all *my* fault.

The moon had started to rise as I dug. Constant movement was the only thing keeping me going. Yet, I knew I couldn't keep digging until the pain faded. I could make it to the other side of the world, and it still wouldn't be enough. It terrified me knowing that if I stopped, I would fall apart and not be able to put myself back together again.

My father had sent multiple people offering to handle this for me, but I refused wanting to pawn the planning of the ceremony off on the others while I hid down here. Reluctantly, they had left me to it. There was no way I was going to be able to make decisions on how we said goodbye. I was going to hide in this manual labor until I couldn't.

Dirt smeared across my forehead as I swiped at it. There wasn't any sweat to wipe away; it was just a habit at this point. The time had come. There wasn't anything more I could do. The hate I held for myself broke free of box I had tried to lock it away in, and it started to slice through me. Like a tsunami tipped with razor blades, it crashed over me. Overwhelmed, I slid to the ground, curling in on myself. The tears came fast, and there was no stopping them this time. It seemed like all I could do was fail. Why was I even here? What good were my abilities if I couldn't use them to save the people I loved? It felt like it had all been for nothing.

Atty's laugh echoed through my mind. Thoughts of Marco surrounded by a gaggle of children all reaching their hands out for the candy he was giving came unbidden. My heart felt like it was shattering all over again. Marco had given his life to save another solider. He knew his fate, and he chose it. Atty, on the other hand... I was fully to blame for his death. How would Gwen and the others ever be able to look me in the face again?

Jasper had been racing toward Atty, and I didn't get there in time. I could still hear the sickening thud as Jasper threw him into the ground. His wet gasps as he struggled for his last breaths. Jasper was my problem. I was the only one who could match him. I should have been able to stop him before ended up anywhere near Atty. Why wasn't I strong enough? Why wasn't I fast enough?

My tears splashed in the bottom of the grave. The sobs escaped me, and I shook under the weight of them. Absolutely exhausted, I couldn't even try to mask my cries. Anyone who walked by would hear me, but I couldn't stop myself. I wasn't strong enough, even now. I couldn't live with myself. Guilt and grief were drowning me. The group was going to fall apart, and it was all my fault. They would never forgive me. I couldn't even blame Gwen if she never wanted to see me again. I wouldn't blame any of them.

Someone was coming this way. The grass quietly crushed beneath their feet. Even more dirt smeared across my face as my hands wiped at my tears. I'd be covered in a coat of mud soon if I kept this up. Shoes appeared, attached to legs. Looking up, I saw they belonged to David.

"Hey, you," he said and jumped down next to me. I had no idea when he had arrived. He was supposed to be on his way to Soland with the other refugees from Neria.

The tears kept coming as I fell into his arms. His grip tightened around me; he must have known it might have been the only thing that could keep all my shattered pieces together. He pulled me close as I clung to him.

"It's all my fault."

His shoulder was already wet from my tears.

"In your heart, you know that isn't true. Even if it's what your mind is trying to make you believe." He rubbed my back as he talked in his most soothing tone.

I was cold and numb. I had been through so much in my life. Yet, this pain was all new to me—feeling so completely at fault for the death of someone so close to me. It had hurt when Chase's mother died to save us, but that didn't compare to this.

"I can't face them." I shook my head against David. "I can't ever face them."

"Come now." He ran his hands through my hair, something familiar from when we were young. "No one blames you. You're the only one doing that. You won't have much choice in the matter; they'll be here in a few minutes. We've given you time to be alone and beat yourself up, but we're going to get through this together. We need you; Gwen needs you, and you know you need us."

I was sure I seemed like a deer in the headlights. "Please, no. David, I'm not ready."

He just shook his head and kissed my forehead. "You don't get to make others' decisions for them."

As they came near, I wiped quickly at my face. Someone dropped into the grave behind me, but I refused to turn around. Arms wrapped around me, and someone's cheek pressed into my shoulder.

"It's not your fault," Gwen said as she squeezed me tightly. "You did everything to save him. You did *everything* you could. I wouldn't have been able to say goodbye if you hadn't kept Jasper away from us. You were the wall that gave me the time I needed, and I will never be able to repay you for that."

I turned in her arms and hugged her. She put her head on my shoulder, and we just stood there for a while. As she shook slightly in my arms, I could tell she was fighting back her own tears.

"Jasper never should have been able to get to him." As soon as I said it, she pulled away to catch my gaze.

Her face scrunched up in her your-an-idiot look. "We all did our best, and something could have happened to any one of us. It's a risk we all knew and took anyway. This doesn't fall on your shoulders. Plus, Jasper isn't going to hurt anyone ever again, is he? And that is all thanks to you." She wiped some of the tears and dirt from my cheeks. "Now, can we please all grieve together?"

Instantly, three more people jumped down with us before I could even nod. Joseph, Benson, and Chase were there. There wasn't a ton of room, but we all sat down and cuddled close. Chase wrapped his arms around me, and I leaned into him, finally able to take a deep long breath. It was probably weird that we were here hanging out in the grave I had just dug, but it was like our own little bubble outside of the real world. Maybe we could leave some of our grief down here too.

"Weren't you headed to Soland?" I asked David.

"We were able to split from the group, and we headed here as soon as we heard." He grabbed at my hand out of habit.

There hadn't been any chatting on the way home, and I had come straight here to dig. I realized I had no idea what had happened to anyone else in the palace. "What happened to the rest of you? I didn't have comms on during the raid."

"I managed to get tons of data on how Neria had been giving assistance to Esmeralda from the king's computer," Chase said. That made sense since I had to go looking for him and found him in the king's office.

Each of them started to recount what had happened since we split upon entering the palace. After getting as many rebels inside as he could, Chase made his way to the office just as the explosions started to rock the building.

Benson had stayed with Naya and her entry squad. They had been the group that captured the king right after Jasper and I had moved our fight outside. The palace guards had surrendered easily once they had been surrounded and outgunned. That was when Benson had run to find the hover copter for it to be ready for us.

Quietly, Gwen told everyone how she and Atty had gone in together. How they had been the ones placing the explosives around the building. It was hard to think she had been with him just hours ago.

Just this morning, they had still been alive.

Gwen's voice caught. "Atty told me to split off as there was another section that needed to blow at the same time. I hadn't thought anything of it. That's why Atty had been alone when the bombs blew."

I could still feel the slabs of stone pinning me down after the collapse. The bite of its ragged edges cutting into me. Jasper and I had fallen through the floor to where Atty had been. My footing had slipped on the rubble as I tried to reach him in time, but Jasper was too close to Atty for me to catch him.

"Because of the way the building had collapsed, I had to loop back around to an area that hadn't been damaged when you called for help. I ran into Marco and the medic, the one he saved, at the top of the stairs to the lower area where you all were." Her voice wavered as she spoke.

We all knew the rest.

Benson eventually broke the silence. "Do you remember the time someone stole Atty's clothes when he was down at the pond skinny dipping? He had to walk all the way back while using a handful of leaves to cover himself."

All of us laughed because of course we did.

"He had to walk straight past both of your dads." He pointed to Chase and me. "And honest to the gods, he just said, 'Is it a little chilly outside to you?'"

Gwen quietly raised her hand. "That was me by the way."

All eyes swiveled to her.

"You're the one who stole his clothes?" I couldn't believe it. Sweet, little Gwen. "Why did you never tell me? Oh gods, that's amazing."

We all exploded into laughter again. As the night wore on, we laughed and cried as we told stories of our friends. Eventually, another set of footsteps headed our way before Thea, Chase's little sister, popped her head over the side with a liquor bottle in hand.

"Can I join?" It didn't seem much like a question, more of a fact that she was indeed joining us.

While I had been held captive, Thea had been living a wild life with her mother, Alice, under the nose of Esmerelda. The two of them had stayed in Longdale, the capital city beneath the shadow of the palace, running a club and living above it. They had been instrumental in gathering intel and support for the rebellion, as it had slowly grown over those six years, using the club as a front for their real motives.

The same day I finally got to see them again, the club was raided. Thea and Alice had been taken captive. We had snuck into the palace to rescue them, but in our attempt to escape, we had been caught and Alice sacrificed her life to give us time to get Thea out of there. She had been living here with her dad ever since.

I blamed myself for Alice's death too. The pain and guilt had only somewhat faded over the past few years. She was the closest thing I ever had to a mother, and I couldn't save her either. I knew it was her choice, but it still haunted me in the night. Just like I knew Atty and Marco's deaths would.

"What are you doing with that?" Chase snapped as he saw the bottle in Thea's hand.

"Calm down it's not like this is my first time drinking—but still," she glared at him, "don't tell Dad." She slipped in to join us and took a swig before handing the bottle to her brother.

He gave her a frustrated look for a moment but rolled his eyes, gave in, and just took a drink himself before passing it along to the others.

3

Vi

The lifeless beige ceiling greeted me as my eyes fluttered open. Luckily, I had been blessed with just swimming in darkness while I slept. I hadn't been visited by the nightmares that came most nights.

It was close to dawn when we had finally clambered out of the grave and headed for the barracks. Nothing was expected of us until the funeral tonight, so I used the time to catch up on some much-needed sleep.

We'd contacted Naya and Jupiter, and they had agreed we should bury Marco here. He had always loved the idea of Kabria, and Neria had destroyed him. They would erect a monument to remember him in Neria once the elections were over.

I hadn't realized how exhausted I was until I'd stumbled to bed. The last thing I remembered was feeling Chase slip his arm over my waist and snuggle in close, the warmth lulling me to sleep.

In the afternoon light, I couldn't help but curl toward the safety of his embrace. He made a soft noise and pulled me tighter, nuzzling into me. Half-awake his lips traced up my shoulder to my neck. I couldn't stop the moan that escaped me. Electricity skipped across my skin at his caress. As I turned, his eyes fluttered open and caught my gaze. The look he gave me made me melt with the heat of it.

He tangled a hand into my hair, and without letting another moment pass, we came together in desperation. Our kisses fierce, as if we would disappear if we didn't hold each other tight enough.

All the fear and pain of the last few months finally escaped me. All the worry over something happening to him, and now the relief that he was okay. I knew we both wanted to steal as many of these moments as we could because they weren't promised. That was crystal clear on a day like today.

I claimed him here and now and vowed to the gods that they would have him over my cold dead body.

Chase held my hand and led me to the mess hall. I loved walking just a beat behind him, the tug of his arm a reminder that he was right here. As the door swung open, I caught sight of the others already at our table. At least we hadn't missed everyone. It was a relief when I noticed the others seemed to have gotten some sleep too. Except for Gwen. Her face was pale, her eyes hollow, and her gaze unfocused. She seemed to be just staring at a random spot on the table. Thea was tucked in tight next to her, and I was so thankful for the girl I thought of as a little sister. I needed to remind myself to thank her being so amazing. She always knew what the best thing to do or say was for people. The opposite of me. I just tried not to say anything, otherwise I might make things worse.

Amelia, the main cook at headquarters, gasped and dropped the pan she was carrying as she saw Chase and I. "Oh my stars. They said you were back, but I'm just pleased as punch to see you again!" She came around the tables.

I headed for her, and she pulled me in for a hug.

"It's really good to see you, Amelia." I hoped she could sense that I meant it with everything I had. For everyone I saw, it felt like a second chance to tell them how much they meant to me. That I was grateful they were still here. Knowing how easily it could all slip away.

"Here! I made your favorites." She beckoned us over to grab a plate. She piled it high, and my stomach growled. "Well, off you go. You look as skinny as a bean pole; can't have you wasting away on me." She made a move to shoo me off, and I couldn't help but shake my head. The look she gave me was filled with pain before she patted flour off her apron and busied herself again as I headed for my friends.

"No offense, Benson, I loved your cooking, but I'm so glad to be home." I dropped into my seat, already salivating.

"True. Nothing is better than Amelia's fresh cooking. The produce in Neria was laughable, but if you twist my arm, maybe I'll make something occasionally. You can see how good my cooking is with fresh Kabrian ingredients," Benson said, waving his fork with a flourish.

"Watch out, Amelia!" David crowed. "Benson's coming for your job."

Amelia stopped and narrowed her eyes at us. "You better get in here and help me sometime, boy. Making this old woman carry all those sacks of potatoes while you, this huge man, sit around taking naps in the sun." She waved a large wooden spoon his way. "Don't think I didn't see you, young man. Plus, I won't be around forever. Someone's going to have to do it." It seemed like she regretted the words the moment she said them. The reminder twisting a knife through me, and by the look of everyone else it might have for them too.

"I'd love to help Amelia; I'll be around soon."

As I took a bite, the pastry melted in my mouth, and I moaned around a bite of croissant.

"I can only hope you look at me like you look at food for the rest of my days," Chase joked as he dropped down next to me.

"I could eat you up all day."

Thea turned bright pink while Chase coughed.

"Gross," Thea whined but grinned at us anyway.

Everyone dissolved into fits of giggles, and I was happy we could still find some joy after all we'd been through. At the very least, when we were together, there was a comradery which would always be there. We had spent so much time together that it felt so natural to be here with them. It might have felt like one of our limbs was missing now, but we would be able to keep going.

I glanced at David and Joseph. They would be gone soon, helping the refugees from Neria start new lives. They were starting a school for all the kids displaced from not just Neria but Kabria as well. To give them a place to live and grow in safety. It was important work, but I would miss them. At least I would see them again, even if only via a vid-screen or a quick flight.

"When does everything start?" I didn't need to explain further. They all knew I was talking about the funeral. My emotions had wrapped me up so completely that I hadn't paid attention to much else since we arrived.

"At dusk," Thea provided. "Dad's been organizing everything."

That wasn't surprising. Ethan was one of the most organized people I had ever met. I knew Chase got that from him. Chase wrapped his arms around me. His touch fought off the numbness that was trying to swallow me.

We spent the remaining hour in the mess hall, talking, waiting until it was time to go. At this point, we were the only people left. It was time, and we couldn't put it off any longer. We all got up to head to where our friends would be laid to rest. It was peaceful there under my tree, and seemed like the perfect resting place.

There was already a group in the field. It wasn't hard to find our dads. My father stood at least a good head taller than everyone else, and Ethan was by his side as always. No one was in any finery, mainly because none of us had any. It was lucky my clothes were even clean. Not that it mattered; both Atty and Marco had seen me on death's door. Atty would have hated all the pomp and circumstance of a traditional burial anyway. I guessed Marco probably would have felt the same.

As we got closer, I got a better look at the sleek black pods that hovered a few feet above the ground. They hummed slightly. Nothing except for their shape gave any indication of what could be inside. People split to make way for us. As I reached out to touch one of the coffins, a field around it pushed gently against my fingers. A slight shock ran across my skin as I pressed through the field. The hairs all over my body stood on end at the feeling.

David must have had a hand in their creation. The material reminded me of the nanobots that created our suits.

I focused on the hum of the coffins, not wanting to hear any of the whispers of the crowd. There was bright movement at the edge of my vision. I was surprised to see CC1 standing by my father.

We'd met the android when we got Marco to his position at his headquarters prior to the raid on the palace in Neria. CC1 had worked in reconnaissance for him, always keeping an eye on the security footage from all of Neria, including access to cameras within the palace. CC1 had given us the info we needed for pulling off the coup successfully.

Curious, I walked over to them. "Hello, CC1."

They nodded in greeting. They looked relatively human, except for their electronic neon blue eyes and corded metallic hair that gave them away. "Hello, Vi. I am happy to see you again."

"It's good to see you as well. Although, I am curious what brought you here?" I asked and my father shrugged. He must not have known either.

"He was my creator. I felt the compulsion to come," CC1 replied. "Marco had also asked me to help you in the event of his demise. I will follow whatever your directives are."

"Thank you. That is very kind. I'm sorry for your loss. I won't have any directives, but I'd like to have your friendship." We exchanged nods before they stepped up a few paces and fell still, their gaze locking onto the coffin.

Ethan cleared his throat to get everyone's attention. It was time. Someone in the back gave a thumbs up as a camera hovered just above the heads of those gathered with us. This was being broadcast to Jupiter and the others in Neria, which eased some of the pain from knowing they could be a part of this. Marco had meant so much to so many of them. So many owed him their lives.

"I wish we were gathered here under better circumstances," Ethan started. "I wish we could spend time with our Nerian friends in person. While we cheer for you and your success, we know the work has only just begun. We know the loss you feel with what you achieved yesterday. As with many things in life, pain and joy often go hand in hand.

"I did not know Marco personally, but I understand what drove him. It's what drives us all. There is still much to be accomplished, and you will not find yourselves there without a fight to hold on to what you have taken back for your people.

"The plight on all Nerians was something close to Marco Diaz's heart. He took risks for what he believed in. He sacrificed for what he believed in. He gave his life to save another, which gives us such a profound insight to who he was as a man. Your lives will be forever changed without him in it, even for those who hadn't spent time with him like myself. He was a beacon for fair and just leadership and the pursuit of change to obtain it. Our hearts go out to our friends who shall feel his loss even deeper. Know that if there is anything you need, just ask. If it's in our power, we shall make it so." Ethan paused. "Does anyone wish to say anything?"

I stepped forward, my hands shaking. I didn't really want to talk in front of everyone, but I felt like I owed it to him. "I didn't know Marco for long, and I didn't get to learn about his life the way I wished I could have, but I understood him. We both saw suffering and would do anything in our power to try and save people from it. He looked out for the people of Neria. He put everything on the line to create the army that achieved his dream of freeing his people from oppression. He can rest easy knowing that has been accomplished.

"We may live across an invisible line, but suffering is suffering. It doesn't matter where you come from; you deserve the right to live your life in peace. To have your rights protected. Marco risked a lot for people he would never meet. He brought my friends and I in as allies and the people I got to meet because of it changed my life." I looked at the camera.

"I see you; I see all you've done. I see why you fight, and I know many of you are there because Marco gave you the path to do so. Do not lose faith, do not wonder if the loss was worth it. It was. He was at peace as he passed, knowing that you had accomplished the first step up a long and winding stairway toward a better future. Please keep going. Don't lose hope. Create the future he envisioned in his memory." I stepped back, and the others pulled in tighter, calming me and helping me felt less exposed.

Ethan moved to address everyone once more.

"Many of you here knew Atty. He had come to us as a young man —alone. No family, on the run, just looking for a place to feel safe. As many of you have. That's why Nolan and I created the Kabrian resistance in the first place, knowing the damage Esmerelda has caused to many of the people of Kabria.

"Atty was dedicated to our cause, to his peers, and to those he chose as family. We are heartbroken at the loss and will forge on so his death will not be in vain." Ethan looked to us, to see if anyone wanted to say anything.

Gwen moved forward, tears shining in her eyes. "Atty was a quiet person. Unless you got to spend time with him, but you should know he believed in what we do with his entire being." Her voice cracked. "He loved so fiercely, and he knew this might be how his story ended." Tears started to fall, and I saw that she couldn't continue.

I reached out and grabbed her hand and continued for her.

"Atty was kind and brave and silly. And he enjoyed nothing more than to make things explode." That got a quiet chuckle from the crowd. "He would want us to remember him in those good times. The times he reminded me there was sun just past the clouds that would be shining on us before we knew it. That everything would work out for the best. He was sure we would be victorious, no matter what. I know myself and my friends," I put an arm out toward the group, "will never give up; we will not let his death be in vain. We will continue this fight, and we will see the future both Atty and Marco knew would come."

Benson squeezed Gwen's arm before walking forward. "I'm sure some of you never managed to speak to him. Heck, it took a while for him to speak to us. While he may have liked people to see the dark and brooding side of him, he was incredibly caring, loving, and funny. He was loyal beyond a fault. He was always there when we needed him, no questions asked. He'd want us to carry on. Like Vi said, I think he'd want today to be a celebration rather than a day of grief."

With that, David pressed a button and the coffins lowered into the graves I had dug. I couldn't stop the tears from falling as I watched them go to their final resting place. I looked up to the tree that had given me so much comfort while I healed from my imprisonment, my arms clutched to my chest, hovering over my heart, and hoped it would provide them peace. The buzzing stopped as the coffins touched the ground, the force fields around them dissipating now that they had completed their task.

We each took a handful of dirt and tossed it in. I let mine slip through my fingers, cascading over the curve of the coffin. I didn't want to acknowledge that we were saying goodbye. Chase wrapped his arms around me, kissing my neck, but I felt his own tears wetting his lips. He clutched me tight, and I grasped on to his arms. Each of us holding the other together.

Benson and Thea both hugged Gwen as her shoulders shook with her silent sobs. I saw Joseph grab David's hand, and Chase and I reached out to pull them close.

Ethan was grave as addressed everyone. "As we stand here today, we lay our friends to rest, knowing they have come to find peace, that their struggle has ended. But this was not our only tragedy. Our Nerian friends have lost others in this fight. And soon, we will head to the feed factory and mourn our losses there. As we take our dead and give them the sendoff they all deserve, this is the stark reminder of why we are here. Why we are fighting. Our people are dying, and we are the force needed to fight back and save who we can. We believe there is a better world than the one we live in today, and the loss we share in our attempt to move toward that goal will weigh on us forever. Yet, one day they shall look down upon us from beyond the veil and see the fruit of the seeds they have sown. We will persevere, and we will be victorious. We shall not stop until everyone enjoys the freedom they so deserve. Atty and Marco have made their final journey. May we feel their presence as they watch over us until we join them after this life."

With that, everyone started to chat amongst themselves, and many headed for the mess hall. It had been stocked with food and drinks, ready for everyone to mingle and celebrate the lives our friends had lived.

Ethan and my father joined us.

"We won't forget them or what they've done. We will win this fight," my father told us before they left to follow the others.

We were the only people left, spread out around our friends' graves, where we had voiced our memories just the night before. There were a few shovels lying against the tree, and we grabbed them. I might have dug the holes alone, but we would fill them together. It would give us all this one last moment with them.

I had told Marco he would love the stars in Kabria, and now he had a perfect view.

4

ESMERELDA

"Your Majesty," came a small voice from my assistant Morgan.

"What is it?" I replied with an exasperated look her way.

"It has been confirmed that Marco Diaz was killed in the attack on your father's palace. I thought you might want to know."

I waved a hand, dismissing her, and she turned and scurried away.

What was this feeling in my chest? I hadn't thought about him in years. It couldn't be regret, could it?

He had been one of the only people to treat me like I was a normal person. He didn't tiptoe around me like everyone else did because I was a princess or because of my illness. We had grown apart as we got older. Then, come to find out he was part of the rebellion. I reminded myself he deserved what he got for turning traitor.

With that, I banished him from my thoughts.

I turned back to the tablet gripped by my blood red nails. I swiped through the videos I had ordered to be sent to me. It was every video that contained Genevieve from the last few weeks. Interrupting an execution, causing chaos at the Nerian Tech Summit, raiding a doctor's office that had been a front for moving my prisoners. My lip curled in a sneer.

I had spent years weaving the story of her being sickly and claiming that was why she never appeared in public. While this was still the story of record, of course, the rumors whirled. The information about my testing facilities was out there, spreading through those who wanted to resist me. The whispers of where she had really been.

Let them talk; let them fear me. They should know what would happen to those who crossed me.

Just like Alice. I smirked, thinking of her cutting her own throat, surprising everyone long enough to give her children time to escape. It had been inconvenient that they got away, but I had been searching for Alice for years, and she had done my work for me by taking her own life.

Now that Genevieve was free, she was becoming a menace, and the rebellion followed her wherever she went. Nolan, ever the strategist, had to have been behind her face popping up everywhere. I felt it in my aching bones. I doubted she was that smart. One thing I had found with our limited success in the experiments was that it turned the subjects into nothing much more than beasts to be let off their chain with a specific target in mind. Nothing more than cold-blooded murdering machines.

I felt a certain amount of glee at the destruction she had caused though. At watching her become more and more rabid the stronger she grew. How much longer would it be before her bloodlust started to consume her? Who would follow her then? She wouldn't be much of a saint to worship when her true self appeared.

I just needed to get her back before she caused too much damage. I still had many questions about my first success. If anything, these last few weeks had proven she was much more than we ever expected. I needed to see what made her different.

Jasper had been a blunt object; she was more like sharp knife. He had been a pale comparison. If I could engineer the next ones to be more like her, no one would be able to stop me. Just thinking of an army of them sent a shiver of ecstasy running through me. I could almost taste the power.

At least with Jasper, we had realized how to keep them more compliant.

I stopped scrolling when one dark video from a CCTV camera in the city caught my attention. There was a young girl she had protected from a large man in an alley. I flipped through a few more and saw her talking with a different young man. Her screaming at a felled solider about his attack on an orphanage.

Look at that, a possible weakness. She had a soft spot the young. I went back to the video of the girl and pulled up facial recognition. *Ah, a troubled youth named Jessie, and she has a younger sister.*

"Morgan," I snapped, and she came running in. I showed her the file on the two girls. "Tell anyone we have left in Neria to find them and bring them to me."

I knew who my next test subjects would be.

Leaning into my high-backed chair, I grinned at the thought. It wasn't likely these two would survive the process, but if they did, they would be exactly what I needed.

Genevieve's mercy would be her undoing.

"Your Majesty." The captain of my guard nodded as he entered.

"What is it?" I raised my eyebrow, conveying he had better not be wasting my time.

"During the attack on the rebel base at the factory, we managed to intercept some messages being relayed to the city of Fairhaven before we jammed their communications." He stood at attention, waiting for what I would do with that information.

"Are you saying Fairhaven is housing traitors?" I leaned forward and to his credit he didn't shy away.

"Yes, ma'am we believe that to be the case."

"We'll have to send them a message. Bring me a holo-recorder and prepare the local troops for action. They'll be moving out within the hour. Expect some prisoners, but not many."

He looked up from under his eyebrows, his chin still slightly tucked. "And the rest?"

"Raze the city and kill them all."

He started to leave to do my bidding.

"Capitan," I called after him and he turned back. "Keep an eye on the city. When their rescue efforts begin, be prepared to launch another attack. I don't want anyone left alive."

5

Vi

We had to have our noses and mouths covered with rags as we walked through the smoldering ruin that was the feed factory. Some of us were digging graves, others moving bodies, more working through the debris to see if anything was salvageable. We'd been at it for two days now, working to honor our fallen and trying to figure out how much damage had been done in the attack. Not just the loss of lives and supplies, but also what type of intel our enemies might have acquired.

I had volunteered to dig again, putting my skills to good use. I dug and dug and dug, trying to ignore the sound of others putting the bodies of our allies in after I was finished. To ignore how many of these graves I had created. Just focusing on the shovel and the dirt.

"That'll be enough; we have almost everyone now." Chase's voice floated down to me from above.

I relaxed as I saw him. Every time he came into view, a wave of gratitude washed over me. He was still here, and I still had more time with him. I passed him the shovel before I jumped up and out of the grave.

"Our dads want to see us," he said. As we walked by the line of graves someone took the shovel from him as we passed. I wrapped my hand in his, and he pulled me toward the half-standing factory.

"What about?" I asked.

He just shrugged in return. We walked in silence; the only real noise here was the sound of hard manual labor going on around us. No one spoke. There was a hush over the entire camp as everyone toiled away.

We made our way inside and headed for the rooms at the back. As we entered, Nolan, Ethan, CC1, and a man my age who I had never met before were all leaning over a table with a map on it. They gave gestures of greeting as they saw us.

"Good, you're here." My father motioned for us to join them.

Ethan ran a hand through his hair in the same way Chase did. It was uncanny how similar they were. He grabbed the back of his neck, rubbing at the muscles bunched there but still managed a smile for us even though he looked dead-tired.

"So, we've tracked their movements from here," the young man said, drawing his finger east from our location toward a medium-sized town called Fairhaven. "They have a satellite camp here; we haven't seen movement of them leaving this location yet." He blinked a few times as he realized who we were. "Oh, hi. I'm George Rivera." He stuck his hand out, and I shook it.

"Nice to meet you, George. Are you in charge here?" I asked.

He flinched, and I felt guilty for asking. "I guess I am now. Everyone else is gone."

I couldn't guess at his pain; he had lost so much so quickly. All the people he had lived and worked with. The devastation was all around us. We lost so many rebels in Neria, but I couldn't name them, not all of them.

I caught his gaze. "I'm so sorry for your loss."

"Same to you. I just heard." A moment passed where we shared our combined grief before we turned back to the task at hand.

I looked at the map. "So, I guess we're headed there?" I tapped my finger on the town.

My father crossed his arms and just stood for a moment, not saying anything. I mimicked him with a scowl on my face. He shook his head with a small chuckle. "Yes, we need to send you there. I just wish we had someone else to go."

I sighed. "This is what we do. Put us to work. We need it." Turning quickly to Chase, I had an idea. He raised his eyebrow at me quizzically before I faced our fathers again.

"Send Thea with us," I said, and Ethan instantly frowned. "She is going to go crazy if you never let her leave. She was in the thick of it with Alice, and I want to train her. I want to make sure she can take care of herself. I think she needs this too."

I could see my father mulling the idea over.

Chase came up behind me and put his hand on my shoulder. "Dad, she's right. Thea needs a change. She's growing up, and no matter what you want, she won't stay at headquarters forever."

My father gave his long-time friend a reassuring look, and finally, Ethan deflated.

"Keep her safe," he said.

"We won't let anything happen to her, I promise," Chase agreed.

Chase gave me a quick low five, as I stood by him, like no one could see us, but I could almost feel our fathers rolling their eyes. "George, tell us what you know about Fairhaven."

"They're the closest city, so we have many allies there. We're not sure if any or all of their information is now compromised. Many of our refugees come to us through them. Many people who traveled there were just looking for someplace safe. The military has a presence there, and we've been experiencing the same patterns that everywhere else is with kids and people without family going missing. With the threat of execution for any who refuse the draft or are found helping us. I don't know what's going to happen, but it's going to be bad. We need to figure out the level of threat and make sure as many of our people are as safe as we can." George was propping himself up with both arms against the table. His hair was falling into his face as he started at the map.

I rubbed my temples as a headache came on fast. My stomach was turning. This was so similar to Neria. So many people were in danger. I didn't know if I could go through that again, but there wasn't much of a choice. This was my duty. We had to put all our advantages to use, and I was one of our best weapons.

"Vi, can you go round up the others, please? George, give me the details of our options and assets." Chase was already in strategy mode. I leaned in for a quick kiss on the cheek before I turned and made my way out of the room to find my friends. As I slipped out, I saw CC1 leaning in to brainstorm with the others. I had a feeling they might be able to revamp our logistics.

The others weren't far. I caught sight of Gwen, Thea, and Benson on the other side of the large open space in the factory. Thea was pushing a broom around while Benson and Gwen were organizing medical supplies. I jogged over to them, and they all noticed me as I made my way closer.

"Hey, what's up?" Benson asked.

I couldn't miss the haunted look in Gwen's eyes that showed she still wasn't totally present with us. "We have a mission; we're going to be rolling out soon." I saw Thea deflate at the news. She had been so happy when we'd finally come back from Neria. "You too kid."

She lit up like the morning sky.

"Really? Dad is going to let me?" She was almost vibrating with excitement.

"Yeah, but you need to do whatever we say when we say it," I told her, and she nodded vigorously before doing a victory dance with the broom. "Come on; we'll get you all up to speed. We're headed to Fairhaven."

Vi

We piled into the armored van. One of the feed factory rebels was going to drive us to Fairhaven. We pulled the door shut behind us, and the driver nodded in greeting before starting it up.

"Thanks for the ride," Benson said. "What's your name?"

"Anthony Hawkins, sir," the man said. "It's an honor to meet you. You're legends."

As always, that sentiment made me uncomfortable. "We're just doing our jobs, like everyone else. It's an honor for us to meet all of you too."

His blush was visible in the rearview mirror. We bounced as the van bumped and jerked over the uneven ground, but we didn't slow as time was of the essence.

Chase turned to Thea with a concerned look. "This is serious, Thea; you need to follow our instructions, no questions."

"I will, I promise." She saluted to me.

"We're glad you're here, little sister." Benson punched her in the shoulder. "You'll be a pro in no time."

"We're going to need to blend in, get a lay of the land before we start reaching out to people." Chase glanced at Anthony. "George said this town is known for its textiles, right?"

"Yeah, there is a single factory where most of the town works."

"We should be showing up close to the shift change. If anyone asks, we're just headed to work." Chase glanced from one of us to the next, ending on Thea, making sure we all understood.

Out of our entire group, though, Thea might be the most experienced in blending in. She had lived in the capital city of Longdale, right under Esmerelda's nose, for years.

Thea had been well versed in slipping through the city undetected and had been handy with guns and weapons already. I knew it would come back to her easily. Just like I knew she would pick everything else up quickly. She always had.

As we rode in relative silence, I couldn't help but get wrapped up in the what-ifs we might find there. I was crossing my fingers, hoping that it would be relatively quiet. That we could slip in to talk to who we needed to without any hassle. But I had the sinking feeling that it wouldn't be that easy.

With the devastation to the feed factory, it was clear Esmerelda was escalating the conflict. I wasn't even sure how she had obtained information about the location. She must have launched the attack as soon as she was aware of our breach of the palace.

We had effectively cut off her supply of prisoners from Neria when the king was removed from power. She couldn't have been pleased to find out what was going on. I hadn't realized how closely they had been in contact, but it was clear she knew.

My father had called us, saying something had happened before the final lock down of the palace was completed. We had raced back right away, but the feed factory was already decimated by the time we made it there.

Esmerelda was already slightly unhinged, and her baseline personality was fury. I worried what this would push her to do next. She had the full might of the Kabrian military behind her. If she moved to a full-on assault against us—I shivered at the thought—the death toll would be incalculable. She didn't care about the collateral damage. She didn't care about my people, *her* people.

Anthony sucked in a breath. "Oh gods," he whispered.

We all turned our attention to the view ahead of us.

Fairhaven was burning. Anthony sped up, racing toward the edge of the city. He skidded to a stop a few blocks in, seeing the damage. Throwing the door open, we all jumped out. We had to help who we could.

"Thea, stay right behind me," Chase snapped.

Panic was written across her face. She hadn't been to the feed factory until all the fires had been put out. She hadn't seen the devastation right after the attack like we had. Now it was right before her.

We all tapped to release the nanobots of our suits to start stitching themselves together. They would protect us from some attacks and would reform instantly if they were broken through. They could even spread to create weapons and shields. If the weapons left our hands, they would stay in the last shape they had been set to, which was great for throwing blades. I cursed, realizing David hadn't had time to make one for Thea. On Chase's signal, the others surrounded her. I moved to the front, ready to take the lead.

I stopped short as we came closer to one of the buildings lining the street. There were bodies hanging from ropes off the edge of the roof. My breath caught in my throat, and I cursed Esmerelda with every fiber of my being.

There was nothing we could do for them, but I held out hope that we would find survivors. We kept our weapons at the ready as we moved further into the city. It was hard to breathe; the smoke was thick in the air.

"How did we not know? When did this happen?" Chase cursed.

I went to call my father, but there was just static on the comms. Just like with the feed factory, they had jammed everything.

The city was eerily quiet, nothing to be heard outside of the shifting of damaged buildings and the crackle of fires. It was so similar to the embattled parts of Neria we had just left. As we continued deeper the more bodies were strewn everywhere. Why was it so quiet?

"Split up and look for survivors. Thea, you're with me," Chase said quietly.

He nodded slightly to me, letting to me know to go and do what I could. Taking off, I raced away from my friends and further into the city. I launched myself over debris scattered throughout the streets. With my enhanced hearing, I listened for any sounds of survivors, for any cries for help. I didn't hear anything. How could I not hear anything? Where was everyone?

Then, I heard footsteps and weapons shifting. In a split second, I changed directions, heading toward the closest building for cover. Just as I made it, bullets began flying toward me from the roofs above. I pushed ahead, crashing through the nearest door to get out of their line of fire. As soon as I had a second to orient myself, I peeked out to see what I was dealing with. There were at least five snipers on each of the two roofs in my line of sight, which meant there were probably more than ten in total.

The entrance to the stairs was across the lobby, and I headed for them. Putting extra power into my legs, I launched myself up, grabbing on to a railing a few floors above. Using my momentum, I jumped up the rest of the way to the landing that opened onto the roof.

Slamming through the door, rage bubbled within me. I could barely breathe as it gripped my core. My steps were quick, and I broke into a run straight at the closest person, who was on the next building.

He looked up in surprise as I reached him. They had obviously been expecting me to emerge again from my place on the ground. He didn't even have time to start turning in my direction before I barreled into him.

Snarling, I grabbed his rifle before he could recover and pulled it from his grasp. He started to cry out, to catch the attention of the others, but I grabbed him by the throat. The others started to fire at me, but I kept him between us. He jerked as the bullets slammed into him. When they paused to reload, I threw him down and he gasped a last wet breath. It made me sick how little they cared for their own. No wonder they had no issues razing an entire city to the ground.

Sliding under the next soldiers' line of fire, I kicked out at his knee. It crunched and buckled in the wrong direction. He screamed in pain as I grabbed his rifle and twisted the metal of the barrel before dropping it. I was on the next sniper before the discarded gun hit the ground. I blew through them like a vicious wind.

Their screams echoed in the empty streets. I couldn't control myself. My fury was all consuming, red creeping across my vision. They were out for blood; I wouldn't be any different. Not this time.

I heard one of the last men calling for backup into his radio. As I reached him, I took him by the throat. He didn't beg for mercy. There was resolve in his eyes, but there was a flicker of fear underneath. He believed in his mission, in Esmerelda. He had picked his side. Glimpsing the destruction over his shoulder, I bellowed my anger and frustration as I threw him from the building. He careened straight into the wall of the one across from us and then tumbled to the ground below. There was no holding back. They didn't deserve compassion or mercy.

Standing on the lip of the building, I gauged the best direction to search next. I decided to head toward the middle of the city. Toward the main square where the markets for trade would be, a place that was normally bustling with people at this time of day.

I leapt from the edge of the roof. Landing lightly, as always, I pushed myself into a sprint once more. As I moved through the city, I still didn't hear any calls for help, but I also didn't run into any more soldiers. My mouth was dry and my pulse was quick. It wasn't from exertion but rather from seeing the extent of what had happened here.

Coming into view of the square, I stumbled to a stop. It was empty, but stalls and carts were damaged, their wares scattered across the ground. In the middle flickered a hologram of Esmerelda that was more than a story high.

"Fairhaven, you have been found to be riddled with collaborators of the terrorists. This is treason against the crown and Kabria. This cannot stand. By my order, the entire city will be made an example of. If you are not a collaborator, submit yourself to the military voluntarily. Any who resist will be found guilty of treason and executed for your crimes. Make your decision as the sentence will be carried out within the hour." The hologram of Esmerelda paused for a moment before the message repeated.

Walking up to the device that the hologram was being cast from, I crushed it under my heel. She had decimated the entire population of the city. That was why I didn't hear any cries for help. No one was left. They were taken or killed.

Someone *had* to be left.

I made my way out of the square and toward the factory that employed most of the city hoping some people might have been able to hide in the huge building. As it came into view, I couldn't breathe. The building was smoldering, and the doors were chained shut. I dropped to my knees at the sight. Everything in my stomach came up with a heave. I heard the roof start to creek before the damaged materials started to shift. I lifted my arm to protect my eyes from the wave of glass, bricks, and dust that exploded out from the building as it collapsed.

Looking at the destruction in front of me, I couldn't stop the tears. They slipped silently down my cheeks. How could she do this to her own people? The city wasn't huge, but it was large enough. There had been so many innocents here. So many who had nothing to do with us. So many who were just going about, living their lives.

I pulled myself up and started to dig my way into the rubble in search of survivors. Someone had to have made it; someone had to be here.

I had to be delicate to not shift anything in case there were air pockets below or to cause more of a collapse. Somewhere, someone might have survived. Finally, I heard coughing and whimpers below me. I dug toward the sounds.

"I'm here. I'm coming, just hold on," I called and managed to unearth a way inside.

"Help," came a soft voice.

The rubble tore apart the skin of my hands as I ripped away chunks of cement and rebar. The building started to groan. I didn't know how long it would last before it came down the rest of the way.

I broke through and saw a soft light from a lantern. It seemed to be a tunnel, and there were more than a few people cowering together. People cried out when they saw me. I could practically feel their relief. Only moments later, I felt the building start to shift again, and I dropped down before it could be caught in the collapse.

Wails erupted as their hope was crushed along with the building. The hole I had made was gone, but the tunnel was still intact.

"It's okay." I held my hands out in what I hoped was a calming gesture. "It's okay. I can still get us out of here. Where does this go?" I asked one of the men who seemed to be lucid.

He pointed farther down the tunnel. "This connected many of the buildings in the city, but it's collapsed near another exit."

"If this connects the buildings, it should lead under the street, right?" I asked him, and he confirmed it. "Show me where." I pointed to another woman. "Keep everyone as close together as you can right here."

She started to give orders to start moving everyone together. The man led me down the tunnel. Eventually, he pointed toward the ceiling. "This should be close."

With the comms down, my team would have no idea where I was. It was up to me to get these people out of here. I could do this. Luckily, the top of the tunnel was relatively low. "Get back to the others," I said, and he did so. I could do this.

I bent my knees and protected my head with my arms. Steeling myself before launching myself up as hard as I could, I slammed into the ceiling. Nothing happened but a bit of dust falling around me. I saw the man watching me like I was crazy.

I ignored him and jumped again. This time, a few pieces of

cement broke off and dropped. I did it again and again, using my body as a battering ram. Finally, a hole started to materialize, and I shook the dust out of my hair and wiped my face.

One more should do it. As soon as I hit, a large piece of the street fell right on top of me. I heard gasps and screams as I went down. My muscles bunched, and I braced myself under it, managing to keep it from crushing me. With a little effort I was able to toss it to the side. A cheer erupted as the sun started to filter into the tunnel. I hooked my hand on the edge of the street to pull myself out.

The cave-in left a hill of debris that the others could crawl up, and I reached down to help them.

Some of the people around me cried and held each other as we got them onto the street.

"Let's go; there's a transport that can take you out of here." Turning, I led them to where we left the van, some of them helping along others who were injured.

I came across Anthony as we got closer. He had been canvasing the area by the van. He brightened as he saw the people with me and ran over to help someone.

I saw another person struggling and asked if they wanted help, picking them up when they agreed and carrying them over. Anthony went to help more of the women and children to the vehicle. We weren't going to be able to fit everyone; some made no move to try to pile in.

"We need to keep searching for others," the man who had helped me said.

"Anthony, get these people to the feed factory. Send some other transports back. We *will* find others." There had to be others. I had to believe there were more.

Right? A whole city couldn't just be gone.

After we got as many as we could fit into the van, Anthony hopped in and started off toward the safety of the rebels. Our reinforcements would be here soon, it was only a twenty-minute drive between us.

I looked at those who were left. "Let's get searching."

We split up to start canvasing the rest of the city. Luckily, it turned out some of the people, like the man, were indeed our allies. I followed him as he led me toward other likely hiding spots where we might find more people.

Now that I had found survivors, again the thought tugged at me about how it was strange that after that first group of soldiers I encountered, we didn't run into any other resistance. Especially since they had called for backup. We searched for almost an hour before I heard a familiar roar, and saw two huge bombers flying directly for us.

"Get to cover!" I screamed.

Everyone looked around in confusion, but within moments, they were scattering for shelter as they saw what was creating the noise.

The city streets rocked and buckled as the first bomb hit. I covered my ears and crouched down as bomb after bomb hit the city. I whimpered as the noise overloaded my senses. I prayed to the gods we wouldn't lose anyone else before heat hit me with full force and I went flying as a bomb landed nearby.

7

Vi

I couldn't move. I couldn't breathe. My ears were ringing, but I was alive. Flexing, I tried to see if anything was broken, but everything seemed to work the way it was supposed to. After catching my breath, I groaned and pushed myself up to my hands and knees. I could barely see through the dust swirling in the air. I got to my feet and started to stumble around, searching for the others.

Through the haze, I saw people starting to stir nearby. I reached out and helped some up, most of them holding bleeding wounds and limping. We all started to search for anyone else who survived. Eventually, I heard people screaming. More bodies were strewn throughout the area, and I gagged at the sight of displaced body parts. I didn't know how much more carnage I could take. Yet, there was no choice; I had to keep going.

A bus come into view, and I sighed in relief. We had split up throughout the city, so I hoped they were sending vehicles to multiple areas. As the doors flung open, medics raced out and headed toward us.

More of the rebels poured out and started grabbing people and helping them to the buses. I caught the eyes of a few others and motioned them over.

"Once everyone is loaded, I need all of you to start searching the rest of the city. We've been covering it from the square and working our way out. We're going to be here as long as it takes to search the whole city," I said, and they saluted before some spread out to tell the others. Many of them went straight to work, searching the surrounding buildings.

I took a moment to get myself under control. Deep breath in and out, in and... I couldn't help but cough from the toxic air.

I tried to keep the panic at bay. I had no idea where my friends were. I hoped they were all okay, but I had to focus on the people nearby. I moved quickly, using my super hearing and shouting out to find any survivors. I dug through pile after pile of rubble. Luckily, we found some. Not many, but some.

I ended up running into the others as I made my way through the city. The tightness in my chest loosened with each one of them I found. Chase visibly sagged as soon as he saw me and I was glad to see Thea was still with him. I hugged everyone tight as I found them, but our moments were brief. We had others to worry about now.

The night dragged on, and eventually, Chase grabbed my arm to pull me away from a pile of rubble. "Come on; they just sent a fresh group. Let's get on the bus."

I didn't want to leave but couldn't argue that I was dead on my feet. I didn't know how much longer I could make it anyway. At least the search would continue. I promised myself I'd be back just as soon as I got some sleep.

The others were at the bus already by the time we made it there. It was clear we were all exhausted. As Thea came by, I grabbed her and placed a kiss on the top of her head, ignoring the dust coating it. She wrapped her arms around me and burrowed her head into my chest. I just held her for a moment before I pushed her toward the waiting transport.

All of us were cut up and bruised, but we were alive. We all looked haunted as we took our seats. Chase pulled me down next to him, cocooning me with his body. I leaned into him, reveling in the warmth and safety of his presence, and darkness enveloped me before the wheels even started to turn.

Chase shook me awake. Blinking slowly, it became clear we were back to the relative safety of the feed factory. With a groan, I pulled myself up and headed off the bus with Chase close on my heels. Blearily, and with stumbling steps, I managed to make my way inside. Our fathers rushed over as soon as they saw us enter. Dad pulled me into a tight hug when he reached me. I just leaned into him, too tired to bear my own weight. Ethan was visibly relieved as he saw his kids and pulled both of them close.

George was there, standing slightly behind the others, not saying anything, just watching us. As I caught his eye, he gave me a grave nod before waving his hands at the cots. The others might have been talking, but I didn't have the energy to listen. I crawled onto the closest cot. Within moments, I was out again.

I woke to the bustle of the rebels. Some were cooking, some were helping the medics helping the wounded, some were talking about the events of the past few days. I groaned as I blinked the sleep from my eyes, and I rolled myself up to place my feet on the floor. This looked exactly like every cell in Neria we had visited, but this was Kabria, this was *my* home. Angry didn't even begin to cover what I felt seeing all the pain and suffering.

Glancing around, I saw Benson and Gwen sleeping in cots nearby. Pushing myself up, I went in search of Chase, as I didn't see him anywhere in the main room. I found Thea a few rows over with her arm thrown over her eyes just like how her brother often rested.

I headed for the small area where we met George the day before. I slipped in and caught sight of not just Chase but our fathers, CC1, George, Joseph, and David as well.

"Morning," came the murmur from the others. Everyone seemed exhausted, except for CC1 who I was pretty sure couldn't get tired.

At least it seemed we all agreed it was not a *good* morning. David filled a cup with coffee and handed it to me silently. I squeezed his hand before he went to stand next to Joseph.

Chase tapped a tablet, and a video of Esmerelda came into view. She was sitting on her throne, looking regal as usual. I hated the fact that she was unarguably beautiful. I wished there was some hint of how ugly she was on the inside.

"My dearest people of Kabria. It is with a heavy heart that I must bring you news of the losses our country feels today. In the wake of the terrorists' work in Neria, now they have brought their chaos home again. They have attacked our own city of Fairhaven."

The view of Esmerelda switched to the burning city. Then, it changed to a video of my run in with the soldiers, including the one I threw from the building. I chewed on my lip at that, feeling guilty for the rage I couldn't contain. I had wanted to hurt them for what they were part of. The video returned to Esmerelda, who was holding tight to a golden staff as she stared into the camera.

"We have yet to uncover why these terrorists are attacking our people, but I give you my word as your queen that they will be stopped. In the interest of safety, all cities will be under a curfew. Anyone found out after curfew will be arrested and interrogated. Fear not, we will get to the bottom of this and restore peace to our land."

Chase stopped the video. I couldn't believe she was spinning this against us. Well, I could, but I hadn't expected it this morning. I had expected her to cover it up and make sure there was no news of it at all.

"We're getting word out to our allies to be careful and not to communicate unless absolutely necessary," my father said.

I jerked my gaze to his. "You need to pull them all back."

He raised his eyebrows in shock and scoffed. "We can't just pull everyone out."

"You need to figure it out." I pointed to the tablet in Chase's hands. "You've been planning this for years, you have the funds, you have locations planned for bases, pull everyone out *now*. Organize and set up the settlements. It's too dangerous. She'll burn the whole country down to defeat us. This isn't us trying to weaken her hold anymore. It's a war; she made it one." I ran my hands through my hair to hide their shaking. "We need to make a stand, and we need to cut her off. Block off her access to the farms and the food, cut her off from this part of Kabria."

"She's right," Chase said. "Things are changing, and if we do block her off, we'll want the people with us out of the cities anyway. We don't want them to starve when we do this. It's time. The civil war has already started."

My father rubbed at his temples. "Yes, okay, you're right. Ethan, CC1, let's get the list together." He turned to David and Joseph. "If we get you a list, can you help us start contacting our people?"

They agreed just as Benson, Gwen, and Thea came into the room. David went to make them cups of coffee as well. I wrapped an arm around Thea and pulled her close. She leaned into me before taking the cup David handed her.

"What's going on?" Thea asked, and Chase showed them the video. Everyone agreed to do what they could to start working on the evacuation plans.

Chase came over and took my hand. I saw the raw emotion laid bare in his eyes. The grief, worry, and love all vying for dominance. I understood it all too well. We had been through too much in a matter of a few days. We had seen too much.

"Can I talk to you?" He gestured toward the door.

"Sure." I gave Thea a quick squeeze and followed him out. I couldn't help but wonder what he couldn't say in front of the others.

Once he stopped and turned to me, and I wondered again what was making him act strange.

"Vi..." He paused. "After all of this..." He waved a hand around in our general area before grabbing mine. "It's proven we don't know how much time we'll have. How we need to take what happiness we can find while we can, and I just can't wait anymore." He swallowed and seemed almost shy, before he set his shoulders, steadying himself. He brushed his thumbs across the back of my hands before brining my fingers to his lips. "Will you marry me?"

My heart skipped a beat, and my insides felt like fireworks were going off. There was only ever going to be one answer to that question. I pounced on him, wrapping my arms around his neck. "Yes!"

Tears started to slip down my cheeks as he pulled me close.

He was right. We had to live our lives to the fullest in spite of everything we had lost. Or what kind of life would be left? There was no need to feel guilty for finding joy after all the heartbreak. It was all right to be happy even in the darkest of times.

His smile lit up his face. He kissed me so passionately that I couldn't help but melt into him. Once we finally unwrapped ourselves, we beamed at each other.

"Let's go tell the others." He tugged me off toward our friends, who erupted in cheers at the news.

CC1 nodded and turned to us. "I am happy to hear of your upcoming union. I believe Marco would have been as well."

Thea's face lit up and Ethan already had tears in his eyes. My dad looked like this was no surprise. I guessed Chase had been a gentleman and asked him first. He gave me a nod, but I saw a twinkle in his eye. The big guy still wasn't much on warm shows of affection, but I could tell he was happy.

David grabbed both of us by the neck and pulled us in close, and we just held each other for a moment. "About time," he said before leaving big sloppy kisses on our cheeks.

"Congratulations." Joseph said sticking out his hand, but I just took it and pulled him in so we could both hug him.

Benson punched Chase in the shoulder and pinched my cheek. "I'm really happy for you."

Then Gwen was there. Tears were shimmering in her eyes, but her smile was radiant. "I'm happy for you, he would be too." I knew she was speaking of Atty. I hoped this wasn't too hard on her.

Thea had rounded the table and slammed into me slipping her

arms around my waist, and she stuck out her tongue at Chase. "I thought he'd never get around to it."

"I realized there was never going to be a perfect time, and I wasn't going to waste another second." The look he gave me had a blush rushing to my cheeks.

My heart was so full. This was one of the times I remembered how loved I was. How lucky I had been to find all these wonderful people who wanted nothing but the best for me.

I might have been a princess, technically, but he was so much more than a prince charming. He was the voice in my head to remind me to keep going, he was my shield, he was the warrior who would always fight by my side. He was my partner, he always let me know I wasn't alone. He was my lifeline at times, anchoring me while I fought the storm inside.

He was my everything, and I would be his forever.

8

ESMERELDA

"You better be here to give me good news." I wasn't in the mood to hear anything else as the captain of my guard entered.

"I do actually," he said.

Narrowing my eyes, I gave him a look that said I better agree or there would be consequences. "And what might that be?"

"We have the sisters. They are en route here."

Well, that was indeed good news.

"Alert me the moment they arrive." I didn't want to waste any time. If this worked, they would be the perfect weapons for my needs. If not, I could make sure Astor knew they were dead because of her. I couldn't help but hope that if it worked on one of them it would work on both. With the shared genes, it seemed likely. "You're dismissed."

He turned and rushed from my office. It always improved my mood when they did that. I loved their fear. I loved the power. It was the least I deserved.

The pain in my head pulsed. I pressed lightly on my eyes, trying to lessen it. My blood boiled under my skin.

I had lived with this my entire life. The disease that rotted my bones. The disease that turned my entire body against me.

Yet, I wouldn't be controlled by it. I could replace the bones. I could temper the fire within me with science.

"Morgan," I snapped, and she appeared.

"Yes, Your Majesty."

"Get the doctor." I couldn't see her response, but I heard her steps receding. My vision swam. My pulse roared in my ears.

The door opened and closed again. The doctor didn't even bother saying anything before a cold metal touched my skin and ice spread from the injection site. Slowly, my vision returned to normal and I saw concern on his face.

"This isn't lasting long enough. Why have you not figured out the cure yet," I hissed.

He just shook his head. Doctor Howard Netzel was one of the few people who didn't cower in fear from me. I had brought him with me from Neria; he had been my doctor for most of my life. The whole point of these experiments was to fix me. Yet, everything we tested lasted no more than a week. At one time, it had been down to days, and before that it was only hours. It was improving, but it wasn't enough. It had turned the brat into a superhuman freak, but it couldn't even rid me of this weakness.

"It's still only compatible with a few specific genes, none of which you possess."

"I have given you years of testing. I want results." Venom dripped from each word.

"You cannot rush science," he said matter-of-factly. The same answer he gave every time.

"If you can't do this, I'll replace you."

While he did know too much to be left alive, it was still a hollow threat. He was the only person who had been with me through it all. He understood what I had overcome, how it had forged me into who I was today. That, and I couldn't waste the years of knowledge locked away in his brain.

"It will come in time, but..." His expression softened. "Our most recent scans show it has moved into your femur. We may have to replace it soon."

Before long, I would be nothing but metal underneath. Who knew how long I had before my organs started to fail. The older I grew, the faster the disease was spreading. Yet, once we found the cure, I wouldn't have to fear time. I would conquer even death itself.

He rested a hand on my shoulder lightly.

"We're working as quickly as we can. It would be faster if we got Joseph Acron back. He was the brain behind the things that have worked. We haven't been able to crack his research completely. Not everything was in the data we seized after he fled."

"Work faster." I waved a hand, and he turned to leave me.

My thoughts wandered to my family. My father wouldn't pass his empire to me, saying this disease left me too damaged to rule. He had always looked at me with disgust. He would have left everything to my idiot brother.

The day the palace had been taken by the rebels; my family had begged me for asylum. Which I enjoyed denying them. After how they treated me, I hoped they were captured and killed as well. Eventually, I would retake Neria, as was my birthright. Out of them all, I was the only one capable of leading; the rest were worthless.

I had been forged in this fire.

I wouldn't be sated until I was unstoppable.

9

VI

Over the next week, we had fresh teams cycled to Fairhaven three times a day. The search for any survivors went on twenty-four hours a day as the shifts kept moving through the city.

Finally, today, we pulled out our last team and called off the search. We had worked through the city in a grid, and at this point, if we found anyone else, they wouldn't be alive. After some sleep and food, the last shift would be cycled out to other jobs either on the blockade, evacuations, or setting up for the influx of newcomers.

We spoke with our allies from every city in Kabria and started creating the evacuation routes. As new refugees started to arrive, they pitched in to help us build the infrastructure of the first new base while many of those who had already been with us helped plan the blockade to the cities and started to reroute all supplies to our own stockpiles. The movements were quick and concise, and the air of the camps were subdued but focused as we tried to execute these gigantic feats as quickly as possible. I was incredibly impressed with the resolve of everyone I met as we worked.

I and the rest of the team were headed back to headquarters, which was a few hours west of Fairhaven, weighed down with exhaustion. By the end of the day, the feed factory would be empty. Nothing more than a burned shell of what it once was.

My mind wandered to our time in the penthouse in Neria before things went sideways. Of the fun we all had living together. The laughter, the lightness we felt, the fact that Atty had been there with us. Now, just a few months later, our entire lives were flipped upside down. I had been surrounded by constant death in the prison, but it was nothing like what I had seen in the past few weeks.

"Do you own anything white or red?" Thea asked me, startling me back into the present.

"Um, a white shirt or two maybe? I don't think I have anything red," I replied, and she scrunched up her face. "Why?"

"You can't get married in that," she said, like it was obvious.

I scoffed. "What is wrong with this? I wear it every day."

Thea rolled her eyes and gave me her most exasperated expression.

"That's the point," Gwen said lightly, but it wasn't followed with her usual giggle. "I probably have something we could put her in."

"It's just going to be us; everyone knows what I look like," I grumbled, but if they wanted to dress me up, I wouldn't complain. A girl didn't get married every day. I couldn't believe that this was happening. It didn't seem real, but we weren't going to waste another moment now that the work at Fairhaven was done. I knew I'd be with Chase forever, but it hadn't crossed my mind with everything else we had been dealing with. Still, I was overjoyed Chase had proposed.

"Is no one going to fuss over me? It's my wedding too." Chase pouted.

"I'll fuss over you," David cooed from his spot in the back.

"Thank you." Chase winked at him, which made us all chuckle, even Gwen. It was nice to see those cracks where she was starting to shine through again, even if they were just for a moment.

They wedding was going to be tonight. As soon as we arrived, I was whisked away from the others by Thea and Gwen. Over my shoulder I saw Chase get pulled in the opposite direction by the others. We caught one last glimpse of each other, sharing that look that was just for us. The next time we saw each other would be at the ceremony.

They pulled me along to Gwen's room, and I threw myself onto the bed while they went through her closet. Garments came flying out, tossed this way and that with the two of them nodding or frowning depending on what they pulled next.

At a certain point, I couldn't keep in the giggles. "How do you have so many clothes?"

"Because some people like to have more variation than five copies of the same outfit." Thea cocked her eyebrow at me like I was ridiculous.

"I don't just have white shirts... I also have tan ones, thank you very much," I countered, and she just shook her head in defeat.

"Ah yes, here it is." Gwen pulled out something red.

"Yes, that's perfect!" Thea exclaimed.

They held up the dress up by the hanger to show me. It was a bright red silk dress that cascaded down and slid across itself as they turned it this way and that.

"I don't think I can pull that off." I chewed on my lip. I wasn't the type of person who did *fancy*. During the mission to infiltrate the Nerian Tech Summit, I was posing as a wealthy investor, and I still wore pants, flats, and a black turtleneck.

"Hogwash," Thea said, which surprised both Gwen and I.

"Hogwash?" we both asked, and all of us fell into giggles.

"Shut up. You know what I mean. You are going to look amazing. My brother isn't going to know what to do with himself," Thea said.

"Oh, I think he'll have a pretty good idea." Gwen elbowed her, wiggling her eyebrow.

"Ew, gross," Thea complained but grinned and then jumped onto the bed with me. "I've always thought of you as a sister, and now, it's going to be official!" She squealed and pulled me close.

I hugged her. "Same here," I told her. "I hope you know I'd always be here for you, no matter what, even if we weren't getting married."

"Yeah, I'm so happy we finally got you back," Thea said as Gwen watched us, slightly subdued. I grabbed her and tugged her down into the dog pile on the bed.

"Okay, but you should probably go get cleaned up before we start getting ready," she told me as she eyed the dust covering us. "You still have rubble in your hair."

"Not just there it's everywhere," I said, and we untangled ourselves.

"Yeah, me too." Gwen grabbed her things, and all three of us decided to go hit the showers.

As I waited for it to heat up from the frozen water that first comes out, I mindlessly rubbed at my shoulder where my scars used to be.

When Esmerelda experimented on me while I was in the prison, my body had been covered in scars. My powers didn't start to show until I had been with the rebels for a while, as Esmerelda had kept me close to starvation on top of everything else. If I'd had my healing, then it must have been doing everything just to keep me alive. As I started to rebuild my strength, I got faster, my hearing was heightened, I saw clearer, and more as the days wore on.

Yet, throughout all of that, even as my enhanced healing came about, those scars never faded. I had seen them as proof of what I had lived through. They had reminded me of who I was and what I could endure on the hard nights.

While in Neria, I had been exposed to a bioweapon that was targeted at me directly using my DNA. It had started to rupture my cells faster than my healing could repair them; I'd almost died. Joseph and David had come up with a serum using the intel on the weapon we had stolen from the summit to reverse engineer a cure for me. It worked but a little too well. My scars had healed, and now, I was even stronger than I had been before.

I was devastated when I realized they were gone. I still wasn't over it. It had happened less than a month ago. As my fingers slipped over my unblemished skin, I flinched. Everyone reminded me I was still just as strong and had lived through it all even if the scars were gone now. It didn't change my experiences, but I missed them. I shook my head and stepped under the warm water, letting it wash away the dirt and grime from my skin and hair. I couldn't help but sigh in relief; we had been without warm water in Neria when staying with the rebels, and this felt divine every time since.

I spent far longer than I needed to under the water, but I hadn't been ready to join the real world yet. Shutting off the water, I wrapped myself in a towel. I poked my head out and saw the girls drying off as well. I smirked; I hadn't been the only one making noises of contentment as we cleaned off. Gwen seemed as relieved as I felt.

"Come on. Are you two ready?" Thea asked, almost bouncing with excitement. "I can't wait to do your hair and makeup!"

I groaned but also grinned as she dragged the two of us to Gwen's room.

"I'll be right back. I'm going to grab my stuff," Thea said before running to her room. I heard cat calls from the hallway, and I poked my head out and glared at a few of the young men I saw standing in the hallway. They noticed me and gulped before returning to their rooms or heading off to wherever they were going. Within moments, she was throwing a huge bag down on the bed. I heard a bunch of items rolling around inside it and felt something like horror as she opened it and revealed almost all of it was makeup.

"No fussing," Gwen said, and I rolled my eyes but surrendered.

We chatted as the girls dried my hair then heated it, straightened it, twirled it, and braided it until it was a beautiful piece of art that I was afraid to touch. I also felt like I might have had at least a few-pounds-worth of bobby pins stuck in there as well.

I reveled in how normal all this was. Was this what life would have been like if Esmerelda had never come into our lives? Would it have been sleepovers filled with makeovers to the tune of gossip? Would we have sat around chatting about first kisses and true love? An ache thrummed in me. It was moments like these that made me truly aware of what had been taken from all of us.

I took a breath and thought of the good. The small things. These moments. They would have to shine brighter than the dark or I would drown in its inky depths.

Gwen finished my eyeliner with a flick of her wrist. Her hand rested against my shoulder as she held my gaze for a moment.

"Are you okay?" I worried that the wedding would make things harder for her.

Slowly, she smiled sadly. "I will be, but don't worry about me tonight. I'm so happy for both of you. I can't wait to celebrate with you. Atty would be happily telling everyone he told us so."

My lips pressed tight, but one corner quirked up. I grabbed her and pulled her into a fierce hug. She clung to me, and we just sat for a moment. Gwen pushed herself back and dusted her hands off on her pantleg.

Thea poked her head over Gwen's shoulder, and she gasped. "You look amazing!" She squealed. "All right, it's time," she said, shaking the dress and handing it to me.

I grabbed it and headed behind a screen in the corner to change. The material was cold and soft as it fell across my skin. My shoulders bare, the rest clung close to me and slipped down my legs, pooling around my feet with just the smallest train. There was a slight slit toward my thigh that made it easier to walk.

I came around, and the girls gasped as they saw me. Thea had her hands covering her mouth, and tears sparkled in her eyes. When I saw myself in Gwen's mirror I stopped short at my reflection. I couldn't help but think back to when I used to catch sight of my reflection in the prison. Then, I had been gaunt, pale, covered in wounds—healed and new. I used to appear half dead.

That girl wouldn't have recognized this version of me.

Some curls fell from the braids and framed my face. My skin was radiant, and the makeup was relatively natural, which fit me just fine. The dress hugged in all the right places. I seemed delicate and fierce at the same time. I looked like a princess. The girls came behind me and wrapped me in a hug, and I tried my best not to cry so I didn't ruin the amazing job the girls had just done. My heart swelled with the love I had for these women and the love they had for me.

10

VI

The sun worked its way toward dusk as we headed out to the training fields. David had let us know to go to my favorite tree when we were ready. My chest tightened when I saw the graves ahead, but I was also happy I could still share this moment with my friends. No matter how macabre that thought might have been, it brought me some peace.

I gasped as I saw the lattice archway that was placed under the boughs of the tree. Some flowers were weaved throughout the trellis. It was beautiful, and I didn't know who put it together so quickly. My gaze landed on Chase waiting near it with the others. Benson, David, Joseph, Ethan, and my father all stood together, chatting as we walked up.

As Chase turned and caught sight of me, he froze. My cheeks instantly burned with a blush at the heat in his gaze. It was passionate and wanting and amazed all at once.

Someone had managed to find him a suit. With the way accentuated his toned form, I had to guess it was his father's because it fit him perfectly. I'm not sure how many moments passed as we just stared at each other.

Shaking my head and coming back to reality, I glanced at the others and saw tears in my father's eyes. He came over and wrapped me in a hug.

"Hey, watch the hair. I'll never be able to get it like this again." I couldn't help but laugh as he pulled away.

"You're so beautiful—you look so much like your mother. I love you," he whispered.

Our relationship still wasn't perfect but holding a grudge at this point seemed pointless with everything else going on in our lives. I decided I would make the best of every day, and we needed to spend time with the ones we loved while we could.

"I love you too, Dad," I said, and he shifted so I could loop my arm through his.

I hadn't budged on one detail when getting dressed. I was barefoot because I refused to wear anything with a heel, and they wouldn't let me wear my boots. The grass was soft and still slightly warm from the day under my footsteps.

Everything else fell away as we approached. I couldn't take my eyes off Chase. As soon as we were close enough, he held out his hands to take mine, and gave me a smile that was just for me. shiver raced its way through my body.

My father gave me a quick kiss before stepping to the front, he was going to officiate too. The king always had the ability to perform these ceremonies.

This was really happening. I squeezed Chase's hands tightly.

I saw our friends over his shoulder. David winked to me, and the others were beaming. I saw Chase's eyes flick behind me to his sister and Gwen, his gaze alight with love.

"We'll make this short, shall we?" my father said, chuckling, and everyone else joined in.

I was all for a quick ceremony. Our friends and family were here, and that was all we needed.

"We're gathered here today to join these two lives together under the gods." My father took up a red candle and lit it. Chase and I clasped hands below, and after a moment, he dripped the hot wax over them. It slipped between our fingers. "We mark this day with pain and pleasure as the road ahead will not be smooth. Here today, you make a vow to support each other through the hard times, as well as the good. Chase and Genevieve have decided to say their own vows today," He held out his hands out toward us.

I was supposed to go first, but I just stood there, unable to make any words come out. Chase watched me patiently, waiting for me to be ready. He would be here for me when I was. As always. There was no hurry; we had the rest of our lives.

"Chase." I paused again, my mind racing, forgetting everything I had planned to say. Flashes of the deepest pain twirled with the memories of him always being there for me. He was always there to pick me up when I fell. "I have lost so many things in my life. I was scared to trust anyone when you found me. You showed me not through your words but through your actions that I was safe with you. I know I'm a lot..." A small chuckle came from our friends. "That I'm stubborn and argumentative and stubborn." Another round of laughs rang out at that. "You have never made me feel like I was too much, or not enough. I always knew, no matter what I did, no matter how I messed up, I could come to you. You've been there for me for my entire life. You *saved* my life. I know I'm far from perfect, but I will never stop trying to be the person you deserve. I love you more than anything."

I took his ring from my father. Chase's eyes were shining as he held out his hand so I could slide it onto his finger.

He squeezed my hands before reaching to take my ring from my father. He took a quick breath. "Genevieve, you have been and will always be perfect to me. I have known you for our entire lives. Almost every one of my memories has you in it. Even in those years you were torn away from us, my thoughts were always with you. When we got into trouble as kids, you always took the blame. Most of the time, it was your fault in the first place but still." That got more chuckles. "You always made me feel safe too, you always made me feel loved. I know you haven't always had that. I will be here for the rest of my days to give that to you and to remind you of how loved you are. Not just by me but by everyone—here and afar. I will never let you forget how amazing you are. You always inspire me to be my best self. You lead by example, you never give up, no matter how bad things may seem. You always push through, and through your actions you make the world better, just by the people you inspire. You are loyal, loving, and strong. You are a spark that lights the flame of change wherever you go. I am honored that you chose for me to be part of your life." He squeezed my hands again, the sincerity thick in his voice. "I love you and I will never stop loving you, even if the God of Death parts us for a while. We'll find each other again. Know that I will always be your safe place."

I couldn't breathe, and tears filled my eyes. So many emotions swirled through me. Love washed over all the years of pain and fear. He had said it in front of the others, but it had only been for me. I already knew he felt that way, but hearing it said out loud erased all my fears. I didn't know what life would bring, but we'd figure it out together.

My father raised his hands and his voice. "Chase Rodgers, do you vow to support Genevieve through this life and the next?"

Chase had never looked away from me and beamed so radiantly it was impossible not to feel his love for me. "I do."

"Genevieve Astor," my father choked up a bit as he said my name, "do you vow to support Chase through this life and the next?"

I nodded as tears came to my own eyes. "I do."

My father blew out the candle. "May the God of Time watch over your journey, may the God of Will bless you to overcome any obstacles, may the God of Mirth bring you joy in the dark, and may the God of Death join you together once again past the veil. We pray for your lives to be blessed, and we cheer for you as you carve this new path forward together. With that, I pronounce you partners in life."

Cheers erupted from our friends as they jumped and clapped, but my focus was on Chase as he wrapped his arms around me, pulling me close and dipping me to capture my lips with his. Fire flared from his touch along my skin in stark contrast to the cold of the silken fabric. I felt Chase smirk against my lips before he broke our kiss.

I smiled wickedly back up at him. He was mine. All mine. Our little bubble burst as our family and friends surrounded us with hugs. We were soon enveloped in a pile of our favorite people. I heard a pop and then the fizz of bubbles as someone opened a bottle of champagne and Gwen started passing out small paper cups to everyone.

"Cheers!" we all called as we clanked the cups together, spilling more than we didn't.

My heart was on the verge of bursting as I watched the group of them over the rim of my drink. It was like watching something in slow motion as I tried to memorize the feeling of this moment.

Chase folded me into his arms and nuzzled my neck.

"Can you believe how lucky we are?" I whispered to him.

"Some days." His cheek brushed against mine as we watched our friends. "It's nice to have a reminder like this though, isn't it?"

"Yeah." It was nothing more than a whisper.

I was a wife. I was *his* wife. He was *my* husband. I was surrounded by my friends, my family... It was more than I could have ever fathomed. I couldn't hold back the giddy feeling that was bubbling within me at those thoughts.

Ethan and Thea came over to us. Ethan held my shoulders and the peace on his face as he gazed at me filled my heart even more.

"You've always been a part of the family, but I'm really happy to make it official." He hugged me and I couldn't help but take a deep breath, just enjoying the feeling of being held.

"Thank you, Ethan." I grinned up at him. He winked, and Thea hooked an arm through his and led him away to talk to Benson.

A large hand landed on my shoulder, and I looked up to see my father there doing the same to Chase with his other. He pulled us both in close. So tight it was hard to breathe.

"I'm so happy for the two of you." He was visibly emotional over the whole thing. "I wish Aria and Alice could have been here, but I know they're smiling down on you two."

He didn't talk about my mother much, and today must have been hard on him not to be able to share this with her. Just like he hadn't been able to share my birthdays, first steps, or all the other firsts. I knew it hurt when he thought of her. He had loved her with every fiber of his being, and it had almost killed him when she died. At least, that was what I had heard over the years. When I was young, he had used all that love to dote on me. Everything had felt so perfect back then, even if I didn't have a mother of my own. He meant to love me enough for them both.

Now, after growing up and being through so much, I saw how that had been through the rose-colored glasses of childhood. Things weren't perfect right now. My father still always thought he was right, and he hid things he shouldn't, but we were both trying our best to take another step towards a normal relationship. The older I got the more I started to understand how my father became the way that he is. The things that almost break you can change you, and he had been through the ringer. Just like me. I made decisions others didn't understand too, because they couldn't understand what had made me this way.

"Chase, I can't think of anyone better for my little girl." He clapped Chase on the shoulder, and when he turned to me, I just wrapped my arms tight around his waist. He stood still for a moment —it was probably a shock to his system—but eventually he softened and embraced me.

"I love you, Dad."

With a soft tremble that might have been him holding in a small sob, he whispered into my hair, "I love you too." He finally pulled away and wiped quickly at his face. "Well, I shouldn't hog you. Off to your friends, you two."

After the champagne was gone, they started to pull us along to the mess hall, but I told them we'd be right there. I took Chase's hand

and guided him over to the gravestones. I reached out and rested my hand on Atty's.

"You told us so," I said quietly.

Chase pulled me close, and we just stood there for a few moments. Then, he twisted his fingers through mine and led me toward our friends.

As he pushed the door open, shock rocked me to see the mess hall was filled with more of our friends from the base. Cheers rang out as we entered. The room was decorated, and a feast lay before us. My stomach growled at the sight, and some people nearby chuckled. I made a beeline for the food as I waved at some people.

My hand never left Chase's. I couldn't keep my hands off him, and there was an electric buzzing where we touched. Anytime he saw me it was like he was devouring me. I couldn't wait to spend the rest of my life with this man. He smirked as if thinking the same thing.

"Oh, my precious! Look at you!" Amelia's called, which reminded me that it wasn't just me and Chase here. I finally spotted her behind a tower of cupcakes. She came around and gave us both a big hug. "Here, you must be starving." She started making plates for us with our favorites.

"Thank you; this is amazing. You really didn't need to do all of this," I said, waving to the giant feast. "You were the first person here who made me feel like a human again. I just really want to thank you for everything you've ever done for me."

Her eyes seemed misty, but she shook her head. "No thanks needed. You are wonderful and deserve all the happiness in the world." She winked at Chase. "And remind that friend of yours to come and help me in the kitchen soon," she teased and pinched our cheeks and sending us off with our food.

"Thank you," Chase said, which made her wipe quickly at her eyes, then she turned back to the table and started to organize deserts again.

It took us a while to return to our normal seats as we made our way through a crowd of well-wishers. I looked longingly down at my plate, my mouth watering. Soon. Soon, I could enjoy the potatoes and steak and all the fixings. A rumble of laughter vibrated through Chase's chest as I leaned against him and thanked another group for their congratulations.

Finally, we made it, and I jumped down, fork already filled and halfway to my mouth before my butt landed in the seat. I moaned as soon as I got the first bite. I loved Amelia's cooking. Feeling everyone watching me, I smiled innocently. Chase kissed my cheek as he slipped into the seat next to me.

My heart was singing. Even after everything we had just been through. I was glad to see other people from base here. I thought they might have needed this celebration just as much as we did.

I watched the people I loved. I wished we could stay here forever. I knew we couldn't ignore reality, but that was a problem for another day.

After taking his and some others plates to the wash, Benson reappeared with his guitar. He started to strum and then broke into one of his shanties, and soon everyone was singing along and holding their cups aloft.

Chase cocooned me in his arms and settled his cheek next to my neck. "Want to sneak out of here?" he whispered, sending goosebumps flickering across my skin. A slight moan escaped him as I agreed, and he grabbed my hand. I waved at Thea and David as they caught my eye, and they gave us a wink and a nod.

We raced to the barracks and up into our room, slamming the door shut behind us. We were a tangle of limbs as we pawed at each other. I caught his lips with mine as he spun me to him. He grasped the zipper of my dress and tugged it down in one quick movement. Heat flared where his fingers lightly slipped over the skin of my back. It was my turn to moan as I clutched his shirt and ripped it open, buttons scattering with the force. A moment later, I remembered that wasn't his shirt, but then the thought was lost again as my eyes roamed over him.

He stood for a moment, his eyes raking over me, drinking me in. "My wife," he said it slowly, like he was testing it out. The words unfamiliar on his lips.

"My husband." I gave him a mischievous smirk as I took a few steps toward him and let my dress fall to my feet. He bit his lip before he reached out and tugged me to him.

We crashed into each other, and I lost myself to the passion of wanting him, needing him. It was like we would never be close enough until our souls merged as one.

———

We decided to spend the entire next day in bed, and no one bothered us. Though, someone did drop off plates of food outside our door. When they knocked, Chase opened it to find no one there but came in with a tray of fruit and juice for breakfast.

He ended up propped up against the headboard, and I leaned back into him. I took a bite out of a strawberry, and the juice slipped through my fingers. As I looked his way his thumb caught it and I bit at him lightly before leaning into his palm, smiling.

"We've barely had any time to talk. What prompted you to ask me to marry you?" Not wanting him to think I was having second thoughts, I quickly added, "I'm glad you did!"

"Everything, really," he said softly. "Losing Atty and Marco, spending all that time with the rebels, coming back and seeing the same thing at home." He sucked in a deep breath. "Fairhaven." He shook his head, trying to rid himself of the images, I assumed.

"Was the apartment really only a few months ago?" I asked, and he grunted. It felt like it had been ages. We had all shared it for over a month while working on infiltrating the Nerian Tech Summit—the reason my father sent us there in the first place. Well, outside of sowing ideas of revolution and stirring the pot over there until the rebels overthrew the monarchy. It turned out my dad had an idea of where that mission would really land us all along.

"Is it ever going to feel normal again?" I asked Chase.

"I think our definition of *normal* is going to be different for a while." He ran his fingers through my hair, and I leaned my head against his chest. "David is leaving tomorrow."

A quick, sharp pain hit me, and I made a sound deep in my throat. I had forgotten he would be leaving for real this time. He needed to get to Soland to help with the refugees they were helping get out of Neria. We had been so busy that it had totally slipped my mind.

I took a deep breath. I had accepted this before; I just had to do it again. It wasn't the end. I would see him all the time, just maybe not in person. It wasn't going to change our friendship.

"Tomorrow, we go back to real life," I whispered, wishing it wasn't true.

Chase tightened his grip around me. "Tomorrow, yes, but not today."

He started to jokingly snarl and nip at my neck while tickling me. I squealed, and the bowl of fruit went flying. Superhuman strength did not stop me from being ticklish, apparently. I turned to pounce on him, and we spent the rest of the day enjoying the rare time we allowed ourselves not to worry about the rest of the world.

11

Vi

Slipping out of bed before the sun rose the next morning, seeing Chase still sleeping with his arm laid over his face, covering his eyes, I couldn't keep the smile off my face. It always reminded me of when we were kids; he's slept like this most of his life. I could always see that little boy hiding just under the surface of everything we'd been through.

I grabbed my boots and snuck out of the room. I hopped through the hallway as I pulled them on. When I stepped out into the crisp chill air, I took a deep, refreshing breath. We had been gone for so long, and everything had been a mess since we got back. This was my first moment to feel like I was finally home. I soaked it in before jogging away from the barracks.

I started on my normal route around the base, picking up speed as I did so. Running had been something to ground me since I was rescued. Normally, after a while, I'd feel the burn in my muscles, but it didn't come. I pushed myself faster, launching myself over the fences, not missing a step as I landed and raced on.

My mind wandered to David. He was leaving again today. I didn't know if this time would be easier or harder. We had already said goodbye once, but he had come straight here after hearing what happened. He and Joseph had then stayed after the attack on Fairhaven, helping us look for survivors. Yet, he couldn't stay forever, and I wasn't sure how my heart or my head would react to saying goodbye once more.

I lapped the base a few times before I decided I wasn't going to get the burn I craved. Ever since the mist had changed me, the only time I had felt any type of exhaustion was in the fight against Jasper in the palace. At least the cool air had cleared my head.

I made my way to David's lab as the sun started to break over the horizon. I heard the rattle of metal before I even made my way inside. It was a coin flip whether he was just here already or if he had been here all night. Poking my head through the door, I saw David searching through shelves on the far side of the room.

"Hi," I called, and he snapped his head around in surprise.

"Oh, hey," he said, smiling at me. He waved me over. "Help me search. It's a box about this big." He held his hands out to show something about the size of a breadbox.

I started to poke around on the shelves closer to me. I grabbed the handle of a black box and pulled it off the shelf. "Is this it?"

David's eyes went wide, and he raced toward me. "No!" He grabbed it from my hand before setting it gently on the table. "No, not that. Don't jostle that one."

I raised an eyebrow at him in alarm, and he gave me his lopsided smile.

"It's a very sensitive explosive."

"Why do you have it just sitting around? And why does the box even have a handle?" I snapped.

"I forgot about it," he said sheepishly.

I shook my head with a laugh. "I'm going to miss you."

"I'm going to miss you guys too." He elbowed me. "Now, help me find this stupid box."

"Is there anything else I shouldn't touch?" I asked half in jest, but he seemed to be taking it seriously.

"Maybe just tell me if you see anything and I'll check it out," he said, turning to the shelves.

Rolling my eyes at him, I continued searching but made sure not to touch anything else. "What are you even looking for?"

"It's got a pile of my journals and some of the research from when you first got here. I thought it would help Joseph and I compare against what we find while working with the refugees. It's around here somewhere." He stood back, rubbing his chin, clearly deep in thought. He perked up and headed for another spot in the room and started digging through a pile, throwing books and pieces of metal haphazardly behind him.

"What are you going to do with the rest of this stuff?" I asked.

He shrugged. "Nothing for now. I'll make another trip sometime and bring more with me. Once we know what our setup looks like and how much room we have. Until then, who knows? Maybe someone here can do something with it."

"Maybe you should label the things that explode," I muttered.

"Ah, good idea." He nodded gravely, grabbed a label maker, and typed into it. The label started to print, and he grabbed it and slapped it across the box he had set on the table. Peering over, I saw it read, 'it goes boom, don't jostle'.

"Mmm, yes that does the trick, doesn't it?" I said, and we fell into a fit of giggles. "I'll call the others so we can help make sure at least all the hazardous stuff has warnings."

I sent a message to the rest of our friends and got quick replies that they would be right over. All the windows in here were covered, and the room was lit only by the bright lights of the lab, so it was always impossible to gauge how much time had passed. It was half the reason he ended up in here for days and we would have to come in and make sure he'd eaten.

As they started to filter in, David handed everyone a label maker.

Why does he have so many? Oh well, at least it was handy. He stopped Thea and handed her a bracelet, which had her jumping up and down before she pounced to hug him, smacking a kiss on his cheek with a thank you. It was such a relief that she finally had her own suit like the rest of us. It was another layer of protection, and I knew we'd been getting into hot water before too long. She'd need it.

"Thanks for all the help, everyone. Okay, so, overall, most boxes are open. Feel free to just label them with whatever you might see inside. Metal scraps, screws, tools, etcetera. Please call me or Joseph over if you find a closed box; we need to check those just in case."

"Just in case of what?" Benson asked.

I mimed an explosion with a whistle. Everyone except for Joseph, David, and I, visibly gulped but then dove in to help anyway.

Chase threw me some breakfast bars, and I grinned before tearing into them. I was starving. He came up, kissed my temple mid-bite, and whispered, "Good morning, wife."

He took my label maker and went to the shelves to start looking through things. A wave of giddiness washed over me at the words. I was Chase's wife! I held back a squeal at the thought.

David rushed around as people called out for him to check boxes. Multiple answers of, "be careful, set it down softly," or "no, don't touch that," or "gods, do not move," rang through the lab throughout the morning.

"David, seriously what have you been doing in here?" Chase laughed at a one point.

"Very serious experimentations," David said, seemingly trying to keep his face straight, but it didn't last long. "What, I like to make things that explode, and you guys like to use them."

That made me think of Atty but didn't change the fact that it was true.

"You're not going to be making bombs in the school, right?" Joseph asked.

The school they were going to was found for us by my old friend Nathan Kelter. It was based in Soland and most of the kids who were going to be there were orphans from the fighting in Neria. Nathan was the King of Soland and had been giving us help in secret for a while. His nobles wouldn't allow the kingdom to get involved with

Nerian or Kabrian politics, but he never was one who could just watch people in pain. He had asked if David and Joseph would be willing to run it while they also continued to work with us in finding out more about Esmerelda and her plans. David had always wanted to help the kids who had no say in any of this violence and was happy to take up the assignment.

"Well, I mean, at some point, we're going to have to teach them how," David replied.

"We are not going to teach young adults how to build bombs. We're training the next generation of leaders, not terrorists," Joseph said.

"Well, gods forbid, we don't manage to finish this war quickly, it might be a handy skill to have. It has been for us." Benson shrugged.

"Exactly. See." David pointed to Benson.

"We'll discuss this later, but no bombs until then," Joseph said in defeat. "Anyway, I'm sure you'll win this war before they even graduate."

"Fine, but I learned how to make them when we were just kids. I can teach it safely; everything will be fine." David waved his hand in a calming gesture.

"You blew off your eyebrows like every week," Chase reminded him.

"I was self-taught, so it's not surprising. It's all part of the learning process." He huffed.

I couldn't help but remember seeing David's face covered in soot and his eyebrows indeed missing when we were just kids in the palace. David's father laughing when he saw him.

The man had been the head blacksmith for my father and had moved into the palace once the three of us had become best friends. So, he was probably used to accidental eyebrow removal. He had passed a year before Esmerelda kidnapped me to force my father to fake his own death and leave her the throne. David's mother had passed before they had even moved to the palace. We had bonded over not having a mother, and Alice had practically adopted us both.

With the help of us all, most of the lab had been labeled before lunch rolled around. Everyone still had all their digits and limbs attached by the end, so that was a win. I had noticed the closer we got to being done, the slower everyone had moved. It meant we were getting closer and closer to our little group being split apart.

Eventually, I couldn't hold it in any longer and grabbed David and Joseph into a tight hug. The dam broke, and all our friends surrounded us in a giant dog pile. With my arms around them, I felt both relax.

David put his forehead to mine. "We'll see you soon. You guys can't stay out of trouble long. You'll need us before you know it."

"We'll always need you," I said.

"We're happy for you. You have some important work to do over in Soland," Gwen said as she reached to squeeze Joseph's hand.

"We're just a call away," David said, nodding firmly, as if to reassure himself of that too.

"Well, I think it's time," Joseph said.

Some of us grabbed their bags from the lab and followed the two out to the hanger, where their transport waited. More of their bags were already loaded onto the hover copter. My heart hitched, wondering if it was the one we had flown in from Neria that had brought our friends' bodies home.

Our migration had caught the attention of some of the rebels, and the pilot ran over to start the takeoff inspection.

"We'll be ready to go in just a bit." He held out a hand, and I gave him their bags to load. "The generals will be here shortly."

He was right; within moments, I saw dad and Ethan rounding the side of the hanger. They waved as they came our way.

"David, Joseph," my father said, clasping arms with them in turn. "We want to thank you for everything, and Nathan has been prepped with your flight path into the country."

"Thanks, Nolan," David said.

"I've always thought of you as a son, and I just wanted to say how proud of you I am," my father said, and I saw David getting slightly choked up at the proclamation. "You'll always have a home here."

David grabbed my father into a hug but let him go quickly before straightening his jacket.

"Thank you for all of your support and for letting me stay to help," Joseph said to both men.

"Thank you for being willing to help," Ethan replied.

Behind us, the hover copter's engine roared to life. David and Joseph looked at each other and then back to us.

"We'll talk soon!" David yelled over the noise. We all waved as the two of them hopped into the copter. They returned them before someone slid the door shut, and we watched as they rose into the sky and started their path to Soland.

"Talk soon," I whispered after them. Chase slung his arm around my shoulder and pulled me after the others. We walked in silence. Life would be different, but it wasn't goodbye, not really.

Chase and I had made our way to our room as everyone disbursed from the hangar. He had dropped me off before running to the mess hall to grab us something to eat. Standing at the window, I watched as everyone buzzed around the ground below. My heart was breaking. Everything I had put off with exhaustion and adrenaline swept over me. My breaths came quickly, and I turned and slammed my back against the wall. I grasped at my chest as I tried to control myself, but I felt like I was drowning. I slowly slid down the wall until I was sitting with my knees curled up to my chest.

I just sat there, locked in place. My brain wasn't working. I couldn't complete a full thought. The words *failure, alone, death,* each one stuck on repeat. Each one like a stab to the heart. Flashes of the bodies, the wreckage, the destruction flooded my mind.

Someone shook my shoulder, and I blinked, pulling my focus to the room. Chase was on his knees holding on to me with a concerned etched on his face. "What's wrong?"

"I don't know if I can keep going," I said in a whisper. "I don't know how much more I can take."

He slid next to me, wrapping his arms around me and tugging me to him. "Take a deep breath. Everything is going to be okay."

I did as he said. The pressure of him against me instantly helped fight off the panic.

"We just need to take all this one step at a time. They need us; we can't give up."

I closed my eyes tightly and leaned into him. I tried to switch my internal mantra to something more positive, but I still felt like I was suffocating. Chase continued to sit there and hold me as I spiraled, whispering to let me know I wasn't alone. At this point, that was what I needed. Time to just break in a place I was safe, and someone who could help pull me back together when I was done.

12.

VI

I was out on my morning run when my comm unit chimed. Surprisingly, it turned out to be Dad asking me to meet at his office. I made a loop around the training fields changing my heading. I slowed as I reached the building in the early morning light. I slipped in through the front door and down the empty hallways before making my way to him.

As I pushed inside, I saw him leaned over his desk—the only one here. He looked tired. Had he been here all night?

"Hey, Dad."

Even though his face did light up as he saw me. "Morning, darling."

Yep, that still felt weird, but I grinned nonetheless. "What did you need?"

He turned around and sat against the edge of his desk. "We've been pulling as many people as we can out of the cities since Fairhaven, but we're receiving reports of some areas getting overrun by the military. They need help."

I wasn't surprising, Esmerelda was escalating daily. She had been subtle with her moves before. She was on an all-out warpath now and had the media blaming us for it. Everyone was in danger.

"Okay, where are you sending us, then?" I knew that was what was coming next.

"The capital." He shrugged and still didn't seem very sure of himself.

"Do you think that's a good idea?" I asked.

"It's not a good idea, but we need Thea's help," he said, sounding defeated.

"Have you talked to Ethan about it?" I asked.

My father rubbed at his chin, his fingers sweeping through his beard. "He's not thrilled, but he agrees it's necessary. She has the most experience in the city out of anyone. She knows where all the escape routes, safe houses, and weapon caches are."

"True." I looked around the room again, half-expecting someone to barge in for the mission update. "Are the others coming?"

"No, I just reached out to you. I wanted to talk," he said.

I grabbed one of the chairs by his desk and dropped into it. "What did you want to talk about?"

"I just..." He took a deep breath. "I know this is too little too late, but I just wanted to apologize."

"Apologize for what?" There were plenty of reasons I had to be upset with him, so I wasn't sure which one he might be referring to.

"Everything." He sighed. "I should have found a way to get you out of the prison as soon as she had you. I didn't know she'd hide you so well so quickly. Then it took forever to find anything on you. Since we got you back, I'm sorry I wasn't more open when you first got here, and I should have explained what I expected to have happened in Neria."

I studied him; he appeared older than I remembered. I wondered if he'd been taking care of himself. Probably not. The last few months must have been a lot to deal with here.

"I should have told you more since you got here. We'd been working in the shadows for so long, everything was need-to-know with everyone, but that shouldn't have included you. I just wanted you to know I'm going to include you and Chase in everything from now on. This is going to be your country, after all. You should be included in the decision making. You proved that when you made the call to evacuate everyone. It was the right call."

I tried my best to keep my emotions off my face, but the confession surprised me. Ever since I was rescued, I had been angry with my father for leaving me with Esmerelda as long as he had. I'd spent six years thinking he was dead, and he had known Esmerelda had me while he hid and built the resistance. I know it wasn't as simple as that, but it was hard to convince my heart.

I had a terrible time learning to trust people after I was rescued and found out he was alive the whole time I was being tortured. I had lost everything during those years. I was twelve when she first locked me up. Those are the years most people learn who they are, and I spent them on deaths door. I had wanted him to apologize, but he never had, not really. Not until today. But seeing him like this... It shocked me. This wasn't the tall, stoic man of my childhood. He appeared his age, and he looked exhausted.

"Thank you," was all I could manage. I still wasn't sure how to handle this confession and my brain felt frozen. I meant to tell him the country wouldn't be mine; I should have. I needed to tell him I wasn't taking the throne, but I knew what that conversation would look like, and it wouldn't be pleasant. I needed to wait for a better time to talk to him about it.

I had been saying I wouldn't be queen since I arrived, but no one believed me. Everyone says I'll change my mind when everything is over, but. I won't. I *know* I won't. The people need someone better than a solider covered in blood. They need a leader who can show them a new future. I am the past. I am what must be done for the greater good, but that's all. I deserve to be able to put it all down. If I live that long.

We ended up sitting there in an awkward silence for a few moments. We had spent so much time apart and had such a rough reunion that we still didn't know how to act around each other.

"So, um, do you want me to tell the others?" I asked.

"Here." He tapped on his tablet and my comm chimed. "I just sent you some of the recent communications we've received from allies in the city. Thea should know the best way to get in contact. We need you to provide cover for the escape. They've just finished creating a new route. It's not going to be easy, which is why you and your team are our best option. We have squads going to the other cities to help the evacuations there, but the closer to the palace, the more security they have. The outer cities will be easier since they're spread thin at the moment."

"Okay, we can be headed out by this afternoon." I sent the data to the rest of the team, along with a message that we were leaving today. I moved to stand up, but my dad caught my wrist.

"I need you to make a statement while you're there. We need to let her know we're bringing this fight to her."

"That is my specialty, after all." With a smirk and a shrug, I turn to leave.

"Good luck," he said to my back as I walked out of his office.

My dad and Ethan had been waiting for us in the hangar as we arrived to load up. Ethan gave Thea a huge hug and clapped Chase on the shoulder as I threw my bag onboard. I gave a quick salute to them but slipped straight into our armored van, not wanting to think about goodbyes or the idea that some of us might not make it back.

Chase hopped in last and pulled the door closed behind him. Benson started the engines, and we pulled out at top speed so we could make our way to the capital city. The drive took a few hours, and we cycled between talking, games, and eventually silence as we all started to think about what we were would be walking into.

I tried to calm my racing heart. My hands were sweating, and I worried the others might see how much this was affecting me. Flashes of the destruction in Neria, the feed factory, and Fairhaven flew through my mind. I could still feel the heat of the fires and smell the smoke. The charred smell that I couldn't think about too long lived in my head. What were we going to be walking into? How much more of that would we see before the end of this war? Would I even make it to the end? Would any of us?

I thought of Atty and Marco, and another piece of my heart chipped and fell away. I would be able to pull myself together eventually if I made it that long, but parts of me would always be missing. I was sure I'd never be whole again. It was just a question of how much more of my heart and soul would be gone by the end of this?

I snapped out of my thoughts as Thea tapped my arm lightly. Anxiety was written clearly on her face.

"Hey," I said quietly, leaning over and putting our heads together.

"I haven't been back since everything," she said. "I thought I was ready, but I don't know if I am now."

This was harder on her than any of us had realized. The last time she was here, she'd watched her club get raided, her home attacked, her friend died in the streets, and she and her mother had been taken prisoner by Esmerelda. Where we lost Alice as we tried to escape from the cells deep in the palace.

"Everything is going to be okay," I told her, trying to reassure her, but I knew this wasn't something I could be sure of. "We'll just do what we can and get as many people out alive as we can. There will be some we won't be able to help, and it's hard, but just focus on the good we do manage to accomplish. You *will* be fine."

I grabbed her hand and squeezed it tightly in mine. She leaned her head against my shoulder and didn't let go. I caught Chase's gaze over the top of her head. I saw his face pinch in pain as he looked on at his sister hurting. We'd all be okay. We had to be.

13

Vi

We slipped through the streets of Longdale as the sun started to set, and I tugged at my hood again. I couldn't afford to be recognized, not yet anyway. I was doing my best to try to stay in its shadow. We were in the outskirts of the city, and Thea was leading us toward an old safe house.

We had spread out as far as we could to seem less conspicuous, and I trailed along a few blocks behind the others. I couldn't see anyone, but I could hear them, so I followed their sounds through the tight alleyways.

The beat of boots moving in time together wasn't far off, and I slipped into an alcove before the patrol passed by. We had already run into multiple patrol teams, and we had barely made it into the city. The streets were quiet compared to what I remembered. It used to be teeming with people giving the area its own personality. But now, barely anyone was outside. We were mixing in with the groups just getting off work and rushing home. Doors were closed, and windows were shuttered.

I could only wonder what it would be like living here. My cheeks burned as my anger boiled within me at the thought of how my people were being forced to live. The towers of the palace were just barely visible, and I glared at my childhood home.

The young version of myself would have never believed how things had turned out. I never would have thought I'd be sneaking through the city streets, exiled from my home, and fighting a war for my people.

Yet, would I ever have gotten to know my people the way I did now? Had the gods given us this path, or was all of this just some sick entertainment for them? Would they give a round of applause if the world burned, or would they step in and save us before we could destroy ourselves? I had to hope this was all planned and leading us to our true purpose.

Once the patrol had gone, I started to follow the others once more. I listened carefully for anything out of the ordinary and evaluated the lightly crowed alley before me. I filed away the best ways to escape, the count of people who were large enough to cause a problem, the way they pressed into each other or stepped apart. All of it was analyzed to help make snap decisions if it came to that.

Thea said we didn't have anything to worry about besides the patrols, but I wasn't taking any chances of someone recognizing me while this close to Esmerelda.

Benson was far enough ahead of me that I could barely glimpse him, but I saw him jerk, heard the clink of something from a pocket and a quiet apology. The kid was thin and gangly, and they slipped through the crowd ahead of me. Every few people, they would bump into someone or cause some sort of distraction before dipping their hands into pockets and bags before moving on.

I couldn't keep the smile off my face as they came close. They went for the pocket of my coat as they passed, but I caught their arm, and they jerked to a stop. Their eyes narrowed as they tried to pull free, but my grip didn't waver.

"Let me go," they said in annoyance. "I'm just a kid." They were maybe in their teens, in baggy clothes and had hair buzzed short.

Overall, they were forgettable. Except for those fierce brown eyes that bore into me with their glare. Exactly what a kid on the street might need to be these days.

I tapped their bag that hung at their hip with the tip of my boot, and it jingled with the jostling of metal.

"That's mine," they grunted.

"It wasn't a few minutes ago," I said, covering a laugh with a cough. I turned to continue after my friends but tugged the kid after me. They struggled but realized they couldn't break my hold and begrudgingly started to follow me. They kept kicking the dirt and working on ways to slow us down, but I didn't stop.

"If you're trying to kidnap me, this isn't going to end well for you."

"Are you hungry?" I turned to catch a glimpse of them over my shoulder, hoping it was still dark enough that they couldn't see who I was. Their stomach grumbled in response.

"What's it to you?"

I knew plenty of kids like this when we were in Neria. Distrustful of anyone, angry at the world after life had kicked them around. I didn't say anything else. I heard a door squeak open and shoes shuffling through, and I just managed to catch the sight of Benson dipping down to enter a building a few hundred feet ahead of us.

"Come on." I sped up to reach the door the others had entered. It had already closed by the time we arrived, so I knocked. A metal slit opened, and eyes blinked at me then looked down to the angry kid behind me.

It swung open, but as soon as it did, the kid kicked at me and tried to jerk their arm free again.

"I'm not going with you. I'll kill you," they hissed, so I tugged a bit harder, and they went stumbling into the building. Two steps in, and I was through and shoved the door closed behind me.

"Calm down, kid." I pulled my hood down, and their eyes

widened in surprise as my hair started to spill around my shoulders. "You hungry?"

They started to glance around, not answering me.

I checked Benson over and after a quick sweep, saw his watch was missing. "Give my friend his stuff back."

I pointed to Benson, and the kid slowly started to pull out the watch and one of his knives. Benson gave me an exasperated look and I just shrugged with a smile before he reached out to take them.

"Vi, what did you do?" Chase said, worry thick in his tone as he turned around to see us.

"I just thought I should get Benson's stuff returned, and the kid is hungry." I noticed the people hanging around the edges of the room. Some of them seemed in awe, others were probably apprehensive. Which I didn't blame them. Hardly anyone seemed older than Thea, except for one woman, who might have been my parents' age.

Chase rubbed at his temples. "You need to stop bringing home strays."

"Hey, who are you calling a stray?" the kid asked, anger clear in their voice.

"What if they turn you in for the reward?" Thea mirrored her brother's stance. They really were so similar.

"Like anyone can catch me even if they do?" I turned to the kid. "Are you going to turn me in..." I paused, hand out, waiting for them to fill in their name.

"Parker," they provided. "I don't know; it depends on what you're going to try to do with me."

"We're going to feed you, see if there is anything that needs to be returned in that bag of yours, and then let you go on your way," I said simply, to which Chase groaned. I looked around the room. "Do you guys have food?"

Everyone turned to the older woman for her answer. She waved at someone, and they ran off, hopefully to go get something. She walked over to me and stuck her hand out.

"It's nice to meet you, Princess. My name is Kora."

I grabbed her hand and shook it. The woman had a firm grip, which I respected. "Just call me Vi, please. I'm not a princess anymore, just a soldier like everyone else."

She raised an eyebrow like she didn't believe that. "Nice to meet you, Vi, but I very much doubt you are just like everyone else."

During the exchange, the kid had turned to race to the door but ran straight into Benson's large chest instead. They hit him so hard, they bounced, and their hand instantly went to their nose.

"Looks like he isn't hungry," Benson said with a chuckle.

"I prefer *they*," Parker said with a frustrated glance at Benson.

"They aren't hungry, so I guess I get theirs." His giant grin broke across his face. The kid seemed to take a deep breath but continued glaring at Benson.

"No one is going to hurt you," Kora said, and pointed to a table with some chairs. "Go on, take a seat. Relax for a bit and then you can decide if you still want to go, but if you want to stay, I'm sure we could find a place for you."

The person who had run to get the food returned with his arms full of ration packs. My stomach growled at the sight. I moved to the table as he dropped them and grabbed one before crouching against the wall. I kept everyone else in my sights as I tore into the first one. A moan escaped my lips as I swallowed my first bite.

Parker just cocked their head as they watched me. I had seen them searching the room, gauging everything, just like I normally did. I wondered what they had lived through to have those reflexes already.

Benson leaned over their shoulder to grab one of the packs, and I saw Parker flinch away as he loomed close. I rolled my eyes. I knew Benson was just acting intimidating to get back at the kid for stealing his things, but from the glint in his eye, he liked their pluck.

Slowly, Parker reached out and grabbed their own ration pack. They glared around the room before opening it and keeping it close to their chest. They were rigid and ate quickly, and I felt that same sadness I had felt so many times. The sadness that always filled me with conviction. I was going to make the world better so I could save as many people as I could from this life.

VI

Thea waved me over, so I pushed myself up and tossed the empty pack into a trash can across the room. It went straight into the basket without even a bounce. Parker was watching me closely, and I gave them a soft smile. Hopefully, they'd give us a chance.

Thea, Chase, and I followed Kora into another room farther into the building. Benson and Gwen stayed behind and were chatting with everyone else, trying to ease the tension.

Kora turned to us as the door quietly clicked shut behind me. She crossed her arms and leaned against a filing cabinet.

"Nolan sent us to help evacuate," Chase started, which just had Kora smirking.

"Yes, I'm sure he did." She ran a hand through her thick, curly salt-and-pepper hair. "He gave you instructions to get everyone out, including us, didn't he?" She gave me a side-eye.

"Well, yeah, of course," Thea said.

"You told him you weren't leaving, didn't you?" I asked.

She turned to me and touched her nose with the tip of her finger. "Nolan never was very good at listening."

A sharp laugh escaped me at that. Her gaze softened.

"You sound just like her," she said quietly. "You look just like her too."

My eyes snapped to hers, and then I scanned her, trying to see if I remembered her at all, but I didn't. "You knew my mom?" I whispered.

"She was an amazing woman. She cared so deeply about the people, her friends, and her family. She loved you so much."

"I don't remember you," I said, and it seemed Chase apparently hadn't recognized her either.

"You wouldn't. I was a ghost for your father. When everything happened, I worked with Alice to help him set up the original resistance. I've been keeping things running since we lost her." Her sad gaze settled upon the siblings. "I am sorry for your loss."

Thea ran over, and Kora wrapped her arms around the younger woman. Of course, that was how Thea knew Kora. Thea had been living here in this city for those six years I had been locked away. Kora must have been a big part of her life.

"It's good to see you, Slip," Kora said to her.

I raised an eyebrow as Thea's cheeks turned pink. "Slip?"

"Speaking of a ghost, Slip here can give me a run for my money," Kora said with a smirk.

I reached out and playfully tapped Thea's shoulder. "Keeping secrets, I see, little one, but I'm not surprised. You always were able to follow us around without us noticing."

"And would tattle if we didn't let you come with us when we were already in the middle of doing something we weren't supposed to," Chase chided, but he pulled her back to ruffle her hair and then swung his arm over her shoulder.

I couldn't miss the look of pride on her face as she glanced up at him. I knew she worshiped her older brother; she always had.

"So, anyway, we've made plans," Kora went on. "Over the last few days, we've been moving the people we need your help to evacuate to our best egress routes. Once we've helped you with that, our people are going to re-enter the city. We can't leave. There are going to be people here who need help and won't evacuate. Or won't know they should have left until it's too late. This is my city. I won't run from it. Not now." She looked at me as she said it.

"Kora, it's going to be dangerous. So much more than before. Please come with us. We can regroup and return to take the city back," Thea pleaded.

Chase shook his head. "We won't be able to retake the city. Not anytime soon. This city won't be free until we've gotten rid of Esmerelda completely, and Kora is right. People are going to see things change soon. People who don't see what's going on yet will, and when they do, they'll be helpless. There are some cities we'll be able to free fully, but not here. Not right underneath the shadow of the palace."

"My people who are staying know the risk, but this is their home too." She sighed.

"I understand, and while we'll help cover the escape, there is something we need to do first." I ran my hand through my hair, it was time for the message my father wanted me to send.

Kora raised an eyebrow at me but just shook her head. "I can't wait to hear about what you have cooked up. But right now, we need to start sending messages for everyone to get ready to move. Thea, will you introduce Chase to Declan? He took over communications from Gerald."

"We lost Gerald?" Thea's shoulders slumped as Kora confirmed it, but she turned and headed for the door to do what she asked.

Chase grabbed my hand for a quick squeeze before following his sister, taking the hint. The door shut behind him, and Kora turned her attention to me.

"I assume you have questions," she said, resting one hip against the wall.

"Will you tell me about my mom?" It was rare to meet someone who knew her.

"Your mother loved everything about life. She always saw the silver lining in any situation. Your father became so much freer once he met her. He started to see the light beyond the clouds. I've known your father since school. Ethan too. When your father met her, something changed..." She snapped her fingers, and her eyes brightened. "Like that. It's not easy being raised as a royal."

She gave me a wry smile. "Your father and Ethan were raised to hide feelings like they were a weakness. They were a feedback loop to each other, but she brought in something new. Your mother." She sighed. "She got Nolan to dance. I remember the first time I saw them dancing and joking. He seemed like a completely different person."

She walked over, set her hand on my shoulder, and looked deep into my eyes. "That part of him died before you ever got to meet him. She died so suddenly. It was a shock to us all. He loved you the best way he knew how, but he was never the same after her death. She would be so proud of you."

I shook my head and pulled away. "She would hate me. If she was like you say, then she would hate what I've become."

Kora pushed forward, catching me. "Maybe right now, you just need to see the light beyond the clouds as well. You're changing the world. Just remember, you're half of her too. You can become whomever you want to. You aren't destined to become just another carbon copy of a ruler. You never could be; you are your own person. You're going to become so much more than either of them could have ever imagined, all because of what you've lived through. And that would make your mother so happy, seeing you not just survive but thrive. Look at you now." She threw her arm toward the others beyond the door. "You have people who love you, and you are free. I know your path must weigh on you, but you are forged from the brightest light and the strongest steel, and nothing will be able to break you if you remember that."

"What if I can't do this?" I wasn't sure if she could even hear me with how quiet my words were. What if I couldn't lead the charge? What if I couldn't beat Esmerelda? What if I couldn't save my people?

"There was something she always told Nolan when times got

tough," Kora said, dragging me from my doubts. "Everyone fears they might fail, but as long as you keep getting up, it's never over. Even if you stumble and fall, and you fear you've done the wrong thing, just get back up and try again. It's only ever truly over once you've given up." She quickly grasped my chin and forced me to look straight at her. "You don't seem like someone who knows how to give up."

I chuckled sadly as a tear slipped down my cheek. "I don't."

"Of course not. While your mother was fun, she was just as stubborn as your father. You couldn't have turned out any other way. Trust me, you would be the light of her life." Without missing a beat, she moved toward the door and pulled it open. "We should start getting everything ready."

She left the door open as she headed to the others. I just stood there for a moment, trying to wrap this idea of my mother around me for a moment before I had to follow. I tried to think through my life, to see if any of those parts of her were in me, and tears came as I did. I felt connected to her in a way I never had before.

I pulled out my tablet and found a picture of my mother. Pictures of her delicate at a ball, strong at my father's side in a throne. The last one was a picture of her holding me close, right after my birth. I reached out a finger and ran it across the image. "I hope you'll still be proud of me when this is all over. I love you, Mom."

15

VI

Thea and Chase were huddled together when I made my way back into the main room. I focused my hearing away, not wanting to eavesdrop. This city and these people were a big part of Thea's life, and I could tell he was checking in on her. She would come to me if she wanted to talk.

Searching for something else to focus on, I dropped into the seat next to Parker, and just watched them for a moment. The longer I did, the more their face scrunched up in what I could assume was anger. I got it. It was easy for anger to be the first emotion when you were always just trying to survive.

"Are you going to let me go now?" they asked me finally.

"You could have left whenever you wanted. Are you sure you really want to?" I was hoping they would open up.

They quickly pushed themselves to their feet, and I reached out and placed a hand on top of theirs. I didn't grab them or try to hold them, just letting them know I was here and had something left to say. They dropped into the seat after shooting me a quick glance.

"What?" Their tone was annoyed, but they were still here.

"What do you want your life to be?"

That seemed to surprise them, but the answer was simple. "Alive."

That was a good but heart-wrenching answer.

"You can be alive but not living." My hand absently went to my neck to run over the scars that no longer existed. The tiniest knife still sliced through me when I remembered they were gone.

"What are you asking of me?" Parker narrowed their sharp eyes.

"I'm asking you to think about what options you have to make your life the way you want it to be. You want to disappear and run? I get it. I've wanted that so many nights, but have you ever had someone have your back? Really have it?"

Parker's defenses instantly went up. "Putting trust in other people is how you die."

"Some people, yes, that's true. But sometimes, it's not." I gestured around us. "I trust every single one of these people with my life, and I haven't met most of them until today."

"Why would you do something that stupid?"

"Because we're all fighting for the same thing. We have all decided that our lives are worth the price of protecting the people of Kabria. My friends have died for this. I won't let it be in vain. Anyway, I'm not asking you to fight if you don't want to. I'm asking if you want to join everyone else when we evacuate them out of the city. You can start a new life. One that doesn't have you stealing to survive. You do have some useful skills if you ever change your mind though and want to join us." I gave a half-smirk before pushing myself up. "Think on it, but if you decide to take off... be safe, Parker."

Parker just kept watching me with a look of confusion as I saluted and turned away.

I went to join Benson, Gwen, and the man with giant head-phones around his neck, who must have been Declan, were all huddled together by a desk full of gadgets, with a radio crackling in the middle.

"Confirmation, we're a go in two hours," Declan said into the radio. Gwen gave me a quick grin as I sidled up next to her.

"Roger that. May the gods bless this day," came the reply.

As much as I wished it would do any good, I couldn't help but wonder again if the gods cared at all about what happened today.

"That was the last message to the teams to start getting into position," Benson said over his shoulder.

"What happens in two hours?" It was Parker who had asked, hovering a few feet behind us.

"We're going to go cause chaos, kid," Benson said, excitement clear in his voice.

From the look on their face, that didn't answer their question.

"We're going to cause a distraction, get the bulk of the queen's forces to circle up on us, and that'll give everyone else time to get to our waiting transportation. Then, we'll circle back and help cover the escape route for any stragglers," he clarified.

I watched as that seemed to sink in for Parker. Their eyes flicked to mine and then to the others. "Why would you do that? Cause a distraction, I mean. Can't you just sneak everyone out?"

Gwen shook her head but gave them a friendly smile. "Not with the number of people we need to move, and it's just what we do, I guess." She shrugged. "We are kind of known for getting their attention and keeping it anyway, so here we are."

"You put your life on the line for people you've never met before, and you trust them not to turn you in for the reward money?" Parker scoffed. "That seems like a bad plan."

I snickered at that. "Seems like it, doesn't it?"

That seemed to knock them off guard.

"I told you, we're all here for the same reason. I trust them, they trust me, and if we work together, we can change the world. It's the right thing to do." I locked eyes with them.

"The lines are being drawn in the sand, and we will do whatever we must to get these people somewhere safer."

Parker jumped as Thea spoke, not noticing she had come up next to them.

"You should really go with the groups we're getting out. Things aren't going to get any easier around here. We're finding places for anyone who doesn't want to join the fight, and then we're going to blockade the supply routes in." She glanced back at Kora, who just waved her off.

"It's not the first blockade I've had to deal with. We'll be fine."

"We should start getting ready. Declan, we've already started the evacuation of the distraction site, haven't we?" Thea asked.

The boy from the radio nodded. "Yes, we've already received word that it's almost completely cleared."

She looked to Parker but didn't say anything, seeming to try to convey that it was time for them to decide what they were going to do.

"Where's the distraction site?" Parker asked.

"The city precinct." Gwen rubbed her hands together. "We're going to go blow some stuff up."

As we started toward the door, I turned to Parker. "Do you know what you're going to do?"

I thought they might follow us out, but they paused and glanced around the room. Kora gave them a patient smile. Parker sighed and turned back to Kora.

"I want to help," they said.

"All right, well, let's find you something to do." Kora sent me a knowing wink.

I nodded and gave them a quick salute. "Welcome to the revolution, Parker."

16

VI

Chase and I relaxed as we heard Thea. Both of us had been terrified to let her walk into the precinct on her own, but we trusted her, and she had gotten in without incident.

"Okay, do your job and get straight out." Chase was using his big brother voice, and I could practically feel the eye roll from Thea on the other end.

"I know the plan," she sniped in return.

Chase and I were hidden in the shadows of an alley next to the precinct, and I gave him a playful punch to the shoulder, silently telling him to leave her alone. He just shrugged but then gave a quick smirk.

"We're ready," Kora said through our comms.

"We've got access to the city's cameras. We'll get everything on video," Declan said.

I held out my fist, and Chase tapped his own knuckles to mine. With a quick nod, I slipped out of the alleyway and into the city streets surrounding the precinct.

"I've got eyes on you," Gwen said in my ear. She was my cover and was already set up on a roof nearby.

I walked across the street and stood on the walkway in front of the entrance to the precinct. Looking up at the towering building, I pulled my hood down, letting my hair spill around my shoulders. Shrugging out of the rest of my coat, I let it drop around my feet. My suit was hidden under my street clothes, and I flicked a dagger to life in my hand.

Heads started to turn my way as I slowly walked to the steps of the front door. Catching the eye of one of the officers outside, he tugged on his radio.

"All units, Genevieve Astor is here. She's heading straight for the entrance," the guard yelled into it before holding up his weapon and moving to block my path.

A commotion stirred from the people in the building and the troops out in the streets flooding our way. Calm washed over me, just like it did every time I was ready for a fight.

I was finally on the offensive, and they would regret treating my people the way they had.

More guards rushed out of the precinct and started to surround me from the streets, and I just stood there, watching the crowd I had drawn. Their guns were up and trained on me.

"Drop the weapon and stay where you are," the one who had first seen me called out.

With a smirk I raised my hands and let the dagger dissolve. The man took a step forward, jabbing his gun closer to me, like it would make a difference. I cocked my head and just stared at him, still wearing my slightly unhinged smile. I saw him flinch, but he didn't back away.

Some of the others did though.

"Genevieve Astor, you are under arrest," he yelled and shuffled another step closer.

"You don't seem to understand what is going on here," I replied as a blinking metal box was tossed into the middle of the group. It blinked twice more before it flared to life and every single piece of metal nearby that wasn't bolted down, came flying toward it, including all of their guns. Our weapons had been outfitted with a repulsor field, leaving my friends the only people who were armed.

David had pointed out the box before he had left, and I was glad Thea had thought to bring it.

The man just looked at his empty hands in confusion as I created two daggers and lunged at him. I sliced through tendons in his shoulder and kicked out at his knee.

Before he could even scream, I was working through the crowd behind him. Chase and the others made their way into the street. They shot around them to move the mass of officers like sheep dogs. It was enough to keep them off balance and distracted.

"Anytime now, Thea," Chase said into his comm as he shot an officer in the foot and the knee, dropping them to the ground. Instantly, he sighted another. We were working to incapacitate as many of them as we could, with wounds where they couldn't just get back up and return to work. They would be in recovery for a while before we'd have to worry about them again. Thinning out Esmerelda's force was the goal. Hopefully giving the people who stayed here a reprieve, if only for a while.

"Give me a minute." She sounded breathless, and a part of me worried about her, but I didn't have time to focus on it.

The street had erupted into chaos, and I dropped into a slide, slicing through ankles, legs, and knees. I launched myself up to my feet and pressed forward before the line behind me even hit the ground.

I smashed the butt of my knife into the temple of the man directly in front of me, and he dropped too.

Movement from the front doors caught my attention, and I saw Thea racing out of the building with blood dripping down her face. She was booking it as fast as she could across the street.

In the moment, I was distracted, a big meaty fist crashed into me, sending me stumbling. My eyes snapped to him, and I saw the flicker of fear but then his anger returned.

Launching myself at him, I managed to swing around him,

grasping his arm and jerking it up his back. The sound of the snapping bone made me shiver with excitement, and then a twinge of horror rushed through me at my initial reaction. Unpacking that would have to wait.

Then, I heard it. The rapid beeping from deep in the building. The man was between me and the building, and I slipped close to him just as the building exploded. His body blocked me from the worst of the blast.

Screams echoed through the street as the guards tried to protect themselves from the launched debris. As the man I had used as a human shield fell, I watched the building start to collapse from the damage.

A feeling of retribution washed over me at the sight. Finally, one of her buildings would be nothing but rubble. This was the first step in getting revenge.

I dodged a wild attack from someone covered in dust that had already recovered from the shock. I glared at him and kicked out with all my strength, and he went flying back, knocking the group of people behind him to the ground.

I heard the short bursts of gunfire as the others continued to incapacitate anyone we could. We were going to cripple them in this city. Not only had the building been taken down, but Thea had placed an explosive in their armory. They would lose their building, their weapons, and their manpower all in one fell swoop.

The best part? This would pull every available enforcer here, into the heart of the city, leaving the outer edges clear to evacuate everyone we could. As if on cue, alarms started to blare nearby, and the sweet song of sirens came this way.

Some of the troops had made it to the pile of weapons made by the magnet box and managed to rip some free. Pushing off, I launched myself over a volley of fire. Then, dipping and weaving this way and that, I made my way toward them.

I dropped and swept one of their legs out from under them. As they hit the ground, I used their chest as a launching pad and tackled another. One of them seemed frozen in shock as I appeared in front of them. I ripped the gun from his hands, and a beat later, he turned and ran. On instinct, I raised the rifle, sighting straight for his head, the bloodlust swimming to the surface as I fought. I ground my teeth, and the bullet ripped through the back of his knee instead. We weren't here to kill in cold blood, even if my body was aching to get my revenge.

With a quick slide backward, I managed to step out of the way of someone racing toward me with a scream of anger. He had too much momentum to correct, and as he went flying past, I swung the rifle into him like a bat. He went toppling to the ground.

"Declan, patch me in." It was time to make my announcement.

We had cleared most of the guards, and they were scatted around, holding their wounds, some screaming, some probably in shock. I saw a camera pointed toward the street, turning to face it and then made sure to do the same to any others there.

I held up my arms, gesturing to the carnage surrounding me. "Esmerelda, this won't stand. You want me to be a terrorist? Fine, here you go. I'm coming for everything you have. I will protect my people, and I will free them from you. To all the people of Kabria, flee the cities. Come to us; we'll protect you. I can't say the same if you stay.

"Anyone who follows orders given by the queen is my enemy, and as you can see, you won't be able to stop me. Esmerelda was the one to bomb Fairhaven. They locked people in buildings and set them on fire. They killed innocents in the name of making us villains. This is your warning. You wanted a villain? You've got one."

The sirens were getting closer, and my friends started to slip into the shadows of the alleyways and disappeared. The first vehicle came screeching to a stop nearby. I grabbed up one of the rifles and tossed it into the air a few times, testing the weight. The doors to the car swung open, and two officers stumbled out. With all my strength, I launched the rifle at the car. It crashed through the hood and straight into the engine. The sirens went silent. The two officers just gaped as they looked from me to their destroyed car.

I made a move like I was going to run at them, and they both flinched, which pleased me to no end. As they peeked toward me, I flashed them one last grin then I took a few running steps, jumped, and landed on the roof of their car. Then, I leapt to the roof of a building lining the street.

Before I headed off to catch up with the others, I took a moment to behold the destruction. People were crumpled in the street, and there were fires starting to burn within the building as another chunk of the walls went crashing to the ground.

My skin itched to return and finish them off. I felt like I did in Neria when I had been fighting Jasper. A rage I could barely control roared through my veins. The need to cause pain to those who had wronged me. To dominate anyone who would cross me.

Again, I wondered what I was becoming. Each time I fought; this feeling grew stronger, harder to lock away. Would I eventually be unable to control it? Would I lose my soul to win this war?

Part of me already knew the answer.

I would if that was what it took.

17

ESMERELDA

The video was paused on the moments after the explosion, parts of the building hanging in midair. Morgan was tense at my side, obviously worried about my reaction. That alone would have given me some satisfaction if I wasn't currently seething.

I fast-forwarded the video to where Genevieve held her hands out giving her speech.

"Um, Your Majesty?" Morgan squeaked.

"What?" I snapped, twisting to glare at her.

"The video has been uploaded to the web. It's been shared four thousand times and already has over one million views."

"Take it down," I hissed.

Heat rushed through me. I felt dizzy with the wave of rage. The Longdale precinct had twenty percent more officers than any of the others. Not only did Genevieve take out those in the building, but she managed to draw in those nearby on patrol as well.

I'd have to increase the numbers for the draft, but even then, they wouldn't be trained soon enough. I'd have to pull in people from other cities to compensate. We had to get Longdale under control, and we'd come down hard on them to do so.

The rebels had broadcast this to the entire country, so we'd have to double patrols and lock down the cities. I pressed my fingertips into my temples, trying to ease the pain.

The door slid open, and Howard walked in. He gestured for Morgan to leave, which she did in a hurry. She might seem meek, but I kept her around because she had a spine when it came to giving orders to others. She was quite the little enforcer, and she was great at organizing my schedule.

My attention turned to Howard. "What?"

Not fazed by the anger in my voice; he crossed his arms and gave me a long look. "I just wanted to check on you."

I growled as my gaze went back to the frozen video. "I'm going to destroy her. She thinks she's won something, but she's just shown everyone her true self. I'm going to make the people suffer for her actions, and when I finally get my hands on her, she's going to beg me to kill her before I'm done with her."

"Well, we have something that can help you obtain her. Or we will. Would you like to see them?"

"The sisters?" I asked.

He tapped a few things into his tablet, and as he swiped his finger, another video came up on the screen. "They will be. We don't want to rush; it could be anywhere from a few months to over a year. We have to make sure the conditioning will hold while they're on a mission, but they survived the first phase."

The screen showed a firing range with two girls emptying clips into the targets. Then, it switched to a room with them hooked up to monitors and running on a treadmill. Next, was an open room where they launched themselves into the air, jumping farther than any human could.

This was going to change everything.

I knew Astor, and she wouldn't fight someone she cared for. And now, she would be fighting not one but two people just as strong as her. She wouldn't know what hit her, and then she'd be all mine.

"Morgan," I snapped, and she poked her head in.

"Yes, Your Majesty?"

"Call for the car; we're going to the facility." I couldn't wait to see my new weapons in action.

PART II

THE FALL

18

Vi

1 year later...

"You've got to be kidding me." Thea cursed.

"I said you were going to jinx us," Gwen called back, cackling manically as we ran through the streets with guards right on our tail.

"It was going fine," Thea barked.

We raced through a bustling area filled with stalls, their workers, and a swarm of shoppers. A cheer erupted when the people saw us. The guards behind us started to get pelted by food and who knew what else. One of them went down as a child ran out and caught his legs before slipping away into the crowd again.

"We're almost there, just keep going," I yelled.

Thea grabbed up a metal sheet that was leaning against a nearby building as we came to the steps. She threw it down against the railing and jumped on it in a fluid motion and started to slide down the stairwell.

Gwen rolled her eyes at me. "Kids," she muttered before running to take a few stairs at a time. I skidded to a stop and took stock of my options. There was a large cart brimming with fruit. I found the owner and tossed them some money and a shrug of apology as I toppled the cart and threw it in front of the entrance to the stairwell. The fruit rolled down the street, and some of the guards chasing us crashed to the ground. The man tipped his hat to me before I turned and raced after the girls. I launched into the air in a flip, landed at the bottom of the stairs, and hit the ground running.

The girls threw the doors to a car open as I caught up. Gwen roared the engine to life. Thea left the door open behind her after she crawled in, and I jumped through the opening. We slammed the doors shut, and the tires screamed and smoked as Gwen threw the car into gear and we shot off.

There was a bag in the seat with me, and I tugged on the zipper. I reached in and grabbed the guns that laid within. I threw one to Thea, and she caught it out of the air. I took out another for myself. We each rolled down our windows. Everything swung to one side when Gwen took a sharp corner at top speed. We tore around a corner and down the next street.

When we straightened out I saw three cars racing up behind us.

"Company is here," I called.

Thea turned and leaned out of her window, gun in hand. "Let's give them one of our favorite welcomes!"

I followed suit, and we started to fire at the lead car. They started to spray bullets back at us, and I had to drop into the car to evade some. Gwen launched us over a bump in the road, and it felt like we were floating for a moment before we crashed down to Earth. She took us around another corner at top speed, and I kept a grip around the edge of the door so I didn't get flung across the seat.

One of my favorite songs was blasting through the speakers, and I couldn't help but let out a howl of excitement. I stuck my head out the window again, my hair whipping sharply in the wind. As we swerved, I worked on aiming at the tire of the first car following us. I heard Gwen whoop from her seat, and then Thea joined in on the calls of chaos.

I landed a shot and one of their tires exploded. The car jerked sharply before it overturned and went flipping end over end. The one behind it wasn't able to stop in time and crashed into it. The third went through full speed, just knocking the others out of the way.

Gwen threw us around another corner, and there it was. We raced toward the train tracks. I could hear the train rumbling up the tracks, its horn blaring. Right on time. Gwen got us parallel then sped up as the train was catching up to us.

I slipped through the window and sat on the edge of the door. Reaching over, I grabbed Thea's arm from her position hanging out the other side of the car. I helped her pull herself up until she was standing on the roof. She ducked down as bullets ricocheted off the car. She shot at the last car behind us. The train was coming up on us, and it was going fast enough that it would speed past us in moments, no matter how fast we got this car to go.

"Now!" I yelled.

Thea dropped her gun and jumped. She managed to catch the handles on the outside of the train, and once she was secure, she started to pull herself to the roof. I crawled onto the top of the car and covered us, firing at the last car, which was making a move to hit us. "Gwen!"

Her door flew open. Quickly, I grabbed her hand and used the momentum from her jump to toss her toward the train. She managed to catch the same handhold, and Thea helped pull her up. As soon as Gwen let go of the wheel, the car started to drift. I jumped for the train.

Thea and Gwen reached down to help me up. The car that had been chasing us fell farther and farther behind.

The train was carrying supplies to the palace. We were here to make sure they didn't make it.

Walking toward the front, I had to brace myself every few seconds. The speed made the gusts of wind vicious. Luckily, David had created some magnetic shoes, which were helping us stay grounded. Gwen and Thea were right behind me, and we didn't have much time; the bridge would be here before we knew it.

Someone's head popped up between the cars ahead. It seemed like they knew we were here now. I ran forward, weaving back and forth as they shot at us. As soon as I reached them, I jumped into the opening. All it took was one well-placed punch, and he went flying off the train. A sharp sting sent a skitter of pain through me, and with a glance at my side, I saw blood. Someone had shot me. I tapped my neck, and my suit slid across my skin. In the same movement, I turned and loosed three daggers. Everyone in the car fell clutching their injuries.

The radios throughout the train blared the warning that we were here. I pushed toward the engine car. More bullets hit my side, but then I saw Thea's head come swinging in upside down as she shot through the door at the people following me.

"I got it. You go," she called to me.

"Toss out who you can before the bridge." Then I kept moving.

Two people crashed into my stomach when I opened the door to the next car. They had been couched on either side of the doorway. I stumbled back a few steps but glared at them. I slammed my foot into one, sending them flying. I grabbed the other, spun, and tossed them into the far wall of the car. Boxes smashed beneath them. Neither would be getting up anytime soon. Grabbing them, I drug them to the opening and tossed them off. I stalked ahead once more; the next car was my target. The door was locked, but there was a window, so I smashed my hand through it, grasping for the lock. It hissed open, and I saw the driver under the console, his hands up in surrender.

"Please, please, don't hurt me," he cried.

"Sure, I won't hurt you," I said with a mischievous grin. I grabbed him by the shirt and pulled him up. His eyes went wide as I held him out, the ground moving past in a blur under his feet. "I'll just let you off here."

I let go, and he dropped. Within seconds, he was out of view.

I turned to the console and started to slow the train. The track was curving ahead, and a wide chasm with a lone bridge spanning the expanse came into view. The train slowed and eventually rolled to a stop. The metal of the bridge creaked under us.

"We're in position," I said into my comm.

"Be right there," Benson said as I worked my way back through the train to see if Thea or Gwen needed any help. I didn't run into anyone as I made it to the cargo car we were here for. I found them opening the door on the side of the car, and I saw the hover copter being flown in by Anthony, with Chase and Benson on board. They slid open the side of the large hover copter and lined up next to the train. We started to throw the supplies across the gap.

When we were done, Chase held out his hand and helped Thea across, and Benson reached out for Gwen. Chase caught my hand last and tugged me over. I spun into his arms, and he kissed me as Anthony flew us away.

Benson threw Gwen one of the rocket launchers, and they shared a wicked look. They both leaned out the door, each targeting one end of the bridge. As they pulled the trigger, a plume of smoke trailed behind the rockets as they raced forward. The sound of the explosion and the tearing of the metal echoed through the valley. I could feel it in my bones as I watched everything crash to Earth, the bridge falling to pieces.

The copter started to turn, heading toward Nexus camp. We were going to drop off these supplies for the newest camp we had built for the refugees. They needed food, medicine, and the clothing we managed to get from the train, and we had destroyed that route for Esmerelda to get any further supplies. I reveled in the victory.

Gwen and Thea both leaned in, and we exchanged high fives. Over the past year, Thea and Anthony had become an integral part of our team. We had been doing missions throughout the entire country, being sent where we were most needed. It had been a struggle to build camps and cities fast enough for the droves of people who came for our protection.

We had been blocking Esmeralda from being able to import anything from the agricultural part of the country, which was firmly in our grasp. We had blocked a supply chain, and she'd create a new one, but we would take that one down too. Neria had cut Esmeralda off, and we were stopping as many imports into the cities as we could. We hoped it was only a matter of time before her own military turned against her due to the conditions.

19

Vi

We landed, and the engines slowly started to power down. As I opened the door there was a group of people waiting for us, who came running over to help unload. Many of the people we had evacuated out of Longdale had ended up here at the Nexus camp. Everyone here was working to expand it from a camp to a small town.

Seeing two people struggling with one of the boxes, I headed their way. "Mind if I take this one?"

I grabbed it from them easily, hefting it onto my shoulder and taking it to the depot, where most of the building supplies were being stored. I dropped it, and the clatter of the metal hitting the cement echoed through the large open building. We had been sourcing most of our materials from our allies up and down the countryside. We had a major advantage since almost all the food, lumber, and brick came from our side of the divide. Esmerelda had the cities, but not much else.

I was surprised at how quickly we had managed to expand Nexus and other camps like it just in the past year. We had people of all walks of life who'd joined us; we had engineers, scientists, doctors, artisans. They had helped us plan and build our little cities.

As our resistance grew, the calls for help only increased. So much so that we had to break up our crew sometimes for multiple missions.

We had eventually moved to Nexus because we had decided to move the highest levels of command evenly through the new camps. I didn't see my father much since then, but he was putting in an effort. He called just to talk and would make time for us to see each other if we did manage to get back to headquarters. It was nice to have a relationship with him in this new dynamic. I was glad to have him around, glad he was *trying* to be around.

Sometimes, Chase and I reminisced on our time in Neria. How, at the time, working with the rebels to fight the king and the military was the hardest thing we ever dealt with, and now we saw it was just the tip of the iceberg. How our war, as it dragged on, was so much more difficult and terrifying than we ever could have expected.

But when we did think of Neria, we both agreed that time was the most carefree we had ever been... in that little apartment, before the world started to fall to pieces. Remembering that month of living a somewhat normal life surrounded by our friends had been something we both clung to. A reminder of what things could be like if we won this war.

It wasn't that I didn't love what we had now. It was beautiful in its own way, but it was different. We were older, and there were more consequences from our decisions now. We'd been through so much since then. Lost so much.

Back then, the memory of the prison weighed heavily on me, and now, while it still was a part of me, I knew it made me who I was. I wasn't the girl who was rescued from the prison; I wasn't the girl who was trapped there. I was something new, and if I made it another few years, I would be a new person then too. At least, I hoped. I hoped I would keep learning and growing, becoming more of the person people needed me to be. The person I needed *myself* to be.

"How's my little train robber?" Chase asked, walking up and wrapping his arms around me.

"I'm hungry," I complained, and he pulled a protein bar from his pocket and held it out to me. My eyes widened at the sight. I grabbed it quickly, and I leaned in to give him a kiss. The feel of him there settled my nerves, his mere presence calming me. I always soaked up every moment with him, building my reserves so I could call on them when I felt myself slipping into chaos.

"Come on. They said there was something we needed to see." He took one of my hands and led the way toward the square.

"Do you know what it is?" I asked, and he shook his head.

"Guys, over here!" Thea called. We headed her way at the far edge of the square.

"Look who's here!" she said when we got closer, holding her hands out toward someone.

I squealed and leapt on David when I saw him. He laughed and threw his arms around me as I almost knocked us both over. I saw Joseph over his shoulder. They had become an item not long after they ended up in Soland, and we couldn't be happier. We hadn't seen them in person in months, and I was so excited for them to be here.

"You didn't say you were coming!" Chase said, as he grabbed Joseph for a hug.

I let go of David, and we switched. I squeezed Joseph tight.

"We wanted it to be a surprise." David shrugged, but he couldn't hide the smile plastered on his face too. "Naya came too, but apparently Benson has stolen her away already."

I saw that Benson was nowhere to be found, which made me chuckle. They had kept in touch since we left Neria and tried to see each other as much as they could, but Naya was busy helping to create the new Nerian government, so she couldn't get away often.

"Well, come on. Let's go to our place." Chase started away, and everyone followed him. I let Anthony pass me to walk with Thea and Gwen.

"Thanks for having my back today." Thea knocked her hip into mine, which bumped me into Gwen.

I wrapped my arm around the latter's shoulders. "Gwen, as always, wonderful driving."

"It was so nice to get some girl time, don't you think? We should ask for more missions with just us." She raised her eyebrow at me.

"I'll see what I can do." I turned to Thea. "By the way, I was going to ask, where were you the other night? We thought you were coming over for dinner."

"Oh, Jenna had come by. We hung out, and I lost track of time," she said quickly.

"I haven't seen her in a bit. Tell her I say hi, will you?"

Gwen caught my eye and gave a tiny shrug. Thea would tell us more when she was ready. We had all seen the completely obvious glances between the two of them for a while. I hoped something was finally happening there. I liked Jenna, she joined the force with us a little less than a year ago, and thought she'd be good for Thea. They were spending a lot of time together recently.

Thea had always been a bit more like me than Chase personality wise, and Jenna kept a calm head in a storm. Thea was still young, not even seventeen yet, and always wanted to prove what she could do. Which often had her running headfirst into trouble. I was proud of her, but I did hope she wasn't trying to prove anything to me. I just wanted her to stay safe, but she had shown us time and time again that she could protect herself. So, I just did everything I could to give her exactly what she needed to do so.

I was the last one to slip through the door of our house and closed it behind us. Just like every time I came back, a contented little sigh escaped me. I felt safe here, and it swirled with memories of Chase and me.

We finally had a little privacy. Chase had made the call when we started to build Nexus. At first, it had been just a tent away from the others, but we built this place together, with some help from our friends. We weren't here all that often, and home was always wherever Chase and I were together, but I loved our little house.

Outside of the room at the barracks, I had never had a place I could call home. Having this meant the world to me.

Chase was already digging through the cabinets to pull out

glasses for everyone. I went to the little bar nook we had, grabbed some bottles, and took them to the large table everyone gathered around.

Right on time, the door opened, and Benson bellowed his hello as he and Naya came in. We all cheered and went to go say hello, swarming her with hugs. We led them into the great room, and I handed each of them a glass.

"Not that we don't love to see you, but what prompted the unexpected trip?" Chase asked David and Joseph.

"Oh, we have news," Joseph said, and I could practically see the excitement vibrating from them both. He pulled David to him, and my heart started doing flips. I hoped this was exactly what I thought it was.

"We're getting married." David looked deep into Joseph's eyes, who squeezed his hand in response.

The room erupted with congratulations as we all jumped up from our seats. We may or may not have been making bets on how long it would take before they made the leap.

I watched my friends amid all this joy, the time seeming to slow as I tried to memorize everything about this moment. I wanted to remember this forever. As we were all painfully aware of at this point, we never knew when it would be the last time you saw the people we loved. So, we always made the most of every second we had together. I closed my eyes and soaked up the love in the room.

20

Vi

The chimes of our comm units sounded throughout the house. We made sure we had enough room for all our friends to stay if necessary, and everyone had. I heard the groans from the others as they awoke to the harsh noise. One of the best parts of my changes was that, although I couldn't get drunk, I also couldn't get hungover. I looked at the message that came through.

Top priority mission. Alpha team requested for the briefing in 30 minutes.

Chase was rubbing the sleep from his eyes, but I was already up and headed for a shower.

"Wait, let's save water," he said in a groggy tone, still rubbing at his eyes.

"Hurry up, or I'm going without you." I winked before slipping into our bathroom. I heard him jump out of bed and run after me. He had a wicked grin plastered on his face as he sauntered in and closed the door behind him. I couldn't help but bite my lip at the view. After all this time, that never got old.

Exactly thirty minutes later, we all huddled around a holoprojector, and the image of my father came to life.

"Good to see you all," he said as he saw David, Joseph, and Naya with us. They saluted in response. "And I hear congratulations are in order."

"Thank you, Nolan." David smiled in response. I didn't ask how my father knew; he just always seemed to. It stopped surprising me, but I also kept that in mind just in case I did something he wouldn't approve of. I was grown, but he still had his I'm-disappointed-in-you look on point.

"We've received word that Fort Mercy is under attack, and there are reports of a super being used in the assault." His gaze lingered on me. "So, we need you out there as soon as possible. We've already prepped your transport; they're ready for you."

"Sure," Chase replied. "We'll head out now."

"Be safe," my father told us before the hologram flickered off.

"Want to help us out from here?" I asked David and Joseph with a mischievous grin.

"Sure thing. We've been looking into the fact that Esmerelda has been working on new supers. Apparently, she's done it. We'll provide you as much information as we can when we see what we're up against." David laid a hand on my shoulder and squeezed it tightly. I rounded on him and gave him the biggest hug before breaking away.

"I'm not scheduled to ship back for a day or two. I'll help here where I can," Naya said. Benson cupped her cheek, gave her a quick kiss, and faced us again.

We all said our goodbyes, and the team raced to get to the transport. Luckily, Fort Mercy wasn't far from us; it should take less than an hour to get there. The copter tore through the air. We knew there was no time to lose. The attack must have started right at dawn, using the rising sun to their advantage.

As we neared, we saw the smoke and fires throughout the base. I could hear the gunfire from here. We were still high above the base, working to circle our way into a safe landing, but I opened the door.

"See you down there," I said to the others and jumped out of the copter. The wind whipped through my hair, stinging my face as I made myself as aerodynamic as possible. As I landed, the ground gave slightly beneath me from the force of the impact. Instantly, I pushed power into my legs and sprinted off into the fray.

I took in everything around me as I raced through the fort. I needed to find the new super. Hearing screams, I sprinted in that direction. As I skidded into the alleyway, I saw a thin girl in a form-fitting, redesigned Kabrian military uniform throwing someone into the opposite wall. I stumbled to a stop as I recognized her. It was Jessie, one of the girls I had come across in Neria. I didn't understand. She had been working with us to overthrow the king, and she hated Esmerelda and everything she stood for.

"Jessie?" I whispered.

She looked at me but didn't seem to have a shred of recognition in her gaze.

"Jessie," I called again, reaching toward her. Faster than the blink of an eye, she was on me. Her attack was swift and brutal. It took everything I had just to try to evade her. I slipped under her punches and twisted out of the way of her kicks. I grabbed her wrists to stop her if only for a second, but she used my grip to her advantage. She pulled me close before slamming her knee into my stomach. I stumbled back.

Something was terribly wrong. I wouldn't attack her. I couldn't hurt her.

"Jessie, stop," I yelled. "What is going on?"

She launched herself at me. Her tackle sent us both crashing into the ground. I tried to grab her again and twisted so I was straddling her and trapping her under me, holding her arms above her head. She screamed and thrashed in my hold.

"Look at me. We know each other; we fought together. Why are you working for Esmerelda? What happened?"

She screamed again and managed to break loose and hit me hard enough to knock me off of her. She pulled daggers from behind her and slashed at me.

When I had fought Jasper, he had been strong but slow. Jessie was different. She was like me. Lean, fast, and flexible. This wasn't going to be easy, but I had to capture her. We had to fix this. Esmerelda had done something to her. How had she even gotten Jessie in the first place? How long had she had her? My hate for my stepmother only grew.

"Converge," Jessie said.

Whatever that was, it couldn't be good. Then I heard light foot-steps racing our way. We were going to have company. I had to get them out of the fort, away from the people here, and out into the open.

Turning, I raced away. I crossed my fingers, hoping she would follow, and within seconds she was. I just prayed I was faster. My mind tumbled through the time since I had last seen her. It had been a few days before we overthrew the king and took the Nerian palace. Naya and Jupiter hadn't said anything about her going missing. Had anyone even noticed? How long had she been in Esmerelda's clutches? What had she done to her? The memories of the torture I had been through flooded me. My heart broke for my friend.

I was almost out past the edge of the fort, but something slammed into my side, and I screamed in surprise as I went crashing through a building. I cursed at the fact that I had been so distracted I hadn't even heard them coming.

That hit. It wasn't from an ordinary solider. Were there two of them? I shook my head, trying to clear it, but someone grabbed my ankle, and I was tossed through another wall. Behind me, the entire structure started to collapse.

I had to focus. I had to get outside of the base, especially if there were two of them. I twisted and raced away, needing some space to think.

I heard them both on my heels as I ran. I couldn't even spare a glance behind me or they would catch up to me. I rushed into open territory, the buildings disappearing behind us. Just a bit farther, there was the cover of the forest up ahead. I flew into the trees as fast as I could.

But they were right there. I could hear them right on my heels.

Fine.

I dug my feet in and threw my arms up as I stopped. I caught them both in the throat, and their feet went flying out from under them. There was a firm thud as they crashed into the ground.

I snarled but it died in my throat as I saw who the other super was.

Cecily. Jessie's little sister.

My stomach dropped to my toes.

No. How? How did Esmerelda get her hands on them both?

How had I not known they needed help?

I screamed in frustration. What was I supposed to do now?

Jessie twisted and swept my feet out from under me as Cecily pounced and rammed into my shoulders, and we went down hard. The air was knocked out of me, and my vision swam.

Cecily slammed her fist into my face repeatedly. I managed to get one good shot right into her chin and knocked her off of me. I flipped to my feet and crouched, ready for an attack.

"Jessie, Cecily," I pleaded, holding my hands up in front of me, like I was dealing with two wild animals. "Don't you remember me? We're friends."

"You are Genevieve Astor, and we're here to collect you." Cecily's voice was monotone, empty. There was no recognition in either of their eyes.

Part of me was crushed. They had clearly been through some kind of hell, and now their job was to bring me to Esmerelda? Terror flared through my pain, but I pushed it into a box and locked it away. No time to worry about that now. I needed to figure out a way to get through to them.

Completely in sync, they both came for me. Blades in their hands, they slashed, and I did everything I could just to evade them. I raced into the trees to have at least the smallest amount of cover. I grabbed a branch, swung myself over, and ended up landing behind them. They turned and snarled. I didn't know what to do, but I wasn't going to get out of here if I didn't fight back.

Gods forgive me. I summoned two batons into my hands and parry a blow from Jessie. My forearm crashed against and incoming attack from Cecily. They came at me with unforgiving speed and power. I dipped backward underneath a slice from Jessie, only to barely block Cecily's next attack.

Could I even match the two of them? I had never been in this position since I got my powers. Jasper had been a deadly opponent, but he was nothing compared to these two. They matched me in every way.

I launched myself up into one of the trees, trying to escape them. They jumped up after me. I finally had an opening and kicked out, sending Jessie falling to the ground. Cecily screamed and came flying at me. I managed to deflect her and caught her by the throat. I threw her with all my might, and she went crashing through branches on her way down, before hitting the dirt with a sickening thud. I went to race away, but Jessie fired a cable, which caught me by the wrist and pulled me down. I managed to land on my feet, summoning a blade in my other hand and slicing through it.

Jessie dug in and ran at me, crashing into me and sending us both to the ground. I scrambled back, trying to get to my feet. For the first time, I went for my comm.

"Guys, I need hel—" I couldn't finish as Cecily rammed me and knocked the air from my chest again. I roared, grabbing her shoulders and twisting so I crushed her into the closest tree, but Jessie ripped me off of her.

I heard Chase's concern as he told me they were coming, but I didn't have time to reply. My attention had to be here. I created shields to protect my arms as they both jumped me again, the sheer force of their attacks driving me to my knees. I threw my arms up to protect my head and shoulders and used a tree to keep myself from sliding backward. I gritted my teeth. The nanobots couldn't reform fast enough to keep the shields up.

I reached out, quickly grabbing a wrist of both girls and tugging, and they collided together.

"We're almost there. Hold on," Thea yelled.

I pulled the batons into my hands and went on the offensive. The speed of my attacks pushed them back, giving me some room to maneuver. I started seeing a pattern in their attacks, and I was able to slip within their weak points. I screamed with rage at what had happened to them, putting everything I had into giving the others time to get here.

Jessie managed to get through, and her blade sliced into my side, breaking through my suit. Cecily took the opening, and her dagger pierced my thigh. Blood quickly spread from the wound, and the flow pulsed in time with my heart.

In quick succession, Jessie stabbed me multiple times before I could manage to jump out of their reach. Pain bloomed as blood started to spill across my skin under my suit that had managed to knit together again. I heard the running steps of my friends and turned to race toward them.

"Get the net," I rasped into my comm. Moments later, I saw Benson ready with the launcher. I pushed myself to get away from them and worked to lead them toward him. I stumbled to a stop, looking behind me. Jessie toppled as the net wrapped around her. She screamed and writhed as she struggled to escape, but blood started to stream from the cuts from the razor wire the net was made of. I watched as Cecily came up short, seeing her sister.

I held up my arms, the batons in each hand, but I couldn't stand straight between the pain and the sudden exhaustion. My vision started to blur. They had to have hit an artery or two. The others came up to the scene, making a semicircle behind me. They had their guns raised and trained on her. Cecily snarled, baring her teeth, before turning and sprinting away.

As soon as I was sure she wasn't coming around for another

attack, I dropped to my knees. I coughed up blood as I caught myself from falling on my face. Chase rushed to me.

"What is it?" he asked with terror clear in his voice as he reached out to hold me up.

My vision swam again as he tapped my neck and the suit started to withdraw. I slumped into his arms and struggled to keep my thoughts straight.

"No, no, no. Where is all of this blood coming from?" Chase cursed as he pressed his hands to my side. "Get over here now," Chase screamed, but I didn't know who he was talking to. I used everything I had to lift my hand to cup his cheek, my bloody fingers smearing red along the stubble that lined his jaw. He was the most beautiful thing I had ever seen.

"You are my everything," I whispered as I thought about our lives together. My body was racing to heal as the blood continued to spill from the wounds. I marveled at his eyes—the eyes I had spent hours admiring—staring down at me. I would be nothing without him; he brought out every good part of me and loved me when the terrible parts came to the surface.

There was a sharp pain in my side, and I slowly looked down to see a metal cylinder pressed there. I followed the arm up to see Thea. I couldn't remember exactly what that was for, but a warmth spread from the spot as darkness flooded my vision. I would just take a little nap. That was all I needed.

21

Vi

I blinked against a blinding light hovering above me. Groaning, I blocked my eyes with my arm. The memory of what happened slowly came back to me as I pushed to sit up on the cot. I glanced around and saw David, who looked overcome with relief when he saw me.

"Oh, thank the gods," he muttered. He sent off a quick message—to the others, I assumed.

Joseph hurried over, pulled out a light, and started to flash it in my eyes. I let him do it for a moment but then batted him away. I had a headache, and that wasn't helping.

"I'm fine." I swayed for a moment, but then I steadied. "See, fine."

"At least Thea had that med shot with her, or you wouldn't have been." David's gaze bore into mine.

"That's why we don't leave home without it." I smiled, trying to get him to lighten up.

Joseph had created the serum of healing nanobots. It gave me enough time for my body to catch up and do the rest. This wasn't the first time they'd had to use it, and I got a lecture every time, but I knew it was out of love.

"We had no idea she had even managed replaced Jasper, and how was I supposed to know there would be two of them?" We had heard Esmerelda was working on it, but I thought we'd know if she managed it. With one, much less two. "Where is Jessie? We still have her, don't we?" I hoped she hadn't managed to get away. If we had her, we could try to fix this.

"The devices worked as expected. She's in the holding cell." David nodded.

We knew this day was coming, so we had been developing technology that could be used to take someone like me down and keep them down. I had managed to convince the others to test it on me to make sure we had something that could protect them if I wasn't there.

The net was made from razor wire that would cut deeper the more the person struggled. The bars of the cell we had created were made from our strongest metal, as well as lasers and a force field around that. We had armor-piercing rounds and energy shields that could stand a blast from an RPG at close range. All the technology had come from David and Joseph and their students at the school.

I swatted them away as I got up, heading for where we were she would be. David and Joseph stopped fussing over me and followed right on my heels. They muttered about me not taking care of myself, but I couldn't wait. I needed to see her.

As I reached the right building, I ached at the thought of what the sisters had gone through. I took a deep breath and straightened my spine before I pulled the door open and marched inside.

I gave a quick hello to the guard who was posted there and pushed into where the cells were. Jessie's eyes were on me as soon as I stepped into the room. She watched me like a predator tracking its prey.

"Jessie, what happened to you?" I couldn't help but remember the hug she had given me when we had reunited her with Cecily in Neria. Now, she didn't say anything in return.

"We managed to get some blood to run tests, and she has the same mutations you do," Joseph said. "The mental conditioning... we don't know what she was put through, but we've got everyone searching for data or anyone who might know something."

"Did anyone tell Naya yet?" I asked.

"Benson did; she came by earlier. Jessie didn't show any recognition with her either." David put a hand on my shoulder, and I covered it with mine.

"I'm so sorry," I whispered to Jessie. She just snarled at me in return. "I think I'm just going to stay for a while." Leaning against the wall, I slid down and sat across from her as they left.

Pulling my knees up, I wrapped my arms around them. I closed my eyes and flinched at the memory of scalpels slicing into my skin. The pain, the hopelessness, the terror washed over me in waves. With effort, I thought of the time with Jessie in Neria. How I had bonded with the people we had met there. Bonds that would last forever.

"Do you remember anything?" I finally asked her. She just glared back at me. "When we first met, you were searching for your sister. We managed to get her out of that orphanage with the Nerian rebels during the attack. You and your friends used to eat with us. Don't you remember any of it? That old apartment building with no heat the rebels had to move to after the attack on the base in the school? I loved it there, as weird as that might seem."

I might have imagined it, but I could have sworn I saw a flicker in her eyes. Something other than blind hate. Then, it was gone.

"Meeting all of you, seeing the plight of the Nerians, you changed everything. Seeing you all fight to change the lives of your people... We realized we could do the same thing."

The corner of her eye twitched.

"I will do everything in my power to help you. I will never give up on either of you. Never."

She wasn't going to say anything, it seemed, so I sighed and settled in just to sit with her for a while.

Chase had been waiting in the lobby of the building and raced to me when I finally left. He pulled me into his arms—one hand tangling in my hair, the other wrapping tightly around my waist. My hand automatically went to his neck, pulling him in for a desperate kiss. He broke away and nuzzled his face against my neck, breathing deeply. Over time, he had stopped chastising me when I got hurt and just enjoyed the fact that I was okay. He knew I was never going to change; it was just who I was.

"I came home." Our mantra after a bad mission.

"You were brought home, but point made," he muttered but grinned at me nonetheless. "David and Joseph want to transfer her to Soland." His brow creased in concern.

I knew why he was worried. "That's a long way to go, and we don't have any transports converted yet."

"They can't stay here; they need to get back to the school. It's the best option to try to help her. We just don't have what we need here. I don't see any other option." He pulled me out into the open, and I took in the setting sun.

I felt like the ground was being pulled out from under me again. The world would keep turning as if nothing had happened. I felt like I was racing to keep up with the changes but was always a step too slow. That no matter what I tried, I couldn't find my balance, and the world was mocking my attempts to take some control in my life.

"We'll just have to manage it." We'd figure it out like we always did. "I'll go with them."

"We're taking off in the morning, but until then, you're all mine." He pulled me close and nipped at my ear. I couldn't help but giggle as we headed to our house. Just his mere presence helped me feel calmer. Even if everything else was crazy, Chase was my constant, the one thing I could always count on. No matter what.

We'd figure this out. We had to.

22

Vi

In the morning, Chase and I made our way to where Jessie was being held. David had sent us a message that they were ready to transfer her into the new mobile cell he had finished putting together. As we pulled the door open, I saw a cell that looked almost identical to the one she was currently in, except it was hovering a few inches above the ground.

"Oh good, you're here," David said with a relieved sigh. He pointed to Jessie. "We're going to need you to move her. We don't trust anyone else to do it."

This was the perfect time for her to try to escape; we had to be ready. The others held stun guns and were stationed around the edges of the room as I moved toward the door to her cell. I nodded at David when I was ready. He pressed a button, and the lasers to the cell powered down.

I put all my attention on Jessie. I took a deep breath, put the key into the lock, and twisted it. I saw her thigh muscles twitch just before she launched herself at the door with all her might. I growled as I slammed my hands into the bars of the door, holding it closed. She slashed out, her nails ripping through the skin of my face, but I wouldn't budge. I cursed and grabbed her hands quickly as they came through the bars again.

"I'm so sorry," I said before I crushed her wrists against the bars. I heard the bones snap, and she roared in pain and pulled her arms in. In the blink of an eye, I had the door flung open. With all the speed I had, I picked her up and tossed her into the other cell. I managed to get the door shut right before she came crashing into it, and I clicked the lock shut.

"Move," David barked. I pulled away, and the lasers ignited along the bars. Jessie let out a frustrated scream as she held her arms close to her chest. I knew they'd heal before too long, but it didn't help the nausea that overcame me at what I had done.

I clenched my jaw tightly as I watched her. She looked more like a wild animal in that cage than the girl I knew. I could see her assessing the situation, working out the best way to escape.

"Let's get this over with. I don't know how long this is going to hold." I turned to the others and saw they were ready. I kept pace as they moved the cell out of the building and toward the hangar. I didn't take my eyes off her. Every part of me was on edge; my nerves buzzed with electricity. I had to be on high alert, to be ready for anything. We couldn't let her get away. We had to help her. I swallowed past the lump in my throat. This *was* to help her. I hoped she'd see that one day.

We loaded everyone into the cargo plane, and the engines roared to life. I sat across from the cell and settled in to keep an eye on her the entire flight. "Jessie, we're going to get you help."

She just glared at me. I sighed and leaned my head against the metal wall. We flew in silence, but the others were chatting amongst themselves up front. I mostly tuned them out, needing all of my focus here.

Maybe twenty minutes into the flight, the alarms started to blare.

"We've got incoming. They're moving in fast," Anthony called from the cockpit.

"We're going to kill everyone you love," Jessie said with a laugh.

My eyes jerked to her before returning to the others. I felt like I might be sick. She meant it, and almost everyone I cared about was on this plane.

Benson ran to the weapons console and started to bring the guns online. The plane rocked violently, and a hole was ripped into the side, air rushing out from the cabin. We weren't going to be able to fight them off.

"Everybody strap in!" I screamed. I knew the best way to keep my friends safe was to get what our pursuers wanted away from them. I raced to the back of the cargo hold and threw a lever, and the ramp started to open. I ran to Jessie's cell and cut through the ties holding the cell in place.

"Vi, wait!" Chase yelled.

I gave him a quick sad smile before I rammed my shoulder into the cell. I just prayed they'd break off the assault and come after us instead. The lasers sliced through my arm and side, but I ignored the pain and pushed hard enough to send the cell sliding down the open ramp. Before it slipped out, I grabbed one of the bars, flinching as my hand flared with pain, and we fell toward the earth together. I saw Chase panicking near the edge of the ramp, but I shook my head and ripped my gaze away to turn my focus to the ground that was racing up at us.

The wind tore at my hair, skin, and clothes as we fell. I braced myself for the impact; this wasn't going to be pretty. I pushed off from the cell moments before the crash, but it wasn't soon enough.

I wasn't sure how long I was knocked out. My body felt like I had just been hit by a truck. I couldn't breathe for the first few moments, and terror gripped me. The flash of the memory of Atty struggling for breath as his chest filled with blood overwhelmed me. I finally managed a gasp, and my entire chest lit with excruciating pain, but I could breathe. My vision slowly started to come back into focus, and I looked around. The cage seemed to have exploded on impact; pieces of metal were strewn all around us. Jessie was coughing on the ground a few feet from me.

Ignoring the pain, I got an arm under me and slowly pushed myself up. My head hung low as I got a knee under me, my chest heaving, trying to recover from the fall.

I spared a glance toward the sky and saw smoke billowing out from the plane my friends were on. It was careening toward the ground miles from us. Gods save them, please. Just save them. At least no one was following them from what I could see. I hoped I had been right, and they were paying attention to us now.

I turned my attention back to Jessie. She had rolled onto her side and her eyes landed on me. We glared at each other from our positions just feet apart, but neither of us could stand yet. We just worked to catch our breath, never taking our eyes off the other.

My body screamed for me to stop as I pushed myself to stand. I ignored it. Needing to favor my right side I pressed my arm against the pain and lurched to Jessie. I grabbed her arm to pull her up after me. She jerked it out of my grasp, but she was hunched in pain the same as me.

"Jessie, please let us help you. Come with me." She took a step away from me as I reached for her.

I heard twigs snapping under boots running toward us. That couldn't be any of my people. The look on Jessie's face was full of victory as she started to straighten and walked backward in the direction of the people coming our way.

This wasn't good. I had to get out of here, and there was no way I'd manage it while trying to get Jessie to come with me. I gave her one more glance before I spun and tried to run the other way. All of me hurt, but as I went, I started to get better control of myself. I went from limping to jogging to running, but I wasn't nearly fast enough. I could hear them gaining on me.

"She went that way; get her," Jessie wheezed to the others behind me.

I pushed myself faster, my legs burning, my chest tight. I stumbled and fell but clambered up and forced myself to keep going. I had to get away. I couldn't be captured. I couldn't go back. I felt like I was going to be sick as terror gripped every part of me. Why hadn't we been prepared for an aerial attack? Why hadn't I thought about being ambushed? We had been worried about her breaking out, not others coming for her. How did they know where we were? Then, I thought about the jammers we had for anything not on our specific frequencies within Nexus and how we had just left that barrier. I cursed to myself; they must have some sort of tracker in her.

I heard men to my left, so I turned and raced in the other direction, but then I heard more ahead of me. They were flanking me. I tried to calm myself, clear my mind. I had to think.

Something crashed down from above ahead of me, and I had to skid to a stop. Cecily stood right in front of me. I spun on my heel, meaning to sprint away, but I was surrounded as men started to come through the trees with weapons raised.

All right, fine. I'd fight my way out.

Cecily appeared next to me. Her fist connected with my jaw, sending me off my feet. Pain flared throughout my body. She leaned down over me and placed a mask over my face, and I couldn't help but breathe in some sort of gas. My last thought was that I hoped my friends were safe.

23

ESMERELDA

My steps echoed through the hallway as I rushed through the facility. I wouldn't believe it until I saw it with my own eyes. When I turned the corner, Jessie and Cecily were standing there already. I had told them not to leave until I arrived. Jessie had some bruises, but I knew they'd be gone in a day or two. Cecily just stood there, barely giving her sister a glance, and her eyes snapped my way as soon as she saw me.

Cecily saluted, and Jessie followed a beat later. Ignoring them, I paused, wanting to be ready to absorb the monumental moment. Then I peered through the window in the cell door.

And there she was. The bane of my existence was prowling back and forth within, but when she saw me, she stopped.

There was fear in her eyes, and the feeling of complete victory almost took my breath away. Finally, after all these years, I had her back, and she would give me all her secrets. I would take what I needed, destroy everything she loves while I do it, and then crush her when I was done.

I watched as the fear in her eyes bled into anger. She used all her strength to attack the door, but it didn't budge. I had created this entire facility to contain people like her. I had accounted for everything.

There were enhanced security measures, materials that would contain them, and a new gas we had perfected to accommodate for their metabolisms. When we had her last time, we hadn't known what type of changes she would undergo. Now that she was here, we could collect all the data we needed. She had been the first, and the success rate was still minimal. There had to be something hidden away in her cells that could give me the answer.

She stood right in front of the window, nothing but a few inches separating us. I stepped closer, and we were almost eye to eye. I noticed she was just a touch shorter than me. Fitting. She would always have to look up at me.

I just smiled as I watched the gears turning in her mind. Her realizing what her life was now. She'd be telling herself she could escape, but there was no way out for her. She'd learn that soon enough. I couldn't wait to watch her resolve fade over the days and weeks ahead.

"Your Majesty, we delivered her as ordered," Cecily said from my side.

"Yes, you did very good Cecily. Your sister, on the other hand..." My eyes narrowed as I watched the older girl. "We'll need to increase your training. It's a disgrace you were able to be captured in the first place. If you aren't up to the task, we have no need for you."

There wasn't even a flicker of emotion from Cecily at the threat to her sister.

Good.

She was shaping up nicely.

I turned as someone came our direction and saw Howard. He made his way to us and looked through the window at the girl inside. Astor's eyes narrowed as he came into view.

"I heard there was good news." He turned to me, ignoring the others.

"Yes, we've finally managed to get our hands on her. Gas her, take her for testing, get the blood samples, and get to work." I couldn't wait; I wanted this started as soon as possible.

"Of course. At once, Your Majesty." He bowed his head before facing the cell again and keying something into the pad by the door.

Gas filled the room. Astor visibly started to panic, holding her breath as long as she could, but it was no use. I didn't move until I saw her drop unconscious to the floor. Howard snapped his fingers, and two guards who had been following him came to his side.

Taking a step back, I watched as they opened the door and each of them grabbed one of her arms. She was limp when they dragged her down the hallway.

The two girls were still here. "Both of you, go to conditioning."

They both turned and headed down the hall toward the rooms waiting for them.

I returned to my quarters to wait for news. I felt like I was floating. I had struggled with this for years, and here she was. She was the key to my cure.

I could feel it in my aching bones.

24

Vi

I hoped the hate I felt radiated from me. I hoped it made the doctor want to pull at his collar, as if it was just a little too tight and he was a little too warm. If that was all I could do while strapped into this chair, at least it would be something.

This wasn't the first room I had awoken in without knowing how I had gotten here. I had been strapped to a table last time, the man I had seen with Esmerelda outside of my cell taking all sorts of blood and making notes. I wished I knew how long I had been out when they gassed me.

I jerked against the restraints, but there was little movement. I was locked in tight. As always.

"Now, now, you know better. Settle down. We'll be ready soon," he admonished me and went back to typing at his computer. He didn't even bother to look my way.

I was going to bite his nose off when he got close enough.

The door hissed open, and the doctor jumped to attention as he saw who it was. *She* was there. Her red lips and her glossy black hair were a shocking contrast to her pale skin and the white walls of the room they had me in. She had always been a striking figure.

"I just wanted to come and say hello. I'm sorry I couldn't get here sooner, but you know, duty calls." She grinned at me, but it was twisted, hateful. "I hope we've been making you feel welcome, now that we have you home. We have missed you very much. Running away like that was such a shame. But you're home now." She clapped and asked the doctor. "What do we have planned for today?"

"Conditioning, Your Majesty."

Her lips turned up slightly at that news. Schooling my features, I tried not to show my fear. I recalled the data we had stolen that went over the protocols they had around this. Within a helmet were speakers, videos, and an injection system. The audio was set to a resonance that caused psychosis. The videos showed either something they wanted you to like or hate, and the injections pumped you with chemicals to produce the reaction they desired.

They could make someone hate the thing they loved most and love something they hated. The results were mixed on if the subject survived or took their own life before the process was completed, but the person was always changed. And these doctors could take as much time as they wanted with me. They had been doing this to Jessie and Cecily for who knew how long. No wonder they hadn't even flinched when seeing us. My blood boiled, and I tried in vain against the restraints again.

"Well, then, don't let me stand in your way." She turned her smile back to me, and I could have sworn her eyes swirled with an inky black. Like evil was trying to crawl its way out of her soul.

The doctor grabbed the helmet I hadn't seen behind him on the table. Nodding to the queen, he came to me, arms outstretched with it. I couldn't help but flinch as he reached out with it toward me. I hated that she saw me do it.

The door slid open again, and the doctor turned to see who it was. Another man in a lab coat came in and bowed to Esmerelda.

"What?" she asked, and he leaned over to whisper to her.

The look she gave me had goosebumps rippling across my entire body.

"Isn't that interesting?" she mused. "How much can it withstand?"

What did she mean by *it*? What was going on now?

"We don't know, Your Majesty. This is a first. We don't know anything just yet. If it's anything like her, one would probably assume quite a lot."

"No matter. If we lose it, we can just try again. Now that we know it's possible, it would be easy enough to recreate. You're dismissed."

The man bowed and exited the room quickly.

She came to me and lightly caressed my cheek. "Oh, my dear. I have just the best news." She leaned down so she was at my eye level. "I'm going to be a grandmother."

I felt like I was staring into the maw of a predator, her teeth glinting with her malicious sneer. I froze. My mind couldn't compute what she had just told me. It was like the gears were grinding and grating against each other. I was trapped in that moment. Unable, or unwilling, to believe it.

Fear started to spread through me. She must have seen me putting the pieces together, and it seemed to give her such joy.

"Yes, my dear," she cooed. "It's so good to have the both of you home." She placed a hand on my stomach. "Well, I'm not one to throw off a schedule. I won't keep you any longer, Doctor." And with that, she left.

As the doctor began to move, I wrenched against my restraints, but they didn't budge. I bit at him as he came near me with the helmet, but he still managed to lock the thing on me.

"No, no..." I screamed in terror at the top of my lungs as the helmet flickered on.

Apparently, I was so befuddled that they didn't bother with the gas. They hauled me up because I couldn't hold my own weight. My vision swam before me as I stared at their boots while they dragged me from the room. There was something... something I needed to focus on, but it was all so hazy.

My ears started ringing, and I closed my eyes against the harsh light in the hallway. Every move of my body made me want to throw up.

Why did I feel this way? What had just happened to me? All I knew was that the only feeling I had besides pain was terror. Something was wrong. Something was *very* wrong.

A few other pairs of feet came toward us from down the hallway. I used all my energy to lift my head to see who they might belong to. It was two girls surrounded by more guards like the ones dragging me.

At least they can walk on their own.

Something tugged at my mind. They looked familiar, but I was too exhausted to place them. I let my head drop again, unable to hold it up any longer.

They continued hauling me along until we came upon a metal door that hissed open and they threw me inside.

The cement floor was cold against my heated skin. I managed to roll onto my back to touch more of my skin to the sweet bliss of the cement.

This seemed familiar. Why did it feel like home?

I didn't bother to think about it as my eyes slipped closed and I fell into sweet empty darkness.

I awoke with a start as a chill ran over me. Sitting up made my head spin, and I clutched at it to try to make the nausea fade. Once it did, I found myself in a cell with nothing more than a bed, a toilet, and a bucket.

It came back to me in a rush. *She* had me again. I was *here* again. As my memories returned to me, tears threatened to fall. I put a hand on my stomach.

"What have I done?" I whispered. A feeling of such fierce protectiveness washed over me. "I'm going to get us out of here. I won't let her have you. I *will* protect you."

I had never thought about being a mother. It had never seemed like something that would even be possible with the way my life had turned out. Yet, as soon as I'd heard it, I knew I had to do everything in my power to protect this life. I tried to force my mind away from the fact that I had no idea how to be a mother and that I would probably be a terrible one. I could worry about that if I managed to live through this. All the questions I had about myself, I had none of them about Chase. I just had to get the two of us home so he could take amazing care of this baby.

I shook my head free of the swirling thoughts. *Time to get to business.*

How was I going to get out of here? My mind flashed to the girls who had walked past us.

Gods, it was Jessie and Cecily. It made my blood run cold. What if they got the conditioning to work on me?

Shaking my head, I banished that idea. I had to stay positive or I wouldn't last long. I had lived through this before. She wouldn't break me now. Not now that I knew what I had to live for. There were people who loved me, and they would be looking for me.

I would get out of here. I was forged from the brightest light and the strongest steel; I could do this.

I just had to bide my time and find the perfect opportunity. I only hoped it wouldn't take too long for it to come around.

25

Vi

Two guards neared the small window of my cell door. I had spent the night before trying to break the door down. My shoulder had just started to recover. I wasn't getting out with brute force. So, it was on to plan B. I tensed, preparing to attack as soon as they came inside.

One of them smirked at me like he could tell what I was planning.

I heard the low hiss and saw gas pouring into the room. Quickly, I held my breath and went to the window. His smile was still plastered on his face as he watched. I pulled my arm back and tried to smash through the window, but I knew it wouldn't do any good. I tried to hold off as long as I could, but soon my lungs were burning, and I had to take a breath. Stupid traitorous body.

As soon as I did, the room started to spin and I dropped to one knee. Swaying before I fell to the ground, unable to keep myself conscious, I swore as my eyes fluttered closed.

I awoke in what seemed to be a field. My head was foggy at first but slowly cleared. Where in the gods' names had they put me now? I couldn't help but be frustrated that plan B hadn't worked. Now, I knew they wouldn't be taking any chances while they moved me for testing.

So, what was this going to be? I looked around but saw nothing on the horizon. Where was I?

"Welcome back to the living," came a voice from somewhere above. "Test alpha will be commencing in five, four, three."

I cursed under my breath. What was this?

"Two, one." A buzz sounded from wherever that voice was coming from.

In the ground, circles slowly opened, and rising from them were humanoid-looking robots on some type of platform. All of them had guns.

They raised them as one and sighted on me, and my instincts took over. I jumped to my feet. The first volley came at me, and I launched myself into the air to arc over them. I aimed for the closest robot and came down on its shoulders. I grasped around its neck, ripped its wiring apart, and threw the head to the ground as the body dropped.

I dashed across the field in a zigzag formation to try to outpace their bullets while heading for my next target. Pain flared through me as a bullet hit my calf, but I didn't slow. I slid beneath the reach of the next robot. When I stood once more, I was under its arms. I grabbed one and snapped the metal of its wrist then ripped the gun from its grip.

In one swift movement, I lifted the gun and fired a quick spray into its head. The light of its eyes flickered before going out. More fire came at me, and I grabbed the robot by the neck and held it between myself and the others as a shield. I pressed forward, letting the metal catch most of the attack aimed at us. Most, not all, but that was a problem for later.

There was a small pause as they had to reload, and I dropped my impromptu shield, spraying bullets at the others. One went down as I severed its knee joint. Another had fluid spraying from a wound, and its movements turned into jerking steps before it collapsed. I walked to the next and sent a few quick rounds into its head, and it stopped moving.

I didn't see anything else moving. "Is that the best you've got?"

The voice came again, "Beta test commencing."

The sky started to flicker as a whine sounded above me. I saw a red light just before a laser came to life heading straight for me. I jumped out of the way. As the sky flickered again, I realized I must have been in some type of simulation room. Which meant there had to be a way out of here.

More lasers appeared, and I had to jump, duck, and weave to keep out of their path. One of them got too close and cut across my arm. I winced at the pain but had to keep moving as they kept sweeping around the room in random patterns.

I started running straight ahead. I was going to go until I hit a wall, find where the edge of this room was. I launched myself upwards and over an incoming laser, instantly having to push off my hands into a backflip and twisting to miss the next. I leaped and spun as I made my way forward. I couldn't be sure if that was a flicker I saw ahead of me, so I put my hand out to keep myself from running into it face first. My hand brushed against metal, and I tried to slow as fast as I could but still crashed straight into it.

Finally. With a sigh, I put my back to the wall and searched around me. *Well, I found one side. What now?*

As I was looking from one side to the other, the wall jolted me with a rush of electricity, and I couldn't hold back my scream. Partly in pain, partly in surprise.

An aggravated huff escaped me. *Time to move.*

I pushed off a few inches from the wall. I turned to my right, holding my hand out, and every few feet let the shock guide me around the edge of the room. *There must be a door around here somewhere.*

The voice returned. "Gamma test commencing."

The lasers started to disappear, and as they did the robots were returning. They came up through the floor again, but there were so many more this time. Groaning, I stopped to try to formulate a plan. This time, they didn't have any guns, so it would be a fistfight. Me versus metal. I rolled my eyes. *Just perfect.*

I gave my hands balled into fists with a preemptive apology. No pain, no gain, and I was hoping to gain a way out of here. I shook my arms out, pumping my fists and bouncing on the balls of my feet.

Here we go.

As the first one reached me, I kicked out hard, impacting its chest and sending it toppling back into the others behind it. More began to swarm in from the edges. I crushed the first one's neck in my grip, and it sparked and sizzled as I did. I threw it into the one coming in from my left.

My head snapped to the side as one hit me right across my jaw. Glowering, I slammed my fist into its chest, and the metal casing crumped beneath my blow. An arm appeared over its shoulder and grabbed my neck, jerking me forward. My forehead cracked into the robot I had just disabled.

I could not go down; they would be all over me.

I grabbed the arm still holding on to me. Apparently, putting too much oomph into my attempt to break free because I crushed it. I started to wheel backward as the arm severed, and my calves hit one of the downed robots behind me. I was free falling toward the ground, but luckily, I was caught by a very helpful robot, who wrapped my throat in its hands.

With a quick movement, I threw my elbow back and it crunched into its head. The hands released me.

There were so many. I shook my head and got my feet under me again. I had seen worse odds before. There was a small pile around me of destroyed robots, and the others were starting to have to step or climb over them to get to me. But it wouldn't be long before I was completely overwhelmed.

One came up on my right, and I went for the neck, trying to get it down as quickly as I could, but as soon as I did, another latched on to my back. One of its arms got a hold around my neck, and its legs locked around my waist. With a roar, I slammed into the wall, crushing the robot between us. Above me, the simulation flickered.

Well, wasn't that mighty interesting? I grabbed the next nearest robot and spun, crushing it into the electrified wall, and it flickered again. This time, it seemed to cause a ripple effect across the room. I happened to catch a glimpse of a viewing window about ten feet off the ground with a few people standing behind it. Esmerelda was there, flanked by the girls and some of her lab lackeys.

My heart clenched at the sight of Jessie and Cecily. Now that my head was clear, I knew I would have to find a way to get them out. I couldn't leave them to my stepmother and the things I knew they were going through.

I used one robot's knee as a foothold and then another's shoulder as a launching pad to leap over the pile of them. I landed on the other side and raced straight for where I had seen that window, now hidden within the simulation again.

I looked over my shoulder, and the robots were hot on my heels.

Perfect. And this time I meant it.

I wasn't being careful this time and ended up running smack into the wall taking the shock as I did so. I turned and charged into the line of robots who had yet to slow and were headed straight for me.

I roared as I crashed through them. Putting myself right into the middle of the first group. They grabbed for me, but anything that came near me, I ripped apart. I tore at their arms. As punches rained down on me and I was driven to my knees, I grabbed their legs. My hair was tugged back, and I ripped off a head that was hovering above me. I tossed the pieces behind me, kicking lifeless bodies in that direction as their husks got in my way.

The bottom of the growing pile of destroyed robots had slid to the wall. The metal was connecting with the electrified boundary. The simulation flickered until it was more of a flash, and then it started to fail altogether.

In the times it disappeared long enough that I could see through the observation window Esmerelda's anger was as clear as day. Jessie and Cecily's faces were both blank, like they weren't even paying attention.

I stepped up the hill until I was almost level with the window, fully planning to smash my way in as soon as I was able.

I couldn't hear her, but I saw Esmerelda shout something that looked like *enough.*

As I turned to tear another robot apart, its hand swiveled up from its wrist and a small pipe extended. It sprayed me right in the face with a gas, and I screamed in rage before the room started to sway and spin.

I toppled down, the pile of wrecked metal tearing into my skin as I fell. More robots came to stand over me, each using their own gas on me.

I blinked up at Esmerelda. The hate on her face was the last thing I saw before I fell into darkness.

26

ESMERELDA

"What was that?" I snarled at the technician before me.

"That was... quite ingenious actually," he murmured, rubbing his chin and looking over his readouts before realizing that was not what I meant. His eyes were wide with fear as he turned to me. "Um, well... I mean."

"Stop blubbering," I commanded, and he snapped his mouth shut. "Get her back to her cell and figure out something that can actually hurt her next time." I turned on my heel, and as I snapped my fingers, the sisters turned to follow me. I was surrounded by incompetence. Someone was going to have an idea to get me what I needed, or I would just get rid of the entire lot and start fresh.

It would help if we could control Genevieve while we worked to get what we needed from both her and the baby. Either way though, I can never allow the child to live, obviously. I can't have another Astor running around. As much as the idea of raising my own possibly powered child with my teachings enticed me, I had learned my lesson. Astor's wouldn't be allowed to live. At least with her, we could see how resilient the fetus would be. The two following me could be the true mothers of the next generation.

It was outstanding that the testing had worked on them both as I had hoped. Now, I had two enforcers that could double as brood mares once we knew what we needed. If these children were everything I hoped, nothing would be able to stop me. Just thinking of the power, a generation of superhumans would have while being raised to believe in my mission gave me goosebumps.

The doctors also said it seemed promising that the stem cells from the child could be exactly what they needed to get the serum for me to work. That they could finally stop this disease and give me the control I had always craved. I would no longer be tethered to the whims of my body.

I was so close to everything I had dreamed of.

It was all going to be mine.

I led us through hallways until we came upon the conditioning rooms.

"It's time for your program," I told them.

"Yes, Your Majesty," they said in unison.

I opened one of the rooms and pointed inside. The younger one, Cecily, entered where a doctor waited with the helmet. As the door slid closed, I took the older sister, Jessie, to the next door, and she walked in automatically.

I couldn't keep the grin off my face as I left them. I had struggled for so long to get to this point, and things were finally going my way. It wouldn't be long now, and I couldn't wait to crush the Astors under my heel once and for all.

It was about time I sent Nolan a message to show him exactly what kind of power I was about to have over him. Genevieve had always been his weakness. That was why I took her in the first place. Only later did I realize I should have just killed her instead of using her as a test subject. Even now, part of me couldn't help but wonder if I should just get rid of her, but the knowledge we could get from her was too valuable. This time, I was ready. I wouldn't let her out of my grasp until I was done with her. I had taken every precaution when building this complex. Everything

On top of the gas and the precautions on the interior of the building, the exterior was fenced, patrolled, and had multiple other deterrents. Sensors, lasers, guns, electrified barbed wire, and some of Marco's robots we had repurposed. No one knew the location. I hadn't had it put in any databases. They would never be able to find her, and she would never manage to get out.

I circled back through the building and made my way to her cell. Through the window, I saw her unconscious on the floor. I knew her wounds were already healed, but she was still covered in blood from them. A satisfied shiver ran through me. She would pay for everything she had put me through.

I was just getting started.

27

Vi

I awoke in my cell, but this time it was easier to get my bearings. That was something, at least. If that gas was affecting me less each time they used it, maybe one of these times, I would wake up before they expected. But I wasn't going to just sit around and wait for that to happen.

Pushing myself up on my elbows, I focused on the wall where it met the ceiling, where the gas had come from. As I focused, I saw a change in texture between one section and another. Stepping onto the bed, I ran my hands along the wall. There were the smallest of pinpricks where the gas must come through. I felt around it to try to see if there were any screws, but the most I felt was a seam.

Good enough.

What could I use? The cell didn't leave me many options. My attention snagged on a bucket. I got down and slammed my foot onto it. It crushed as easily as a cardboard box. I grabbed it from where it had crumpled and pulled it apart. I ran my finger over the jagged edges of the rough triangle and blood bloomed beneath it. That should work.

I gazed at my improvised blade. I lifted and turned it against the light. I reminded of the scalpels they had used before... The blood coating me from cuts they made.

I shook my head. I didn't have time to waste. Gingerly, I folded one of the edges over so at least one side wasn't razor sharp. I dug it into the seam, but even with that flatter edge in my palm, blood dripped down my arm as I worked. It was warm where the blood splashed my cheek. I ignored it, but it dripped again and again, until it was more of a steady flow.

I wasn't getting any purchase against the metal, no matter how hard I dug. I twisted and turned it, but it wasn't doing anything. Whomever made it did quality work. I shouldn't have been surprised, but I was annoyed.

I dropped my arm and leaned my head back against the wall with a huff. I could still feel the blood dripping down my fingertips, staining the bed. I reveled in the pain, just a bit, and thumped my head against the wall once more.

I couldn't get discouraged. I wasn't a kid this time. I was stronger than before. This was now, not then. I survived this once; I was going to do it again.

Squeezing my eyes shut, my fist tightened around the knife, creating a fresh flow of blood. I meant to take a deep breath, but it was more like a gasp, as tears tried to fall. I *would* figure out a way to escape. I just hadn't found the right method yet, but I would. Staying here was not an option I was willing to entertain, and I would fight Esmerelda every second I could.

I was not terrified anymore.

As many times as I said it to myself, part of me knew it was a lie.

I was absolutely terrified.

I was terrified I'd die here. That I would never see the people I loved again. That Esmerelda would hurt my baby. That I wouldn't be able to save Jessie or Cecily. That I would never see Chase again. That I was a failure in every way that matters.

I wanted to curl up into a ball and cry, but I didn't have the time.

The makeshift knife clattered to the ground as I tried to pull myself out of my swirling emotions. I redirected my fear and anger to finding a way to escape. Banging the heel of my hand against the section of wall, I wanted to see if I could pop anything loose, but nothing budged. The pounding of my hand matched the racing beat of my heart.

I need to get out.

I have to get out.

Let me out.

In the privacy of my own mind, I screamed with the panic.

Something clattered outside my cell, then I got a face full of gas.

You have got to be kidding me.

I fell backward as I lost all control and faded out before I hit the ground.

Cold metal licked my skin, and I was covered in gooseflesh against the chilled air. Groaning as I went to move, I realized I was locked in restraints again. My arms were held out straight to my sides but were cuffed at my wrists. There was one at my neck, multiple between my chest and my knees, and I was locked down at my ankles as well. They apparently weren't taking any chances.

"What are you doing to me?" I asked, but it was barely more than a whisper.

The face of one of the doctors appeared above me.

"Oh, good you're awake. We need you conscious for this." Then she disappeared again.

I tried to move my head enough to catch a glimpse of her. She was typing away at a computer with a tray of metal tools at her side. Scalpel, needles, and bottles of liquid. I tried to swallow the fear, but I could hear my pulse racing in my ears. I closed my eyes and tried, and failed, to take deep breaths.

The conditioning helmet left you completely out of it, but this pain and the memory of tests like this were what haunted me at night. The nights when Chase would have to hold me close to keep me from falling apart.

I bit my lip to keep myself from whimpering in my terror. This is why no doctor except Joseph was allowed anywhere near me.

The door opened and the smell of her perfume as it mixed with the memories of a room like this, almost made me sick. Even without seeing her I instinctively knew it was her, and my body went into flight mode, with nowhere to go.

Be brave. Show her you are not afraid.

I felt her drag one of her manicured nails up my calf, to my thigh, skipping over where the restraints were in place. Instead making a raking noise against the metal when she crossed them. My muscles instinctually clenched as she drug it over my abs, to my ribs.

"Look at me," She hissed as her nails dug into my neck as she cut off my air. I could feel the skin breaking as she had me in her grasp. Her grip was unnaturally strong, a reminder of her cybernetic arms under the false skin. She could snap my neck easily, she twitched like she might, but never did.

I opened my eyes and all I could see was her. The joy in her eyes gave me the impression that I was not selling the idea that I wasn't scared.

I felt like I was twelve again. Returned to the time when she first had me. Terrified of this woman and now I knew what she would put me through. I remembered the grief of thinking I would be at her mercy for the rest of my life because there was no one left to save me. That I was too young and too weak to save myself.

Tears slipped from my eyes and dripped onto the table beneath me.

My friends got me once, I hoped they could help me again, but I wasn't going to wait around. There had to be a way. I just needed to be ready.

"That's a good girl," She cooed and wiped a tear from my face only to wipe it away on my bottom lip. To make me taste the salt of my failure. She turned to the doctor. "You'll be able to get what you need from the fetus?" She asked as the doctor.

"Possibly, this is earlier than recommended, but it seems promising."

"What are you doing?" I begged as I tried to jerk out of my restraints.

"You're going to need to stay still for this if you don't want us to hurt the baby," the doctor said calmly.

The doctor started to wipe something cold across my stomach. I bit into my lip so hard it started to bleed, but I also wouldn't move. I couldn't risk it. More tears escaped as I felt a pinch of something biting into my abdomen. The feeling was so violating. Hate flared and I memorized this doctor's face. She would regret doing this to me.

I had to be strong. I just had to keep us both safe long enough to figure out how to escape.

"There, that should do it," The doctor said, and I saw them releasing a tube filled with fluid.

Esmerelda snatched it away, her eyes shining as she looked at it. "Beautiful," She breathed. Her gaze snapped from me to the doctor. "Carry on with the scheduled testing, I have what I need for now."

With a swirl of her gown, she disappeared out the door. The doctor was loading a green liquid from a bottle into another needle. Tapping it twice as a little drop escaped the tip making sure there was no air within.

"Now, we need you awake, I need you to answer some questions as this circulates through your system."

Without any warning, the needle was jabbed into my neck. As she pushed down on the plunger; it felt like my veins were on fire. I forced myself to take deep breaths but soon I could feel my entire body shaking from the pain. I was so hot It felt like I was burning up from the inside.

"What is your pain level?" She asked me.

I hissed at her in response. Which just made her arch an eyebrow at me.

"I do require you to answer me."

My breathing was ragged as I spasmed from the pain. I couldn't even form words if I wanted to. My jaw was locked tight like every other muscle in my body at the moment.

"Fine, I'll take that as moderate." I heard metal clatter, and I couldn't have been anymore terrified even as she picked up a scalpel, even though that was one of the things I feared most.

"Now, let's see how long this takes to heal over." A bright red line bloomed down the inside of my arm as she sliced it. "Please tell me if you feel any discomfort."

"All I feel is discomfort." I meant to snap at her, but it came out slurred and garbled. She waited for a few minutes before poking at my arm.

"Good. How would you rate the pain from the cut on a scale of one to ten."

The cut was nothing compared to the pain the rest of my body was already in.

"I'll make sure to ask you that when I get my hands on you." My body felt heavy but I rolled my head enough to try to get a good look at her.

"I'll mark that down as a one." Her gloved hands poked at my arm and he made thoughtful noises over me. "Quick healer. Even after extensive nerve damage." Her head popped over mine again. "How are you feeling from the serum? Is the effect still in place?"

As she hovered over me I jerked my head up and smiled weakly as I heard the bone in her nose break from my headbutt.

"It seems as if it must be clearing out of your system faster than we expected," She muttered nasally, holding a rag to stop the bleeding. "Interesting." Her own pain was seemingly forgotten as she wrote down some notes.

Next, she took a bottle that contained a red liquid and filled another needle. She pressed it to my neck again and the pain I had felt before was nothing compared to what flowed through me now.

I couldn't hold back the scream that ripped through me. The pain was so intense I couldn't even see, I couldn't think. I was all consumed by it. I couldn't remember a before or even contemplate an after.

"Good, just as we thought. I'll code that one as a six." It was the last thing I heard before I blacked out.

My cheek stung as the doctor slapped me awake again. The pain had receded slightly. More of a burning ache than a sizzling slice.

"I told you we needed you awake," She admonished me.

My mouth was so dry I could barely open it, my entire body was on fire, and my head was spinning. I tried to remember... something about light and steel.

She grabbed a vile filled with yellow liquid and smirked as she stared down at me.

"We assume this one should be around a nine. Please let me know if you agree."

Quickly she pressed it into my neck and the scream was instantaneous as my entire body convulsed from the sensation. It was like I had been hit by lightning. Like it was bouncing around behind my eyes and liquefying my insides. I bucked so violently I popped open one of the restraints by my hips.

"Now let's try this again." She sliced my arm open again before my head even started to clear.

With each deep breath I tried to remember anything that would keep me sane, but a scream ripped from my throat as the pain crackled through me on another wave of lightning.

***

Time means something different when you're locked away like this. It doesn't flow like it does in the outside world. I didn't know how long they kept me in that room filling me with different concoctions and slicing parts of me open.

As I opened my eyes, I slowly realized I wasn't in my cell. They were dragging me along the corridor. I took foggy stock of the situation, but it was obvious I didn't have enough energy and was in too much pain to manage any type of an escape. I let my head drop again and through slitted eyes, I watched as the building moved before me.

Everything looked the same so I couldn't say for sure where I was within the building, but they drug me past an open door where I saw multiple people sitting inside working on gigantic computers.

I filed that away for later. I would find that room and destroy it before I left. I would leave them with nothing. I would do everything in my power to make sure they never benefitted from what they were doing to me.

As we passed a group of people, I took the chance to look up and saw Jessie being led by guards to a room. As the door slid open, I saw the chair inside and realized it was one of the conditioning rooms.

I'd make sure they wouldn't be able to benefit from what they were doing to us.

I made a silent promise that I would get her and her sister out of here. Just as soon as I had an actual idea of how in the world I'd manage it.

28

ESMERELDA

I didn't do anything as undignified as running, but I did make it to Howard's office at a quicker pace than normal. I couldn't wait; the answers could be here, right in my hand. I could feel it. This had to be what we had been searching for. A way to break the mystery around my cure. Stem cells from the child of the seemingly indestructible bane of my existence. Revenge would be sweet.

Howard looked up from his tablet from where he sat behind his desk. I held the tube out ahead of me as I entered. His eyes softened, and I chastised myself for showing my desperation.

"I told you I'd have someone take care of that." He sighed and pushed himself up then took it from me.

"It's fine. I wanted to make sure nothing happened to it on the way." I swirled into a chair in front of his glass desk and watched him. "What's next?"

He turned to me with the same expression that my old tutors used to give me when I exasperated them. I tried my best to tamp down the anger that raged in me at the memory. He understood why I was impatient and why I needed him.

"We need to get it down to the lab and start running some tests. We'll know more in a few days, a week maybe."

I glowered as I leaned back into the chair, not defeated, just delayed. "You need to be faster."

"You can't rush science."

As always, the reply drove me insane. I huffed, and he released a soft laugh.

"Buck up. This is what you always wanted, isn't it?"

I thought of the brat's screams ringing in the hallway as I hurried here. Someone to punish for always ruining my plans, to hurt for everything I had been through. Someone who would provide me with my oldest dream. Yes, even with these delays, I had everything I wanted, or I would soon.

"How is it going with the girls? They seem more obedient than before," I said.

He pushed a button and then turned to lean against the wall. "Very promising. I believe their age is making them even more malleable than Jasper was. The first test went well; they managed to capture Genevieve."

"Yes, they didn't even seem to recognize her, but with them here in the same complex... We need to make sure the conditioning is foolproof. I wouldn't put anything past Astor. She's thrown a wrench in every other plan," I growled.

"The science is sound, but we can have them scheduled for double treatments."

It would have to be enough for now.

There was a chirp as someone came to the door.

"Open," Howard called out.

There was a younger man in a lab coat there.

"Take this down to my lab. It's for Project Bloodstone. I'll be down shortly."

The man took it, nodding before he disappeared.

"Remind me again why you chose that name?" I asked as the door slid shut.

"Bloodstones were once given to warriors. They were coveted to keep wounds from being fatal back in the dark ages. How has it been today? It's been a few days since your last injection."

I glared at him. "It's fine," I muttered, but I could sense the next attack would be soon.

"Truthfully?" he asked in that knowing way of his. By now, he knew I wasn't telling the truth.

"I can feel the headache starting." Then, my hands would shake, my vision would blur, and the burning inside me would make me want to scream.

"And your leg?" He raised an eyebrow at me.

"It's nothing I haven't dealt with before". There was no point trying to skirt around it. He was the closest thing to a father figure I'd had in my life. One who didn't despise me anyway.

My femur burned almost constantly, with every movement flaring the pain so sharp it could steal my breath.

"We need to replace it." He had been saying this for a while.

"We're so close; I can hang on. I want to save it. There is so little of me left." I could deal with the pain. I wasn't sure how I would take losing another piece of myself.

"Two weeks, then we're having this conversation again."

"You don't tell me what to do," I snapped.

"Two weeks." He got up and extended his arm to the door. "If you'll excuse me, I have some work to do."

My hackles rose, but I swallowed my snide response.

"You better figure it out before then." My empty threat hung in the air behind me as I swept out of his office and headed back to my quarters. I needed to check on the imbeciles I'd left in charge of the kingdom. They could handle simple tasks, but if left alone for too long, I didn't know what they would manage to bungle. I would have to make an appearance soon, but it was going to be hard to tear myself away from this place.

My mind turned to the other thing I had been holding off on. It would be time soon. I had things to prepare.

29

Vi

They threw me into my cell, and I was shaking so violently I couldn't push myself up. Spasms still ripped through me. Aftershocks from the most recent tests they had put me through. Tears slipped silently, some dripping off the edge of my nose to the cold ground I had collapsed on.

The despair was setting in. The feeling that I would never find a way out of here and she'd do this to me until I couldn't take anymore.

A thought flickered on the edges of my mind, but I couldn't give it any attention. That I could remove myself from the equation, just give up, and not let Esmerelda have what she wanted. To take myself away from the terror and the pain, but I knew I wouldn't. I knew I couldn't. I had someone to protect besides myself. I had to be strong. Stronger than I ever had been before.

I wrapped my hands around my stomach as I curled into myself.

"Please be as strong as me," I whispered. They hadn't done any tests recently to give any indication if the baby was still there. After everything they put me through, I wouldn't be surprised if I had lost it, but as soon as I knew about the baby, I wanted them so fiercely. I wanted to love and protect them. I wanted to finish this war to make a better world for them to grow up in.

I would find a way to rid the world of Esmerelda. Painfully, if I had any say in it. She would pay for everything she had put me and others through. She would regret the pain she had doled out.

While I gave into despair in some moments, the hate burning through me fueled me in others. I would have my revenge. I would tear this place down around me if that's what it took to destroy it. I'd watch with glee as it burned.

The involuntary shaking had finally stopped, and I rolled onto my back. Reaching my arms up, I let them drop heavily to the ground, landing on my hair splayed around me.

I was exhausted. I hadn't spent much time in here. I was being gassed constantly and waking up in new horrifying places. My body was taken to the very edge of what I could live through and then deposited here. Then, the cycle would start all over again. Every escape attempt from this room had failed. I was too broken to fight my way free when I managed to come to as they dragged me through the hallways back to my cell.

There had to be a way. I just hadn't found it yet. I couldn't give up.

My eyes started to droop as the exhaustion took over, and I hoped for a dreamless slumber. Just as I could feel myself drifting away, the lights in the cell died.

Blinking, I looked around, hoping the power had gone out. Pushing myself up, I caught sight of a smiling guard in front of the window.

One of the loudest things I ever heard blasted into my cell. It was a cacophony of noises that forced me to clap my hands over my ears. My heightened hearing sent stabbing pain into my head.

Then, the lights turned back on, but not for good. They started to flash on and off, flickering without a pattern.

With my hands still clasped over my ears, I watched as the guard walked away, and my stomach dropped. How long were they going to leave me here like this?

I jumped up and ran to the door. I screamed as I slammed my hand against it over and over.

"Stop," I begged. "Let me out." I kept pounding my hand against the door, but he didn't turn to me. "Please, let me out," I begged before leaning my back against the door and sliding down the wall. I wrapped my hands over my ears and curled into as tight of a ball as I could. Closing my eyes against the strobing light, I started to pray.

Gas filled my cell as soon as the sound and lights stopped. I knew I should be worried about where they were taking me next, but I had prayed for the reprieve of being unconscious. Anything had to be better than what I had just been through.

I awoke to pain flaring through me, which made me buck against the restraints locking me in. I was on another metal table, but this one had been tipped almost upright. My heart skipped a beat, hoping I would find out something about the baby. So I could at least know if it was still there.

"About time you woke up," Esmerelda chastised me.

"You're the one drugging me," I slurred.

"Is that any way to act when I have a present for you?"

I flinched at the thought. I didn't want whatever she considered a gift.

"Such an ungrateful brat. You always have been." She turned from me to the person in the lab coat, but as I looked around, I realized I wasn't in the normal operating room.

This room was large, and I could hear there were guards posted at the door behind me. The sound of their hands moving on their weapons was unmistakable. A part of me hungered for a real fight. When I got free, I would destroy them.

There was a large screen on the wall in front of me, and I couldn't figure out why I would be here. I heard the door slide open, and a grin spread across Esmerelda's face.

"Girls, good, you are right on time."

Jessie and Cecily came up and stood at either side of the table I was strapped to.

"Jessie, Cecily, look at me." I tried to say it quickly, but it came out slow, my body unable to do what I asked of it yet.

"Ignore her. She isn't why you are here." The screen before me flared to life. "They are."

As the image came into focus, my first reaction was to flinch away before a sob escaped me. On the screen in front of me were my father and Chase in what I knew was my father's office. The horror on their faces made it clear what they must be seeing, what *I* must look like. I hated that my first reaction wasn't one of relief in seeing their faces. The conditioning was already starting to change me bit by bit.

"Nolan," Esmerelda said with an air of superiority.

"Vi, are you okay?" my father asked quickly, his eyes racing across the view he must be seeing.

"Peachy." My speech still came out distorted. Whatever they pumped me with was stronger than normal. I tried to smile, but the pain I saw in Chase's eyes broke me. I saw realization hit him as he noticed the girls flanking me.

"Release them." My father's voice boomed.

"Disband your silly resistance, turn over everyone who has ever helped you, and I will bring you together again. Those are my terms."

"Don't." I shook my head, but it made my vision swim. My heart hammered at the sight of them.

"We will get them from you. We did before, and we will again." He slammed his fist down on the desk he was standing behind.

"Give in to my demands or you will never see your daughter ever again."

I could feel the triumph in her voice as she waved a hand toward me.

"Or your grandchild. Don't test me, Nolan. I will kill them just like I did your wife."

Confusion, anger, and terror flashed across their faces at the casual delivery of those two insane revelations. My mind swam. My mother? What did she have to do with my mother's death? The shock on my father's face was clear. This had to be the first he'd heard of it too.

"What do you mean?" he asked.

Esmerelda just laughed. "Didn't you think it was strange she got so sick so quickly? I had her poisoned, you bumbling oaf. You had to need a wife for me to get to where I wanted to go." She raised her arms, gesturing to herself in her luxurious gown.

"I'm going to kill you, Esmerelda." My father seethed.

Esmerelda put her hand to her forehead like this was giving her a headache. "Nolan, you have no cards to play here. Do what I say or I will be the one killing someone, or I guess it would be someones now."

The last thing I saw before the video disconnected was the pain on Chase's face, and I felt like I was drowning. I had just managed a true breath while seeing the people I loved, only to be dragged back into the depths now that they were gone. I ached to be with them.

I hated that they found out this way. I hated that this was how I had found out. This should have been a time of celebration and being surrounded by love. Not pain, terror, and death.

My fury boiled inside me, burning off the effects of whatever they had dosed me with. I had something else to add to the long list of things I would make Esmerelda pay for. My mom. Another layer of rage and sadness washed over me for her. For the woman I never got to meet.

I was light and steel, and I would rain them both down on my enemies.

A scream ripped from me as I used every ounce of my strength to try to break the restraints. One by one, they started to pop. The pure terror on Esmerelda's face as I did so only spurred me on. She jabbed an arm at the doctor.

"Get her under control." She flinched away from me, taking a step toward the door.

She'd better run. She was mine if I got out of here.

I roared, got my left arm free, and managed to grab the doctor by the throat as he came for me. I cut off his air, and he dropped the needle he had been holding. He scratched at my hand. I tightened my grip, feeling his bones break before he fell limp.

I kept thrashing as Esmeralda continued screeching for someone to do something as she stood angled away from me in case she needed to flee.

A guard reached me and cracked my skull with the butt of his rifle.

As I slipped away, I held on tight to the fact that I could have sworn Jessie flinched as she watched the exchange. She had looked up to Chase and me in Neria as we helped the rebellion there. That had to have been a flicker of recognition, a hesitation to do what Esmerelda wanted.

I hadn't seen Cecily, but I hoped it had been there with her too.

I could save them.

30

ESMERELDA

Taking some deep breaths, I ran my hands over my hair, working to regain my composure. I watched warily as they dragged Genevieve down the hallway. Even though she was unconscious, they had put her in chains to do so. I wasn't taking any chances. She shouldn't have been able to get out of those restraints.

Cecily came up to me, her gaze flat. "Are you all right, Your Majesty?"

"Yes, I'm perfectly fine." Over her shoulder, her sister stood behind her with her eyes locked on the ground. She hadn't made a single move to restrain Genevieve. "Both of you, off to conditioning. You'll need another treatment today."

A guard followed them as they turned to do so. Jessie was keeping close to the Cecily as they left.

That would not do. But I could lock them away if they fell out of line without a second thought. No use in letting a dangerous dog roam free when it might bite. I could always make new warriors eventually. The recent round of testing seemed promising for more to live than the percentages we've seen in the past.

I'd give it a few days before I made my decision, but I would keep

166

the younger one with me for now. She seemed to be well under control.

I let my mind wander as I headed for my quarters, reliving the sight of Nolan seeing his broken daughter, finding out about a grandchild he'd never meet. The pain in his eyes sent power thrumming through me. I would destroy his entire world and enjoy every second of it.

That boy with him seemed devastated. I remembered him vaguely from when I had first arrived in Kabria. One of the children endlessly causing chaos in the palace with Genevieve. There had been three of them. I wondered where the other one got to. Maybe he was dead. No matter, really.

Nolan was my target. If he had just gone away quietly, I wouldn't be dealing with any of this. Then he deprived me of my experiment and weaponized her against me. They had decided to stand against me, and they would pay the price for it. The Astor line would die with them.

As I stepped into my room, a flare of pain shot through my leg, causing me to topple to the ground. The door had slid shut behind me seconds before, so no one saw, thank the gods. My head started to throb. Trying to think through the agony, I pulled myself to the side table and opened a drawer, digging out a pre-filled syringe. I stabbed it into my neck and took a few deep breaths as the icy feeling spread its way from the injection.

My arms were weak, but I managed to pull myself up onto the couch and lean back against it. I didn't have it in me to call for anyone, especially Howard. I couldn't have that talk today. We were so close to the cure I could feel it. I wouldn't give up another body part to this gods-cursed disease.

I wouldn't let anyone see me like this. Not after almost running from that girl. I slammed my fist into my leg, the pain washing over me once more. This time in punishment. How could I have let myself flinch like that? I looked like a fool when she broke through the restraints.

I cannot show fear. I cannot show weakness. I was better than this.

I opened a video of the call we had just had, and I froze the frame on Nolan's face, soaking in the pain I had caused. My momentary lapse today was nothing, just a blip that I wouldn't let anyone remember.

Nothing would be able to stop me soon. I leaned my head back against the couch, coded the door to lock itself, and relaxed as the medication spreading through my body.

31

Vi

I hung heavily; my arms were clasped above me. I was in shackles hooked high enough that my toes barely scraped the floor as I swung there. My shoulders felt like they were going to slip out of their sockets.

A moan of pain escaped me before I tried to figure out where I was. I shivered, and my breath clouded as it slipped through my lips. Looking down, there were circles stuck to me with wires trailing from them across my bare skin. I was in nothing but a bra and a pair of skintight shorts. The room around me was frosted over, and there was an observation window in front of me.

"Welcome back," a voice came through the speakers.

"What is this?" I mumbled; my tongue was still numb.

"We're tracking your vitals when exposed to extremes for long periods of time. Buckle up; it's going to be a long day." With that, the room returned to an eerie silence.

I could see my toes starting to turn slightly blue, and glancing up, I saw my fingers weren't faring much better.

I tried to remember what I had learned about how long someone would last if caught out in freezing temperatures. I wished I had paid more attention, but I knew people didn't last long. I only guessed that meant I would be stuck here being very cold for a very long time. Stupid healing. I wished it meant I didn't feel pain, but I felt everything. All I could do was try to ignore it.

But no matter how many times I tried to clear my mind, I could feel the cold seeping into my bones. At least it wasn't sleep deprivation. Although, many of these tests were starting to stack up against each other, fighting for the most hated tactic she had used thus far.

Trying again to distract myself, I counted the tiles in the room. Then, I counted the robots I had destroyed. The number of times I had been in the conditioning helmet and felt searing pain as I looked upon the faces of those I loved. The number of times I felt desire as images of blood and death were shown to me. How fear and mistrust was starting to seep into me when they showed me pictures of my friends. Yet, I never once felt anything but hate whenever I saw Esmerelda, so that was something.

I counted the number of times I had told Chase I loved him. The hugs I had given my friends. The number of awkward conversations with my father. Grief washed through me, thinking I might never be able to forgive him. To completely fix things with him. That I was losing the time I thought I would have.

The cold had my jaw clenched so tight that I thought I might be cracking my molars. My attention kept snapping away from my distractions to the pain. The chain above me rattled from my shaking. I was losing feeling to multiple parts of my body.

"Please," I begged quietly through chattering teeth. "Please, stop."

Each time I awoke in a test, the amount of time before I begged for it to end diminished. My strength to hold on was fading. The eternity it felt like I had spent here was wearing me down. The despair kept whispering to me. *How easy would it be to just find a way to end it all?*

I could have sworn I heard a thump from somewhere, but my mind couldn't focus on it. It was probably only my imagination again.

The door slid open, and a gunshot rang out. I flinched away. A figure rushed in, my shackles clicked open, and I dropped like dead weight to the ground. The person grabbed my shoulders and shook me until I managed to focus on them.

"Hurry up. They'll know what I've done if you don't cause a bunch of destruction right now," Jessie told me.

My thoughts started to thaw as I stared at her. What was she doing here? The security camera was sparking and I realized that shot had taken it out..

"Come on. Get up. It needs to look like you managed to break your way out of here." She grabbed my arm and pulled me to my feet then shoved a gun in my hands, but my numb hands dropped it. I scrambled to pick it up, trying to get feeling back into my fingers.

"Come with me."

She just shook her head. "I'll never leave her, and she'll never come. Not yet. Give me time to get her back."

Cecily.

"Sorry about this," she said quickly before she hit me with a right hook. "The pain is going to get the drugs out of your system faster."

She was right; just like when I had seen my family on that screen, my pulse quickened, and my head cleared. Within moments, my limbs started to feel like my own again.

"I'll keep trying to get you both away from her," I promised.

"For now, start with burning this place to the ground."

I saw the blaze of fury in her eyes before she slapped one more thing into my hand and turned to speed from the room.

She had handed me a gas mask like the ones Marco created. Smiling, I held it up so it molded to my face. I whispered a prayer for my friend before pushing myself to my feet and tightening my grip on the gun. No one was going to gas me today.

It was time for a reckoning.

I stumbled out of the room and found the door to the observation room propped open by someone's leg. Inside, bodies were scattered on the ground with puddles of blood pooling around them.

Red clouded my vision. With a smirk, I stalked down the hallway searching for prey. My body begged to spill their blood. It didn't matter which way I went yet. I wasn't leaving until I had destroyed this entire complex.

There were limited guards, as almost the entire place was filled with doctors and scientists. Everyone I came across froze like deer in the headlights, recognizing their fates after what they had done to me and who knew how many others.

A pair scrambled backward as I moved toward them. I didn't rush, just raised my gun and fired. They dropped with a thud that rang with the finality of it. There was no nagging voice of a conscious, not right now. All I heard was the call to take my revenge. To show no mercy.

The more people I ran across, the less control I had. Any hesitation I held before was gone. They made me a monster, so they would see what a monster could do. My thoughts degraded into nothing more than the need to hunt.

As I turned a corner, I came upon a line of guards. They started to yell into their radios as I jumped the distance between us. I slipped between them, and before they could move out of the way, they were collapsed at my feet.

I hissed as a bullet hit the back of my arm. Spinning, I returned fire as more sunk into my skin.

I focused on the last of them, who had terror in his eyes. I recognized him as the face that haunted me from the window of my cell. He put his hands up and was about to say something, but I didn't give him time.

His scream echoed down the hall.

Popping out my clip, I saw I was almost out, so I dropped it and grabbed one from the bodies lying at my feet. I started down the hallway once more, leaving a trail of bloody footprints behind me.

I wasn't a princess or a prisoner—today, I was the god of death. The sheer power I felt being free in these hallways to exact my revenge made my blood sing.

The alarms finally started to sound as red lights flared to life, casting the entire place in a deadly glow.

I twisted and turned through the building, taking down anyone who was unlucky enough to cross my path.

Halfway down another hallway that was identical to the others, something nagged at me. I went to the closest door, pushing it open, and grinned at what lay within.

The computer room. The one I had seen the first time the gas had worn off too early. I ripped an ax from the emergency box and slapped it into my hand. Some people had scurried out of the room as I had grabbed it, but I didn't chase them.

Releasing my tension and rage and hate on those computers and servers, I hacked them to pieces. A scream ripped from me as I slammed the ax into them. I couldn't keep the images of everything I had been through here from crashing around me. Parts of the wiring sparked and started fires within the metal shells.

The screens flickered and shut down one at a time as whatever information they had here was destroyed. I hoped.

One of the last things to shut down were the controls to all the doors in the building. The lights on a console all flashed green before winking out for good. I had no idea how many other prisoners they had here, if any, but I hoped they would cause even more chaos.

I turned to find two guards in the doorway. They both had their guns raised, and I only had a second to react as they pulled the triggers. I leapt up and out of the way of their fire, landing just to the right of them.

I snapped my arm out and knocked the closest one into the other. The gun of the man behind him went off and sprayed across his partner as they fell. Soon enough, the other fell silent.

Should I feel something? Horror at what I was doing, or maybe guilt? I didn't. It felt good, and I would have to deal with that realization later. For now, I just reveled in it.

I turned a corner and caught sight of the doctor who had shot me up with the serums that made my veins burn and had taken something from my baby. I saw the fear in her eyes as she ran into the closest room.

I took my time; she had nowhere to run. I was flooded with memories of how many ways I had thought about killing her after the pain had been racing through me for hours on end. The door didn't open as I came up to it. It was either locked or jammed, but that didn't matter.

My kick crumpled it from the middle, and I managed to rip it away.

"Well, hello there." I grinned.

She was on the floor and crawled away from me, backing into the farthest wall. "Please, please, don't hurt me. I was just doing my job," she wailed.

"I'm tired of that excuse," I told her. They had said it in Neria too. My mind echoed with the number of times I had heard it today. I noticed two canisters of chemicals in the corner and cocked my head.

Interesting. Through the observation window I saw one of the tables I had been strapped to. They had been following orders and saw the pain they caused when they did so. With no remorse for me or any of the people they subjected to the things that happened here. Rage rushed through me again. On a desk were a pair of the cuffs they used on me. I snatched them up and turned back to the doctor.

She screamed as I grabbed her and locked one of the shackles to her wrist. The other I linked to a metal bar that was keeping the canister in place against the wall. The doctor's eyes widened, looking from me to the cuffs. Then I saw the realization in her eyes. I wasn't going to just lock her up and leave her here. There were flammable warnings plastered across the canister.

"I need you conscious for this," I said. As I walked through the threshold I shot the canister. Her screams didn't last long.

I continued my search. Within a few minutes, the hallway rocked with an explosion, almost knocking my feet out from under me. Many testing rooms were grouped together, so it was likely more would explode soon enough. I could already smell the smoke.

The building was in chaos. I listened for the mass of bodies, as everyone was fleeing by now. A guard came crashing into the hallway I was in, and I raised my gun to shoot, but nothing happened. It was empty. He gave me a wolfish grin, and I just shrugged and flung it at him with all my strength. His head whipped to the side, and he dropped to the ground. I bent down to take his gun from him, and as I did, I caught sight again of the bloody footprints I had been leaving in my wake.

I was mesmerized by it for a moment, knowing it wasn't just mine and it wasn't just theirs. A mix of the pain I had felt here and the pain I was dolling out. No one who faced me on my trek through the compound would live to tell the tale.

When I straightened, I saw the door to the outside and made my way for it. As I pushed my way through, the stars were shining high above me. I gasped, like I was finally able to breathe, finally able to see the sky once more. Twice I had been locked away from it. Never again.

"Stop," someone shouted.

A group of guards all aimed their barrels at me.

With my gun hand, I swiped my arm across my forehead, stopping the blood that threatened to drip into my eyes. Glancing down, I saw more was smeared across the rest of me. I smiled at the guards, and they flinched before they started firing.

I jumped and twirled out of the way of their attacks, leaping onto a stack of crates and firing down on them. They toppled like dominoes.

I heard more screams and I caught a glimpse of Esmerelda being spirited away into an armored van. Cecily followed the queen in. Jessie was last. She saw me, and we shared a look before she turned away. Giving herself willingly to this torture because of the love for her sister.

Heat licked my skin as explosions ripped apart the building behind me. My hair blew around my face, and I reveled for another moment in the carnage. Eventually, I made my way to one of the vehicles. As much as I wanted to go after the queen now, I wasn't in shape to attempt it. Better to find my way home and regroup. I hoped if there were any other prisoners, they would escape, but I couldn't do anything more than save myself right now. I'd send a team back to investigate once I reached safety. I couldn't take the chance of them figuring out how to capture me again.

I slid in and pressed the ignition, and it hummed to life. So cocky, leaving these vehicles unsecured where anyone could use them. Like nothing could have ever touched them here, in their guarded fortress.

I put the van into gear and drove straight. I'd just keep going until I had some idea of where I was and how I could get home. As I saw the explosions in the rearview mirror, I couldn't keep the smirk off my face.

I guessed I'd find out if I would be able to live with myself after today, but at this moment, I felt nothing but vindication.

32

ESMERELDA

The alarms were blaring, and I pulled up the security camera feeds. It couldn't be her. It just couldn't. I cursed under my breath. The camera in her testing room was offline, and the ones covering the area closest to her were littered with bodies.

How had she gotten out? I had thought of everything. My eyes caught on the bloody footprints down the hallway, and I flipped through the security feeds to track her. She wasn't headed for the exit; she was making her way through the belly of the building.

Sucking the air between my teeth, I turned for the door. We heard running footsteps, and my guards turned toward the noise with their weapons drawn, but it was just the girls.

"We need to get you out of here, Your Majesty," Cecily said stonily as she came to a stop next to me.

The older one was quiet behind her sister, but her face was void of emotion. They took the lead as my guards closed formation behind me. I stumbled as the floor shook from an explosion somewhere deeper in the building.

The complex would have to be abandoned. I turned to one of the guards.

"Order an airstrike. We can't have any of the building left." I knew they wouldn't make it in time to catch Astor in the blasts, but the lab was already lost. I couldn't take the risk of those rebels obtaining any data. The man started speaking into his radio.

At the worst possible moment, the pain in my leg flared to life and I crashed to my knees. I hissed as Cecily hauled me back to my feet. I glared at her and pulled my arm away. I went to take another step and stumbled again.

She slung my arm over her shoulder and started forward again. At least there was no pity from her, just a solider doing her duty, no questions asked. She was living up to being my most devoted convert.

I had been focused on testing adults to be ready to fight Astor right away, but perhaps it would be better in the long run to start younger. They might take a few years for their full strengths to emerge, but they could be trained in that time. I'd put that to the test as soon as we got arrive to the palace. That might be the path to the army I wanted to create. With a force of super humans, no one would be able to stand against me. Not Kabria, not Neria. Even Soland would one day be mine.

We made our way outside and rushed for one of the armored vans. Cecily reached out and opened the door, helping me inside then slipping in after me. Jessie came last, but she hesitated for a moment, and behind her I saw Astor standing over guards who were scatted around on the ground, unmoving. There was another explosion, and I flinched, but she didn't move an inch as the power of the blast hit her. She was a striking image. The flames raging behind her casting her in shadow giving the impression of a burning crown.

Jessie finally hopped in, and the driver took off from the site. I turned and watched out the back window, snarling as I caught sight of Genevieve calmly stealing one of the vehicles.

I screamed, thinking of the stem cells we had lost, and now I didn't have a way to get any more. My hands shook with fury.

Well, we'd have to fix that. I had two test subjects right here.

It had taken ages and cost a fortune to build that facility, but no matter. I'd just raise the taxes to offset the cost for the construction of the next one. Then again, I could arrest one of the rich thorns in my side and seize their assets. Maybe I'd just do both.

Out of the corner of my eye I caught Jessie staring at me. There was a light in her eyes I hadn't seen in some time. That would not do. I'd have to step-up her conditioning again. I'd rather break her than let her get any ideas in her head about disobeying me.

33

Vi

I drove until the van ran out of fuel. Sliding the door open, I slipped out, grabbing a shotgun just in case. I still had no clothes or shoes, and the blood on me was starting to dry. No matter how uncomfortable I was though, it was nothing compared to what I had just escaped.

I walked through fields and forests with nothing but the wind for company. Wrapping my arms around myself, I tried to get my head straight. My emotions swirled from grief over what I had endured at Esmerelda's hand once more to the power thrumming through my veins at the destruction I had wrought.

I thought of Chase and the others, but the moment I did, I felt like I was going to be sick. The conditioning still had a hold of me. I pushed the feeling down and focused on memories of the others that hadn't been tainted, reminding myself of how much I was loved and how lucky I was to have them in my life.

But my mind kept finding its way back to the screams of my captors. Especially when my eyes caught on the crimson smeared all over me.

Was I a monster? Did I even deserve to return to the people who loved me? Would they recoil from me when they learned what I had done?

I heard the burbling of water and made my way toward it. It was nothing more than a small creek, but I knelt beside it. My reflection wavered there, the moon behind me. I was covered in blood. I pushed my hands down into the water to wash them. I cupped some and took a long drink. It cooled the fire within me as I swallowed. Once I had my fill, I thought about washing the rest of me, but I stopped myself.

They had to understand what I had done to know if they could ever accept me. I couldn't trust their love for me if they didn't understand who I was now. I needed to know what they thought of the person who was coming back to them.

As I sat there, I found a sharp rock and worked on making it sharper. Once it was able to cleanly slice my finger, I dug it into my thigh and started to root out a bullet that had lodged there. To keep from screaming, I bit down on a stick I found nearby. After extracting it, I tried to get one in the meat of my tricep, but I couldn't reach it. Someone would have to help me with that. I managed to extract a few more before I decided the rest would have to wait.

Slowly, I pushed myself to my feet and continued on my journey. I guessed I had a ways to go before I made it home. If it would even be my home when I got there was something I could worry about later.

The sun rose, and I saw my feet were bleeding again as I walked through a field that had been harvested. The broken stalks were cutting into my skin, but I hadn't felt it at all. I wasn't tired, my muscles didn't burn. The wounds to my body were healing, but I knew the scars to my mind and soul might never leave me.

I tried to keep my mind off what they had put me through, but the thoughts came unbidden. I was so wrapped up in them that I didn't notice when someone yelled for me to stop. Dirt erupted before me as bullets ripped into the ground.

Instantly on alert, I snapped up my shotgun and sighted who had fired at me, but I realized they were high up in a guard post. I instantly dropped the gun and held my hands up.

"What are you doing here? Who are you?" they yelled down to me.

"I'm Genevieve Astor," I called, which seemed to confuse him. He called it in on his radio.

The man in the guard tower motioned to some others, and they walked toward me. I kept my hands up and stayed where I was. I didn't need to get shot again. I'd had my fill of that during the escape.

The guards whispered as they got close enough to really see me. I must have looked worse than I thought. We stood there, feet apart, just staring at each other. They had nothing to say to my face, and I didn't know what to say in return.

A van came racing up and slammed on its brakes as it neared the fence. The doors flew open, and I sagged as I saw Chase, Thea, and our dads jump out of it and rush toward me. By some miracle I had made it to headquarters and the people I wanted to see most were already here.

Chase crashed into me and wrapped me in his arms.

"I'm covered in blood," I muttered, before he squeezed me tighter and I collapsed into him. Nothing felt better than being surrounded by him. Eventually, he pulled back and held me out at arm's reach. His hands instinctively reached for me to check me over for wounds before he frowned and dropped them back to his sides. There was so much blood the exercise was pointless.

"Are you okay?"

Part of me shattered at the question. I saw the others coming toward us over his shoulder.

"I will be." It was all I could manage, and I prayed it wasn't a lie.

"Gods," my dad whispered before he put a hand to my cheek, and I leaned into it.

"I love you, Dad." I had felt so much guilt when I thought I might die without being able to make sure he knew. I grabbed him, clung to his waist, and buried my face in his chest. He held on like I'd disappear if he let me go, and we just stood there for a moment.

"We've got this; you all get back to your posts," I heard Ethan telling the others. They shuffled away, but then the whispers started.

"All hail the bloody red queen," one said before I forced myself to ignore them.

I squeezed my eyes shut and just held on for dear life. I was terrified if I looked up that they would be shying away from me and what I was.

Thea's small hands rested softly on my back, and I couldn't stop the sob that ripped from me.

"Thea, please. I don't want you to see me like this," I pleaded.

"I'm happy you're home," she said, and I felt someone pulling her away. My father dipped and hooked an arm under my knees to lift me close to his chest. I curled into myself as tight as I could, too afraid to open my eyes.

"Come on, let's get you looked at," he said, starting to walk away.

"There are some bullets I couldn't get out," I mumbled. His muscles tensed beneath me.

"It'll all be okay now." He pressed a kiss to the top of my head and slipped me into the van, where Chase crawled in next to me. He grabbed my hand and wouldn't let it go. I could feel his eyes on me, and I was scared, but I finally met his gaze.

I fell apart as soon as I saw the love and the pain there. "I'm so sorry," I cried.

He pulled me to him, holding me tightly. "Shh, you have nothing to be sorry for. You're home now."

I wouldn't let a doctor near me, so we sat in a small room as Chase worked to remove the bullets I hadn't managed to get out on my own. My father left, saying he was going to get me some clothes, and Thea said she'd let the others know I had made it back.

Chase came to stand in front of me, holding a wet cloth. One of his hands reached up to cup my cheek while the other wiped at the blood that was coating me. Every touch was gentle, like I might shatter with too much pressure.

"How long did she have me?" It was so quiet I wasn't sure if he heard me, but then he took a deep breath, as if he was steeling himself.

"Two months." The answer skewered me. I wasn't sure if it would have been better to always wonder. Time had meant nothing, and it had felt like an eternity, but I had held out hope it hadn't been that long.

Two months of the people who loved me having no idea if I was alive or dead. Two months of my family having to worry. Right now, I was more concerned about how it had impacted them because I still had no idea how it was going to affect me.

I would have thought being home and safe would have lifted a weight, but I felt just as heavy as I had before, tensing as flashes of the memories of pain came unbidden.

Chase tipped up my chin and waited until I looked at him. "She didn't break you. You escaped, and you're home now."

"But what if she did?" My voice cracked as I asked the question that had been haunting me.

"Then, we'll help put you back together again." He kissed my forehead before he went back to wiping the blood from me.

"You don't know what I did, what I went through. I was a monster. She made me into a monster." There was no stopping the tears that fell.

"I would love you even if you burned down the world." He kissed away my tears. "I will be by your side no matter what."

And he did. He sat with me as I hid in that room, unable to face whatever was going to come next but knowing whatever did he would be right there with me. Knowing he saw me as I was and wouldn't turn away.

I didn't deserve him.

I settled my hand on my stomach. I hoped the baby was all right. I might not deserve Chase, but this baby did.

34

Vi

A light knock came at the door, and Thea slipped in. I cursed myself for flinching as she did.

"Hey, sis," she said softly.

Getting over my initial reaction I reached out and pulled her to me, hugging her tightly. "It's so good to see you."

"I was thinking the same thing." She squeezed me tight before slipping onto a nearby table. "Are you okay?"

With a gasp, the tears were back. All I could manage was to shake my head, letting her know I wasn't. I pushed the heels of my hands into my eyes, trying to reign myself in. I wouldn't want many people to see me like this, but it felt good for her to know. I knew she'd love me even if I was broken. That was what family did, right? Loved you even when it was hard to?

Right?

I didn't know how I'd handle her turning away from me.

Thea and Chase exchanged a glance.

"What do you think about going to see David?" Chase asked.

"There is so much to do. We can't just take off."

He sighed. "You need to get out of the field right now. We both need David; you know we do. The three of us can get through this together; just like everything else. Also, you know need a doctor and Joseph is the only one you'll let near you." He raised his eyebrow at me, and I knew he was right.

"It would be good to see them," I agreed.

"Good, because the plane will be ready in a few minutes. The others wanted to come see you. Is that okay?" Thea asked.

So, it hadn't been a question. Chase and I were going, and I was officially being taken off duty. In my state I wouldn't be worth anything anyways, and if I hadn't lost the baby, we had to hide it. It was clear Esmerelda would do anything to get us back, and I had to protect them the best I could. We had to hide, and the school was a surprising convenient place to do so.

I wanted to get out of here as soon as possible. I needed to see David. He helped me heal after being rescued originally. I knew I'd need him this time too.

When I agreed, Thea tapped out a message to the others, and within moments, they were there. Gwen ran up to me, and my first instinct again was to step away. Her eyes going wide as she saw it.

"Sorry." Shaking my head, I pulled her in for a hug, and she sighed as she leaned against me. I rested my chin on the top of her head, and Benson smiled at me from behind her.

"We're so happy you're back," he said.

Gwen let me go and went to sit next to Thea, and Benson wrapped me in his giant embrace.

I had held on to this thought so tight to keep myself from losing my mind. That I would get home to them. But it was still overwhelming to finally be here.

"Are you guys coming too?" I asked them.

"I'm going to stay here and work with Thea," Gwen said, throwing her thumb over her shoulder at my little sister.

That was good. I knew they would look out for each other.

"What about you, Benson?"

"I'm headed to Neria to see Naya and Jupiter. They'll be sending some people back with me to help us look into helping Jessie and Cecily.

I steadied myself knowing I had to say it. "They have condition-ing. Brainwashing. It... can make you feel things you never would on your own. Believe people you shouldn't. Jessie seems to be free of it—at least, at times—but Cecily, she's under Esmerelda's complete control. Like Jasper was. Jessie was the one who freed me, but she wouldn't come without her. We need to draw them out and see if we can capture them. I promised I'd come for them. We can't let Esmerelda keep them. We have to save them." I was begging. "I need to go after them again. I can't waste time." But his expression told me that wasn't an option.

"We'll talk about it once we get there." He took my hand in his, and our fingers intertwined. "It's time to go."

He was right. I was exhausted, and I knew I wouldn't be of any use right now, but the guilt of doing nothing felt like it would eat me alive.

The others walked with us as we headed to the hangers and the plane that was ready to go. As usual, our fathers were waiting there for us.

I wrapped my arms around my dad and squeezed tight. "I love you," I whispered. Every moment felt precious. I was tired of not knowing how to act around him.

He kissed my forehead. "I love you more than anything. Go, spend some time with your friends and heal, and send me a message when you're ready. I'll be here."

Ethan hugged both Chase and I, and I gave him a kiss on the cheek before Chase pulled me into our waiting transport. With a wave to our friends, he shut the door, and Anthony prepared for takeoff.

I dropped into the seat heavily and ran my hands through my hair. Chase slipped in next to me, and I leaned into him.

"Get some sleep," he murmured into my hair. That didn't sound like a bad idea. The hum of the engines quickly lulled me to sleep.

I jerked awake with a scream as the plane rocked in some turbulence. Anthony looked over his shoulder at us in alarm but turned back quickly enough. Chase had locked his hands around my wrists as I had lashed out on instinct.

"Sorry. I'm sorry," I muttered, and he pulled me so we were eye to eye.

"Do not apologize." His tone was firm, like it always was while trying to get through to me when I was being stubborn. Yet, he was still gentle; the relief he felt that I was home was obvious. "We're going to set down a few miles from the school and walk the rest of the way. We're almost there."

I rolled out some of my stiff joints. We started descending, and Chase got ready to throw the door open as we landed. I jumped out as soon as he did, and we said goodbye to Anthony before he took off to head back to headquarters.

Hiking my bag over my shoulder I headed into the forest that surrounded the school. It was reminiscent of the forest around headquarters. The fresh air automatically triggered the need to take a deep breath, then another. The stars shone through the breaks in the canopy.

I was free. I was safe. I was with family.

Yet, it wasn't long before the memories of the tests crawled to the surface, and I had to force them back into a box.

Clear your mind. Think of the positive things you have.

Ground yourself in this moment.

I am safe.

How did I protect myself from my own mind?

The echoes of my screams bounced within my skull.

Chase grabbed my hand and pulled me back to the present. He just gave me a small grin and tugged me after him. His thumb ran over my knuckles in a soft steady pace. Back and forth, back and forth. Breathe in and out, in and out.

I could start to see the school through the trees. It really was breathtaking. It was a massive brick building with towering spires and a large open courtyard in the middle of the three-sided, square-like building. There was also a track with bleachers near the open back of the courtyard.

Chase shot off a message, and the doors swung open. The silhouettes of David and Joseph stood there.

We hurried up to meet them, and I only hesitated for a moment at the first sight of David's face before shaking my head and diving in for a hug. I wouldn't let what Esmerelda's conditioning did to me come between me and the people I loved.

They didn't let me go for a long time, and I felt David trembling slightly in my arms.

I was so happy to see him. He was an integral part of my life, and now that I finally had him with me, another knot in my gut loosened. As soon as I was free, I grabbed Joseph's arm.

"I need to know about the baby." Now that we were here, I had to know.

David and Joseph shared a quick confused look. Chase must not have said anything. Joseph squeezed my hand and just pulled me after him. "Let's head to my lab."

35

ESMERELDA

The girls were quiet as I glared down the hallway we were passing through. Looking over my shoulder, I saw Jessie watching her feet uncomfortably while Cecily just stared straight ahead. The older girl shifted under my gaze as I came to a stop.

"Jessie, what did you see in there?" I asked her.

She stiffened but returned my gaze. "Nothing. I came straight to protect you, Your Majesty."

"You didn't run into Astor?" I leaned in, but she just shook her head.

"No, ma'am—" She stopped talking when I hissed at the word.

"Do not call me ma'am," I snapped, and she nodded quickly in response.

Something was different with her. It was time to separate the two. Put her through some extra conditioning and give her a few nights of sleep deprivation. We'd see how she was then, and if she still wasn't under heel, I'd get rid of her.

Jessie slid closer to her sister and went to grab her hand, but Cecily just glanced down at it in confusion. It was enough for Jessie to pull her hand back and watch her sister. Jessie bit at her lip, and my hackles rose at the movement.

Something had happened, and it had Genevieve Astor written all over it.

"Jessie, go see Dr. Netzel."

She tried to cover the quick flash of confusion, but I saw it anyway. She turned and headed toward his office. I analyzed Cecily up but as usual, there wasn't any reaction from her. I moved to head back down the hallway again and motioned for her to follow. Instantly, I heard her steps behind me.

I'd keep her close. She had been exceeding my expectations. She had less of a mouth on her than Jasper and was more controllable than her sister. She was perfect. Finally, someone who was competent. She had almost bled out Astor with her attack back in Fort Mercy.

She was going to be my prized weapon to eviscerate Nolan and his followers.

As soon as we reached my office, I sent a message to Howard to prep Jessie for conditioning, and that we'd need to investigate the creation of a new child to replace the lost stem cells. If she wasn't going to be a useful weapon, she could be a useful tool in a different way.

"You've done very well," I told her.

She didn't move.

"You'll be reporting to me from now on. Come see me every morning if you haven't been given other instructions. You're dismissed."

She gave me a small nod before turning on her heel and leaving.

About an hour later, my door opened and Howard entered. As he did I looked up from the reports I was reading.

"How long until you can get me more stem cells and finish your work?" I snapped.

"That all depends. We'll have to run some tests to see if she's even able to bear children. She has levels of scarring; I'm not sure what happened to her before she ended up here."

"She better be able to. She's becoming less and less useful, and if I don't have a use for her, we don't need her anymore."

"Of course." He dipped his head toward me. "We'll start testing immediately."

"Oh, and for the next round of test subjects, include children. Provide me with a report on what should be the best age range to start with." I watched him carefully to see what his reaction would be, but he just agreed and left.

Good. As I expected, he had no qualms with what needed to be done.

PART III

THE INNOCENT

36

Vi

We walked through the empty halls, which wasn't a surprise. While this was a boarding school, it was late. The kids were probably all in their dorms. They led us down a stairwell built of brick, and as we descended, my heart started to race. The farther I got from the open, the more the terror set in, but I bit my lip and tried to ignore it. Tried to calm myself.

Joseph slid a door open, and I froze at the sight of an operating table. I couldn't breathe as I stared at it.

Chase stepped into my field of view and gripped my wrists again. "What do you need?"

How was I supposed to know? I was completely paralyzed by my fear. He softly tugged me forward, but not toward the table. He led me to a stool near the wall and turned me so I couldn't see it.

I could guess they were exchanging looks behind my back. I hated that I was too weak to be able to get past this. Logically, I knew I was safe, but it didn't stop the waves of terror that took hold of me.

I was so broken.

Joseph sat on a stool next to me and pulled it up closer. "I'm going to need to take some blood, but we can do this later if you need."

I shook my head, closed my eyes, and stuck my arm out to him.

"This can't wait. I have to know. Just do it. I trust you." It didn't matter that I knew it was coming; a snarl ripped through me as the needle pierced my skin. Joseph wasn't fazed though and got it done as quickly as possible and released me. I snatched my arm back and stood to start pacing away some of this tension. I tugged at my hair as I ran my fingers through it.

Just breathe. You are safe.

"Vi." David put a hand on my arm, pulling me back to the present. "You aren't alone; we're here for you." He had helped me put myself back together before, and he knew some of what I had gone through in those six years. So, he didn't need to hear what happened this time to know it was bad.

I wrapped my arms around myself, shaking my head. "I know," I muttered it again and again, trying to believe it.

It was starting to feel like these past two months had been harder on me than those six years. I didn't know if it was the time since I had been first rescued that had dulled the pain and this was still fresh or if it was because it really had been that much worse this time. The scientists hadn't been waiting for something to happen. They knew what I could do, and they wanted to see what it would take to break me.

"We're here when you're ready," David said, and Chase nodded behind him. He walked over to Chase, and I couldn't help but eavesdrop on them. "She's pregnant?"

"According to Esmerelda," Chase replied.

"I am, or I was, at least. She took stem cells. She thinks it's going to cure her," I blurted out. Everyone turned to me, and the tears sprung free again.

They both rushed to me as I sunk to the ground. Chase wrapped me in his arms and David grabbed my hand.

"I didn't even know. *She* told me. If she hurt them..." I didn't finish the thought; they knew what I'd do.

I saw Joseph's feet as he walked toward us. He squatted down in front of me and waited until he had my attention.

"You're still pregnant. We'll keep an eye on you, but it seems like they might take after you."

Chase tightened his grip on me, and I took his face in my hands and kissed him with all the desperation that was weaving through me. When I pulled back, his smile was shining brighter than the sun.

Joseph helped David up as Chase wound his hand in my hair and pulled me back to kiss him again.

"I love you so much," he whispered against my lips. "I can't wait to be a parent with you."

Joseph coughed awkwardly, and we finally untangled ourselves. "You must be tired; we have a room made up for you. It's right down here."

"Thank you," I said quietly. I could tell they were concerned, but I moved to follow them.

It really was right next to the lab, and he opened the door for me. The first thing I noticed was there were no windows, which made sense because we were underground. Still, I hesitated. Chase must have noticed, but I had done it so much today that he only glanced at me before I followed him in.

"There is breakfast in the great hall upstairs in the morning, but we can grab you something and bring it down here for you. We'll be making an announcement to the school. Many of the kids know you already, but we'll let them know no one can say anything about you being here."

"You think we can trust them?" Chase asked.

"They are good kids. Most of them worship you two as heroes. I don't think we have anything to worry about." David's assurance calmed me slightly.

"We get major cool points being your friend." Joseph used finger quotes to emphasize the coolness.

"We'll see you in the morning. Get some sleep." David squeezed my hand once more before Chase shut the door behind them.

I walked over to the bed and flopped down on it, surprised by the give of the mattress. Because I wasn't in a cell. I was in a bedroom. With my husband. In my friend's hidden school.

An arm snaked around me as the bed rocked and he joined me. I scooted back into his firm embrace.

I'm safe.

Chase started to hum and run his hands lightly over me. The vibration of his chest and the slow circles his hands traced calmed me until, all at once, I was overcome by exhaustion.

I struggled against the restraints, and the table was so cold it burned against my skin.

Esmerelda towered over me as she sneered. Lightning exploded from her fingertips; the pain was so intense, but I couldn't scream. No matter what I tried, I couldn't speak.

A doctor appeared over me with an oversized scalpel and started to dig into my stomach.

"Here she is, my queen." The doctor held up a baby already swaddled with piercing green eyes and brown hair.

I jerked and tried everything to get free, but I was sitting now as the helmet was lowered onto me.

The videos they showed me were of my family and friends, and I felt nothing but fear. Pain ricocheted through my bones before it felt like my skin was on fire.

I was ripped away and found myself in an empty hallway. The cries of a child and the laughter of my stepmother echoed around me.

Limping at first, I tried to push myself faster. I had to get to them, but the faster I ran, the farther the hallway expanded.

Doors started to appear, and I ripped the first one open to stumble into the room covered in ice. The door slammed shut behind me. I ran back to it and looked out the window, banging on the metal of the door. I tried to scream for help but still couldn't make a sound.

I rushed the door, putting my shoulder down to ram it, but when it opened, I went falling through space.

I screamed as I launched out of bed. I saw nothing but blank walls. Terror flared through me. I focused on the door and ran for it, vaguely aware of a sound behind me. I had to get out.

The door splintered as I crashed through it. I slid into the hallway and saw windows with a lab beyond.

A hand grabbed my arm, and I spun and punched at whoever it was. My vision flickered, and a guard stood in front of me. He was fuzzy at the edges, but I wasn't going to be taken again.

With a scream, I pushed forward as they blocked the blows I threw at them.

I heard another commotion behind me, but I couldn't tear my eyes away from this person who deserved my wrath. I wouldn't be dragged away this time.

Arms caged me and pulled me backward. I roared my fury as cold expanded from a prick on my neck.

"No, please, please don't take me back. I can't. Please just kill me," I begged as the lights above me started to sway. I expected the fire to rip its way through my veins, but all I felt was numbness instead.

37

Vi

Blinking my eyes open, fear gripped me as I saw bright lights above. I went to launch myself forward before I saw three people in chairs between myself and the open doorframe. The door was hanging in pieces, barely still attached to the hinges. There were chunks of it in the hallway beyond.

Chase pushed himself up but lifted his hands in front of him. Most likely so that he could block me in case I ran. I sighed as I realized it was just him, David, and Joseph.

Chase had a black eye, and I scrambled off the bed to go to him. He leaned into my hand as I ran it across his face, lightly touching the bruise. I started to remember the terror and a fight.

"No... did I do this?" I asked, aghast.

"It's fine. Are you okay? You had no idea where you were. No idea who we were."

I pulled out of his grasp and backed away. "I can't believe I hurt you. I wasn't—it wasn't you. I wasn't here." I shook my head, trying to put the pieces together of what I saw and what I knew.

What I had said before I passed out came back to me. I had begged for them to kill me. They had seen just how broken I was, and

I couldn't make them forget it. It was agonizing feeling like they may never see me the same again.

"It's okay. I'm fine, I promise. You only got in one good shot." He tried to laugh, but it died as soon as he saw me flinch.

"I don't think I can stay in here. It's too enclosed. We should go." I tried to skirt around them to get out of here.

David grabbed me as I went past him. "You are staying right here. Well, not here. I think I have a better place we can have you stay." He took my hand and pulled it. "Come with me."

Reminding myself he was my best friend and would only have the best intentions, I followed. He guided us through the main hallway that held the doors to the courtyard and front entryway. Dawn had just broken, so the place was still rather empty. We ran into a kid or two, but they just stared as we passed. Joseph nodded to them, and David gave them a smile but didn't stop.

Turning left down the next hallway, we made our way to a stairwell at the end of it, and we started to climb. This building was huge, and we didn't stop till we reached the top floor of one of the towers. He pushed open the door, and I got a sweeping look at the room inside.

It was expansive and filled with boxes that had dust-covered tarps over them. It seemed like it was used for storage, but my attention was drawn to one thing. At the far side of the room, part of the roof was a circular glass cone that rose to a metal-tipped point. Next to it was a hatch that had direct access to the roof.

My legs moved on their own, pulling me toward it. The first light of dawn streaked through and swept across my face. I closed my eyes and took a deep breath. I would always be able to see the sky.

I turned back to my friends and gave them an exhausted smile. "It's perfect," I breathed.

Leave it to David to know exactly what I needed.

"We'll get the stuff cleared out of here today," Joseph said. "The kids would love to help."

"Or they might not, but they'll help anyway." David and Joseph chuckled, sharing a look. "Breakfast should be ready soon; want us to grab you something and bring it up?"

"Can you show us around?" Chase asked, and I understood he wanted to get the layout of the building and grounds memorized.

"Yeah, sure thing. Vi, do you want to come?" David asked, and I agreed. It would be nice to know the lay of the land here.

We all headed down the stairs to the main areas of the building.

"Down this way is the lobby, main dining and gathering area." He pointed toward the area that we had walked through earlier that also had the stairs down to Joseph's lab. The building front was flanked on either side by other sections of the building that jutted backward. In the courtyard the layout created was a fountain surrounded by benches and trees. I could just see the track and bleachers in the distance.

The northern wing was where the classrooms were located. The southern wing was the dorms. Our new room was at the top of the southern wing. I could see the glass ceiling in the tower from our place in the courtyard.

My mind raced with the different routes attackers could approach and the best defensible positions. It wouldn't be too diffi-cult to get all the kids together and defend a single wing. It was habit by this point, and I tried to remind myself I wasn't on the front. And I wasn't with Esmerelda. The point of being here was that we were off the grid.

A door flung open, and footsteps raced toward us. Someone crashed into me, and I rocked as arms wrapped around me. The moment I saw it was someone younger, I managed to stop my reflexes from lashing out.

Under the beanie I saw it was Doug. I sighed and hugged him back.

"I heard it was you," he said, smiling at me. He was as tall as me now. "I'm so happy to see you. Did you know Lilly and Bunny are here too? A lot of the kids came here after you all won against the king."

"It's good to see you, Doug. You'll have to take me to see the girls."

He was one of the kids we had met when we were working with the Nerian rebels. My heart tugged at the thought that he might not know about Jessie or Cecily yet. They had been close in the camps. I'd have to figure out how to break it to them. All of them.

"It's almost breakfast. Come on, you can get all you want to eat. There is plenty." He chirped.

It had been no secret how much I needed to eat to replace the calories my enhanced metabolism burned through. It was sweet he had thought of it.

"Lead on." Over my shoulder, I saw Chase letting out a deep breath and giving me an encouraging smile. His love was palpable. I tried to wrap it around myself like armor. I'd hold on to it like a life preserver when I began slipping back into the darkness of my mind.

As we made our way through the halls to the dining room, a crowd started to gather behind our group. The whispers had started, asking if it was really us. As soon as we entered the dining hall, there was a squeal, and a little missile came careening straight for me. I caught Bunny and hugged her tight. She had grown quite a bit since I had seen her last, but she was still small for her age. She had to be around ten now.

"Did you miss us?" Her grin was so wide it looked like it might crack her cheeks.

"I missed you a whole bunch."

She giggled, and I glimpsed Lilly behind her. She gave me a wave.

I walked over and gave her a hug too. "It's good to see you." I clasped her on the shoulder. Lilly was one of the oldest; only Jessie had been older in the group. "You did good." Which had her beaming with pride.

"Someone said there was breakfast." I was starving, and then bustled off in the middle of a group of kids who led me to the buffet table. I couldn't understand them as they all talked over each other, but it put me at ease. This was a feeling, and a memory, Esmerelda hadn't managed to taint. She hadn't had any video of the kids with the rebels. She couldn't use them against me in the conditioning.

A man walked up to me, patting his hands on an apron before sticking one out. "Hi there. I'm Theo O'Doherty. I'm the cook here."

"Ah, so I have you to thank for this amazing-looking breakfast. It's nice to meet you," I said as I shook his hand.

He blushed a bit. "It's an honor to have you with us. I came over from Neria, and I just wanted to thank you. And young Doug wanted me to tell you not to worry, there will always be plenty to eat here. Just come on by if you ever feel peckish."

"Thank you. That's very nice of you, and I probably will take you up on that."

He waved to the table. "Go on. Don't let me keep you."

Before I knew it, I had a plate piled high with food and I was shuffled to a table as the kids surrounded me and asked me all sorts of questions. I peeked over the heads of the nearby children and saw the boys grabbing another table on the other side of the room.

Turning my attention back to the kids, I answered questions and listened to their stories until the sun was high in the sky and my plate had been empty for quite some time.

For the first time possibly since I had escaped, my mind was completely focused on the present. Their enthusiasm helped me forget just for a bit, which was enough for now.

38

Vi

A storm was coming. The smell wafted in on the wind through the trees. Bracing my arms against my knees, I dropped my chin into my hands. How long had I been sitting out here on the bleachers? I wasn't sure.

The clouds on the horizon had been hanging around, blocking most of the sunlight. The contrast of the deep green of the trees against the backdrop of the storm was one of the most beautiful things I'd ever seen. The colors were so vibrant the view took my breath away. I'd just been sitting and staring at them, and my mind had been blissfully blank. It reminded me so much of watching the storms roll in back home.

Footsteps were headed my way, and their gate seemed familiar.

Doug clambered up the bleachers to sit next to me.

"Hey."

"Hey," I replied.

"Do you remember when we first me?" he asked as he settled in on the metal bench.

"Of course." I did remember. He was in one of the last groups to evacuate the rebels' bases hidden in a school in Neria after the military had bombed it. We had hung at the back of the group and chatted about what he might want to do when he grew up.

"You told me helping others could help me heal myself." His glanced at me before he went on. "There are a lot of people you could help here. Without having to be a weapon."

So, he remembered it too. He had said he wanted to be like me, but I had told him I was just a weapon that got pointed in a direction and all I did was hurt people. I had been trying to show him there was a different path and that he and the other kids shouldn't look up to me.

"I don't know if I'm endangering any of you by being here. I'm still not sure I can stay. Your safety is the top priority."

There was a sad smile on his face. "You've protected us all. Let us return the favor. I don't know what exactly is going on, but I can tell something is. I just want you to know it's all going to be okay; you can trust us."

A tear slipped down my cheek, but I didn't move to wipe it away. Staring up at the sky, I took a deep breath. I could let my friends and family take care of me. At least, I could try. I didn't have to bear this all alone.

"That sounds really nice, Doug."

The first drops of rain speckled across my skin.

"Are you going to go inside?" he asked.

"Soon. I think I just need to sit for a little longer."

I gave him a wave as he scampered down from the bleachers and ran to get inside before the rain started in earnest.

Raising my face to the sky once more, I closed my eyes. Each drop felt like it might be washing a small portion of my sadness away. Rinsing away the invisible grime left on me from that place. Maybe it just felt nice for the weather to match my mood—my emotions whipping through me like a twister, coming on without warning.

Sometimes, all I could do was grit my teeth and wait for it to release me. Other times, I could remember that I wouldn't feel this way forever. There was a way to move on; it would just take time. For now, I just had to trust that the people here wanted only the best for me. That they would do what it took to help me get better.

I could tell the drops of rain were cold, the wind making it even colder, but I didn't feel it. Wiping at my face and clearing the droplets from my eyelashes, I stood. I ran my hands through my hair, dislodging pieces stuck to my face, and made my decision. Every day, I was going to do the best I could, and that was all I could ask of myself.

David slipped in next to me, and my flinch was so minute I didn't think he saw it. I was dripping wet and squelching through the pristine hallways of the school.

Steading myself, I walked close enough that I could lightly bump his shoulder, and he bumped mine right back.

"Want to go watch the rain in your room?"

I had been seriously lacking in alone time with David, so I couldn't think of anything I'd enjoy more right now. He seemed to notice my mood perking up slightly, and we headed for the stairway to the tower.

"This place is amazing, David. Honestly, it's really impressive what you two have built here."

"I mean, technically, Nathan built it." He waggled his eyebrows at me as he glanced over his shoulder.

Which also was true, Nathan had bankrolled the entire project of setting up this school. Nathan was the King of Soland and he found the location, had the school built, and worked on getting the kids and teachers here in the first place, but the day to day is what made this place special.

"It's still amazing, and you've done something incredible for these kids. So many of them wouldn't have a chance at something like this back there. This place wouldn't exist without the two of you. You're here every day teaching these kids how to be good people. I think that makes you more responsible for this success than Nathan. Don't tell him I said that though."

"I really enjoy it, and the kids love Joseph. There is a group of the older kids working with him down in the labs. Most of the older group are planning to return to the resistance. I wish we had a better option or something they wanted to do more than going back to the fight. I understand it though. It's what we chose."

We reached the top floor, and he pushed the door open but paused and glanced at me.

"We wanted to know if you would want to teach physical education while you're here. I know you'll go crazy if you don't have anything to do."

Me teaching kids? Me teaching kids how to exercise, getting to be outside and run. It sounded perfect because he was right. I would go crazy if they expected me to just hole up in here, hiding away, doing nothing. And if I was being honest, I had a soft spot for all these kids. So, I just nodded, and he beamed at me.

"Oh, good!" He clapped his hands together. "The kids are going to be so excited."

The room had been cleaned out, and there was nothing more than a mattress and a few blankets up here, but it was enough. Catching the edge, I dragged it to lay right under the glass.

I dropped onto it and threw my arms wide against the mattress. David thumped down next to me. As we laid there with our heads close, we just stared up at the droplets hitting the glass and sliding down the curve of it. The sound was relaxing. We had done this dozens of times as kids in the palace, when no one would let us outside.

"I don't think I'm a good person anymore. I don't know if I ever was." It surprised me how easy the truth came out.

"That's ridiculous. You are selfless. You always put others ahead of yourself. You care so deeply for people. You feel their pain and turn it into hope. That is something beautiful."

"Oh, David." I sighed and pressed a hand to my eyes. "You don't know what I did, and I didn't even flinch. I reveled in hurting the people who hurt me."

"You mean going through that building, setting it on fire, and destroying their servers and data with an ax?"

My eyes wide, I rolled to my side to look at him. He propped himself up with an arm. If he had seen that, he'd seen everything. He knew. I didn't know how, but he knew, and he wasn't fleeing from me.

"Yeah, I managed to use an old backdoor into palace security. Someone had uploaded all the camera footage until they stopped transmitting because of the damage. I also found out they have the data they collected, but the stem cells were destroyed."

"You saw." I was still trying to process that fact.

"I must not be a good person either because I'm glad you got revenge. Even if it was nothing compared to what they deserved." The words slipped through his clenched teeth, and his fists were clenched.

I put my hand over his.

"I will never turn my back on you. I will always be on your side. This is war, and sometimes people have to get their hands dirty. But if you want to stop, if you want to give that life up, you can stay here. You know I'd never turn down more time with you guys."

Absentmindedly, my hand fell to my stomach. I hadn't had time to really think about what this meant. I had been focused on just keeping us alive. What kind of life could we give a child if we went back? What would Esmerelda do to get her hands on them? Was there even a place fit to bring a child into the world?

I could still hear the laughter of kids downstairs. It might not be an easy life, but it didn't have to be a bad one.

"David."

He waited for me to go on.

"I want to leave the baby here with you."

The confusion was plain on his face.

"Just listen. Right now, Esmerelda won't know if I lost the baby or not. Who is to say I didn't lose it during the escape or even from one of the last tests? I mean, they had me chained up in a frozen room when Jessie let me loose." Now that I had thought of the idea, I could feel in my bones it was our best option. I had always sworn since I was rescued that if I had a child, I would never leave them the way my father left me, and now, here I was thinking I might do the same thing.

I saw my father in a completely different light. Esmerelda had threatened to kill me if my father didn't give her control. He thought leaving was the best way to keep me safe. Deciding to live to fight another day, and we both have.

"Vi, this is all new, and I'm sure it's overwhelming…" he started.

"If it looks like I lost the baby, she won't come after them. There is nothing for her to test, no one for her to hurt. You know if Esmerelda finds out they're alive, she will not stop until she has them. Can't you see this is the best way to keep them safe? They'll just be another orphan."

"Come on. Chase isn't going to go for this. He would be an amazing dad. You would be an amazing mother."

"You need to help me convince him. The best thing I can do for them is to get back out there and finish this war. Make a better place for them to grow up. You can keep them safer than I ever could. You know I have to go back. We have to use every tool at our disposal to win, and I couldn't live with myself knowing I did nothing to stop her."

David shook his head, but I could tell he saw sense in it.

"Okay, fine. We'll talk to him, but I still don't know if it's the best option. We have plenty of time to figure this out."

With that at least slightly settled, we both flopped down to the mattress and stared up at the rain.

"You don't think it's going to be a super baby, do you?" I asked.

"I have no idea, man. With your luck, probably."

"Oh no…" I whispered, and that got a laugh out of both of us.

39

Vi

The door was quiet, but I still heard it swing open, and I rolled over to see Chase walking in. David and I were still sprawled on the mattress, watching the rain. We had been catching up, reminiscing, and just enjoying each other's company.

"This is where you two have been hiding." He started toward us with a chuckle. David and I scooted to give him room to join us.

"Where have you been?" I asked.

"I've been hanging out with Joseph." He turned to David and raised an eyebrow. "He asked if I wanted to teach strategy to the kids."

"And you *said?*" David asked, drawing out the last word.

"Are we staying?" Chase looked at me.

"Yeah, we are. I'm going to teach kids how to run around and kick stuff. While we're here, anyway."

"Good, because I already told him I would."

We rolled into each other as the bed dipped under Chase's weight.

"I see you decided to hang out in the rain," he said, poking my wet clothes that were soaking him as I cuddled up to him.

"It was soothing. I feel a lot like that storm most of the time. It was kind of cathartic." I was tucked in tight next to him, my head leaning lightly on his shoulder. I couldn't help but start to nip at his neck, which elicited a deep, rattling moan from him.

"Could you guys please wait until I leave?" David groaned and scooted away from us.

Chase's arm slipped over my waist, tugging me closer. "We'll see you later."

He caught my eye, and I was trapped in his gaze. The world seemed to slip away.

David got up and chuckled. "Lunch should be ready soon."

His steps receded, followed by the soft click of the door closing. I couldn't keep my hands from roaming across Chase's body, and it seemed like he couldn't either. Everywhere he touched burned away the chill from the wet clothes still clinging to my body.

He wrapped his hand around my thigh and tugged me over to straddle him.

"I love you more than anything," he whispered, and I saw the pain and fear in his eyes. "I thought I might lose you."

"I came home." Our mantra. In Neria, he had been terrified I would put myself in the type of danger I wouldn't be able to survive. I almost hadn't, but ultimately, it was Atty I couldn't save. My heart clenched, thinking of his last breaths. The scream that ripped from Gwen as he left us. The look as the life drained from Jasper's eyes when I finally killed him for what he had done.

"I know." Chase's hand cupped my cheek, returning me to the present. I placed my own firmly over his shoulders and leaned in close over him. Our breaths mixed, but our eyes locked, and we just sat for a moment, soaking each other in.

Then, his fingers dug into my hips before sliding under the hem of my shirt, and inch by inch, he worked the fabric up my ribs. As my body thrummed with electricity at his touch and the tension from his slow movements, I arched up and ripped my shirt over my head. I stared down at him, and his eyes roamed my body while my hair dripped on his chest.

His breathing was ragged beneath me before one of his hands slid behind my neck and pulled me toward him. We crashed together, and all the fear and need exploded from me. I finally had him in my arms after not knowing if I'd ever see him again.

This was the first moment I didn't feel like I had to fight or flee. I felt like everything might be okay now that we were together again. His love burned away the fog of everything I had been through.

I tore at his clothes, and he flipped us so I was staring up at him.

"I would destroy the gods to return to you. I will always come home. I never knew I could love someone the way I love you. You make me the best version of myself."

His breath hitched at my words before he leaned down to place a quick kiss on the tip of my nose. He ran a thumb along the edge of my jaw as he held my neck lightly. "I know you would."

As the rain, lightning, and thunder crashed above us, we lost ourselves to each other. Worshiping each other. Making sure the other knew just how much we meant those words. That nothing would ever be able to keep us apart. We would do anything to get back to each other.

Anything.

As soon as the buffet of food was in sight, I dropped Chase's hand and raced toward it.

I was starving. I gave Theo a quick bow when I saw him and mouthed 'thank you'. He just shook his head with a chuckle.

I piled my plate high. It smelled delicious. Doug waved to me, and I gave a quick salute to Chase and went to sit with the kids. Bunny, Lilly, and some others I recognized from Neria were with him.

I flopped down onto the bench next to Lilly and grinned at them before I dove into my food. I couldn't hold back the moan as the flavors mixed on my tongue. It was pure bliss. My body had been screaming at me to eat something.

"I heard you're going to teach us!" Bunny said excitedly, bouncing in her seat.

"How do you know that already? David literally just asked me a bit ago."

The kids all exchanged devious looks.

"It's a small school; word gets around fast." Lilly said with a smirk and a shrug.

"I shall keep that in mind." I laughed. "Yeah, we'll be staying and helping out for a while."

"Chase is too," Doug said. "He's going to teach strategy. I can't wait. I'm going to learn everything I can so I can keep our home safe." His voice had turned grave.

I waved my fork at him. "You all are safe here, but it's a good skill to know. It can help you out in many ways."

"Are you going to teach us how to kick butt?" Lilly asked me.

"I don't think so." I shook my head, but a little girl at the end quietly spoke up.

"Can you please teach me how to protect myself?"

Many others at the table agreed. I saw some of the scars painting their skin. I knew some of these kids' lives hadn't been easy. The hope in their gazes shattered an already broken piece of my heart. The question weighed on me.

"Of course, I will. I want all of you to feel like you are safe no matter where you go, but I'm also going to teach you when it's acceptable to use what you know. No matter how angry you may be, violence isn't the answer."

I was a hypocrite, but I didn't care. I would teach them to be better than me.

I saw Chase being introduced to adults I hadn't met yet. They must have been other teachers here. It shouldn't surprise me. It wasn't like David and Joseph could teach these kids everything they needed to know on their own, but my anxiety flared. The old habit of not trusting anyone was rearing its ugly head.

Logically, I knew I should trust them. David and Joseph obviously did. But they were an unknown factor. I still didn't trust that Esmerelda wouldn't find another way to get me or my baby. I didn't know if I was strong enough to stop that from happening. I hadn't been last time.

My plate was empty, so I turned to the kids. "I'm going to go introduce myself. I'll see you all later."

They chorused goodbye as I got up. I dropped my tray off before circling back to the table where Chase and the others were. Without even looking my way, Chase scooted over and made room. His hand found my thigh and gave it a quick squeeze, letting me know he was here for me.

"Everyone," David said as he saw me, "this is Vi, my best friend."

"Pretty sure I'm your best friend," Chase replied, cocking his eyebrow at David.

"I thought that was me," Joseph said, pouting.

David bumped his shoulder with his own, and they shared a smile. Everyone waved and said hello. All I managed was an awkward wave in return.

"Um, hi."

David rolled his eyes. "She's shy."

"This is Riley Shaw; she teaches the arts here. She's one of the best in Soland." He pointed toward a woman with dark skin and hair that hung in long dreadlocks. Her light grey eyes popped from under the gold eyeliner. Her clothes were gem tones, and she was dripping in beautiful gold jewelry.

"Oh, so you're from here?" I asked.

"Yeah, Nathan asked me if I would be interested in coming to help out."

"You know Nathan?" Chase turned to her.

"We went to school together. I've heard all about you three." She smirked as she said it. "Including the frog incident."

"I can't believe he told you that." That helped to make me more comfortable. If Nathan trusted her with the frog incident, she had to be good people. I didn't think he would have told anyone about that. "Well, then, I am honored to meet you. Nathan is one of my favorite people on the planet."

I had only seen him a few times since the squad first rescued me. We completed a few missions that had us end up in Soland. Including rescuing Joseph after his alliances with the rebels was uncovered. Nathan had given him asylum in Soland. Nathan had also come to the Nerian tech summit to ask me about offer for David to move here and run the school. Maybe I would finally manage to get some real time to catch up with him while we were here.

"This is Xander Warren he teaches history." Joseph nodded toward a lean man with sun kissed skin and dark eyes that twinkled when he smiled our way.

"It's an honor to meet you." He bowed his head as he said it. "I'm from Neria. You actually saved my niece when you were evacuating the orphanage. She's around here somewhere." He gestured to the hall filled with the chatter of all the kids here.

"It's nice to meet you, Xander." I knew many of these people were from Neria. I was glad he and his niece had managed to get here together.

"I'm Monica." A woman with curly red hair and freckles across her nose and cheeks in a combination that seemed to make her glow. She was close enough that she stuck her hand out, and I shook it. "I teach a few different things, but my main focus is law and government."

I couldn't help but be lifted up by the joy that seemed to radiate from her. As much as I wanted to be wary, I also really wanted to like them. They had said they wanted to give these kids the best chance to succeed, and a lot of these classes seemed like they might be preparing them to grow up to lead if they wanted to.

I couldn't wait to see what the kids managed to do in the future. I knew they'd be better than us. They would truly make the world a better place. Of that, I had no doubt.

40

Vi

I made sure I got to the track early. David and Joseph had given Chase and I some clothes because we hadn't brought much. I wasn't surprised that everything fit perfectly as I jumped a few times, getting used to the new shoes.

I shook out my shoulders and hands and rolled my neck. I took a deep breath, and another, then I felt the focus that normally enveloped me when I'd exercise.

I took a few running steps before launching myself into the air. Every time I landed, I pushed myself into another jump or flip. The world spun as I leapt from the ground time and again. The thrill of the power thrummed through my body.

Finally landing, my feet rooted to the spot, I noticed some of the kids collected on the bleachers just watching me.

"Oh, hey," I called and jogged over to them.

"That was so cool." One of the younger girls squealed.

Chuckling, I winked at her. "I can teach you."

The crowd was starting to grow, and was filled with expectant faces. I backed up a few feet to let them grab seats and rested my hands on my hips, waiting until everyone was settled.

"So..." They were all staring at me with rapt attention. It caught me off guard. "I'm Vi." Why did I say that? I sounded like an idiot. I'm sure they all already knew that. "I don't totally know how to do any of this. So, I figured we'd start with stretching."

There were some grumbles. Apparently, they were expecting something a little more exciting.

Going deeper into the field the kids followed. Each of them picking a place a few feet away from the others. I could tell some of the friend groups as they huddled in their own little orbits.

"When do you think we're going to learn how to take someone down with just a thumb?" one of the boys whispered to his friends, who chuckled in response.

"There are multiple ways you can take someone down with a well-placed jab, but you won't be learning any of that here," I said, looking straight at him and he instantly flushed to a bright pink.

"Whoa, it's real. Do you think she can hear us?" another girl said to her group.

"Yes." I turned to her, and her eyes got as big as saucers. "Keep that in mind when you think about sneaking around after lights out." I wouldn't turn any of them in, but they didn't need to know that. Let them try to figure out ways to get around me.

"Now, stretching before you start any type of exercise will decrease the risk of injury. Mirror what I do."

I guided them through multiple stretches, correcting their form, and answering questions as I meandered through the group. After about fifteen minutes, I called for them to stop.

"All right, now that everyone is warmed up, it's time for a game."

That elicited excited chatter from the kids.

"Break up into two groups. We're going to be playing a game of capture the flag."

A cheer erupted, and they started to break into teams. This was one of the first things Chase had Gwen, Benson, Atty, and I do to get to know each other when they started to train me.

Doug and Lilly had come out as the two captains and were bickering over the next pick. I walked over and gave them each a small cloth—one red, one blue. David had shown me where they kept the sporting equipment earlier. As they started to haggle over who would be in which group, I headed to the bleachers, but Chase caught my eye as he tossed a ball into the air and caught it as he came this way. I met him behind the bleachers, and his grin was nothing but mischief.

"Hello, Professor." He smirked at me, and the heat in his words made me bite my lip.

I ran forward and knocked the ball out of his hands, jumping to catch it, and he caught me around the waist. Spinning in his arms, I couldn't contain my squeal as he tickled me. "I am supposed to be a professional adult, and you are making that incredibly difficult."

He pouted as I pulled myself from his grip.

I reached out and tapped the end of his nose. "Boop."

I spun on my heel, raced out from behind the bleachers, and headed for the kids who were finalizing the teams. When I put my hands on my hips, everyone turned their attention back to me. "All right, it's easy. You want to get the other team's flag before they get yours." I held my arm up. "And go!"

"Remember to try to fortify a defensive position," Chase called out from his seat.

"Where is the end of the game arena? What are the rules?" One of them asked.

"There aren't any. Have fun." I dropped into a seat next to Chase and watched as the game unfolded.

"I'm not sure you're very good at this," Chase whispered to me.

"Probably not, but I'm not the one who suggested I teach." I shrugged. "They'll be fine."

Chaos ensued.

"This seems familiar," Chase said, bumping my shoulder with his.

"I have no idea what I'm doing, so I just stole from the best."

"I am the best, aren't I?"

I barked out a laugh. "And so humble."

The bleachers groaned, and I saw the other teachers joining us.

"Who's on what team?" David asked.

"I have no idea," I called back, and that got a laugh out of the others.

The teachers started to get into the game, jumping up and yelling with near misses. The kids were screaming in excitement, and I couldn't keep the smile off my face. This was what they needed—to just be kids for a while.

Maybe this was what I needed—to see that being carefree really was possible.

I reached out and grabbed David's hand. He had a silly grin on his face. I was pretty sure he knew what I meant with that one touch. That I was so proud of him and what he had built here with Joseph. How it was clear this was his path and how he would impact the world.

If there were anywhere I'd want my child to be if not with us, then it was here. In a place with people to look out for them. For them to grow up around other kids. Where they could get to be a kid.

Doug made an impressive feint to get out of a close call and started to celebrate. He held the flag up and chanted, but Lilly was sneaking up behind him. She pounced and grabbed it out of his hands then raced away. He glared after her before taking chase.

It was nice that I was going to see them grow into themselves here. Where they had enough safety to really figure out who they want to be.

"I wish I would have signed up to teach this," Xander said as he leaned back against the bleacher behind him.

"Too late. I called it. Letting them loose to burn off all their energy is my master plan. I don't have to impart any wisdom, just wear them out. You guys have the hard jobs."

"I have a feeling you'll teach them more than you think," Riley said from my left. She winked at me, and it helped to ease more of the tension.

This felt very similar to when I first met Benson, Atty, and Gwen.

The sneaking suspicion that I could let them in, and I wouldn't regret it. The hope that this might be a friendship blossoming.

Finally, I pulled out the whistle hanging around my neck. Everyone headed for the bleachers, and I pushed myself up and went to meet them.

"Good job, everyone. I saw some great teamwork out there." My hands fell to their comfort position on my hips.

"We won!" someone from Lilly's team yelled.

"You did, but do you know what else you accomplished today?"

"We learned how to communicate and work together," Lilly replied instantly.

I nodded to her, and I could see her stand a bit straighter when I did.

"Lilly is exactly right. The real goal was to be in step with your teammates. Able to pivot and make snap decisions when presented with something unexpected. If you learn to trust those you are with and can effectively communicate, anything is possible." I shrugged. "Plus, it's just kind of fun, right?" A cheer erupted. I jerked my head over my shoulder. "Go on, get out of here. I'll see you guys tomorrow."

Doug had dropped down to lay on the grass while I was talking, and Lilly now stood over him. She stuck out her hand. He blushed before grabbing it, and she pulled him up.

Chase walked up behind me and wrapped his arms around my waist.

"You are good at this." Goosebumps rippled across my neck as his breath mixed with my hair. I leaned back against him.

Maybe I could do this.

Vi

Chase started to pull away, but I grabbed him and held him close.

"I need to talk to you."

He spun me in his arms, so I was facing him, with his goofy half smile on his face. His eyes flickered when he saw my expression. I knew this wasn't going to be pleasant, but I felt it was the right thing to do.

"What is it?" he asked.

I pulled us to the bleachers and sat, cutting off the view of the others heading into the school.

All right, I'd start with the easy part first. "We need to convince Esmerelda I lost the baby."

I could see him thinking of ideas. "We can take fake security footage, just have you showing up across the front line. We could even go back for a while, soon before you start to show…" He paused in thought. "I'm sure David and the kids can figure something out."

I put my hand on his and caught his eyes. "Then, the baby is going to live here. And as far as anyone outside of this school is concerned, they're going to be just another orphan."

I could see him trying to reign in his automatic response. Because

224

of course he wouldn't want to do this. I knew he wouldn't. He would be an amazing father, and I would be taking that away from him, but we *had* to.

"You of all people are saying you want to leave your child?" he snapped. It hurt, but I didn't blame him for it.

"Yes, I am." I sighed and looked to the sky. "I never thought I would be in a position like this. You know that." Tears threatened to fall. "But we have to keep them safe. I would do *anything* to do that. If Esmerelda gets even a rumor this baby lived, they will never be safe. She will stop at nothing to get them. This," my hand went to my stomach, "is the reason she didn't kill me this time. She wants them more than she wants me. We can't let them come into this world with that type of threat hanging over their head."

"We can figure out something." But it was clear he was losing his confidence.

It broke my heart to watch him accept that I was right. They could have a childhood here, which they couldn't have with us.

"We could just stay in hiding. We don't have to go back," he tried, but I shook my head.

"I won't be able to live with myself if I run now." I paused for a moment. "You wouldn't be able to either."

Eventually, he grabbed my thigh and pulled me to him on the bench. I wrapped my arms around him as he laid his head on my chest. He held me tightly, and I ran my fingers through his hair and kissed the top of his head.

"We'll just have to end the war as fast as we can," I whispered, but I worried how long it would really take. Would we blink and years would have passed? Would we miss everything in our child's life?

Would I even make it to the end? I couldn't even think about Chase. I would not imagine a world where he wouldn't be there. I didn't know what I would do if I ever lost him.

"Joseph said we can trust everyone here. He said they would take anything that happens here to the grave," he said finally.

"Good, because they'll be some of the only people who know who our baby is."

Chase grabbed my hands and started to twist his fingers with mine. He pulled our clasped hands to his lips and kissed my knuckles. "Why can't we just have a normal life?"

I could practically feel both of our hearts breaking. I had asked myself the same thing so many times I'd lost count.

"You deserve better," I muttered, but he gave me a fierce look.

"*We* deserve better." He reached up and wiped away a tear that was slipping down my cheek. "We didn't deserve any of this." He sighed. "And *that* is why we have to do this—because no one deserves it. Esmerelda must be stopped, and we're going to be the people to stop her."

"It won't be forever." I prayed that was the truth.

David had told us to meet him in the dining hall once it was lights out for the kids. Joseph and Monica were caught up in a conversation, but David noticed us. He held up a bottle to wave us over, and I rolled my eyes. It must be adult-bonding time.

"Oh, Vi, I have something for you," Joseph said when he saw me. He pulled a stoppered beaker from the white lab coat he was still wearing. It contained a thick purple liquid.

I quirked an eyebrow at him. "What does this one do?"

Joseph was the only person who could hand me strange liquids and I would do what he said with them.

"This is a good one." He held it out to me.

I popped the stopper out and sniffed. It smelled like lavender. Well, it seemed pleasant enough.

"Go on take a sip."

I held it to my mouth, but he held out his hands to stop me.

"Maybe sit first. I haven't tested this yet."

It was such a Davidism that it made my heart swell. They really had rubbed off on each other here.

"Okay, safe now?" I asked, my tone full of sarcasm as I sat.

"Yes, safe enough."

Since it was just us, I asked him quietly if it was safe for the baby.

"Like I would give you anything that wasn't. All the ingredients are harmless."

I rolled my eyes and tipped my head back. The liquid tasted sweet and warm. It reminded me of a summer's day, lying in the sun.

The weight I normally carried, the tension, the anxiety, seemed to completely vanish. I had never felt so relaxed. I gasped at the relief, which ended in a hiccup.

"What was that?" I asked, still trying to understand what this feeling was, looking at my hands like they might not be the same ones I was used to.

"I decided to make something to help you relax. I know you aren't used to taking care of yourself, so this should help if you feel overwhelmed you can take it."

So, this was something that might be able to snap me out midspiral. Something to let me take a deep breath. My hand went to my chest out of habit. Normally, I felt like if I just put some pressure on my chest, it might not ache so badly, but now, that hole inside me was gone.

I sat with the feeling, trying to memorize it, trying to come up with words as to how it felt so I could try to conjure it again later. To make sure I knew this was real, that I could really feel this way. My eyes watered as I reached across the table to grab his hand in thanks.

As the others came in, I could already tell the feeling was slipping away and the normal tightness of my muscles was returning, but a calm still resided in my chest. Chase grasped my hand in his. Now that I knew that feeling existed within me, I would search for ways to find it again.

David started to fill some glasses from the bottles and handed them out. "I thought we could use some time away from the kids. So, Vi, Chase, we'd like to officially welcome you to the faculty."

Everyone held up their glasses, and I shrugged and pulled the topper of my beaker. We cheered and all clinked our glasses together. I took another sip, and my eyes fluttered shut as the wave of bliss rolled through me. The weightlessness instinctively had me taking a deep breath. I set the beaker down on the table and grinned to myself as I put the stopper back in.

Bliss in a bottle.

"Um, Xander, Monica, Riley, there are also some things we need to discuss with you." David's tone turned somber. "You know Vi and Chase will be staying here for a while. We trust all of you implicitly, but with them being here, we need to take some security precautions. No one besides the people here at the school can know either of them are here."

"I'm pregnant," I blurted out, which got a round of surprised faces. "No one can know. You'll be some of the only people who know the baby lived." I took a deep breath and closed my eyes, not wanting to watch anyone as I said it. "I'm trusting you all with the most important secret of my life."

They nodded in response.

"Once the baby is born, they're going to live here at the school as just another war orphan. I know this is a lot, but I trust all of you with this information. This is the safest place for them to be. Does anyone have any issues with that?"

Monica reached out and took my hand, her eyes soft. "We're here for the kids. *All* of the kids. We would do anything for them."

Xander had his arms crossed but was nodding. "Not a bad plan."

Well, that was a relief. Their reactions were just another reason I felt I could place my trust in them.

Riley held up her glass. "Congratulations, you two."

Everyone leaned in to cheers again, and the rest of the night passed in a calm haze as they caught us up on some of the crazy things the kids had done so far.

David snuck over to me. "Didn't need my help, then?"

I knew he was talking about convincing Chase.

"No." I placed my hands possessively over my belly because, even though I knew it was the right choice, it was ripping me to pieces inside.

Vi

The spring warmed into summer as we got comfortable in our new normal. We video called with the others to update them up on what was going on with us. David had come up with an encryption for us to use for all communication.

My breath still caught, thinking of the tears my father tried to hold back when he found out our decision. He promised we'd have a heart to heart when we saw each other next. Thea was thrilled she was going to have a niece or nephew. Everyone knew the importance of keeping this secret. If we made any mistakes, the baby would be in danger. Gwen and Benson had given us words of encouragement and said they'd see us as soon as they could.

The kids loved Chase's classes. Many of them, I was sure, just loved Chase. I had to say, the role of teacher fit him well. If we hadn't been living in this time, I could see how this might have been his life. He was patient and caring. He worked with each child to help them in the ways that they needed.

I was standing in the hallway, peeking in through the open door, and I couldn't help but bite my lip at the sight. As much as my heart sung to see him in his element, it twisted knowing we wouldn't be able to give this to our own child. If he had loved anyone but me, he could have had this. While my mind tore itself down, I couldn't help but hear his calm voice in my mind.

This was my choice, and I would always choose you.

I had to stop beating myself up for choices that weren't even mine. He knew what I was, and he accepted me and all that entailed.

It was getting easier to let the voices of my friends drown out my own demons.

Maybe this was what healing felt like.

The kids started to flow out of the room as Chase finished with his class. They waved to me as they passed me in the hallway. Lilly held out her hand, and I gave her a high five as she went by.

Chase was organizing some of the maps he had been using when I slipped into the room. He turned and leaned against the table he had been cleaning. Crossing his arms over his chest, his eyes swept over me and the small bump I was showing now. He licked his lips and moved to me, but I beat him to it. Speeding to him, I pressed myself into the hard lines of him and twisted my arms around his neck.

A throaty chuckle escaped him before he lowered his lips to mine.

The hairs on the back of my neck stood on edge. I snapped my head toward the windows that lined the interior courtyard. There was some type of grinding and then the screams of the kids echoing from outside.

Chase heard it now too, but I was already at the window, throwing it open and jumping through. There was a group of kids huddled together, gasping and pointing at the roof.

One of the kids must have gotten up there, and the railing they had been perched against had broken. They were hanging stories above the ground with a handhold on the crumbling gutter.

On instinct, I was already racing toward the commotion. As I reached the back of the group that had gathered, I launched myself and soared over them.

"I'm coming. Hold on," I yelled. I could hear their cries from above. Pushing off as hard as I could, I jumped up the building. The edges of the roof were sloped, so I got as close as I could and searched for something to anchor myself to. The boy's wide eyes met mine as I leaned over far enough to reach for him.

He was too far away though. I saw that a section to his right seemed to be slightly sturdier. It was my best option. I let go and slid down the curve of the roof. Bracing myself I wrapped my left arm around him and pulled him to me. His arms instantly clung to me, and he buried his head in my chest.

The metal groaned and snapped. Before I could stop either of us, we both went hurtling toward the ground. I curled around him as we fell. The impact pushed all the air from my lungs, stars swimming in my vision as my head snapped back into the ground.

The first intake of breath was painful, but it was something. I pushed myself up on one elbow and saw the boy being hauled up. He seemed unscathed overall. Good.

The crowd parted as Chase and Xander made their way through. Xander went to the boy, and Chase came to me.

"Is he okay?" I wheezed.

"Yeah, he's going to be fine. Are you okay?" Chase asked.

I moved a bit. There were some flares of pain, but nothing that wouldn't be fine in a few minutes. "Yeah, I'm okay."

He held out a hand, and as soon as I took it, he helped me to my feet.

A cheer went up through the kids now that it clear we'd both be fine. I went to the boy and put my hands on his shoulders, twisting him around to look him over.

"You're sure you are okay?" I asked him. He couldn't have been more than eight.

"Why don't we all go see Joseph," Chase said. Xander took the boy's hand, and I followed them into the building. Lilly ran up to catch up to me, a worried expression on her face.

"Hey, can you see how he got up there?" I asked her. "We're

going to want close off those exits, and I'll go up there soon and see about getting all of that fixed."

"We'll get the kids back on schedule and keep an eye on them."

"Thanks, Lilly."

She turned and ran off to the others. I saw them organizing at her instruction, and pride spread through me. Out of habit, I rolled my neck and shoulders, stretching my arms above my head to loosen them.

"What's all this?" Joseph asked as we entered.

"There was a little mishap. We just want to get Jimmy and Vi checked out. They had a bit of a fall," Chase said.

Joseph gave me a look. "What constitutes as a little mishap?"

I held my hands out in surrender. "I was just there to help."

Jimmy was staring dejectedly at his shoes. I walked to him and squatted down so I could be on his level.

"Just a small fall," I told Joseph, but in a whisper to the boy, "Stay off the roof from here on out." I winked, and he seemed to feel better.

Joseph shook his head with a crooked smile. "Hazel, can you take Jimmy and give him a checkup please."

One of the girls learning medicine from Joseph collected him and took the boy to the other side of the lab.

"Come here. I've been meaning to get you in here anyway," Joseph told me and pointed to an upholstered doctor's chair. Nathan had it sent over, along with all the equipment Joseph could ever need to help me until and with the birth.

Nathan had been ecstatic at the news we were pregnant, and I know he felt for us having to leave them here, but he also understood why. That was something about my friendship with Nathan. He understood parts of me without question because they lived in him too. The choices that had to be made for the good of our people. The burden of a duty we'd been born with.

The school already would have wanted for nothing, but I knew Nathan would make this the best place my baby could grow up in.

He had started talking about the field trips he was going to plan for the kids within Soland. I knew they would love it. I couldn't believe the beauty of Soland when I first came here as a child. I would spend hours in the art museums. Then, you'd leave there only to see the cities themselves dripping with precious metals and meticulously planned gardens. The schools were some of the best on the continent. Soland was known for its resources, which also included some of the smartest scientists and most creative artists on the planet. It ran at a slower pace than Kabria and Neria. The people here spent their time imagining, creating, and learning. Whereas, Neria was technology based, and Kabria was known for its agriculture.

I had always daydreamed of all of three of the countries coming together. Becoming one and sharing everything we had with all the people. Not having to negotiate trade arraignments that could delay a grain shipment to a hungry people. Or having to haggle more lumber for machine parts when someone got upset over a noble's offhanded comment in the media. To finally stop the infighting between our countries and just coexist.

Joseph opened one of my eyes wide and flashed a penlight in front of me. He ran a few other tests before he stopped hovering.

"Everything is normal. Lie back." He pushed my shoulder lightly.

I leaned back and pulled my tank top up a few inches to give him room. He ran the scanner over my belly, and the images appeared on a large screen over his desk.

The fast little heartbeat started to pulse through the speakers. Chase finally took a deep breath as soon as he heard it. His hand rested on my shoulder, and I bumped his arm with my temple, but we both kept watching the screen.

As Joseph moved the scanner around, he grinned. "Do you guys want to know the gender?"

Seeing the excited look on Chase's face made up my mind. He wanted to know. So, I did too.

"It's a girl," he said happily.

Chase wrapped himself around me from behind, burying his face in my neck. "It's a girl," he whispered, and I could feel his grin against my skin.

"It's a girl," I echoed.

A perfect, brilliant little girl.

43

ESMERELDA

I threw the folder across the room with a scream of frustration.

"Where is she?" I roared.

Cecily, Jessie, and a few others were circled around the other side of my desk, bringing me nothing of use yet again. Howard was watching the commotion from the corner.

"She was just in Longdale. How did you not manage to get to her in time? How does she keep slipping through your fingers? What use are you?" I was seething. For the last few months, Genevieve had been popping up on video, but every time I sent people for her, she would vanish. Like she was playing some game of cat and mouse.

From the videos, it seemed that she had lost the baby, which was a shame because that meant I couldn't get more stem cells even if we got her back. Although, I was honestly surprised the fetus had lasted as long as it did.

Now, I was stuck waiting for more stem cells. Apparently, Jessie was unable to carry a child, and I wouldn't waste Cecily. Not yet. If she kept failing me, maybe I'd rethink my decision. At least Jessie's conditioning was back in place. I hadn't had problems with her after a few dedicated weeks of the doctors working with her, but everything else was falling apart.

The children's survival rate was even lower than adults. They were unable to handle the changes. We've been trying different ages, but so far, only two had lasted to phase two.

So, we've continued testing on adults, but we've focused those down to only women. They only needed to survive. We wouldn't use them as weapons. Getting the stems cells were my top priority.

The brat destroying that facility had set me back years.

One of the leaders of my elite force started to stammer, but I threw a hand up to stop him.

"Just get out of my face. Next time I see you, bring me good news, or I can find someone else who will." My heartbeat pounded through my veins, my head pulsing in pain with it. Howard motioned for the girls to leave, but he stayed. He grabbed one of the shots from the drawer of my desk and pierced my neck with it. Cold slipped through me and helped against the nausea that had been starting.

I hissed as the pain in my leg didn't calm. Howard leaned against the desk and watched as I rubbed at the limb.

"Es," he said finally, and I glared up at him. He was the only person who knew or would dare to use that name for me. "It's time; we must replace it. If it shatters or splinters, there's going to be more damage I'll have to repair. You know we can't wait any longer. The stem cells are gone. We won't have anything in time."

I grinded my teeth, but he was right. The pain was daily. The shots weren't doing anything for it anymore. Yet another piece of me would be gone, replaced by metal. I raised my hands in front of me, turning them, thinking of the fact that no bones resided within them any longer.

We had no idea how much longer my organs would last. Howard had to pivot most of his research to try to come up with replacements before they failed. My vision was already deteriorating, forcing me to start manufacturing the multiple types implants we still had blueprints for from Neria.

I had made changes to the eye implants to remove the obvious neon blue that was common for Nerian devices. No one could know they had been replaced if it got to that. I wouldn't let anyone know this weakness that lived inside me.

He sighed and put his hand on my shoulder before turning to leave as well.

I would conquer this; my body would not be my tomb. I would find an elixir not just to cure me, but I would defeat death itself.

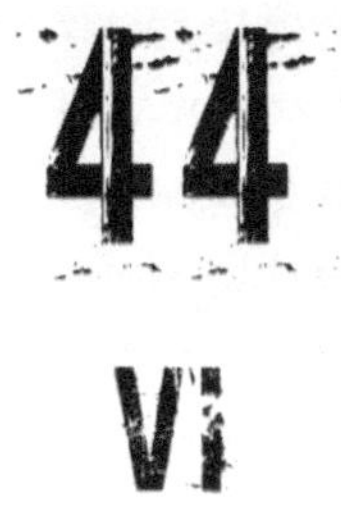

Vi

2 months later...

Everyone had gathered in the interior courtyard for the day. The air had just enough chill that a light jacket was all one needed. I looked out toward the sports field, where the wood was already stacked for the bonfire we were having tonight. Today was the solstice, and we had decided to make it an all-out event.

During the day, the kids had been broken up into small groups for a challenge. Each team was given a kingdom wide crisis event. The goal was for each team to figure out how best to proceed, as if they were in positions of power. As the teams came up to each teacher, they would have to analyze a part of their event that lined up with that teacher's classes.

So, Xander provided historical details up to that certain event. The students discussed how that information would impact or influence their decision.

Chase provided the teams with the current strategic situation at the time. The events ranged from natural disasters to military attacks, even climate change like acid rain. Then, the students had to figure out how that informed their decisions on their next steps.

David shared what type of weaponry, machinery, or technology was at their disposal. They had to decide what was used, how it was used, and how to deploy it where they needed.

Riley gave examples of art created from multiple perspectives—rich, poor, native, or invading. They explained how the art could be analyzed to understand who they were working with or against.

Joseph advised on the types of diseases or wounds that impacted the people and the type of medicine they had access to, depending on the type of event. They then had to decide the best way to manage their assets to deploy the treatments.

Monica dealt with politics and diplomacy and how the students needed to work with others to try to implement their decided course of action.

I wasn't involved in any of that. I had been working with the kids for a few weeks on a top-secret project, which we would reveal at the bonfire tonight. So, I got to sit back and watch the events unfolding.

Their comprehension, problem solving, and creativity impressed me. It was clear we had future leaders here. Not just that they could do it, but also that they wanted to. They wanted to make the world a better place because they had seen how terrible it could be. I was so proud I felt like I might burst.

"Okay, okay, everyone," Joseph said as the kids started to circle around him. "Quiet down. I just want to say I am blown away with what you accomplished today. You all have proven how you can learn to adapt to tough scenarios and know when it's time to ask if what decision you are making is the right one for the people. You all did an amazing job, and I want you to remember that you can do whatever you put your mind to. If you keep empathy and compassion as your guiding light when you make those decisions, you'll be on the right path.

"Now, I know it's been a long day, so the barbecue is ready. Go ahead and grab some food while it's hot." He waved his hands toward where the food had been set up, and some kids raced to get there first.

He shook his head with a chuckle, and I made my way across the courtyard to him and the others.

"So, slacker, what is your top-secret project?" David asked me.

"You'll find out when we light the bonfire. I can't give away the surprise." I winked. I hadn't even told Chase. The kids had been having a blast practicing, and we had even moved our classes farther out from the school so no one could spy on us.

Riley clapped my shoulder as she passed me and gave me a look that said she couldn't wait to find out. Monica skipped to catch up, and the two of them headed for the meat, potatoes, and all the sides one could imagine. That was just dinner. There was also a table piled with deserts. Everything smelled amazing and was making my mouth water. Theo had really outdone himself today. He had been prepping for this the entire week.

Chase grabbed my hand as he was passing me. He tugged and twirled me in a circle before grabbing me for a kiss, his hand slipping to my growing belly as he did.

"I'm sure it's going to be wonderful," he whispered against my lips.

"Either wonderful or it's going to go terribly wrong." But I shook my head with a smirk as I said it. "They're going to do great; they've been working really hard."

As we approached the table, I cradled my stomach. "Well, kiddo, what are you craving today?" It all looked amazing, so I just started to grab a bit of everything. And then, I saw the pickles. I grabbed a few, went to move on but decided to grab just a couple more, and before I walked away, maybe just one more. They sounded absolutely amazing at the moment, and I couldn't wait to dive in, so I took a quick bite while I finished grabbing more to eat.

Most of the kids were sprawled around in the grass, enjoying the sun, so I made my way toward the bleachers, which seemed like a popular decision as the other teachers were there or coming this way.

Monica moaned. "This is so good, Theo," she said around a mouthful of something.

He had taken a seat with his own plate at the bleachers as well. He beamed at the compliment.

Riley was leaning back on her elbows, watching everyone. Today, her normally golden lined makeup was a bit more intricate, with entwining white lines too. I was always so envious of how together Riley seemed. So calm and content. I felt like the opposite, with my feelings swirling around me and no control of when they came or went. She had been starting to work with me on meditation. I was not any good at it, but I was trying.

Monica reminded me so much of Gwen and Thea. She was always so upbeat and excited about everything. Her curly hair made it seem like it might bounce her away. There had been multiple girl nights with them since I arrived, and I enjoyed every second of them.

There was always a flicker of sadness when I realized it reminded me so much of our squad's apartment in Neria. It reminded me of Atty's laugh, us hanging out reading together, that stupid beanie.

It reminded me that I hadn't seen Thea, Gwen, or Benson in person in months. And I wanted so badly to share these moments with them too.

Eventually, all of us were stuffed and I was laid out on the bench, watching the clouds sweep across the sky and listening to the chatter from the kids. Chase was sitting a step up from me, close enough I could nuzzle into his legs. The summer was ending, and this was a perfect way to send it off. Fall was officially here.

I had been tracking the sun, knowing we wanted to get started just soon enough before the sunset to finish right before it got dark. It was almost time.

I swung myself up and jumped down to go find Doug and Lilly. When they saw me, they started getting all the kids moving. A small group worked to wrangle up the younger kids and steer them to the bleachers. I made my way to the giant pile of wood that would be the bonfire.

A boy named Billy had managed to set up a sound system

outside. He was one of the boys who worked with David often on his gadgets.

"All you have to do is hit play." He held a device out to me.

"Thank you. Go on, get out there."

The kids were collecting around the bonfire. It was time. I turned to everyone on the bleachers.

"Happy solstice, everybody," I said while some of the younger kids clapped, excited for whatever was about to happen. "Everyone here," I gestured to all those gathered behind me, "has been working very hard, and they have been doing an amazing job. So enough of me, let's let them show you."

I clicked the play button and jogged off the field. Music with a heavy beat blasted from the speakers. The whole group started to move to from a pattern before the first words rang out and they broke into a choreographed dance.

It was absolute joy; they were so into it. And they all remembered the moves. I felt giddy just seeing how much they enjoyed themselves. A small group broke away from the others, and the four of them began tumbling passes, flipping across the front line of dancers.

The audience erupted with whistles and clapping. The song was coming to a close, but before the end, two people moved into place behind the wood. They were lighting the starters. The wood caught fire at the same time as the last pose.

As soon as they ended, I raced out to them, throwing out high fives and getting pulled into hugs.

"That was awesome! Jenny, you hit that mark perfectly. Dan," I pointed to him, "I saw you. You hit every single move. Great job. Seriously, it was amazing."

Someone clapped behind us. I turned back to the bleachers out of curiosity because that clap was the only thing I heard. Some of the kids gasped when they saw who was standing there.

"Nathan!" I ran over to him. I didn't know if I was supposed to follow some kind of decorum. He was the king here, but I didn't care. He was just my buddy, and I hadn't seen him in ages.

He wrapped me in a hug, his grip so much firmer than before. He had put on some muscle since I'd seen him last.

"I thought today might be a good day for me to come by." He winced. "I meant to be here earlier, but you know how it is. I couldn't get away."

"You could always just run away," I joked. "How are you even here though?"

"You're not the only one who can keep a secret," Chase said, coming up from behind me. He wrapped one arm around me and held the other out to Nathan to shake. "Good to see you, man."

I twisted and hit Chase's cheek with an exaggerated smooch.

"Well, it was a wonderful surprise." I turned to the kids and bumped Chase out of the way. "Kids, if you don't know this is Nathan Ketler, King of Soland and our benefactor here."

We spent the next hour or so going around so everyone had a chance to talk to him. Eventually, we ended up seated around the bonfire and the kids were peppering Nathan with questions about being king.

"I heard about how well you all did today with your exercise," Nathan said to them. "Being in charge isn't about the power. If you are a leader, you are a servant. Everything you do needs to be to try to better the world for your people. Leaders like the Ravensbones wanted power over peace. They have never once thought of what would be best for their people but what is best for themselves. That's why the resistance in Neria and Kabria is so important. If you see something bad happening and you do nothing, you are implicit in that wrongdoing. That's true in all facets of life. Stand up when you see people being bullied or being taken advantage of. Even the planet needs your protection. This world is our home, after all, and we only have one. That's why I'm so proud of all of you and especially thankful to your teachers."

"Miss Vi says that too," one of the younger girls piped up.

"And Miss Vi is very wise," he said, winking at me.

It had happened on accident, but a sort of ethics class had

emerged from a seemingly normal conversation we had after dinner one night. Now, the kids always circled around and we'd talk about what it meant when you had power and how to make sure you were using it for the right reasons. I showed them how twisted Esmerelda and her father were in the way they used their own power. I was excited that they could also learn from Nathan.

So, we sat there, two royals passing along everything we had learned and conveying to them how fulfilling a life of service could really be.

VI

The sky was filled with stars once we all met back up at the bleachers. Apparently, us old people had been given the seating. The speakers were playing something that had the kids dancing around the bonfire.

"We get you for an entire night? You don't have to go rush off to some emergency council meeting?" I asked Nathan. I had grown up in a palace, so I had an idea of how hard this would have been to pull off.

"Only two people know I'm here, and neither of them would tell anyone. Just my aide back at the palace and my driver. Everything else can wait until I return."

"I'm so happy I won't have to worry about meetings and sneaking away." It slipped out before I even thought about it.

"Why wouldn't you?" he asked.

Everyone assumed I would take over when we beat Esmerelda. My father wasn't going to; he said the people wouldn't trust him. I had support of the military, of the citizens, even of the Nerians. Everyone told me it was my job when this was over. That I would become queen as soon as we won.

No one had listened when I said it was not what I wanted. And Neria, as it turned out, was my answer.

"If I'm standing when this is all over, I'm not taking control. I'm not going to be queen." This wasn't a surprise to Chase, and I knew David had an idea I might make a decision like this.

"What are you going to do? Who are you going to pick? Someone needs to take over from Esmerelda." For just the smallest moment I saw a flicker of jealousy in Nathan's eyes.

"I'm not going to pick anyone. We're going to set up an election. The people are going to have a say in their government from now on. We all saw how the elections worked for Neria, and it is reproducible. I'm going to ask Naya and Jupiter to help facilitate when it's time." I wouldn't let myself think of the what ifs on who might still be around or how long it would take to end this war.

"What would you do if you just had a regular life?" His voice was wistful.

"I want a space of my own. I want to have a garden. Maybe I'd take up painting or sculpting or something creative. I just want to feel at peace."

Ever since Esmerelda had me the first time, I had daydreamed of a life of digging into the soil, the sun shining down on me, with only the sound of the wind through the trees.

I thought of being surrounded by my friends, not having to rush off to another deadly situation. Being here was helping me realize what I wanted out of my life. Days spent curled up on a mattress and watching the rain pour down. The chaos and joy of the kids here.

I had thought the world was a terrible place. It was all I had known for so long, but I was so wrong. There were days I might be drowning in my despair, but then it was followed by days like today, where everything was so much better than I could have ever dreamed.

I turned to him. "Are you happy?"

"Me? Oh, you know I complain, but it is one of the most fulfilling things I've ever experienced. It's what I was born for." He chuckled.

"I got it from dad. He really was amazing. I still don't think I can ever fill his shoes, but every day, I do my best. To him, the duty of the king was to do the best for everyone in his kingdom. To provide for them, protect them, listen to them. It's not my kingdom; it's theirs."

"I don't deserve to rule. I'm nothing more than this." I held my arm out and clenched my fist before releasing it and staring at my palm. "After what I've done, I cannot lead them into the new world. I am a product of what we're leaving behind, and I will stay in the past. The people deserve to have a say in the decisions that impact their lives. Let them vote. This horrible chapter can be over, and everyone can move on."

"Have you told your dad this?" David asked as he poked his head over.

"I will." I left it at that. I had no idea when I'd manage to actually have this talk with him, but I wouldn't be swayed. It was the right thing to do.

I looked down, and my hands automatically wrapped around my stomach. I thought about the little house with a garden and Chase and I running around after a little girl in the yard. Just a normal life. Was that even a possibility for us? I had to admit, I daydreamed about it all the time now. Of a time when we could all be together.

"I know I've said it before, but since I'm seeing you in person, congratulations," Nathan said.

"Thanks. For everything." And I meant *everything*. He was always providing us as much support as he could in secret. He obtained this place for the school, filled it with amazing people, and gave them all the support they could ever need.

"I will protect her with everything I have. I promise you. She'll be safe."

My throat caught, and a tear escaped. I wiped at it quickly. "I know you will. I know all of you will. I'll never be able to pay you back."

My friends were some of the most loyal people I'd ever met, and I knew they would protect her like she was their own.

"Good thing I don't need nor want you to pay me back." He stuck out his pinky and wrapped my own around it. Like when we were children, the pinky promise was forever binding.

Riley came over and popped down next to Nathan, which brought the rest of the group in closer. They both made silly faces at each other the moment their eyes locked.

"Ah, so you are as weird as him." I giggled at Riley. It was such a change from her normal measured appearance. It was like I was seeing back in time to when they were in school.

"Our weird just fits." She laughed. "Been like this since the day I met him."

"Has she made you meditate?" he asked me. I knew he understood the struggle of never being able to turn my brain off for a minute by his tone.

"I'm so bad at it," I muttered.

"You are pretty bad," Riley added. "But so is he. Must be a royal thing. You're all too high strung for me."

"Ah, born to be royal and gifted with crippling anxiety and the fear of failing." Sarcasm was thick in my voice.

"But the food's good, so I'll take it." Nathan chuckled.

"I heard you told Riley about the frog incident." A sly smirk spread across my face.

This caught the attention of the others, and they leaned in.

"What's the frog incident?" Monica asked.

I shot Nathan a questioning glance, not sure if he was going to say, but he rolled his eyes and gave in.

"This one," he threw a thumb over his shoulder at me, "decided to attack me with absolutely no provocation. She hid under the dining table and managed to get a frog to hop up my pant leg. I screamed bloody murder when I got up and it wouldn't hop back out."

"You got me grounded. I was completely within my rights," I replied.

"You were the one who had the bright idea to have a sword fight in the room with the crystal dishware," he jibed.

"You deserved what you got." I crossed my arms over my chest before we both dissolved into laughter.

"Where were you during this?" Xander asked Chase and David. They both put up their hands in surrender.

"We had nothing to do with that," David said innocently.

"You guys helped me catch the frogs, you liars," I said, glaring at him.

"We didn't know what you would do with said frogs," Chase countered.

I glared at him. "Mhmm, sure."

Nathan gave a mock hurt look to the boys. "Traitors."

As the night wore on, we eventually sent all the kids back to their rooms. We spent the rest of the night just hanging out. I felt like Nathan was enjoying this small chance to be normal. We learned about his years in school with Riley. Xander told us more about his life in Neria. Monica told us about her life in public relations in Neria, where she had dealt with many diplomats and was privy to many secrets of the elite. It was what had prompted her to teach politics and diplomacy to the students.

As the sky started to lighten, we all gasped at the time.

"Luckily, I'm not driving," Nathan joked through a yawn as we walked him to the front doors of the school. Everyone hugged him goodbye, but he grabbed my hand, and I followed him outside. He pulled me in for a hug, and I melted into him. "It was good to see you. And she'll be one of the safest kids on the planet. I'll worry about her, and you can worry about ending the war so you can come home."

I pinched his cheek and smiled up at him. "You are a saint, Nathan Ketler. Now, off you go before you fall asleep on your feet."

I held his other hand until our arms were taught between us and our fingers slipped apart as he headed for the car. He gave me a quick look over his shoulder, winked, and then slipped into the waiting open door.

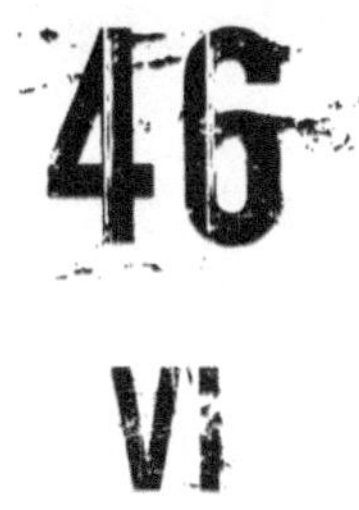

Vi

1 month later...

I worked to knot David's gray tie. It was sharp against his navy suit. I could tell he was nervous but also excited, and I beamed with pride as I looked him over. His gaze caught in the mirror, and he started to tug the tie one way and then the other. I placed a hand over his to quiet is nervous fidgeting.

"It's perfect," I told him, but his eyes slid back to the mirror, analyzing everything. Taking his hands in mine I pulled him away so he couldn't see his reflection any longer.

"I know. I know it is. I'm just..." He paused. "I'm just so nervous."

"Because you can't wait for the rest of your life."

He sighed, and that beautiful smile of his finally came out. "Yeah," he said dreamily.

"You two are so cute I might just die," I joked.

There was a knock at the door, and I opened it a crack in case it was Joseph.

But it was Chase. "Time to switch."

I swung the door open and let him inside. I leaned against his side, and we both took in the sight of our best friend on the happiest day of his life.

David pulled us both in for a hug. "I'm so happy you both are here."

"Nothing would have kept us from it," I said, ignoring the multiple times I almost didn't make it to this day due to dancing on death's doorstep. As we broke apart, I rose up and gave David a quick kiss on the cheek. "Okay, I'll see you down there."

Before I slipped out the door, I turned back and gave him a wink. The door clicked quietly shut behind me, and I headed down the stairs, past the main floor, to Joseph's lab. As I entered, I could see him in the mirror tugging uncomfortably at his own tie. His suit was the same color as David's tie, and his tie was the same color as David's suit.

Crossing to him, I placed my hand over his just like I had done to David. "You look amazing. You're going to take his breath away, I promise."

He smirked at me. "I know. I am gorgeous in this suit."

"That you are."

"You didn't need to come check on me," he said, but I cocked an eyebrow at him.

"Joseph, you're family," I said firmly, and I could see how that had an effect on him. "This might make it official, but you've had a place in our hearts and our family since we met you. I'm so happy you two found each other. I've known David a long time, and there has never been anyone in his life like you. The way you love him, you bring out the best in him. You've changed his life for the better."

Joseph took a deep breath and pulled me in for a hug. "That means a lot. Thank you. He brings out the best in me too."

I straightened his tie for him. "Are you ready?"

He took another deep breath. "Yeah, I am."

We left his office, making our way to the courtyard. The kids had insisted they take care of everything. They had set up the decorations and all the seating. In the great hall, they had set up everything for the reception too.

As we pushed through the doors, my breath caught in my throat and Joseph squeezed my arm. I saw tears brimming in his eyes. It was beautiful, and it meant so much knowing how hard everyone had worked on it.

There were flowers everywhere. Wrapped around an arch that was 3D printed by some of the students in David's shop, wrapped into garlands draped on the exterior of the school. Petals had been scattered across the ground and up the aisle. White chairs were lined in rows, enough for the students and our friends.

I saw many of the kids we had met in Neria, including Doug and Lilly, circled around Gwen, Thea, Benson, and Anthony. The kids were getting to know Anthony, as he hadn't been with us in Neria.

Benson and Anthony were in smart black suits. Gwen was gorgeous in a blue shimmering gown that dropped low across her back. Thea was in a short pink dress that was tight at the waist with the skirt flared out coming to her mid-thigh.

She gasped and clapped her hands together as she saw us. Gwen's face broke out in a beaming smile, and Benson nodded in approval as they noticed us as well.

"Glad you all could make it," Joseph told them.

"We wouldn't miss this for the world," Gwen said excitedly.

Benson and Joseph clasped forearms, but Benson tugged him in for a hug and gave him a few firm pats on the back.

I heard the footsteps of Chase and David making their way through the building and grabbed Joseph once more. I tugged him back toward the doors, positioned him, and then stepped behind to cover his eyes.

"Are you ready?" I leaned into whisper to him.

Chase opened the door but had David's eyes covered too. The crowd had all shifted to turn our way, everyone wanting to see that first between them.

Chase and I shared our own glance, each of us bubbling with excitement for our friends. In sync, we both pulled our hands away. I had the perfect view to see David's eyes and smile widen at the sight. It reminded me of when I first saw Chase at our wedding. With the pride on Chase's face, I can only assume Joseph's reaction mirrored David's. After a moment of just taking each other in, they crossed the distance. Chase came to me to give them a few moments to themselves.

"They're so cute," I said to him as I took his arm and we made our way to the crowd milling around the seating.

"Gods, isn't this great? I'm so happy for them." He leaned in to give me a peck on the cheek.

"It really is," I agreed.

Monica, Xander, Riley, Theo, and our squad made their way to us. Riley was in a billowing outfit of gem tones, her dreadlocks wrapped in more gold than usual and her gold and teal lines of makeup making her eyes pop. Xander had on a cream suit that made his skin seem to glow. Monica wore a shimmering green gown that hugged her body. Theo was in a white shirt with tan pants that may have had a dusting of flour across his right side.

My own dress was a lightweight fabric in a dark teal that was comfortable on my ever-growing baby bump, with a slit that started at my thigh. Monica and Riley had helped me pick it out.

I took another moment to ogle Chase, who was handsome as ever in a maroon suit that complimented my dress. Tailored to him perfectly, it showed off how toned he was underneath. It was everything I could do just to keep my hands off him. He caught me staring and quirked an eyebrow up, with the twist of his mouth in the slightest hint of a smirk. There was hunger in his eyes as he stared right back. He put a hand on my belly and kissed me again. Heat rushed through me all the way down to my toes.

"I can't wait to get you out of that dress," he whispered to me.

"You guys are the worst," Thea complained with a groan as she reached us, which made both of us chuckle.

"You look beautiful, sis," Chase told her.

She grinned and twirled the skirt back and forth. "Thanks. You don't look so bad

yourself." She jabbed him with her elbow.

David and Joseph were headed our way, their hands clasped together.

"Is it time?" I asked them.

"Yes, let's do this. I don't know if I can wait another second," David said and that had Joseph giving him a loving expression.

Riley gestured to the kids that it was time. Everyone else exchanged excited last words before heading to their seats. There was a row of students who were lined up at the front of the seating off to the side of the arch.

Chase wrapped his arm through David's, and I did the same to Joseph. It was time. Joseph squeezed my arm but didn't take his eyes off of David's back. David peeked over his shoulder and winked to him as the row of students started to sing. They had been practicing for weeks for this moment. They sounded like a chorus of angels.

Everyone turned in their seats as Chase and David started to walk down the aisle. We let them take a few steps before Joseph and I followed. I had broken down in happy tears when Joseph asked if I would give him away. It was one of the highest honors of my entire life.

As we reached the arch, where Riley waited ready to officiate, Joseph turned to me and I placed kisses on each of his cheeks before I moved to stand a few steps to his side. Joseph's gaze instantly went to David, who beamed at him.

As the song ended, the entire crowd hushed and Riley held up her arms.

"We're here today to celebrate the union of these two. A Kabrian and a Nerian being united here in Soland shows that there is a way past these borders when it comes to love. We come to share in the bond of these two men, who have changed all of our lives for the better." She turned her focus from the crowd to the two before her.

"David and Joseph have decided to prepare their own vows." She turned to Joseph who would be going first.

"David," he started with a small waver in his voice, "almost three years ago, I met you, and you told me I had to run for my life. You were my savior in Neria and got me here to safety. Our relationship continued as we worked together, and you helped me through my grief, helped me forgive myself for what my work had been used for, and helped me see how much good in the world I could still do. My feelings for you continued to grow as we worked side by side, and eventually, I realized your feelings had grown as well. It was one of the happiest days of my life to find that out, and today now tops the list. I am honored to be able to love you, and I will always make sure you know you are my world. I will cherish every day we have together."

David reached out and grabbed Joseph's hand and squeezed it tightly. Tears brimmed his eyes. "Joseph, I've never been so delighted about being in a firefight than the one that brought me to you."

That got a chuckle from the crowd.

"You understood me in a way few ever had," he continued. "I have always loved our discussions that would go late into the night while trying to crack some problem. You take care of me when I haven't realized I've been locked away for hours at a time. Watching you with everyone at the school has taught me how to be a good role model. You helped me bring this dream to life. I can't think of anyone else I would want to have at my side. You are loving, dedicated, kind, and I will spend my life working to be the man you deserve."

I teared up, watching my oldest friend declare what Joseph meant to him. Memories of us throughout our lives came to me. Every moment that made me love him and how proud I was that he found someone to share his life with. I wanted the world for him, and I knew Joseph would give it to him.

Riley smiled at the two before picking up with the rest of the ceremony.

"David Roberts, do you vow to support Joseph through this life and the next?" Riley asked.

"I do," David agreed, and I could hear the emotion thick in his voice.

"Joseph Acron, do you vow to support David through this life and the next?"

"I do," Joseph said, his other hand went to grasp David's, and David did the same.

She held up a red candle and ignited it. As the wax melted, she dripped it onto their clasped hands. "We mark this day with pain and pleasure as the road ahead will not be smooth. Here today, you make a vow to support each other through the hard times as well as the good. May the God of Time watch over your journey, may the God of Will bless you in overcoming any obstacles, may the God of Mirth bring you joy in the dark, and may the God of Death join you together once again past the veil. I now pronounce you partners in life."

David and Joseph came together in a passionate kiss, and cheers went up in the crowd. A drone flew over, dropping more flower petals down on the entire party.

Tears flowed freely as I clapped and saw Chase's where he stood behind David. He winked at me, making my heart flutter. David and Joseph turned toward everyone and raised their clasped hands above their heads, celebrating with the rest of us.

The crowd mingled and chatted after the ceremony, before we moved into the great hall for the reception. Theo had outdone himself with the cake that towered on one of the tables. There had also been mouthwatering appetizers, and he was setting up the buffet now. My stomach growled as soon as I saw the first warmers. Doug, Libby, and some of their friends were helping. I was so proud of how they had taken leadership roles here and were being great role models for the younger kids.

Joseph and David had spent time with the students as they filtered past, wanting to say congratulations. The adults had congregated around a table. The teachers and our squad were getting to know each other and trading stories from the last few months.

"Oh, by the way, Nathan said his gift would be delivered in the next few days," Chase said when we finally got a chance to talk with David and Joseph.

"That's nice of him," Joseph said.

Like anyone was surprised. Nathan had been doting on this school and the people running it. He was so proud of this place and helped anyway he could.

"I wonder what it is," David mused.

I happened to know it was a new, oversized 3D printer that could print with metals and composites for David. Joseph was getting some new lab equipment that was complicated enough I couldn't explain what it actually did. The gifts, unsurprisingly, were perfect, and they were going to love them.

Once the buffet was fully set up, I booked it over to the table with David, Joseph, and Benson, excited to get our hands on Theo's delicious cooking. The great hall was filled with the sounds of laughter as the kids goofed around, and some were already dancing to a playlist someone had put together. It was chaos and joy, and it made me feel as light as a feather being part of this amazing moment.

David and Joseph both smeared frosting on the other's face when they did the first slice of cake. As the night wore on, eventually, they bid everyone goodnight and took off to spend some time together. It reminded me of my wedding night with Chase, and I bit my lip as I watched him laugh at a joke from Monica. The way his eyes sparkled and he threw his head back without a care in the world. The way his sharp lines softened when he smiled.

I soaked up every minute as we joked and talked late into the night, saying goodnight to the kids as they filtered back to their dorms in waves. I had no doubts that they would be carrying on till the early morning, as kids were known to do, but wanted to be out of sight of the adults. Everyone would be riding the high of this day well into the days and weeks to come.

Vi

As I walked through the halls, my hands wandered to my lower back. It was strange that my muscles were... was sore the right word? I pressed my palms into the tense muscles and stretched a bit, but it was still there. I hadn't felt sore like this since before the mist. At least, not without being in some sort of deadly encounter beforehand.

It wouldn't hurt to check in with Joseph, so I turned and started to head toward his lab. It was a little after lunch, and that was normally where I could find him.

As expected, he was at his computer when I pushed the door open. He smiled as soon as he saw me. "And what do I owe this pleasure?"

A flare of pain radiated through me, and I grimaced. "I don't know. My back hurts, I think."

He pointed to the chair. "Take a seat."

I did as he said, and he started to press his fingers into my back and sides. "Nothing feels out of the ordinary. Did you do anything to bring it on? Twist the wrong way?"

"You really think I managed to twist something?" I went to stand,

and liquid crashed to my feet. I looked down in horror then back up to Joseph.

"You're in labor," he said quietly.

"What?" Anxiety exploded through me. "It's too early, right?" I wasn't ready for this. Was something wrong? What had happened?

"Come on, let's get you to the room." He grabbed my hand and led me out of his lab, but I saw a strange expression on his face.

"What?"

"Well, it's been seven months, and honestly, anything could happen with this pregnancy. There is no precedent here. Take a deep breath. I'm sure everything is fine." He pushed the door open to the room we had prepped for this. As soon as he got me in the chair, he went to a cabinet, pulled out the gown, and tossed it to me. "Get changed. I'll go let Chase know. I'll be right back."

I rubbed my stomach and tried to practice my deep breathing. Now was not the time to freak out. Everything was fine. Everything was *fine*. I stripped out of my clothes, folded them neatly on one of the chairs, and slipped into the gown. There wasn't anything to worry about.

I didn't stop pacing until Chase came into the room. His eyes were shining, but he still seemed concerned.

"Joseph said it's fine," I said weakly, and he wrapped me in his arms and buried his face in my hair.

"Everything is going to be okay." He maneuvered me back toward the bed. "What do you need?"

"I have no idea." And I didn't.

He leaned down to kiss me and didn't pull away even as Joseph and David arrived.

"How are you feeling?" Joseph asked.

"Honestly, fine. I only came to you because I had a sore muscle."

"I'll be outside. I can run to get anything you need." David squeezed my hand before he left. It helped to know he'd be close by.

Chase grabbed one of the chairs and pulled it over. His hand slipped across my stomach.

"I love you more than anything, and I'll be right here." He kissed my forehead, and I leaned against him with a sigh. I was surrounded by love, which helped burn away the terror.

"This came on quickly, so if we're lucky she might be here before we know it," Joseph said as he started to get ready.

As it turned out, I was not, in fact, lucky.

It felt like it would go on forever. I was covered in sweat and incredibly uncomfortable. At least this was a pain born from love. It would be worth it in the end.

"It won't be long now," Joseph said.

I refused to grab Chase's hand during the contractions. I did happen to grab the railings to the bed though, and now the bars were crumpled from my grip. Whoops.

I groaned again, but I saw from Joseph's face that this must be it. So, I pushed with a scream, but I wasn't the only one. The cries of a baby filled the air in the next moment. Tears fell as emotions overtook me.

It was over, and she was alive. As Joseph headed my way with her wrapped in a blanket, I shifted to be able to hold her.

Her tiny face took my breath away. I shifted so Chase could get a good look. Tears lined his eyes as he gazed down at us. Joseph called for David to come in.

David's head instantly appeared in the door. He snuck in and stood next to Joseph, watching the three of us. I moved so Chase could hold her. He gingerly picked her up and cradled her to his chest.

My soul sang, seeing the two of them together. Then, realization dawned on me. This was it. This was the thing we had been waiting for. I thought I had months left of this life, and now we would have to leave. We had agreed we would go back to the front as soon as we could. We didn't want to waste any time to bring this war to an end. We wanted to get back to our girl as fast as we could.

I'd be leaving the school, the kids, my friends, and our little girl.

"What are you going to name her?" David asked.

"Aria," Chase said instantly. I glanced at him in surprise. We had thrown some names around, but we hadn't made a final decision. Aria had been my mother's name.

"Aria," I echoed just as she yawned, and I melted.

"Aria Astor," David cheered.

"Aria Smith," I reminded him.

"In a few weeks, but for now she's an Astor. Enjoy this time," Joseph said. "Come on, David, let's give them some space. Vi, I'll be back soon, and we'll give her a checkup, but by the sound of those lungs, she's perfectly fine."

I scooted over so Chase could slip into the bed and we could watch her together. There was a type of spell woven over us as we soaked in everything about her. She had the tiniest fingers, hands, and toes, and she seemed like magic. Every twitch and coo had both of us exchanging excited glances.

We would be staying for another week or two, so I pushed away the thoughts of having to leave. For now, I was going to enjoy having her here.

"You're a dad." I murmured.

"And you're a mom."

"I can't believe it," I whispered.

He leaned over and kissed me. "Me neither."

This was the start of a whole new chapter of our lives.

PART IV

THE LEGEND

Vi

My hands were braced against the desk as I stared at my father on the screen in front of me.

"Ethan and I can't get away right now. There is so much going on with setting up the new towns. When it calms down a bit, we'll put CC1 in charge and figure out a time we can all see each other. But for now, we need you to head straight to the front lines. We're going to be transferring full control of the army to the both of you. We'll let the others know; they wanted to meet with up with you as soon as you got back. Anthony will be there within the hour. And remember, we're here if you need to talk."

"We understand. Thanks for everything," Chase said from behind me.

"Good luck." With one last sad smile, he ended the call.

"We're doing the right thing," I said, and Chase wrapped me up in his arms.

"We are doing the right thing," he echoed. We had been saying this to each other so many times over the past couple of weeks. Especially when we were alone at night and found ourselves staring out the glass dome at the stars, unable to sleep, both of us dreading today.

I grabbed his hand, and we headed to meet the others to start saying our goodbyes. We had said goodbye to most of the kids from the school at dinner last night. David, Joseph, Xander, Riley, Monica, Doug, Lilly, and Bunny were waiting for us.

As soon as I saw Aria's face cuddled in David's arms, I thought about staying again. I bit my lip and shook it off.

I reached out and pulled both Doug and Lilly in for a hug. After stepping back I looked them both over. They had grown so much since I first met them. I had spent the last few months seeing how amazing they turned out, even after everything they had been through.

"I'm not going to stop until I get Jessie and Cecily back," I told them. Not long after we arrived, they had asked about them one day at lunch. It had been devastating to see their reactions to the news.

"We know," Doug said as he threw an arm around Lilly's shoulders, and Bunny came and wrapped her arms around me.

"I'm going to miss you," she said through unshed tears.

"I'm going to miss you too, but can you do me a favor?"

Her eyes lit up. "Yeah!"

I leaned down and conspiratorially whispered to her. "Keep an eye on everyone here for me. You're in charge." I winked, and she giggled and bobbed her head up and down.

The others wished us well. Then, I finally came to David. He held out his arms, and I took Aria from him. She slowly blinked her bright green eyes open and smiled when she saw me. She had my eyes and Chase's smile. I kissed her softly as I tried to hold back the tears. "We'll come for you as soon as we can, little one."

Chase's face appeared over my shoulder as he stared down at our little princess. He stuck his finger out, and she grabbed on to it.

My breath shuddered at the sight. I didn't know if I had the strength to do this. I closed my eyes, took a deep breath, and then gave myself one last moment to memorize everything about her. Once I had, I handed her to Chase. He bounced and whispered to her, leaving a kiss on her forehead.

My nails were digging into my palms so hard they pierced the skin.

Chase handed her back over to David and came to stand with me.

"We'll never be able to repay you for this," he said to them.

"Thank you for everything," I finished.

"It's our pleasure. Now, go win that war," David said, but I could tell he shared our pain.

With one last look to our friends, and another to our daughter. I turned and pushed my way through the front doors into the chilly morning air.

If I didn't do this right now, I never would.

Our ride was going to meet us a few miles away, so I started walking. The air chilled my lungs. I couldn't stop the tears from slipping silently down my cheeks. Chase caught up to me and took my hand. A quick glance at his taught shoulders and stormy features showed me this was killing him inside too.

I pulled us close together, and we leaned on each other as we walked. We didn't talk. We didn't need words to express the devastation we both felt.

The small plane was waiting in the clearing for us when we arrived, just as planned.

"Good to see you," Anthony said as we climbed inside.

"Thanks for the ride." Chase dropped heavily into a seat.

"Anytime." Anthony started to go through his pre-flight checklist.

Chase handed me a tablet, and we got to work going over the most recent information from the front.

The line between Esmerelda's domain and our forces ran a jagged line from the north to southeast of the kingdom. The palace and the cities still under her control were mostly the affluent areas that were closer to the Nerian border on the eastern side of the king-dom. We had control of the farms and the land to the west that ran all the way to the ocean. Esmerelda was left with only one northern port she could access.

Her troops were making a push for one of our northern most

cities, Dauton, to give them more access to the coast. There had also been reports of sightings of Jessie and Cecily through Esmerelda's territory, and they seemed to be headed north as well. On top of everything else, cities on lockdown were being swept for our allies who hadn't left during the evacuations. They needed our help as well.

We were going straight to the post near Dauton, I assumed we'd find Jessie and Cecily there. Esmerelda needed to take that city to get more supplies, and I knew she sent the girls to make sure their forces prevailed. I wouldn't let that happen, and it was my best shot to get to Jessie and Cecily away from Esmerelda's influence. I hoped I could break through and get them to come with us.

I knew Esmerelda had been making inroads to our border while we had been away. The resistance had been spread too thin to work cohesively. As far as we knew, she thought I was on the front line this entire time, so she probably thought she was pushing her way toward breaking us. She'd be in for a surprise once I finally did get out there. I had plenty of pain I wanted to get revenge for.

I was thankful for David and a few kids at the school who had been working up fake footage of me over the past few months. I prayed she bought it because it was proof that Aria didn't survive. If she didn't, I couldn't even think about what she would do to take her from us.

So, I believed with my whole heart that it worked. That we had pulled it off and I could spend my time taking her defenses apart piece by piece until there was nothing left. Then, I could finally leave this life behind me.

The shudder of us coming in for a landing jerked me out of my thoughts. Chase gave me an understanding look from the seat across from me. I couldn't believe I had been lost in my thoughts that entire flight.

The plane came to a stop, and the ramp lowered. Anthony took off his headphones and got up to stretch.

"Here you are," he said, waving a hand at the camp before us.

"Where are you off to next?" I asked him.

"Here for a bit, unless someone puts in a call, but I'll be around if you need me." He gave me a quick salute before he headed off deeper into the hangar.

I saw George Rivera headed toward us. I hadn't seen him much since Fairhaven; where he had ended up in charge due to being one of the only people in leadership still alive after the attack. It was going to be quite the reunion, it seemed.

"Good to see you!" he called and held out a hand to shake ours.

"Hey, George," Chase said, and I just gave a tired smile. "Glad to see a familiar face."

Mortars exploded off in the distance. The smell of smoke drifted in from the north. As the smell of gunpowder and war wafted in, a calm washed over me.

I was in my comfort zone, and it was time to get to work.

49

VI

I was leaning against the command center's wall when the door popped open. I looked up from the tablet I had been going through the plans on and saw Thea. Pushing myself up, I went to wrap her in the biggest hug.

"I missed you," I whispered, and she squeezed me back before relaxing in my arms. I knew the past few months had been hard on everyone, and I hated that she hadn't been with us.

Gwen squealed as she entered next. She bounced over slung her arms over me and Thea's shoulders. "The squad is back together," she sang and kissed my cheek.

I got a hand free to wave at Benson and Anthony as they came in. Chase had spun in his chair as they arrived.

Chase launched himself at Benson, and they caught each other with firm and manly back pats. Anthony and Chase shared a nod.

I had finally managed to untangle myself from the girls when Thea ran over to Chase. He ruffled her hair, and she yelled at him for messing it up. I knew they would help us get through this.

I had gotten so lucky with the people in my life. I had support here, in Soland, and friends in Neria too. People I knew I could trust with my life. And the life of something even more precious.

Gwen caught my eye and gave me a look that said she was here if I needed to talk, but she wouldn't bring it up otherwise. I gave her a thankful nod.

"So," she punched a fist into her palm, "where are we going, and who are we messing up?"

"We're going to try to set a trap for Jessie and Cecily," I said. "In their territory."

Benson barked a laugh. "It's like you never left."

I just shrugged. "You know you missed this."

Chase took a deep breath and caught my eye. It was time to let them know of another change. "I'm staying here. I'll coordinate what I can for you, but you'll be mostly on your own."

Thea looked at her brother with surprise. "What do you mean? You're always with us."

He rubbed the back of his neck and seemed dejected. "Not this time. Maybe not again for a while. We can't make the same mistakes as dad. Someone needs to coordinate everything for the entire force, not just here. I'm utilizing my skills in the best way I can."

Sadness filled his eyes as he left the other half unsaid. That I was doing the same; my skills would always leave me in the middle of the fighting.

Chase and I had talked about this. It made strategic sense, but also, it left one of us farther away from the danger. If we both couldn't go home to Aria, at least one of us could.

No one was happy about it, but it was for the best. I started to hand out tablets to everyone.

"Here is there location outside of Dauton. They've been shelling the edge of the city, but we've been keeping control so far." I tapped, and the images changed to zoom in. It focused on a section to the east. "There is an area here where some people were seen entering twelve hours ago. It's them. I know it."

Benson slapped me on the back. "When do we leave?"

"Now," Chase said, and I saw the love as he looked at me. This was it. This was life now. There wasn't any time to waste. I made a promise to get the girls back and getting them away from Esmerelda would put us in a better position to end this war.

I felt like I might crawl out of my skin. I was ready to get back to the fight. Memories of the lab I had destroyed washed over me. The red lights flashing, screams echoing, and me covered in blood.

That is who you really are, part of me whispered, but I shook the thought away. I hoped I was more than that, but I knew I'd do anything to end this and get back to my little girl.

Chase had said goodbye to everyone before following me to our room. He wasn't going to be able to see us off because he had a meeting with a few of the generals soon. He had helped me pack my bag earlier, and we finally had to say things would be changing drastically for us. It was real. It was here.

He shut the door behind us and I ran my hands through my hair to pull it up. A shiver raced through me when his arms wrapped around me. My heart beat faster as his chin rested on my shoulder and his breath tickled my ear.

I turned in his arms. He was trying to pretend everything was fine, but I could tell he was breaking inside. I held his face lightly in my hands before pushing to my toes so I could press my lips to his. I wished our lives were different, but this was who we were.

We could have run. Should we have run? Maybe. But we were people of duty. We would watch the news and hear about the losses and deaths and pain and know we could have done something to help. That knowledge would have eaten us alive, and I didn't want Aria to have to grow up on the run, always having to look over her shoulder.

We could do this—focus on the goal and bring it all to an end. This gave us a chance. A chance for a real life. A chance to make the world a better place. For everyone. I just needed to keep convincing myself of that.

"I'll...I'll see you when I get home."

He sighed, closed his eyes, and leaned his forehead against mine "I'll see you when you get home."

Tears silently fell as he crushed me to him. My hand slipped into his hair and pulled him down to kiss me. We let our bodies say goodbye for longer than we should have. Finally, I tugged away and grabbed my bag. Heading to the door, I stopped and hoisted my bag onto my shoulder before looking back at him one more time.

He was standing stiffly, like he had stopped himself from following me. I forced myself to turn away and head out to meet up with the others.

As I left, I heard Chase muffle his scream into a pillow. No one else would have heard it, but I did, and I couldn't breathe past the lump in my throat. I wanted to run back to him, but I couldn't.

This will be worth it. We have to do this. We don't have a choice.

I started to run, wanting to think of anything else. It didn't take long for me to make it to the northern edge of camp, where everyone was meeting. We were headed to Dauton on foot. The girls were about half-a-day's walk from here. Gwen waved as soon as she saw me.

"Hey," I said, dropping my bag down next to hers.

She raised an eyebrow, silently checking on me.

"I'm fine."

She raised it higher.

"I'm relatively fine."

She put her hands on her hips.

"I am absolutely not fine, but this," I waved a hand at the forest ahead, "is the best thing for me right now."

"All right. At least you know how to be honest now." She shook my shoulder. "Growth."

"I can't wait to show you what I learned while you were gone," Thea called from behind me as she came crunching up the road.

"I can't wait to see it." I winked to her before turning to the others. "Ready?"

"Let's go cause some chaos," Gwen said, swinging her rifle over her shoulder as we slipped into the trees.

50

Vi

The rain had begun as we made it to our target. We were flanking the camp and planned to take out the perimeter patrol. The camp was small, remote, and made to keep things hidden. Too bad for them we already knew what we were searching for was here.

The sun hadn't yet started to rise, and the rain was masking the sounds of our movements. I peeked around the tree I was hidden behind to catch sight of the guard a few meters ahead. When he turned back toward camp, I ran out using a burst of speed until I was right behind him.

His eyes widened in surprise as he noticed me, but before he could even think of crying an alarm, my punch was enough to send him crashing to the ground unconscious.

I hurried to hide him and myself in the shadow of the building straight ahead, securing him with zip ties. A soft glow emitted from the windows. I took a quick look, analyzing the room in moments. The tips of the stucco wall pricked my back as I leaned against it and took a steadying breath. The room seemed to be the impromptu armory. It was filled with weapons and empty of people. Getting inside here would allow me to keep anyone I ran into away from the weapons.

The sound of me pushing the window open was hidden by the slap of the rain on the roof. My boots made soft squeaks as I landed on the wooden floor. I snuck to the door and opened it just enough to see someone in the hallway ahead of me. In one swift move, I opened it more, slipped through, and closed it behind me. The sound had him turning to look straight at me.

I gave a quick sarcastic wave before I launched off my back leg and was on him. I crushed his gun's barrel in my grip and ripped it away, instantly reversing the motion and whipping it across his temple. He dropped just like the man outside. I bound this man like I had the other. I listened for other sounds in the building as I did.

"We'll be pushing in with the alpha squad in the morning. Their main forces are here and here," someone said.

"No, we'll be going in right before the sun rises. We'll have the sun at our back." That was Cecily, I was sure of it. "Your team will wait for us to radio to you that we've taken care of their heavy weapons."

From the sounds of it, there were about six other people in the building, including the girls. They were in a room farther toward the front of the building. As quiet as I could, I snuck through the hallway until I was a few feet from the entrance to the larger open room they were in.

I closed my eyes and let a calm rushed through me. *Three. Two.* My eyes snapped open, and I launched into the room. A knife slid into my hand and released with a flick of my wrist. I buried it to the hilt in one of the men's thighs.

Before his scream even ripped from his lips, I had already thrown three more, hitting the other men in the room. As if in sync, roars erupted from them as they all dropped from their wounds.

Both girls turned and paused, only for a moment, before Cecily was coming for me, but my attention wasn't on her. I saw the way

Jessie paused when she saw me. She grimaced at her sister then followed.

I blocked Cecily's first attempt, but her next was nothing but a blur, and the game was on. I fell back as she continued to hit me with a barrage of attacks.

"I just want to talk." I managed to get out between the impact of her punches.

"There is nothing to say," Cecily ground out.

Jessie joined the fight, but I could tell she was pulling her punches. I caught her eyes, and I could see the regret in them. She was still there, but she wouldn't do anything that would give herself away until we could get to Cecily.

"We're friends. Don't you remember? The queen has messed with your head." I ducked under one of Cecily's right hooks, but she had backed me into a corner of the room.

"You're a traitor to your kingdom," she hissed.

"You're not even from here." I growled in frustration. "Try to remember Neria. Esmerelda was the reason your people were being kidnapped. Your people died because of her and her father. She's brainwashed you. Both of you just try to remember," I begged. I was only talking to Cecily, but I couldn't give Jessie away. If this didn't work, she was still going to be our best bet at getting them out from under my stepmother's thumb. Esmerelda must still trust her if she sent her out here, so Jessie must be hiding it enough not to be suspicious.

Cecily roared with annoyance as I blocked another one of her hits. I slammed my foot into her torso, and she went skidding backward. I ducked under a slower punch from Jessie and jumped and flipped over her to the middle of the room.

Cecily grabbed a knife that was laying on a table and dove at me again. I created a baton and kept her from slashing at me. She might be as strong and fast as me, but I had experience on my side. I slipped in and out of the way of her attacks, fighting back, but just barely. I was still holding back.

I got in close, but she feigned left and then charged me, wrapping her arms around me with her shoulder in my chest as she had us both smashing through the window. Rain instantly crashed around us.

She was straddling me as she pummeled my face with her fist, crushing me into the mud with each hit. I grabbed her wrists and managed to turn us over, but she was so slippery I lost my hold on her. She managed to roll us again, but I got a knee between us and rammed it into her stomach. Her breath was forced from her, and I knocked her off me.

I pushed myself to a knee but threw myself down again just as Jessie went careening over me. Her blow missed. It had given Cecily time to get up though, and she came charging at me again.

We traded blow after blow, all of us twisting and jumping to evade what we could. Unlike when I fought Jasper, when we were nothing more than two beasts crashing into each other with brute force, fighting the girls was more like a dance. The longer we fought, the more covered in mud we got, and our hits started to glance off each other from the slickness.

People were starting to yell through the camp; our presence had definitely been noticed now. I heard gunshots nearby, but they weren't aimed at me. I didn't have a second to think about it. It was all I could do to focus on my fight. Even without Jessie really trying, it was difficult to fight two people with the same abilities as myself.

I got in close enough with a burst of speed and locked my arm around Cecily's neck. I tried to put on enough pressure to knock her out, but she just jerked her head back into mine and then grabbed my arm to launch me over her shoulder and into the ground.

She was instantly on me again but ended up distracted by an explosion from our right. It seemed like the others were well into their plan of disabling the rest of the camp. I took the opening and kicked her away from me.

As I pushed myself up, I was pulled backward by Jessie's arm around my neck.

"Let us go," she whispered.

I had one of my hands wrapped around the arm at my neck, and he pressed something into my hand.

"I'll get you intel from inside. Now, make it look good," she finished.

So, she still wasn't ready to leave. I hated the idea, but a spy could be invaluable. I jammed my elbow back into her side, and she let her grip on me loosen. I dropped and spun, sweeping her legs out from under her.

There were more explosions and gunfire, closer this time. Even in the rain, I could see some of the small outbuildings were on fire.

I went to attack Jessie again, but Cecily grabbed me and tossed me back. Bullets sprayed at her feet. Benson had appeared and was sighting his rifle at the girls.

Jessie tugged Cecily to her and whispered in her ear. The younger girl glared at her sister, but Jessie was already pulling her away. With one look back, hate filled the Cecily's eyes before she turned and raced off. Jessie waited a beat and gave me a sad smile then she took off after her.

Benson started to go after them, but I grabbed his arm and shook my head. I saw confusion on his face, but he didn't question me. We both turned back and split up to finish the job. While we didn't manage to get the girls, we still needed to cripple this camp. Then we were headed to take down the troops attacking Dauton.

51

ESMERELDA

"You're telling me, you finally ran into Astor and you came back empty handed yet again," I growled. The girls both stood there, staring at their feet.

"They surprised us; we weren't ready for them. We had to regroup," Jessie said quietly.

"You shouldn't need to be ready for them. What use are you to me if you can't do the single task of bringing me Astor? And while you were failing at that, they ended up destroying our entire advancing line." A headache spread behind my eyes. "Get out of my sight. Go to conditioning."

After months of Genevieve being elusive, we finally had her in our sights, and she managed to cause yet another mess. Anger flowed through my veins as I slammed my fist down on my desk.

The rebels had been interrupting our supplies, and now there was famine in the cities, which was making the draft harder to enforce. The people were starting to fight back, and I had to send more men to squash the resistance.

It felt like everything was falling apart, but would reign with an iron fist. They would come to heel. Just like the girls.

I called for Howard and dropped onto the couch, turning down the lights and pressing the heels of my hands into my eyes. Anger and frustration brought these headaches on more often now. It didn't help that everything set off my temper these days. I just needed something to go my way.

The door slid open and closed again quietly. He didn't have to ask and came straight over. The cold metal of the canisters kissed the skin of my neck, and ice started to spread from the shot.

"Not good news, I take it?" he asked me.

I was able to push myself up a bit straighter, and my eyes fluttered open once it didn't feel like they would burst from the pressure anymore.

"No. Finally spotted Astor and she ended up destroying the entire northern front line. Tell me you at least have good news with the testing?"

"We lost the last thirty percent of the test group yesterday. We'll start a new batch in a few days once they've arrived." He didn't even flinch at the glare I shot his way. He just shrugged.

"You can't rush science," I growled, parroting his line with all the sarcasm I could muster. "Just have good news for me soon or I'll find someone else." The threat was empty as always, and he knew it, but I was just so angry.

There was a chime, and I saw it was a message from Morgan. She advised that the generals were waiting. I had summoned them, and with the mood I was in, if they didn't have any good news, I would be looking for new people to fill their shoes.

I stood, turning on the lights, letting Howard know he was dismissed. He left as the generals all entered my office.

"You better have a plan to fix this," I hissed, and they all swallowed before jumping into their ideas of what to do next.

Vi

We had spent two days clearing out the camps along the edge of Dauton, making our way north and disabling enough of their artillery that they finally retreated and gave up their siege on the city.

All I wanted was a warm shower as we crossed back into our own camp, but I headed for the command center first. I had waved off the others, saying I'd find them later. People saluted me as I walked by, and I returned the gesture. I made my way to where I knew Chase would be.

I pushed the door open, and he visibly relaxed as soon as he saw it was me. He put down his tablet and came straight for me, backing me up so I was leaning against the closed door. He caged me in with his arms as one locked the door and the other wound into my hair.

He put his forehead to mine for a moment before kissing me desperately. I returned it, glad to see him again.

When we finally broke apart, I pulled out the communicator Jessie had given me. I had checked in and let him know what happened after the girls had escaped. He knew what it was when he took it from me. "I'm sorry it didn't work out like you hoped."

"As much as I hate it, this could be the thing that turns the tide." I had been telling myself that over and over to make myself believe it. "I trust her. I know I'd do the same thing."

Chase pulled me close, and I rested my head on his chest, just listening to his heart and his breathing, each starting to slow now that I was close. Then, I felt him tense, and I turned my face up to his.

"I have to send you out again."

"When?" I asked.

"Tonight. We have to help evacuate Radan. Some of our assets were trapped while trying to get people out of the city."

My heart clenched, and I saw the pain mirrored on his face. I knew we would be sent out again, but I had thought we'd at least have a day or two together. Now, to find out we only had hours... I knew I had to make this as easy on him as possible. So, I swallowed my disappointment, smiled, and cradled the side of his face with my hand.

"Well, let's make the most of this time, and then I'll see you when I come home." It was starting to dawn on me that home would now just be wherever we were together. There wasn't going to be one place where we hung our hats any longer. We'd bounce from place to place, turning into ships that passed in the night as I was sent out to the field time and time again. Because we would sacrifice what was needed for the cause, even if it was each other.

I looked around then back to the locked door. Giving him a mischievous grin, I slid my hands under his jacket and slowly pulled it off. I saw my own hunger reflected back at me in his eyes.

He tugged at my shirt that was stuck to my skin from the sweat and dirt, unbothered by how filthy I was. He pulled me close and started to sweep his lips over my skin.

"I missed you." His voice was thick with need against me.

"I came home," was all I managed before we were completely lost to each other.

Chase and I spent the remaining hours together, unable to get enough of each other. He followed me to the shower and helped wash the last few days off of me. He also helped me pack another bag for the next trip. As we went to get something to eat, we always had at least some part of us touching, soaking up every last second before we were torn apart again. The others joined us to eat, and the others caught up with Chase.

I just sat and watched them, once again memorizing this moment, like I did every time we all got to get together.

Chase's tablet chimed. It was a video call from David. Chase answered, and David and Joseph appeared. He turned the tablet around, and we all jumped into action, saying hi and talking over each other, which just made David laugh.

"Hey, guys, good to see you." Joseph came more into frame, and my heart lurched as I saw him holding Aria. It was all I could do to keep from reaching out to run my finger over the screen, wishing I could hold her.

"Is everything okay?" Chase asked instantly.

"Everything's fine. We just wanted to check in," David said. It seemed like he was keeping his eyes on Chase and me. I could tell he was worried about us.

Everyone started to coo, and Joseph moved so Aria was easier to see. I stared at her little smile as she squirmed in his arms. When I could finally tear my eyes away, I noticed Gwen watching me.

It was good to have friends who knew me so well. We had spent so much time together that we could read each other easily. As I watched Aria I lost track of the conversation until I realized the good-byes had started.

Chase checked his watch, and his eyes slid back to me. It was time.

Everything seemed to slow as we all exchanged looks. Then, we all started to move as one. Thea wrapped her arms around her brother and buried her face in his chest as he pulled her close.

"See you soon, big bro." With that she linked her arm in Gwen's, and they waved goodbye then headed out.

Benson slapped Chase on the shoulder and followed them. Anthony gave a quick salute before leaving as well. Chase grabbed my hand and squeezed it before we did the same.

"This is so weird," he muttered.

"I know. You can come with us if you want. I'm sure we can figure something out," I said, giving him a sideways glance, but he just shook his head.

"This will get easier. We'll get used to it." It seemed like he was trying to convince himself of that more than anything else.

A part of me wished that wouldn't be true, but I knew it would. All I could hope for was that it wouldn't be for too long.

We caught up to the others, and Chase finally dropped my hand.

"All right, I've sent you all the information we have on the situation. You'll be arriving there in a few hours. We have a couple of squads in the area we'll be sending to meet you." He paused and smiled with a sigh. "Good luck. Stay safe."

Everyone went in for another hug before we piled into the hover copter. Anthony brought the engines to life, and we started to lift off the ground. I stayed crouched in the open door until Chase gave one last wave and turned away. Then, I finally slid it shut.

I dropped into the seat next to Thea. She kept watching out the window, but she slipped her hand into mine. I sighed and closed my eyes, leaning my head back against the seat. I took a breath, and another, then I blinked my eyes open and reached for my tablet to start going over the information again.

We took the time in the air to come up with a plan of action. There were sewer tunnels that ran under the city we would use to get in and head for the safe house. We had received a message that some of our allies were there. We'd find out what the current situation was and figure out next steps from there.

We arrived without incident a few hours later, and our backup was already there waiting for us.

"All right," I said to the others. "Entrance is right over there. Let's get to it."

We all moved out and started the trek into the city.

Time to get back to work.

53

Vi

6 Months Later...

I flopped heavily in the chair. If I wasn't careful, within a minute or two, I would be asleep, but I still had things to do. Over the last six months, we had been shipped out so often, I could fall asleep anywhere if we had a few free minutes.

The door pushed open, and Chase walked in, followed by George and Anthony. I went to push myself up, but Chase shook his head and came over to kiss my temple.

"Welcome back," George said.

"Great job on taking out the satellite communications station," Anthony said.

I gave them a quick salute. "Just another day at the office." I threw a data storage device onto the table between us. "We managed to get that out. See if you can find anything helpful on it?"

"Jessie checked in." Chase started to rub my shoulders, and it felt fantastic. "We need you to head to the southern barricade. Esmerelda is sending a force to try to re-open her supply line by breaking through."

I ran my hands over my face a few times before they slid into my hair. I was exhausted.

"Yeah, of course. We'll head out once we get a few hours of sleep."

"We don't have any time to waste. You'll need to sleep on the plane." Chase gave me the look that said he didn't want to have to do this, but he didn't have a choice.

Frustration filled me, but I tried to tamp it down. This wasn't his fault; it was just the way of things.

"The team is going to burn out soon. We're not going to be any help if we're dead on our feet and delirious." But I knew he already knew that.

"Jessie and Cecily will be there; I need you there. You know how much damage they'll do if you aren't there to stop them."

"Then, just send me. Give the squad a break." I raised an eyebrow at him, crossing my arms over my chest. I saw Anthony and George trying to pretend they weren't here. They looked incredibly uncomfortable.

"They're the ones used to working with you. I need them there to have your back." Now, he was the one running his hands over his face before they stopped on the back of his neck. He shook his head at me. "I'm sorry. I'll get you guys a break as soon as I can."

"There is never going to be a good time. We've been going non-stop for six months, Chase." My voice was rising.

"Uh, we'll check in with you guys in a bit. Let us know when you've figured," George waved his hand between us, "this out."

With that, both gave us a salute and closed the door behind them as they left.

Chase and I both went back to glaring each other.

"Come on," I said. "You know we can't keep this up."

"I don't have a choice." His tone was pleading. "I have to think of everyone. I have to make the decision that will keep the most people the safest we can."

"Everyone but us," I muttered. I knew he was right; I was just so tired that it made me irritable.

"That's not fair." He crossed the room and put his hands on my shoulders, leaning down to be eye level with me. "I know you're tired. I'll figure it out as soon as I can, I promise. But it can't be today. You know I'm doing this so we can get back to her as fast as we can."

"You don't think I know that?" I snapped at him, stepping away again. "Don't throw her in my face like I'm not doing *everything* to end this." I was being loud, but not enough to be heard through the walls.

"That's not what I meant. I know you are." His gaze turned apologetic. "Come here," he said in a firm tone and closed the distance between us, wrapping me in a hug and setting his cheek on the top of my head as my arms slid around him.

Just the feel of him calmed me. I hated that we had been reduced to this, but this was our sacrifice for the good of our people.

"You need to figure something out, soon. If you don't, someone is going to get hurt." I spoke into his chest, nuzzling the soft fabric of his shirt.

"I know. I will, I promise." He had pulled back enough to cup my face in one of his warm hands.

As soon as our eyes met, he moved in and my eyes fluttered closed as he kissed me. Everything fell away as his hands roamed over my body. With a slight push, he backed me into the wall, never breaking the kiss. I moaned as his body pressed against mine and we collided with it.

One of his hands twisted into my hair, and his touch went from gentle to frantic. I gasped as he moved to kiss his way down my jaw then my neck. I tugged at the hem of his shirt, needing to see him, to feel him.

"Door, lock," Chase murmured as he looked at me like he was starving and only I would sate that hunger.

I heard the light click from the door before I grabbed the back of his neck and tugged him to me. Every scrap of restraint was gone.

Chase gripped the back of my thighs and pulled me up, and I wrapped my legs around him. He twisted us toward the center of the room and dropped me down on the table. His kisses pushed me back so he could reach behind me to swipe everything from the table to the floor.

I ripped off his shirt, and he instantly came back for more. His hands slipped underneath mine to do the same. We crashed together, every part of me heated, and I burned where he touched me. I arched back as he kissed down my collarbone, whimpering, wanting more.

"I love you, Genevieve." He didn't use my full name often, and it made me fall apart when he did. He was the only one who could say it without grating on my nerves.

"I love you. I've missed you so much," I whispered.

The time for arguing was over. We'd spend this stolen moment with one another, worshiping each other, and then we'd figure the rest out later.

Chase and I crowded around the screen, our shoulders crushed together. The call was still ringing through, and when it connected, David was on the other end. Chase and I always called in when we had these few moments in the same place. Joseph was in the background, bouncing Aria in his arms and whispering to her as she cried.

"Someone's having a hard day," David said, and he looked exhausted.

"A hard month," Joseph said from behind him.

"What's wrong?" I asked, worry thick in my voice.

"She's going through a growth spurt, shooting up like a weed. She's twice the size of an average kid in her age group. Twice as far along in her milestones too," Joseph said, trying to be heard over her. She had healthy lungs at least. "Don't worry, I'm not exactly surprised. She's totally healthy."

What did this mean? Was she going to age twice as fast her whole life? How would we keep this under wraps if people outside of the school met her more than once? What did this mean for her development with other kids? I had thought she might be enhanced more as a passing idea, not that it would actually happen.

And we weren't there to see any of it. We missed her first steps, her first word, her first temper tantrum. Would she be a teenager before we managed to end this stupid war? Was I going to miss everything special? I was so frustrated and angry and sad. We wouldn't even be able to video call soon. We had decided to hide who she was from her too.

I missed her terribly.

"Is there anything we can do?" Chase asked.

"No, everything is under control. We've got this. You guys just focus on winning this so you can come home," David said.

I reached out and touched the screen where she was held by Joseph. My heart clenched, and just like every time I saw her, I wanted to give everything up.

"Doug and Lilly have been helping out with babysitting, and she loves it when he reads her stories." Joseph walked toward David to hand her off.

"Have those two finally admitted they like each other yet?" They had been trading glances for months as they got closer at the school.

"No." David groaned.

"It'll be any time now," Joseph said, poking David, "but they can do it all in their own time."

David rolled his eyes. We all thought they would be a good pair. They were different but complemented each other well.

Chase's comm unit went off, and we sighed.

"We've got to go. We'll call soon," Chase said.

They gave us an empathetic smile, and David pointed to the screen, telling Aria to say goodbye.

"Talk soon," David said, and the call ended.

I ran my hands through my hair and sighed. It was time again.

"All right. I have to get over there. I'll see you when we get back," I said.

Chase wrapped me in his arms and kissed my temple. "See you when you get home."

54

Vi

Jessie said they'd be attacking at dawn, and we made it to the barricade with a few hours to spare. We had been able to grab a few minutes of rest, but it wasn't enough. As soon as we arrived, we started checking in to make sure they were up to speed and ready for the imminent attack.

I could see the exhaustion in the others. I wanted to tell them to stay here in camp, but I knew they wouldn't hear of it. We just needed to stick to the plan, and it would give us all the best shot to make it out of this unscathed.

"All right, everyone ready?" I asked once we were circled up.

"And ready for Plans B, C, and D if things go like the way they normally do," Benson said with a laugh.

"Yes, and all of those." I chuckled as I put my hand in, and they all threw one of theirs on top. "We've got this. Let's remind them they can't take anymore from us than they already have, and let's see if we can get the girls back."

We broke apart, and Gwen headed off for one of the closest guard towers that had been erected, her sniper rifle looped over her shoulder. Benson and Anthony went to find the woman in charge of this checkpoint. Thea followed me as we slipped through the barriers and headed up the road toward where Esmerelda's troops would be coming from.

Esmeralda always wanted a spectacle she could use against us, so we doubted they'd come any way other than the main road. Thea and I settled down in our hiding spot to wait. I wrapped my arms around my knees and couldn't help but notice how tired Thea seemed. "You okay?"

She scrunched up her nose to the question but didn't answer.

"Come on, sis. Talk to me. I know you're exhausted. We all are. I need to know if you are okay to do this. It's fine if you aren't. I wouldn't be able to handle it if anything happened to you."

"I'm fine," she muttered. "I can handle it, just like all of you can."

"This is bigger than pride, Thea. If you make a mistake, it can cost you everything, and if you're doing this just because Chase sent us, your brother isn't always right."

She straightened her back and locked her gaze on mine. "I promise you I'm fine. Nothing is going to happen to me, and I'll have your back."

"I know you will." I lightly punched her shoulder and raised an eyebrow at her. "Now, what's the deal with Jenna?"

She groaned and leaned her head back to stare through the canopy above us. "We broke up. We're just gone too much; we couldn't make it work."

"I'm really sorry. Chase said he'd hear me out about giving you guys some time off when we get done here." It was frustrating that Thea had lost someone because of our missions. There was just so much to do, and we were the best option for success.

"What do you mean? You need a break too." She was wearing one of her most stern expressions—the one she used anytime she didn't agree with me.

"I'll try, I promise. But there are some things that only I can do. Things that I can do alone. Everyone is dead on their feet. Someone will get hurt if we keep up this pace."

Something caught my attention, and I cocked my head to the side, focusing my hearing.

"They're almost here." I could hear the stamp of feet coming this way.

Thea moved to a crouch and started to take inventory of her weapons. I closed my eyes and listened for the specific gate of Jessie and Cecily.

Thea sent a message to the others that it was time. I gave her a reassuring smile and walked out to the middle of the road. Within moments, Jessie, Cecily, and what might have been a hundred men rounded the bend.

Cecily held up her arm, and the troops behind her came to a halt.

"Hey, there. Fancy meeting you here," I said, waving at her.

Cecily's eyes narrowed on me. The first rows of troops behind her all raised their guns, sighting them on me. I gave the signal, and Thea tossed multiple smoke bombs our way.

There were shouts as large plumes of smoke erupted from the canisters. I launched into action, racing toward the group. Slipping between the girls, I rushed straight into their forces. I dashed in, the blades I had summoned slashing anyone that came within my reach. I needed to incapacitate as many of them as I could before I had to focus on keeping the girl's attention.

As Cecily grabbed my arm and pulled me back, it seemed that my time was up. I spun, putting momentum in my right hook and connecting straight into her jaw. She crashed backward. Without missing a beat, I pushed forward, stalking after her.

With each clash with the girls, my reservations against fighting them dropped away. There was only one way to make it out of these fights, and it wasn't by going easy on them. Jessie and I had started to recognize each other's moves, helping us make it look realistic while not actually doing any harm. Making it appear like enough of a challenge where Jessie still appeared loyal but also kept both me and her sister from doing any real damage to each other.

Jessie slipped between us and pushed me back to give Cecily

some breathing room. We had maneuvered off to the side of the road, and the bulk of the troops were surging forward toward the barricade. Thea was still in the cover of the trees, waiting for the right moment. As soon as they had all moved past, she stepped out and started to fire on the troops from the back. Blocking them between her and our own force ahead of them.

I made a feint to the right and slipped around Jessie's side as she lunged for where I had been. I moved in on Cecily, slicing out at her, and she jumped back just enough to evade my strike. I twisted out of the way of Jessie as she jabbed at me.

Thea cried out, and my attention instantly snapped to her. Some of the troops had turned back and were advancing on her. She was limping as she headed for the cover of the trees.

Cecily and Jessie turned their heads to see where my attention had gone. Cecily took off, racing for her. I launched myself after her, but she matched me for speed. Terror gripped me, memories of Atty dying at Jasper's hands flooding my mind. I couldn't be too late again. I had to protect her.

Cecily plunged her knife toward Thea's back, but in a flash, Jessie was there. Unable to correct in time, the blade stabbed straight into Jessie's chest.

"No!" I screamed and reached them, grabbing Cecily's shoulders and flinging her away. I put myself between her and the others, crouched, arms wide, ready to block her no matter which way she came at me.

"Traitor," Cecily hissed, but she was looking past me to Jessie.

"I won't let you hurt her." Jessie had her hand pressed tight to her wound. "Can't you see what we're doing is wrong? Please, Cess."

Pain twisted Jessie's face as she tried to get through to her sister. Jessie, with lurching steps, passed me and held her free hand out to Cecily. I put out a protective arm between Thea and the girls, keeping her behind me. I checked on her quickly, my eyes asking if she was okay. She nodded, and a weight lifted from my chest. The men who had been advancing on Thea had turned back when they saw Cecily moving in on her, so at least I didn't have to worry about them at the moment.

"If you're against us, then you are no longer needed," Cecily said as she flipped her knife in her grip and charged at Jessie, who just managed to stumble out of the way.

"Get to the others," I barked at Thea. I wouldn't be able to keep my mind on this if I was worried that she might get hurt. She hesitated but then limped toward the barricade.

Cecily came straight at me. I used the power in my legs to slam my shoulder into hers, and we crashed together. I ducked down while breaking her grip on me. Calling a knife into my hand from my suit, I sliced out at her while she was still off balance.

She roared as it slid into her ribs, and she got in a lucky shot with her elbow, making me stumble back. Jessie came up behind her and pinned her arms to her side. Cecily struggled, but Jessie's grip held. I rushed to them and held Cecily's face in my hands. Her eyes went wide, filled with rage.

"Cecily, it's me. It's Vi. We want to help you. I need you to remember," I begged, but there was no recognition there.

"Cecily, please," Jessie cried, curling around her sister as she held her tight.

She slammed her head back into her sister's, and I heard Jessie's nose break. It stunned her enough for her grip to falter. I reached out, trying to grab her, but she was too fast and my hands grasped air.

She glared at us from a few meters away and raised her arm. That was when I noticed she was holding something. Jessie's eyes went wide.

"No, don't!" she screamed, but her sister had already pressed the button. There was a buzz as a swarm of drones flew over us, racing toward our men. Within moments, behind us, explosions went off at the same time and I saw pieces of the barricade being thrown into the air from the blasts.

I looked at Jessie once before I spun to race toward whatever had just happened. The two would have to decide what to do with each other. I had to check on my people. Those drones had been rigged with explosives.

"Thea, Gwen, Benson, Anthony," I called out, unable to see them through the haze. Walking slowly, I noticed it wasn't just our people. Esmerelda's soldiers were also laid out from the blasts. My hand went to my throat, closing my eyes. To her, no life was sacred.

I screamed out for the others, fear taking over every part of my body. I heard some coughing and ran toward the sound. It was two of ours helping each other away from the wreckage.

"Are you hurt?" I put my hand on one of their shoulders and checked them both over. One had blood dripping down his forehead, but he just shook his head.

"We're fine. I'll call this in. Go check on the others," he said waving me off towards the others.

I headed toward the guard tower Gwen had been in. She was already back on the ground when I made it there, and we pulled each other in for a hug.

"Oh, thank the gods," she said. "I saw Benson over there; he's helping some others. Anthony is already checking on some of the wounded back that way."

"What about Thea? She had come this way." Panic washed through me.

"We'll find her," Gwen said calmly.

We spread out, and the dust started to settle. I saw Jessie making her way to me with Thea's arm draped over her shoulder. Both of them were limping and holding their chests.

"Gwen," I yelled to get her attention and then ran over to meet them. "Thank the gods you're okay. What about Cecily?"

Jessie shook her head. "She wasn't staying, and I wasn't leaving."

She looked defeated, but there was still the smallest glint in her eyes.

"Jessie," Gwen said with surprise.

"I hope it's okay if I'm here. I showed my cards when I got in Cecily's way."

Gwen ran up and gave her a one-armed hug before tapping her head to Jessie's.

"It's good to see you. We've got others wounded down that way," Gwen said.

Now that I knew my friends were safe, I turned and headed for someone leaning their back up against one of the barricades. It was one of Esmerelda's men holding together a gaping wound on his leg.

I hadn't thought Esmerelda could stoop any lower. I was wrong. Did she even recognize these people as humans? Everyone was nothing but a pawn to her. To be used, sacrificed, or discarded when their usefulness was gone.

Jessie's only option was to defect. Esmerelda would have known she didn't have control of her anymore, and with every fiber of my being, I knew she would have killed her. I was relieved to finally have my friend back, and we'd figure out some way to get through to Cecily. We had to.

The man's eyes were wide with fear as I came over.

I knelt and held out a hand. "Come with me. We'll get you patched up."

55

VI

6 Months Later...

I crawled across the roof of the school. The sun had gone down a few hours ago, but Aria was in what used to be my room, coloring. I peeked over the edge into the glass dome that raised over the attic.

She was so big. She looked more like a two or three year old, and this was only her first birthday. Hesitantly, I reached out and touched the glass where I could see her below me. I couldn't stop the tears as I leaned flat against the roof to stay out of sight and try to collect myself. My breathing was short and quick, and my throat had closed up. I was missing everything. I wanted to be with her more than almost anything in the world. Anything except making this world safe for her. I bit the side of my fist and tried to get myself under control.

From a few floors below, someone called Aria's name, and I heard her get up and head to the door. Had she heard that? She had been growing faster than kids her age and blowing past milestones one after another, but this would be something only she could do. Something she could have only gotten from me.

After she closed the door, I opened the hatch that would let me drop into the room. I knelt and spread out the papers she had been coloring in front of me. There were pictures of her with David and Joseph and the school. Pictures of her with other kids and the teachers. A picture of a tree with the sun shining high above.

My eyes caught on one. It had Geniviv written on it, there was a woman that had curly yellow hair standing there, holding an oversized sword and shield. I grabbed that one and folded it up, slipping it in my coat. I replaced it with a little box that had a bow wrapped around it. The tag had Aria's name on it but nothing else.

"Happy birthday, little one," I whispered as I left the way I had come.

I heard her steps pause before turning this way. I pushed myself out of sight and I could just barely see as the door opened and she came back in. She searched around for who had made that noise. Because she *had* heard me.

She saw the box and bent over to pick it up. Still looking around in confusion, she gave a shrug and started to open it. Inside was a leather-bound notebook with blank pages. David and Joseph had told us how much she enjoyed drawing. An excited smile spread across her face, and she searched once more but then held the sketchbook close to her chest and headed out the door. I listened as she skipped downstairs.

The others were waiting to sing her happy birthday, and I stayed long enough to listen. The need to stay washed over me again, but I forced myself to drop off the roof and slipped into the dense trees that lined the school.

Pushing myself into a run, I dipped in and out of the trees until my transport finally came into view. As soon as I was in the waiting copter, Anthony started to get ready for takeoff.

"How'd it go?" he asked as I threw on the headphones.

"As good as it could," I muttered. I was still a mess over having to leave again, but I would do it all over again, and I'd be back here in secret every year until the war was over. We had decided I would be the only one to come because I could stay out of sight.

I put through a call Chase.

"Hey, honey," Chase said, and I could hear him shuffling papers around. "How did she look?" His tone soft. I knew he was missing her as much as I was,

"Huge. Happy. She made a drawing of me, and I stole it."

His melodic laugh came through the line. "Of course you did."

"I think she's got my hearing," I blurted out. "I'm going to send David a message in a minute."

"It's going to get harder to hide who she is." It sounded like he set his papers down.

"I know. At least everyone in the school has sworn they won't say anything. Hopefully by the time any new kids come in who don't know, she'll stop growing as fast as she is now. David can just pass her off as being older, which will help. If we're lucky, we can finish this and get her back before anything happens that we need to worry about." I clung to that shred of hope that maybe in a few months, I could have her in my arms, a year tops.

"It's going to be okay."

I knew he was right. It had to be. My comm dinged with new information he just sent me.

"There's a change of plans though. You can't come straight here; we need you on the front. Esmerelda's troops just made a push into our territory.

"All right." A sigh escaped me. "I'll get home as soon as I can."

"I love you."

"I love you too. Talk soon." I hung up and remembered to breathe, in and out, in and out. Picking up the tablet I read through the details for what I was heading into.

If I could just get the tides to turn. If we could just do some real damage, we would be able to end this soon. Too many cities had been locked down, and anyone who might want to flee didn't make it very far. Not far enough to get to us. It seemed that Esmerelda might have an infinite resource of soldiers until she ran out of people. We had gotten word she was threatening families of people who tried to refuse the draft. I needed to end this. I needed to get home to my girl.

***

6 months later...

Leaning back against the wall with my eyes closed, I took a deep breath, and then another. I was trying to banish the red tinting my vision. Every time we went into the field, it was getting harder to banish the rage when we were done.

Finally, once I felt like I had control again, I used my comm to call Chase. It rang a few times before I heard a rustle on the other end.

"I'm up. I'm awake." He didn't sound like he was awake; he never did at first. It was two in the morning, and we had just made it back to a safe house. But he made me promise I would call every time, so I did.

"You should really just get some sleep," I chided.

"This is more important." He sighed, and I could tell he was wiping his hands across his face, working to fully wake up. "Everyone okay?"

"Yeah, we're all fine. The people we got out are on the way to the Nexus camp." I let myself rest heavily against the building.

"Good. CC1 already has everything prepared for the new arrivals."

We fell into a silence born from how exhausted we both were. Most of our calls had long stretches of just listening to the other person be there. Just enjoying the fact that they were safe.

"How are you? How did the meeting with the southern captains go?" I asked.

"It went fine, but apparently the heads of the new cities are giving our dads some problems. I'm surprised it didn't happen sooner, honestly. Everyone has needs, and there isn't enough to go around. Everything had to be built so quickly, and Jupiter has to smuggle us some of the parts we need. Esmerelda has been blocking our routes from Neria." He paused. "But you know all that."

I grinned, even though he couldn't see it. "Yes, seeing as we're about to be sent to try to break through. *Someone*," I said in a sarcastic tone, "happened to give me that order earlier today."

"Was that today?" He moaned. "Everything is blurring together."

"I guess technically, it was yesterday, but you're preaching to the choir." Because everything had blurred together. Where we were, what we were there for, the people I saw laid out in the infirmaries. The people we had to bury. The cities and camps I had seen burnt to the ground. The scarred land. The suffering and the pain, but also the joy.

"Isn't Aria getting so big in those photos David sent over?" he finally asked.

"I know. How old do you think she looks? At least three, right?"

"I think that was about the size Thea was."

"Remember back at the palace with all of us there. That seems like an entire lifetime ago. I loved your quarters. I miss your mom's cooking and all of us piling in front of the fireplace." I picked mindlessly at the wall behind me.

"I miss her apple cider when the first hints of fall arrived."

I sighed. That cider had honestly been one of my favorite things of the entire year. "You should see if your dad knows the recipe."

"I'll make some the next time you're home."

I was going to hold him to that. "When would that be boss?"

After Thea was hurt at the barricade, we had been given a few days off, but other than that, I had only seen him a handful of times in the past six months. There was always something that needed us.

"After this next one, I promise. We'll get Jessie and her team to cover. I'll get you guys some rest."

"Only if we're really not needed." That was why we had only seen each other for such a short time—because we couldn't just ignore calls for help. The entire team always agreed to go if something came up, and something *always* came up.

"How many times have you lectured me about burning out the team? Which also includes you, even if you never consider that. Plus, I just really need you. I... need some time together."

I needed to see him too. This war was taking a toll on both of us. "Okay, I promise. So, you better figure out that recipe quick because it won't take us long to reconnect the supply chain. For a while, anyway."

"Good. I'll be ready."

The smell of dinner—or breakfast, I suppose—wafted to me from the kitchen of our safe house. We had infiltrated one of the cities for this mission and we'd be heading out tomorrow.

I pushed myself up and headed that way. "Food's almost done," I told him. The others were already gathered and chatting as Benson finished cooking. I put the call on speaker. "Say hi."

"Hey, guys."

Everyone called hello to Chase.

"Get some sleep. We'll see you back here soon."

I clicked the call off speaker. "You should get to bed yourself. I'll talk to you later. Have a good day. I love you."

"I love you too. Talk soon... Actually, I'll see you soon."

We did not see each other soon.

We were stuck trying to clear the supply route for over three weeks. Jessie and her team couldn't get out to us for over a week, and even with both of us, it still took that long. Now, we finally managed to push them far enough back to get some shipments in from Jupiter and the others.

My bag was slung over my shoulder as we stepped onto the hanger floor. We had returned to Nexus camp, and I couldn't wait to get to our house, throw my things down, take a nice hot shower, and sleep in a comfortable bed.

But first, I couldn't wait to see Chase.

I heard his rushed footsteps headed our way, and I dropped my bag just as I saw him. I'd say we met in the middle, but it was more one sided because I couldn't get my feet to move. As he reached me, my arms instinctively wrapped around his waist, and I laid my head on his chest, relaxing into his grip. I wondered if I might cry from how good this felt and how much I had missed it. As always, his hands rubbed circles on my back, waiting for me to be ready.

"Hey, bro," Thea called.

"Hey. I'll catch up with you tomorrow," he told her, and I finally leaned up to give him a kiss. "Let's get you home." He bent down and picked up my bag then knotted his fingers with mine to pull me along.

It felt like an eternity, but finally the house came into view, and I picked up my pace. Chase dropped my bag in the hallway as soon as we got inside. He kissed me on the cheek as he swept by, heading to get the hot water going in the bathtub while I tugged at my boots, almost knocking myself over as I did. Just like we did every time I returned to Nexus.

I tore off every grimy piece of clothing as I made my way to the bathroom, not wanting to be in them a second longer. The room was already starting to warm, and steam rose from the tub. The sigh that left me at the sight released months-worth of tension. I slipped into the tub and moaned as the warm water caressed my tight muscles. Then, as always Chase was there pushing my hair over my shoulder and worked on loosening the knots there.

Words would come later; this time was to slowly return to normal. To remember that I was a human, not just a soldier or a weapon. To bring myself back from being tense and on edge every second of every day. This was a safe place, and I could let myself relax. I never realized how much it affected me until I got home.

When the stakes were life or death. I had people's lives in my hands when I was out there. My people.

Chase leaned over and kissed my temple before he left. Once he was gone, I pulled my knees up and rested my cheek on them. Staring at the steam flickering in and out of view, it reminded me of the smoke rising off the front lines from the cannon fire. I pressed my eyes closed, trying to clear my mind. The sound of gunfire was so normal for me now that I felt like something was missing here in the quiet.

I could hear Chase headed my way, so I popped the drain and grabbed a towel, wrapping it around myself as I stepped out. Chase came around the corner with the cheesiest smile on his face, throwing me some clothes then holding up a mug proudly, which was also steaming. I gasped.

"No," I whispered. "Is this it?"

"It's perfect if I say so myself. Mom would be proud." He handed it over, and I inhaled the spicy scent, memories washing over me. Happy ones for once.

I threw on the clothes quickly and then didn't wait for it to cool before taking a sip. He was right. It was perfect.

"Just like home," I said. "I love you. This is amazing."

"Just like home."

He had a fire going in the hearth, and I dropped onto the couch, curling one leg to my chest and sat back to enjoy this. I bounced as Chase dropped down next to me, and he grabbed one of my feet to start to massage it. This was my love language—touching, soothing something that was sore.

We talked about Aria and our friends, and the goings on of our day-to-day lives that we didn't convey in our middle-of-the-night check-ins. We talked until I could barely keep my eyes open, and he pulled me to bed. With the mix of the comfort, the warmth of his body, and the weight of his arm slung over my waist, it was mere moments before I drifted into a dreamless sleep.

56

Vi

2 Years Later...

Perspiration collected within the gas mask covering my nose and mouth as I raced through no-man's-land. I launched myself over a barbed wire fence that used to show the edge of Esmerelda's territory. We had pushed them back over the past few months. I had been stationed here on the front lines long enough it blurred together. Shells exploded around me from the cannons they pointed this way. The sounds of them whistling through the air gave me just enough warning to dodge when they were landing close.

This war had drug on longer than any of us had expected. I hated to admit it, but her weapons were more advanced than ours. We were only managing to recreate what she had already thrown at us. We had word the top scientists of Neria had defected to her care. Brining their secret work and patents with them. They also had the advantage of not caring about collateral damage when creating these weapons. Something we would never do.

The roar of hundreds of my soldiers rose behind me as we charged forward once more. The enemy had been lobbing mist canisters into our path, but luckily, we had shipped in enough gas masks.

Jumping into a long arc it ended up dropping me in the middle of their trench.

I was a wave of carnage as I sped through the confused men, my knives slick with blood when I finally let them dissolve as my troops came flooding in behind me. I was breathing heavily. It was almost impossible to not go for the deadly strikes. I wanted to end them all. I wanted them dead at my feet. I needed their blood. It took me hours to reign in the bloodlust after a battle now. I was losing myself.

Thea came up behind me and held out her fist, and I tapped my knuckles to it before I turned and took off in the other direction. As I jumped over bodies littering my path to get to the others, I started to hear the enemy troops panicking and fleeing toward the safety of Esmerelda's territory.

The chants from my own men rang out. "For the true queen! Beware the bloody red queen!"

It was their warning call to the enemy. *Beware the bloody red queen because she's coming for you.*

The name had spread through the troops since my escape. It had become their cheer when we claimed our victories. I hated it, but I wasn't going to take it from them. Half of my power was what people built me up to be, what they thought I was. I was their queen and their general, and I would do whatever it took to win. Both sides had seen what I looked like after a tough battle, and many times, the name fit as I was drenched in crimson.

I caught sight of Benson knocking his way through the men in front of him, but the crowd was thinning as they fled. Jumping up and out, I put my hands on my hips and scanned the area. The enemy was fleeing, some toppling from gunshots. I saw Gwen perched in her nest and firing off shots. She must have sighted me on her scope because she waved. I returned it before jumping back in.

I started to wind my way through the trench again, searching for their command post. It ended up not being much more than an area with wood slats perched across the top and a small table with papers strewn around, some knocked to the ground.

Bending down, I grabbed up the papers and started to shuffle through them. Most of them weren't anything helpful, but then I stopped as something caught my eye. I dropped the others and stepped out of the shade to read it better.

I tapped my comm and heard Chase within moments.

"Did everything go smoothly?" There was always a hint of worry in his voice in my first call after a raid.

"Yeah, but I found something." The excitement was clear in my own. "There is a base no more than a few miles from here. That must be where they retreated to. It seems like it might be a weapon manufacturing plant. We're going to go after them."

"Okay, send us the information, and we'll do some digging and get everything prepped for it."

"No, we're going now. They're going to be unorganized, and they won't expect it. This is our best chance."

He sighed in resignation. "Fine. Report in as soon as you can." He paused, but before I could say anything, he added, "Be safe."

"Always." I was sure he was rolling his eyes. "Love you. We'll talk soon." I shut off the call. Turning, I searched for the others and saw Benson headed my way. I waved him over.

He looked at the paper clutched tightly in my hand. "Something good?"

"Get everyone ready. We're making a push due west. There is a base, and we're going to take it."

I started putting out a message to Thea and Gwen. Then to Anthony who was with George in the camp behind us to update them on my plan. They had been stationed out here with us and helped coordinate with the rest of the troops.

Within a few minutes, the rest of the squad arrived. Once I had the squad all together, we pulled up a map and started to go over my ideas. We'd be moving out within the hour.

"Man, it feels good to finally be making some headway," Thea said, and everyone agreed.

Over the past few months, we had been making inroads to

Esmerelda's territory across the entire engagement line. Her forces had been dwindling, and the prisoners we had taken were sick and hungry. We had heard there had been revolts in some of the cities she had locked down. This was it. I could feel it, and I wasn't going to let our momentum here stall.

"I'm going to scout. Gwen come with me. We'll regroup in thirty and get everyone ready to move."

Gwen hiked her rifle strap up on her shoulder, and we both headed out of the trench. She split off to get to higher ground to cover me. On silent feet, I made my way farther out, searching for anyone left who would be still retreating.

The path seemed clear enough. It was time, and we were ready.

Standing on a hill with my arms propped on my waist, I watched the buzzing base beneath me. The rest of my force was just on the other side of the ridge, waiting for the signal, and gave it.

With a roar, they started forward. I took my place at the front of the wave and raced down the hill toward the perimeter of the base. The noise of the stampede rushing behind me was overwhelming, but I could still make out the startled shouts as their people noticed the oncoming swarm.

When I got close enough, in one jump, I landed on the platform of the closest guard tower. I grabbed his rifle and bent it, tossing the guard out and to the ground. I ripped a nearby turret from its perch and crushed it so it couldn't be used.

Once I was sure it was inoperable, I leapt from the tower and down into the chaos below. We were flowing into the area, sweeping through the few guards this far out. I pushed myself faster to make it back to the front, and I saw a line of men ahead who had started to amass, finally realizing what was going on.

Racing ahead of my forces, I jumped and weaved through the gunfire. Within moments, I was on the group and started to slash my way through their formation. I broke up their bulk as they scattered to get out of my reach, and my men took full advantage, charging into their ranks.

A wave of enemy soldiers crushed in around me, and I crouched as they piled in, trying to use sheer numbers to stop me. With a scream, I used enough power to break free and scatter them back. My comm pinged. I tapped it as I bent backward to evade a swing from the nearest man.

"What?" I barked.

"There is a problem." It was David's voice on the other end.

"I'm kind of in the middle of something." I quickly stepped back, evading the slice of a knife.

"It's Aria."

That froze me on the spot, and a volley of bullets ripped into my shoulder. My head whipped to where it came from, and I launched myself at who had shot them.

"What do you mean?" That was Chase. I hadn't realized he had been on the call too. It must be bad.

My movements were delayed as my mind swirled through the list of terrible things that could have happened.

"There was a video from the field trip of Aria using her abilities. We didn't realize, and it's been circulating. I'm worried Esmerelda might have seen it."

I grunted as someone slammed into me and knocked off my balance.

"Vi?" Chase's voice was worried.

"I'm fine," I muttered and slashed out with my blades to give myself some breathing room.

"Okay, David, I'm on my way," Chase said. "We'll figure out what to do about it and see how we can improve security."

"I'll find Anthony and be there as soon as I can." I growled as someone came up behind me and got their arm around my throat. My elbow connected with their ribs, and I threw them off me.

"Be safe," both said to me before I clicked off the call.

I had to tamp down the worry and get my mind back to the task at hand. I wouldn't be of any use if I got myself killed before Anthony got here.

I linked in the others to my comm.

"Something's happened with Aria. Anthony get your hands on anything you can to get us to the school. I have to go."

"We've got this," Thea said quickly.

"Don't worry about us," Benson chimed in.

"We'll take care of everything here," Gwen agreed.

And I knew they would.

57

ESMERELDA

"Your Majesty, I think you'll want to see this," Morgan said.

I was in the middle of a meeting with my cabinet, working on plans to quell the revolts within the cities. I turned to her, hoping my exasperation was clear on my face.

"What is it now?" I sighed. My headache was growing in intensity, and I might need another dose of medication soon.

She just handed me a tablet and then pressed play on the video. It was obviously shot in Soland; there were golden towers rising into the sky from the garden-like walkways. I didn't know what exactly could be of any interest to me there, but then I saw it.

A young girl who seemed to be about seven was jumping between two columns to reach the peak, which was a good twenty feet off the ground. There was a slim beam that connected the columns in the area, and she was doing backflips and twists across it to the cheers of the people below.

The garden was filled with sculptures, and a group of kids ran into one of them. It rocked a few times before it started to topple. Within seconds, the girl was on the ground, and before it could crush the children below, she caught it, holding the weight on her back as the others scattered out of the way. Then, with a hefty push, she tossed it away.

I rewound it for a few seconds and let it play again, and again, and again.

"Everyone get out," I snapped, and they all rushed from the room, leaving me alone with Morgan. The video played a bit further, and whoever was filming ran over to her. I paused it once more as she came into full view of the camera. Her bright green eyes flared beneath sandy brown bangs.

"Well, isn't that interesting." I knew those eyes. I sent a message for Howard to come to me.

As soon as he walked through the door, I pushed the tablet into his face.

"What do you think of this?" I asked him.

His brow furrowed as he watched it. He started to pace, playing it multiple times—something he did when he was thinking.

"You think this is the child?" He looked at me over the tablet.

"Could it be?"

"Possibly." He shrugged, but I saw the gleam in his eye. He thought so too.

I turned to Morgan. "Find out where she is. Get her and bring her here. This is a top priority. Send Cecily with as many men as we have available."

She rushed from the room to get everything ready.

"Very interesting," Howard muttered as he watched the video again.

"It seems Astor managed to keep a secret." I growled. I had been convinced the child was lost, we had seen Genevieve in the weeks and months after her escape. This little girl looked to be too old, but I could feel it. It had to be her, and if it was, I was going to have all the leverage I needed to end this.

Love was their weakness; it always had been. It only proved again that fear was the most effective way to rule.

Not only would I have something that Astor held dear, but I

would have another subject to test to see if she might be the way to unlock this cure once and for all. I had lost two more bones in my leg, and my kidney had to be replaced since the loss of the facility and her escape.

Howard handed the tablet back to me.

"Send that to me. I'm going to start getting some things ready." He put an arm on my shoulder. "This is promising." He turned and headed out; I could tell his mind was already racing with what we might be able to glean from the child.

I dropped back into my chair and couldn't keep the grin from my face.

This was it. I could feel it.

I'd finally have everything I wanted.

58

Vi

"No... gods. No, no, no," I cursed as Anthony flew within sight of the school. Smoke was curling into the air; parts of the school were in flames. Groups of kids were on their knees with their hands up as troops pointed guns at them. "Fly straight over. Don't slow down," I barked and ran to the back of the cargo plane. It was the first plane we had come across, and I hadn't known time was of the essence. If I had, I would have made sure we took something faster.

Terror permeated every cell of my body as I hit the button to open the ramp. Anthony dove to get as close to the ground as he dared. Once we were over the school, I leapt. Wind whipped through my hair as I hurtled toward the ground.

My momentum had me sliding to a stop as soon as I landed. Closing my eyes, I listened for Chase, David, Aria, any of them. I saw David with a group of the kids being guarded in the courtyard. I hoped that meant the other teachers were with other groups helping to keep the children calm.

"Cecily, stop. You know this is wrong," I managed to hear Chase say, and my throat tightened. I sprinted in their direction.

Let me get there in time. Don't let me be too late. Not again.

I crashed through the doors that led from the courtyard to the foyer. The wood splintered and exploded upon impact. I skidded to a stop when I saw Chase with his arms out, Aria hiding behind him and Cecily with a gun pointed at them.

Chase's attention snapped to me, and in that moment, Cecily fired.

As if in slow motion three bullets ripped into Chase's chest, he dropped heavily to a knee, and Aria screamed as Cecily grabbed her by the arm.

"Cecily!" I roared.

She turned to me, and the smile she wore made my stomach drop. It was malicious, and gleeful, but her eyes were also empty. Like killing him meant nothing to her except the fact that she knew it would destroy me.

Then, she was running and dragging Aria behind her. Aria was trying to tug her arm free but was no match for the older girl. They burst through the front doors, and I was hot on their heels, but I stumbled as I came upon Chase doubled over. I could already hear his labored breathing and a wet sound that shouldn't be there.

"Go," he growled at me, so I did. We both knew I had to get to Aria.

As I broke through the front doors, I came face to face with rows of her men. They instantly fired, and I had to jump to escape their reach.

They surrounded me, and I tried to push my way through, but there were too many bodies. I tried to jump up to get free, but hands grabbed me, pulling me back.

I roared, my fury consuming me. I could just barely see Cecily and Aria ahead, making their way onto a waiting hover copter. Tossing the people closest to me away, I tried to break free. I sliced and stabbed. I grabbed any weapon I could and eventually thinned out the crowd before realizing they were turning and fleeing as Cecily's transport was already taking off.

My heart raced, and I felt like I would be sick. I broke free and pushed myself faster, racing for the plane. I couldn't let them get away, but before I could get close enough, it was already speeding away. I kept running, my mind was unable to understand what just happened. It was clear within mere moments, there was no hope of catching them. I pulled my hands through my hair, tugging at it as I doubled over. My vision blurred, I felt like I couldn't' breathe, I was going be sick, and then I heard Chase cough and the splatter of blood.

Snapped out of my terror, I turned and sped to him. He was on his knees, one hand bracing himself as he stared at the other covered in blood.

"Chase." I panicked and knelt next to him. I gently grabbed him into my arms and pulled him back so I could look him over. There were three spots spreading the stain of blood across his chest. "Hey, hey. It's going to be fine," I said, my voice was shaking. I screamed for help. Since the men out front had left, I hoped that meant all the other troops were retreating. Someone had to be close now, didn't they? Someone had to come and help.

Chase put a hand to my chin and turned me to look at him. Pain was clear in his eyes, and tears slipped down my face. His thumb brushed away one of them.

"You need to listen to me." He had to stop to try to catch his breath. "You are going to be okay. You are the strongest person I know. You've survived so much, and you are going to survive this."

"Don't say that." I called for help again. If someone could get here with a med pack in time, he would be okay. He needed to be okay. My heart started to shatter as I saw how pale he was. This wasn't real.

"Genevieve," he said, his tone firm, "you need to go and get our girl. You are going to save her, and you are an amazing mother. You need to tell her how much I love her and how sorry I am."

"No..." I begged. I couldn't see through my tears, and I couldn't breathe past the lump in my throat. "You can't leave me. It's going to be okay. We're going to fix you up." I pressed my hand to his wounds, trying to do anything to help.

"You can do this. I'll always be with you." He gasped, and I heard liquid where it shouldn't be. "I've loved you for my entire life. I'm so happy for the time we had together; it never would have been enough." He wheezed and gripped my hand as he gave one last little smile—the one that was just for me.

I leaned down and kissed him, his blood coating my lips. My tears dripped onto his cheeks and my hands twisted in his shirt.

"You're my whole life. Please, stay with me," I begged. "I can't lose you. Please. I love you so much." I cried for help again as I held him close. His breathing rattled in his chest, and I finally heard people running our way. I couldn't even look up. I just kept calling for help, over and over. Chase's eyes closed as I heard his breathing slow then stop.

"No," I whispered as someone took him from me and laid him on the ground. I saw them rip open a med pack, and start to try to save him, but I heard his heart.

Thump, thump... thump... thump...

Then, it faded until it didn't beat again. They pumped on his chest, trying to restart it, but there was nothing. A scream I had only heard once before ripped from me. It was the same scream that came from Gwen when Atty died. A primal scream of my world, heart, and soul shattering into a million pieces.

Arms wrapped around me and pulled me back into a chest. Riley was there holding me close. Joseph and David were still trying everything they could to save him.

I just clutched on to Riley as I cried. Part of me knew nothing would work. He was gone.

My daughter had been kidnapped and my husband was dead.

And I had been useless.

Aria.

Eventually, I wiped at my face and pushed myself up. My entire body felt like it was made of lead, yet I stood. I stared down on the face that had loved me so fiercely, had gotten me through the worst days in my life, who was my everything, and I knew I couldn't grieve right now. When I put a hand on David's shoulder, he looked up at me. I shook my head. I saw something in him break, but he moved back so I could sit next to Chase once more.

I knelt and pushed the hair away from his face. I couldn't breathe, and my vision blurred again, but I pressed a kiss to his forehead.

"I have to go get our daughter," I whispered to him. "I'll love you for the rest of time. I'll try my best to be the person you saw."

I stood and turned to David.

"Find out where that plane went." I growled.

He glanced from me to Chase and back before he got up to start searching.

Numbness washed over me, but my feet moved as purpose drove me forward. I couldn't break now, not when there was so much at stake. Rage flooded through me, and I conjured an image of Esmerelda and Cecily.

I was ending this. Now.

They were going to pay.

59

Vi

"This is General Astor. All cells that can arrive at Longdale by sunset are ordered to move out immediately. All aerial support is to load with max munitions and be ready for an assault on the palace. The siege will commence at dusk." I clicked off the communications device and turned back to the others.

We were prepping at the edges of Longdale, the capital city. David had been able to track the plane to the palace. Gwen, Benson, and Thea had flown to meet us as soon as they heard about Chase and Aria. Naya had even arrived with Jessie. She had been visiting and wouldn't hear of not helping. George and Anthony were connecting with other cells to make sure everything was coordinated.

We were all devastated, but the others, like myself, were determined. We had a goal to get us through the next few hours. We could grieve when this was all over.

So, this was it. We had been moving towards this goal, but I wasn't waiting any longer. I thanked the gods we had made enough progress in the last few months to make this even a possibility.

The time had come to end this war. We were going to take the city, the palace, and get my daughter back. I'd burn it to the ground if I had to. Nothing would stop me.

"All right, so, I'm going to slip in through the city before the attack. Just like in Neria, I'll be dealing with the palace while they send everyone they have out to deal with our attack on the city."

"We're all going," Benson said, and the rest agreed.

Thea looked like she had revenge on her mind. Everyone did. We were out for blood, and we would get our revenge.

David had made the calls to let everyone know. It was everything I could do to keep myself moving. Moving toward my daughter to save her. I had a singular purpose.

"We're family. We're not letting you go in alone," Gwen said and put a hand on my shoulder. I laid my own on top of it, my thanks in that grip. Anything to keep me grounded in the present.

Anytime my mind slipped from what I needed to be doing, all I could see Cecily shooting Chase, the wounds in his chest, his lifeless body. Aria being tugged into the hover copter and the door shutting her away from me.

I felt like I was crawling out of my skin. The plan was to leave when the sun started to set, but I couldn't wait.

"Let's go, then. George, you're in charge."

He nodded gravely to me. "Good luck."

The others turned, and we all went to grab our weapons and get ready to head into the city. Jessie grabbed my arm and pulled me to the side.

"I heard it was Cecily." The guilt she felt was obvious. "I just want to say I'm sorry. I know that doesn't fix anything, but she's completely under Esmerelda's control. If she was herself... she would never."

I knew what those conditioning helmets could do, but the rational part of my brain wasn't here right now. My entire body felt like it was on fire with my rage.

"But she did it nonetheless," I hissed, and she flinched. Red started to cloud my vision. "She killed him, and she kidnapped Aria. We both know exactly what they're going to do to her."

"Please, just let me deal with her in there." Her voice was quiet.

I shook my head. I wasn't going to make any promises.

I wouldn't be showing any mercy today.

The sun had set by the time we made our way to one of the secret entrances into the palace. Perks of growing up here, I knew every nook and cranny in this place. As we made our way through the tunnel, I held out a light to show the way. Jessie was right on my heels, followed by Thea, Gwen, Anthony, Benson, and Naya.

Jessie and I were both listening for any sign of danger, but hardly anyone knew this route. I wasn't sure if Esmerelda even knew of it. We slipped along silently until the door to the interior came into view.

I looked over my shoulder to the others, who all shifted their weapons to be ready for anything. I cracked door open, checked if the coast was clear, and then made my way into one of the marbled hallways.

Once I was sure it was clear, I moved to give the others room to join me. In the distance, I heard the explosions of the first wave flying over the city. There was also chatter coming in from the outer city calling for help and reinforcements. They were reporting that they were being breached by land and by air.

The alarm was raised, and instructions were being given to organize the response to our attack. People were scattering away from our location, so I moved ahead. The others flanked me as we swept through my childhood home, trying to find where Aria was being kept.

Footsteps came our way, and Jessie froze. She looked to me and then back in the direction of the person approaching.

I growled as she took a step ahead and faced me. She shook her head. I could see how this was paining her, but I pushed forward, and she stepped backward to match me.

"I can't let you."

"Move," I snapped as Cecily came into view. My friends sighted their weapons on her.

Jessie looked at the others, pleading. "Please, let me handle this."

The others shifted, seemingly uncomfortable.

"Go, keep searching for her," I said over my shoulder, but I didn't move. Slowly, they turned and raced away to keep searching the building.

My focus was completely trained on Cecily, my vision bathed in red. She moved into a fighting stance at the same time I did, and Jessie looked back and forth between us.

"Please, both of you," she begged.

The sound of the last beats of Chase's heart pounded in my ears. In the time it took me to launch off my rear foot, Jessie blocked my path. I tossed her away, twisting to aim for Cecily as she sped around her sister. We crashed together, and Cecily managed to get me on my back as we fell.

With a roar, I hit her with a right hook, knocking her back enough for me to get my legs under me again. I pounced on her, using the moment she was unbalanced. A blade came to life in my hand, and I stabbed at her with everything I had. She just managed to slip out of the way, and it lodged in the ground next to her.

Jessie grabbed my arm and tossed me back. Then, she blocked Cecily when she came for me. The three of us jumped and launched attacks, each spinning out of the way of the other. Our powers had always been matched, and now that it wasn't two on one, none of us could get the upper hand.

Our fight took us in and out of rooms as we crashed through doorways and a few walls until we found ourselves in one of the maintenance rooms, where bundles of wires and pipes connected from multiple floors.

Perfect.

I backed Cecily up against one of the walls, where I could slice into the cables behind her. She lowered her shoulder and came charging at me to push me back and give her some room to move.

Jessie slammed her sister into the wall by her shoulders, shearing some pipes. Steam started to spill into the room. A buzzing caught my attention, and I looked to where she had just landed. A live wire was sparking behind them.

"Sorry, Jessie," I muttered. I gripped her arm and threw her into the far wall. Then, I pressed into Cecily and took the wire that was as big as my wrist, pulling it from the wall and crushing it into the back of her neck. She screamed as she convulsed. I could feel the electricity passing through me too, but I held on. When I couldn't stand it a moment longer, I dropped them both.

Jessie screamed and scrambled to Cecily. She pulled her into her arms, the younger girl limp in her grip, and pushed her hair away to see her face.

Now that she was unconscious, all I could see was the little girl we had saved back in Neria. The knowledge that Chase was gone still weighed on me; I didn't feel any better.

"I'm sorry, Cecily," I whispered before I turned and headed back into the palace to find the others, leaving the sisters behind.

She hadn't deserved any of this, she was just a little girl who had been tortured to the brink of death. I knew we had tried everything to get through to her. I knew I had failed her.

But my pain still wouldn't let me forgive her. Not completely. Not right now.

I pushed myself into a jog, listening for my team to guide my path.

Then, I heard it.

Aria was yelling for help.

60

Vi

I burst into the throne room to find Esmerelda there with Aria, whose hands were shackled. They were so small they had to be custom made. She seemed even more minuscule compared to the imposing throne Esmerelda was perched upon.

Rage exploded through me as I saw my little girl furious but also terrified on the floor. A doctor I had seen while being held captive stood behind her. She jerked against the restraints, and if looks could kill, I wouldn't have anyone to fight.

I saw myself in her anger, but also her fear. All I wanted to do was to make everything better. To make it so she'd never have to feel this pain ever again. I could feel my control slipping. The beast was emerging. I just hoped she didn't fear me too when this was all over.

There were rows of guards with their weapons trained on me as I slowed to a stop.

"Ah, yes. As always, if things are exploding, an Astor is nearby. I've been expecting you." She pursed her lips slightly at the sight of me.

"Cecily isn't coming," I told her. "Now, give Aria to me." I took a step, and the wall of men adjusted their grip on their guns.

Esmerelda pulled the chain, and Aria stumbled forward. She put her hand possessively around Aria's throat. Aria tried to pull away, but she held her firm. Blood slipped from under Esmerelda's nails. I snarled at the sight.

"Oh, no. I think not. Your daughter isn't going anywhere."

Aria's eyes went wide. I thought back to the drawing she had made of me years ago that I still had tucked away in my things. So far, we had been able to keep the secret of who she was from her. At least, enough so that Aria couldn't have been sure, even if she had a suspicion.

Then, I saw the understanding wash over her as she realized who Chase must have been when he had tried to protect her. Pain crossed her face, but then the anger returned.

That's my girl. Don't give up.

"You aren't getting out of this alive, Esmerelda." I gestured at the men surrounding me. "You know you don't have enough to stop me. Especially now that you've lost Cecily."

Aria's gaze fell to me. She raised her chin straightened her back. *That's right, little, stay strong. I'm coming.*

I was going to get her out of here no matter what.

Esmerelda snarled, and as one, the men in front of me fired. I leapt clear of most of it and went on the move. I started to make my way through the group, but these men were faster and stronger than the grunts I saw on the front lines.

One grabbed me by my neck and slammed me down. I had to roll to evade the next volley of gunfire. From a crouch, I pushed myself forward and knocked a group ahead of me down. I grabbed one of their rifles by the barrel and swung it around like a bat. I took someone out at the knees, another with a perfect crack across his jaw.

I stumbled as someone managed to get a hit into my ribs. I hissed at the impact but got my feet under me and spun, catching someone by the wrist and getting their gun. I shot someone's foot then their thigh as they dropped.

I made my way meticulously through the crowd. They dropped

like flies. After shooting another in the shoulder, I turned to find the edge of a rifle pressed against my forehead.

I looked up then back at the man holding the gun. Before he could pull the trigger, I took the barrel in my hand and squeezed until the metal crumpled in my grip. He gasped and moved to pull away, but I caught him and headbutted him. He fell unconscious to the ground.

Turning I saw the doctor trying to pull Aria away as he and Esmeralda fled for a hidden door behind the drapes at the edge of the room.

I screamed, announcing the primal fury that had control of me. I was on them in seconds. Reaching Esmerelda, I tossed her into the middle of the room. I grabbed the doctor next with a snarl and slammed my foot down on the side of his leg, and it buckled the wrong direction. He wouldn't be going anywhere anytime soon.

I took a moment to look Aria over, seeing the shock but also understanding in her eyes. Gently I broke the metal of her shackles, making sure not to hurt her, before turning my attention to my step-mother once more.

I stalked after her, but she was getting to her feet and stumbling away from me. Her men groaned in pain behind her. Hate boiled within me, just like it had with Cecily. I wouldn't be calmed. I would finally be free. She would pay for everything she had done to my people, my family, and me.

Esmerelda ripped at her skirt, giving her the ability to move more freely. Then, she stood straight to face me.

"You have ruined everything," she hissed at me. "I should have killed you when you were a child."

"Yeah, you should have," I agreed. "You made me into this. You created your own downfall." I held my hands wide as I continued pressing forward and she kept backing up. "Why? Why have you done all of this?" I asked her. It was something I had always wondered. What would make a person become this? Do everything she had done?

"You'd never understand," she said, her tone heavy. She lashed out at me, but I just stepped out of reach.

"I don't care. You owe me this. You ruined my life for it. You ruined my kingdom for it."

"Please," the doctor said from behind me. "She's just been searching for a cure."

I scoffed.

"You did all of this because you didn't want to die?" It wasn't enough, her excuse wasn't anywhere good enough.

"I deserve to rule. Neria should have been mine. This disease took that from me."

"So, you killed my mother and took my country instead? All because your daddy didn't love you?" I spit at her. "You deserve nothing."

She lunged and landed a punch straight to my cheek. She got another hit straight to my ribs, and my bones broke under her metal fist. I just stood there, taking it. She was nothing compared to me. I was a predator, and she was prey. Her little claws wouldn't hurt me now.

I waited and withstood the blows she landed. Finally, she pulled back, her eyes were wide with fear, and was breathing heavily. Even with her metal skeleton she would never hurt me enough to stop me.

Now, it was my turn. I launched myself at her, but she was quick and evaded me. My anger made me sloppy, but I didn't care. After all these years, I was ready for her. My attacks hit metal as she blocked my blows. For someone who always had others carry out her dirty work, she was putting up a better fight than I had expected, but it wouldn't matter.

I was a weapon. I had spent the last years of my life honing my skills until no one could match me. I finally had her pinned. My next attack pushed her to her knees. In a last ditch effort she jumped up and grappled so we toppled to the ground together.

I twisted so I was straddling her before raining punches down on her. She was caged in now with nowhere to go. My scream echoed in the throne room as I poured every moment of pain in my life into this barrage.

Killing my mother, stealing those six years from me, turning me into this, forcing me to be a weapon, taking away Alice, ruining my country, killing my people, taking my friends from me. Taking Chase away from me. Ruining the only chance for the three of us to live together in peace. She deserved a fate worse than death, but I would take my payment in blood. I wasn't going to make the same mistake she did. She would die here.

She pulled her arms up, her metal bones trying to block most of my hits, but I could feel them crumpling under my fury.

"Mom, stop."

Aria's voice suddenly broke through my bloodlust. My arm was still raised, prepared to land another blow. Esmerelda was covered in blood, just like my fists. I pushed myself up and stumbled away from my stepmother.

I turned to Aria and seeing her pulled me even more firmly back to reality. I glared down at Esmerelda crouched below me. I grabbed her and drug her to the middle of the cavernous space. She was limp in my grip, and I tossed her down like the trash she was. She was whimpering but I felt no pity for her.

The doors opened, and the others entered, looking around at the bodies littering the floor and Esmerelda at my feet.

"I guess we're too late," Benson said, which made an unhinged little giggle bubble up in me.

"Do any of you have zip ties?" I asked, and Thea came over.

She glared bloody murder at Esmerelda as she tightened them to the point of bruising. She leaned down and stared at her for a moment. I could only guess what was going through her mind. Thea too had lived here in the palace her entire life until the coup. Her mother had lost her life here so Thea could escape after they were arrested. Now, she was here right after her brother had been murdered. I wasn't the only one here whose life had been ruined by this woman.

Footsteps got my attention. Jessie entered with Cecily's arm swung over her shoulder. She had to help the girl walk. Thea turned to attack, but I grabbed her arm, watching the other girl. Her eyes were clearer than I had seen since them she had been kidnapped and brainwashed. I wondered if the massive electric shock she had taken might have finally broken through. At least, she didn't seem like she wanted to hurt us, but then her gaze settled on Esmerelda, and she looked ready to kill again.

Once I was sure Thea wouldn't attack, I walked over to Aria. I dropped to my knees in front of her. She just stared at me with wide eyes. Like she was searching for any resemblance to her own reflection in my face.

I had always thought she looked more like Chase than me. She had his sandy hair, even though it laid in waves across her shoulders. Not curly like mine, but not straight like his.

"Are you okay?" I finally asked her. I reached out delicately until I realized how bloody my hands were and I dropped them. I couldn't taint her with my sins.

"I always wondered why I was different than everyone else," she said softly.

"I'm so sorry we couldn't tell you. We thought it was the best way to keep you safe. I'm sorry we couldn't be with you. We never stopped loving you though. Everything we ever did was for you."

"I understand," she said, and the calm that emanated from her surprised me.

That hadn't been what I had expected her to say.

"You had to save the world." She shrugged. "The teachers always said what all of you were doing was important."

"Are you okay?" I asked her again. "I'm sorry. You shouldn't have seen that." A girl her age shouldn't have been exposed to any of this. I worried how this entire situation was going to affect her.

She watched me, strangely stoic, but I could see anger simmering as she glared down at the woman who had her kidnapped. "Justice shouldn't come today. Ms. Monica always said justice should be given by the people."

"Well, seems like that school is doing a good job." I said with a chuckle.

I saw a flicker of movement and Cecily was there standing behind Esmerelda.

I turned towards them, thinking she was trying to escape with her, but it wasn't needed. Cecily took a knife and sliced through Esmerelda's throat. I whirled back and grabbed Aria, pressing her to me so she couldn't watch as Esmerelda clutched at her throat. Blood seeped through my stepmother's fingers. Cecily watched her captor's terror before she caught my eye. We stared at each other for a moment. She gave the smallest of nods to me before she turned and raced from the room. Jessie paused in shock before turning and running after her sister.

Esmerelda's blood started to pool around her as I watched her realize this was her fate. She turned to me, her eyes begging to help her. I pressed Aria into me so she couldn't see and she wrapped her arms around me. Esmerelda slipped to the ground, losing her strength.

"Beware the monsters you create," was the last thing she ever heard before she left this world. I listened to make sure her heart didn't beat again.

It didn't seem real that it was over.

I didn't know what was next. I had never let myself think past this moment, afraid it may never come.

All I knew was I needed to take care of Aria. I'd do whatever that required.

Vi

It was surreal to think it was really over, walking down these halls of the palace with my father on one side and my daughter on the other. It had been a few days since the siege, and we were still working to get things under control. Being here with David, but not Chase... I still felt numb, not quite sure how to accept this new reality.

Dad, Aria, and I pushed our way into the gathering room used for council meetings to find everyone already there, including Ethan, CC1, Nathan, Naya, and Jupiter, on top of my squad.

The argument had gone on for over a day, but my father had finally accepted my decision. We were turning the country over to the people to elect their representatives, like Neria had done before us. They were proof it was a viable option.

I wanted a quiet and normal life, and I had done enough. I had earned it. It was time to do this for myself, and for Aria.

Everyone had been doting on Aria since they had arrived. David and Joseph had helped me explain everything to her. We spent hours telling her everything we could about us.

My friends had helped me pick up the pieces at night when I

couldn't keep myself together. I missed Chase so much it felt like it might kill me, but I had a reason to live. I had a promise to keep. I had a little girl to love.

Jupiter had given me her words of wisdom, helping me let go of this burden I had carried for so long. She had gone through something similar when they had taken control of Neria. She helped me understand that I was allowed to make a life for myself. I could put the warrior away and find peace. That there were good people who would carry on where I left off, and I didn't have to carry the weight of the world any longer.

I had been taken captive at twelve, rescued at eighteen, and here I was almost twenty-six and the war was finally over. I felt like I had lived an entire lifetime in the last seven years. I had endured pain, fought for my life, and had been loved unconditionally.

Here I was, a mother and a widow.

Nathan came over and gave me a hug. He had only gotten in this morning. He held me tightly, and I returned the embrace, enjoying the fact that we were able to be here together. No sneaking, no secrets, just a friend being here for me.

"So, when is Soland going to join the cool club of democracy?" I asked him.

He laughed. "That might start a civil war of my own. Let me work on them." He winked. "What are you going to do now?"

"I'm going to go live at the school, take up teaching, start a garden. It was the last place that felt like home. Aria loves it there, and I've missed it."

"Oh, good. That means you can come visit all the time. I'll make sure we send out invites to all the balls and events," Nathan said excitedly.

"Or you could not do that." I groaned.

"Do I get to go to the ball?" Aria asked.

"Of course, you can," he said. "You can bring all your friends too."

She jumped up and down and clapped at that. I rolled my eyes and gave him an exasperated look.

"If you give it a chance, you might like it. Riley loves them," Nathan said with a smirk.

Jupiter turned to my dad. "Our engineers will be flying in at the end of the week. We're going to send supplies to help rebuild the cities that were damaged."

"Thank you. That will be invaluable. We're also going to keep expanding the towns we had been building for the refugees if we can have help there as well."

"Anything you need. You helped us in our time of need. It's our pleasure to return the favor."

"I've got a crew of our engineers coming as well," Nathan chimed in. His were going to create monuments in the cities to serve as memorials for those that were lost in this conflict.

Seeing the three of our countries in one room, working together, was another thing that was going to take some time getting used to. I had always thought we would be best together, and I was happy I was being proven right.

Sometimes, everything was just so overwhelming I had to take a step back and breathe through the tears that threatened to choke me. Remind myself it was over. We were building a new world. Everything we had ever dreamed of.

My hand went to my shoulder, and I tried to remember the feeling of Chase's there, giving me his strength when I needed it. How he would hold me close when we got good news. How he was overjoyed when we found out we were having a girl. Building our home together at Nexus camp. His lips on mine as we were announced partners for life.

He was going to own my heart for the rest of my life.

Just like the little girl standing at my side would. I looked to my dad took Aria's hand before I walked over to Thea. She stood with her arms crossed, holding herself tight. She had seemed so lost over the last few days.

"Hey, sis."

She blinked up at me, as if just realizing I was talking to her.

"Come with us to the school. I think it'll be good for you."

She seemed to think on it for a moment.

"Maybe one day. I think I'm going to travel. Find out who I am." She had lost her life to the war just like I had.

I pulled her close and kissed the top of her head, the same way Chase used to do. "I think that's a great idea. Come find me when you're ready. You'll know where I'll be."

Gwen came over to us and gave me a playful punch on the shoulder.

"No invite for me?" she joked. "It's fine. I'm actually going to hang around. George said he'd teach me how to organize the logistics. I want to help rebuild."

George smiled and winked at us. "Happy to help. She'll pick it up in no time I'm sure."

Benson came over, holding Naya's hand.

"Are you off to Neria?" I asked him, and he blushed but nodded. "I'm happy for you two."

That got Naya to blush as well. We were all getting a new lease on life. We could do whatever we wanted now. We could be happy. Do the things we had to put off because of the war.

Ethan gave me a small wave, and I extracted myself from the group to go over to him. My heart broke for him. He had lost his wife and his son, and now his daughter was leaving to find herself.

"Hey, Dad," I said, and I could see the tears he had to fight back when I did.

"I just wanted to say it's been an honor to have you in the family. I know you were his world, and I know what it cost you two over the past few years. He thought of you every day, and he'd never been as happy as he was when the two of you were together. Even during the hard times." He coughed, covering the waver in his voice. "I know the thing he would want most in the world is for you to keep living your best life. To hold tight to every spark of joy you find."

"I'm so sorry, Ethan. I should have saved him. If there was anyone, I could have saved..." my voice wavered. "I was the one who was supposed to be in danger, not him."

"You know if it could only be one of you, this is how he would want it. You saved her, and he'll live on through both of you, and me and Thea and all your friends. He'll never really leave us." He clasped my hand tightly.

I shook it. "I know you're right. If you ever need anything, just call me and I'll be there."

"Oh, you know I'll be visiting. I can't stay away from that precious girl for too long. We'll be spoiling her rotten."

"Of that, I'm sure. You'll always be welcome."

He dropped my hand and headed over to speak to my father and Jupiter.

David and Joseph finally came up to me.

"Are you ready for this?" David asked.

"I don't think I've ever been more ready for anything in my life." I felt like the chains that held me down were slowly disappearing.

"Everyone is excited for your return. The kids are throwing a party," Joseph said with a chuckle.

"The kids would throw a party simply because it's Wednesday, but I can't wait to see them."

Aria ran over, wrapped her arms around me, and smiled up to David and Joseph.

"So, can I call you Uncle David and Uncle Joseph now?" she asked.

"I'd love that," David said, tapping her nose.

"You have more family than you'll know what to do with now," I told her, and the look on her face was a mirror image of Chase. I picked her up and hugged her close.

"It's almost time to go," Joseph said.

I looked around the room to the people who I loved most in the world. The sun filtered in, hitting a glass sculpture that made it appear like rainbow glitter throughout the room.

A new chapter in our lives was starting, but we all had one last thing to do first.

62

Vi

It felt like I was flanked by everyone Chase and I had ever met. We were back at headquarters under that tree that had changed my life. A new grave stood empty next to the two other headstones. Another slick black pod hovered nearby as my father spoke.

My attention flickered from what was being said to my own thoughts. As the wind whispered through the trees, the tears came harder. It was like the kisses he'd trail up my neck, the feeling of his arms around me. He was never going to hold me again. I would never get his smile that was just for me ever again.

I choked as the pain gripped me in its fist once more. My brain couldn't understand how I'd never see him again. I'd never hear his laugh again. I'd never be wrapped in his arms again.

David tugged on my sleeve, and I turned to him with Aria's little hand held in his, and it pulled me back to reality once more. "Do you want to say anything?"

I noticed everyone watching me expectantly. I wiped at my face and stepped forward to turn and address everyone. Not just our family, our squad, and others like George and Naya and Jupiter, but everyone who had met us in Neria who was close enough to come. People from every camp and city we had helped and built were here.

Amelia seemed to be holding in tears with Theo next to her. Parker and Kora stood together with Declan and the others. Everyone stood in silent attention to this man who changed their lives.

"I just wanted to thank everyone for being here." I took a breath and tried to steady myself. "The crowd that is here just proves what an amazing person Chase was. His whole life was protecting people. Me and our friends, but also people he'd never met before.

"Every place he went, he made sure that those people felt heard in their needs and did his best to help provide that. He knew how to make hard decisions, understood what those implications were, and did his best to dull the blowback when he could.

"He gave his life over to the people. Not just those of Kabria but everyone. He believed in our fight with every fiber of his being. He believed in bringing about a better world. He would want us to revel in our victory but know the hard work is not done yet. To truly honor him, we need to use this time to build that new world. A *better* world. Protect our future from ever reliving this tragedy. So, I ask all of you, beg all of you, do what you can to improve the world. Whatever little, tiny act of kindness you can.

"Chase knew it was possible. Let's show him we know it too."

I stepped back, David pulled me in close, and Aria clung tight to my leg. I still couldn't focus while others spoke. I just stared at the pod where Chase's body lie. Eventually, it was time, and the pod started to lower itself into the grave. As I bent down to grab a handful of dirt, I was reminded of the last time I did this. I saw Chase standing there with me, dropping dirt onto Atty and Marco's coffins. Tears swam in my eyes as I let the dirt slip through my fingers once more.

As everyone else started to leave, I dropped my knees at the edge of the grave. I didn't feel like I was part of my body. I just existed as I sat there and stared at the resting place of the love my life.

Someone stood next to me, and I looked up as the giant blocked out the sun behind them.

"Dad," I cried. "It hurts so bad."

He took a knee and put one hand on my shoulder, turning me to him as I sobbed. I wiped at the never-ending tears with my wrist.

"I know it does, sweetie." His reply was soft, swirled with his own pain.

"Does it stop?" I begged.

"I don't think so." His own gaze was far off, I assumed thinking of my mother. Of him standing at her grave with me as a baby. His answer hurt but was also comforting because I feared a time when I wouldn't feel the pain of his loss. What would that mean if it faded away?

Here I was at the grave of my own partner, with a daughter waiting for me. I understood another layer of my father, being here with him, seeing how much my life mirrored his own. How similar we really were. How much of his daughter I really was.

"But you'll keep living. You'll take all that love and shower it on that little girl. He'll live on through you and the rest of us. Your life is going to change, and that is the way of the world. I still talk to your mother sometimes. It brings me peace. She never stopped being the person I wanted to tell everything to." He looked over his shoulder, and I could hear Aria headed our way.

I waved for her to join us when she paused seeming timid.

"Can you tell me more about him?" she asked quietly. I patted the ground next to me in invitation. She plopped down between me and my father. The three of us talked until I heard Amelia getting ready to send people to search for us to make sure we had eaten.

I stood and held out a hand to Aria. She grabbed it, and I pulled her up after me.

"I'm starving," she muttered, which just made my dad and me chuckle.

"Me too, kid. Me too."

With one last glance over my shoulder, I swung her up into my arms and smiled, ready to figure out what the rest of my life was going to be like. Knowing he'd always be there to watch over us.

EPILOGUE

"So, you're saying you really are Genevieve Astor, the Bloody Red Queen from the history books?" the man sitting across from me asked.

"I really wish that wasn't the name that stuck, but yeah." I sighed. It was incredibly annoying that I hadn't had a say in what they immortalized me as.

We were seated within a hedge maze that brought us to this circular courtyard within its heart. The table and chairs had a perfect view of the marble statues that were part of the exterior circular wall every few feet. Due north was a statue of Chase, flanked by Thea, Gwen, Atty, Benson, David, Joseph, Anthony, and Marco.

"Are you really two hundred years old?" he said incredulously.

"Somewhere around there. It all kind of blurs together after a while. The older I get, the harder it is to remember."

Many years ago, I had found this plot of land hidden away atop a mountain. It wasn't often that people would come across me. The trek up here was arduous, and only the most dedicated people made their way this far. If they did, I offered to tell them my story. Most took me up on it but then had a hard time believing me.

"They say one day you just disappeared, but the tale goes that you swore you'd be back if you were needed. You're a boogeyman they use to scare children with to be good."

"I've kept an eye on you all. For the most part, you've been on pretty good behavior."

"I can't believe you're real," he muttered. "What do you do with yourself up here? Are you lonely?"

"I keep myself busy. I spent a decade learning to sculpt." I pointed to the statues surrounding us. "I made them before I could forget what their faces looked like. Once everyone I knew was gone, it was hard to stay. Their memories keep me company most of the time."

The years after the war were calm and peaceful. I spent as much time as I could with them all. They aged and I didn't. I watched as they got older, but their families grew. I was still keeping an eye on their descendants.

David and Joseph lived together happily running the school well into their old age. Their kids became teachers and doctors, and one was an adrenaline junkie. Riley, Xander, and Monica ended up being on boards of multiple schools and companies in Soland after eventually leaving teaching. Riley also did drag me to balls and taught me to dance, and they were actually quite fun.

Thea found out she loved traveling and explored not just our entire continent but others too. She always came home with some new wild story of her adventures. Benson and Naya ended up being leaders in the new Kabrian government. Their descendants were still politicians. Good ones, at that. Gwen and George ended up getting married and their children went into public service. Ethan and my father both died of old age. All of them did, and for that I would be eternally grateful.

Nathan eventually did convert Soland to a democracy before his death. It helped that they saw the success of Neria and Kabria. The continent eventually ended up merging the three countries into one and I saw my dream realized. Our people had never been more prosperous than they were today.

Steps crunched on the gravel. "Speak of the devil. I wasn't expecting you for a few years yet."

"Mom, are you boring another traveler with your stories?"

Aria walked down the path from the house. She had grown to be as tall as I was and could be in her early twenties. Even now, I didn't look much older. I could pass for being in my thirties. The changes in us seemed to delay aging. Decades were like mere months to our bodies.

"Leave your poor mother alone," I said. "I don't get to have a good conversation very often. Plus, they ask to hear it."

"Whose fault is that? You're the one who built a house in the middle of nowhere. You know you can come with me back to the cities anytime."

I huffed and waved a hand dismissively. "I leave sometimes. It's a lot of work to change identities that often, and I enjoy the peace up here."

Aria just shook her head in amusement. This wasn't the first time we'd had this conversation.

"I got a message from Jessie. Her and Cecily want to meet up; they have something they need to talk to us about."

"Wait. So, all of you are still alive?" the man asked in surprise.

"Yeah. We tend to meet up every few decades or so. I wonder what they want," I mused.

"She said it was important but wouldn't say more."

"Are there more of you?" he asked, like we might overrun the place and take over if we had spread.

"No, we all decided it should end with us. Besides Aria we agreed we wouldn't have any children. We destroyed all the data so no one could make any more as well. We keep watch, but otherwise, we stay out of the business of mere mortals," I said with a chuckle. "But it's nice not to be completely alone."

He looked at Aria. "What have you done all this time?"

My chest swelled with pride. "She was a diplomat."

"That's a story for another time." Aria rolled her eyes.

"No one is going to believe this," he said.

"Yeah, probably not." Aria laughed. "Sorry to cut this short, but we should get going as soon as we can."

I pushed myself up from the table. It looked like it was time to leave my sanctuary and head back to the land of the living. "If you'll excuse me, I just need to grab a few things." I stood and headed to grab my go bag. Old habits die hard. I always hand one handy in case

I needed to leave quickly. As I walked back to the house, I heard Aria head to the statue of Chase like she always did.

"Hi, Dad. Sorry I have to pull Mom away, and I'm sorry I haven't been here in a while. I'll catch you up when we return."

It warmed my heart to hear her talking to him. I did the same. I still shared everything with him, knowing he was there, watching over us, waiting for us to finally cross the veil to be with him again. It was taking longer than we expected, but I knew I'd see him again one day.

"Would you like to join us for the hike down?" I asked when the traveler and Aria made their way near the front of the house. I closed the door behind me.

He nodded mutely, but it didn't last for long. He peppered us with questions as we made our way down the mountain to the city far below. Once we finally arrived, I turned to the traveler.

"Live well. Remember, we'll be coming for you all if you ever mess up as badly as we did." I winked before Aria and I slipped into the busy streets and headed for the hangar that held the plane I had acquired in the last decade or so.

"You know where to go?" I asked her.

That smile of Chase's broke across her face as she nodded. "Let's go. I can feel an adventure calling."

ACKNOWLEDGMENTS

Hey readers. Thank you for joining me on this journey of Vi and her friends. It seems so crazy to me that it's over! I hope you enjoyed the ride and loved the characters as much as I did. This story has been bouncing around in my brain since 2011. I just want to thank a few people who made this possible.

First off my husband. He dealt with me locking myself away on nights and weekends to write. He is the amazing cover artist for all three of these books. He dealt with my million change requests after he just made all the changes I had just asked for. He's always supported this crazy hobby of mine and I couldn't be more grateful.

Caitlin my amazing editor who I couldn't have done this without. She always has great comments on thing that I could fix to make the story the best possible. She's also an amazing formatter and gives me feedback on my blurbs! I hate blurbs with a passion if you don't know.

Caitlin and Heather are great accountability buddies. Honestly it might have taken another two years to finish this book if I didn't have them.

All my friends and family who have been so supportive of this journey I've been on. Thank you all for buying, reading, and leaving reviews on these books!

This journey has come to an end, but that's not to say you won't see these characters in the future. I might be working on a few books that follow Aria and what she got up to after the end of the war.

I also have some other short stories in mind. What did Gwen and Atty talk about in the kitchen in Neria? What was Esmerelda like in school when she knew Marco? How about what Ethan, Nolan, Kora and Aria were like in school? Do you want to see more of Riley and

Nathan and their shenanigans? I also might have some other missions the squad went on that absolutely did not go to plan. So, keep an eye out!

Again, I just really want to thank everyone for checking these books out and I really do hope you enjoyed the show.

PLAYLIST

Check out some of my favorite songs to write to that really embody
my favorite things about this story.

Theme Songs for the Trilogy
Manhunt by Derivakat & Cartian
Revolution by The Score
War! by Zach Callison
Enemy (From Arcane Series) Imagine Dragons & JID

Mood: Genevieve Astor
Welcome Home by Derivakat

Mood: Queen Esmerelda
Lonely King by CG5

Jams that Pump You Up
Nevermind by Dennis Lloyd
Living for the Weekend by Fitz and the Tantrums
Bad Guy by Billie Eilish
Lonely by Imagine Dragons
Hit The Snooze by The Living Tombstone
Long Time Friends by The Living Tombstone
Waiting for You by Alexander Jean
Baby I'm a Queen by Sofi Tukker
Captain's Call (Feat. CG5) by Derivakat
Hannah by Freelance Whales
Same Old Song (S.O.S. Part 1) by Two Feet
Dark Water by Daphne Willis

Love Me Less (Feat. Kim Petras) by MAX
Dream Song by Finish Ticket
Cali God by Grace Mitchell
Can't Hold Us (Feat. Ray Dalton) by Macklemore & Ryan Lewis
Blinded by The Bots
Don't Let Me Down (Feat. Daya) by The Chainsmokers
Drink You Away by Justin Timberlake
Dark Side by Bishop Briggs
Queen of Broken Hearts by Blackbear
Gotta Be a Reason by Alec Benjamin
Hourglass by Set It Off
Complainer by Cold War Kids
Baby Outlaw by Elle King
Labour by Paris Paloma
Tiger by Chair Model
I Miss U by Jax Jones & Au/Ra
Goosbumps (Remix) by Travis Scott & HVME
Roses (Imanbek Remix) by SAINt JHN
Edamame (Feat. Rich Brian) by Bbno$

ABOUT THE AUTHOR

Marissa has been writing for as long as she can remember. She graduated with a bachelors and masters degrees in creative writing from SHNU.

You can connect with me here and subscribe to my newsletter: marissaallencreations.com

facebook.com/MarissaAllenAuthor

instagram.com/marissaallenauthor

www.ingramcontent.com/pod-product-compliance
Lightning Source LLC
Chambersburg PA
CBHW031439160726
47994CB00005B/1793